**DARK HORSE COWBOYS**
*Do or Die Cowboy*
*Hot Target Cowboy*
*When to Call a Cowboy*

# COWBOY
## *Christmas*
# HOMECOMING

# JUNE FAVER

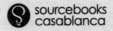
sourcebooks
casablanca

Published by Sourcebooks Casablanca, an imprint of Sourcebooks
P.O. Box 4410, Naperville, Illinois 60567-4410
(630) 961-3900
sourcebooks.com

Printed and bound in the United States of America.
OPM 10 9 8 7 6 5 4 3 2 1

*To my dear friend Stephanie Cover, former firefighter, EMT, and paramedic.*

*Steph is truly a hero, an inspiration, and deserving of her HEA.*

# Chapter 1

It was late November when he found the envelope.

Big Jim Garrett held the letter for a while before opening it. It was from his sister-in-law, Adele, who now lived over in Fort Worth. There was a stack of mail on the kitchen counter, but from what he could tell, it was made up mostly of Christmas cards. He would leave those for the others in his household to open, but this letter was addressed to him personally with no "and family" tacked on.

*What's going on with Adele?* After Big Jim's brother had died, Adele had sold their land and moved to Fort Worth, where she had some relatives.

Big Jim's back teeth ground together as he recalled how she had fallen way behind in property taxes and was forced to sell off the property and stock. The woman had always been headstrong and shortsighted, to his way of thinking. No business sense, and she hadn't come to Big Jim until it was too late.

He took a seat at the counter separating the kitchen from the dining area. Tearing the envelope open, he slid out a single sheet of notepaper.

*Dear Jim,*

*I'm writing to let you know that Zachery is home from his second tour of duty with the U.S. Army.*

*He intends to return to Langston and hopes to
find employment. I hope you can help him get
settled.*

*I feel really bad that I had to sell the ranch,
but I just couldn't manage everything by myself.
I'm so worried. Zach just doesn't seem the same
as when he left. I'm hoping he can find himself
when he goes home.*

*Best ever,*
*Adele*

Big Jim carefully folded the letter and replaced it in
the envelope.

His nephew, Zach, had grown up with Big Jim's own
three sons. They had been like a pack of puppies, insepa-
rable and carefree. After graduating from high school,
Zach had enlisted, while his own sons, one by one, had
gone to college and returned to the land. The land that
Big Jim would never sell under any circumstances.

He was more than a little peeved that Adele had sold
off the land his brother had worked so hard for and that
he must have thought would go to Zach someday.

Big Jim shook his head. *Sad.* But of course he would
try to help his nephew settle in and find his place now
that he was a civilian—a rancher—again.

*Ranchers.* The Garretts were ranchers. It was part of
their genetic makeup.

Even his rebellious middle son, Tyler, now a country-
western singer, had returned to his roots. Of course, he
had returned with his bride, Leah, and her daughter,
Gracie. He had built a home for his new family right

there on the sprawling Garrett ranch. Big Jim knew that Tyler would always return to the place he called home, no matter where his musical career might take him.

Big Jim's oldest son, Colton, had also married and was in the process of building a home for his bride, Misty, and her younger brother, but the snow had hindered their progress. For now, they were living with Big Jim at the Garrett ranch house, happily making preparations for their first Christmas as man and wife.

His youngest son, Beau, had gotten back with his high school girlfriend, Dixie, and their beautiful daughter, Ava. Now, reconciled, they were happily remodeling Dixie's ranch house and getting it ready for their own Christmas celebration.

But now the Garrett Christmas celebration would include Zach Garrett.

Big Jim had made a passionate and somewhat irritable vow to his deceased brother that he would do everything in his power to ensure that Zach would be welcomed and know that he always had a place here with the rest of the Garrett family.

He tucked the letter in his pocket and headed out to the stables. Saddling up his favorite stallion and letting that horse run free would help shake off his own demons. "Bah! Humbug," he muttered.

***

The countryside whizzed by, but Zach Garrett paid no attention. He felt nothing. Only the passing of time.

It was cold, but he was well insulated. Nothing could touch him.

The sprawling metropolitan Dallas–Fort Worth area

made him feel claustrophobic, but now that the bus was speeding along the highway, he could breathe at least.

He wore his uniform because he'd left his civilian garb at home—the home his mother had packed up and sold. She told him all of his belongings were carefully stowed in the two-car garage of the house she'd purchased in a nice, quiet neighborhood. But he hadn't opened even a box.

Maybe his past was in there, along with his dad's. Maybe he would be able to open the boxes someday, but now all he wanted was to get back to Langston, the last place he had been happy. He wanted to see his cousins, the crazy guys he had grown up with. Most of all, he wanted to feel like he belonged somewhere.

Zach heaved a sigh. It must have been loud because the old lady across the aisle from him looked him over. *It's okay, Grandma. I'm just the remains of Zachery Garrett...his outer shell.*

He hoped to find something to stuff himself with. Something with feelings. Something strong that could withstand whatever was to come next.

The old lady was still staring.

He shifted in his seat, turning his wide shoulders to the window. He tried to focus on the images as they passed. Mostly pastureland, cattle grazing in the distance. He tried to identify the breeds. Hereford, Black Angus, Charolais...there were some Brangus, an interesting cross-breed of Angus and Brahman.

Another huge sigh escaped.

He'd always thought he would come home to his family's ranch, to the snug ranch house with barn, stables, and outbuildings. He wondered who was living there now.

Zach snapped out of his trance. His fists were clenched. Every muscle in his body was tensed, and he wasn't sure why. *Is this anger?* He wasn't sure what anger felt like any longer. He had felt anger in Afghanistan. Rage, in fact. Intense loss and fury over the unfairness of life…and death.

It was better to feel nothing.

Be alert for danger, but feel nothing.

————

"I can't wait to meet your friend, Colt." Misty Garrett sat in the passenger seat of the big silver double-dually truck. Her twelve-year-old brother, Mark, sat behind her playing a handheld video game.

"He's my cousin. I hope you like Zach. Sometimes, he was more like a brother to me than my own brothers."

"The two of you were the same age. It's natural you would be close."

Colt snorted. "Probably, but we had so much in common. We were in the same grade and played all sports together." He gave Misty a pat on her thigh. "We showed calves and later bulls at the area fairs. We just had a natural interest in the same things."

He recalled the hot summer days when they would go to the creek to cool off, sometimes trying to ditch the younger boys. Usually his mother would insist he take his little brothers along and be responsible for watching out for them…a task shared by his cousin, Zach.

Now, as Colt drove to Amarillo to meet his cousin's bus, he was excited. He hadn't seen Zach since the day he had enlisted. But he was sure his best friend, from childhood through high school, felt the same way.

He couldn't wait to show off Misty. Glancing at his bride, he was filled with a sense of pride and emotion. He knew the love they shared would last forever. *As long as we both shall live…*

Maybe Zach had somebody special in his life. Colt hoped so. He knew his own life had taken on a whole new dimension since Misty had become a part of it.

As they rolled into Amarillo, Mark chattered about his game, and Misty made complementary comments.

When he parked beside the bus station, Colt realized he was wearing a broad grin. "Hang out here while I try to find Zach." He swung out of the truck, leaving the motor running with the heater on.

A blast of cold air hit him full force. He zipped his down jacket and held onto his Stetson. He couldn't let that fly off his head. Once inside the bus station, he stopped, his back against the wall, to search for his friend. Colt was as tall as his father, Big Jim. At six-foot-plus, he could easily scan the room, but it just took one sweep to find Zach, still wearing his camouflage gear and clutching an enormous duffel bag.

Colt swallowed hard.

Zach didn't appear to be really focused. Perhaps he was tired from all the traveling.

Colt called his name and started across the width of the bus station. But Zach snapped to and rose to greet him. The two embraced and slapped each other on the back.

"Damn, Colt. You're looking great." Zach was staring at him as though he was looking for changes.

This was only fair because Colt was doing the same thing. "Thanks, bud. You look…different. It must be the hair."

Zach ran his fingers over his buzz cut. "Or lack thereof."

Colt hefted the duffel onto his shoulder and motioned for Zach to follow. "Let's get into the truck and on the road. Dad and the guys are waiting for you at the house."

A look of sadness flashed across Zach's face. "Um, yeah. I can't wait."

―――⁓―――

Zach followed Colton outside to the parking lot. Colt had always been tall, but over the years, he had beefed up considerably. He was built like a Mack truck, effortlessly lobbing the heavy duffel bag into the bed of a big silver truck. There was a sign on the door with *Circle G Ranch* emblazoned across it. It had an image of the big horseshoe-shaped arch over the entrance to the ranch.

Zach felt as if he had been sucker-punched. Here was his best friend, living the life he could have been living. Colt was a bigger-than-life cowboy, with a family full of cowboys, born to raise cattle and work the land.

Zach swallowed hard. It was over for him. There was no land or cattle. His home was gone. Someone else owned it now, so he should just turn the page and move on.

He opened the passenger door and stepped up into the cab, surprised to see two other people in the vehicle. A very attractive young brunette woman sat in the backseat along with a dark-haired boy.

She grinned and waggled her fingers in a wave as Colt climbed in front in the driver's seat.

"Zach, this is my wife, Misty, and her brother, Mark." He started up the truck. "Sorry you missed our wedding."

"Um—congratulations. Sorry I missed it too."

"Hi, Zach," Misty said. "Colt has told us so much about you. I'm happy to get to meet you finally."

"Thanks… I—I'm happy to meet you." Zach was stunned. It was reasonable that Colt would get married, but the reality was staring him in the face. Another way in which Colt had moved on, while Zach was living like a rat in the desert, in a place where he couldn't tell enemy from noncombatant. In a place where the enemy wired their own children with explosives to use them as weapons against those they considered infidels.

"Hey, Zach. Are you all right?" It was Colt who nudged him out of his trance.

"Yeah, I'm great. It's great to be here. Everything's great. Thanks for picking me up."

The expression on Colt's face could best be described as uncertain.

The drive to the Garrett ranch was uneventful, with sparse conversation. Zach wasn't able to manage small talk.

Eventually, Colt slowed and turned in at the horseshoe arch with the name *Circle G* overhead, the tires bumping over the cattle guard. This jarred Zach physically and emotionally, as he recalled all the times he had bumped over the same cattle guard and into the same comfortable world where he knew all the players.

---

Stephanie Gayle looked at the check. "Oh, Big Jim. This is so generous. You're going to make sure the children have a nice Christmas."

Big Jim shrugged. "It's the least I can do for those

poor kids." He looked around the room, his gaze falling on a little red-haired girl and a blonde girl maybe a little older. "I think all children need to be loved."

"I feel the same way."

Big Jim's face morphed from sentimental to grim. "How are those two kids you saved? The ones whose mother got killed."

Stephanie tried to control the tremor in her voice. "They—they're still at the children's center. They don't have any family members willing to take them in."

"Well, that's a damned shame."

She nodded. "Rafe Neeley, the stepfather... He's been arraigned and bound over for trial." The image of Rafe's angry face as he screamed threats made her shudder.

"Good," Big Jim pronounced. "I hope that sumbitch gets what's coming to him. I can't imagine a man hurting a woman or a child...much less murdering the woman you're married to."

Stephanie's throat tightened. "Hope they put him away for a hundred years. The children...they witnessed their mother being murdered. They—they were so traumatized."

Big Jim let out a snort and reached in the back pocket of his Wranglers. He produced a worn leather billfold and pulled out a couple of hundred-dollar bills. "Here ya go. Buy them two angels a little something special...and let me know what happens to them. I hope they wind up with some good family."

She swallowed hard. "Thanks, Big Jim. I'll find something special for them." The words *some good family* stuck in her craw.

"Come have a cup of coffee, Stephanie." Big Jim motioned her into the kitchen.

Stephanie took a seat at the counter while Big Jim filled two cups with coffee. He set one in front of her and leaned on the other side of the counter.

That was when Colt's voice could be heard from the front of the house. "Hello! Where is everyone? I brought my brother from another mother."

"Back here," Big Jim called.

Misty and Mark led the way, both grinning. "We got him," Mark announced.

Colton came next, followed by a tall, muscular man wearing camouflage gear. This guy appeared to be on edge, like he'd just been plucked from a battleground. His gaze took in the entire interior and everyone in the large kitchen. When he locked eyes with Stephanie, she felt a jolt like an electric shock. He was a Garrett.

It was the Garrett eyes. Those amazing, smoky-turquoise eyes, ringed with black lashes. They held her in thrall for a moment before releasing her.

Big Jim let out a yelp. "Zachery Garrett! Come here, boy!" Big Jim held out a hand, and when the newcomer reached for it, Big Jim dragged him closer and clasped him in a man hug. "Dang! It's been a long time…and look how you've grown."

"Yes, sir. It's been forever."

Big Jim pounded him on the back and then pulled back to look at him. "I'm glad you're here, son. We all are. Just in time for Christmas."

"Glad to be here, sir." His gaze flicked back to Stephanie.

"Where are my manners?" Big Jim asked. "This fine

young man is my nephew, Zach Garrett. He's just been discharged from the U.S. Army."

Stephanie smiled. *Nephew, huh? Garrett through and through.*

Big Jim gestured toward her. "And this lovely young lady is Stephanie Gayle. Believe it or not, she's a firefighter."

Stephanie gave a one-sided grin and rolled her eyes. "Why do people always find it difficult to think of me as a firefighter?"

"Because we always think of firefighters as big burly men," Misty said. "One has to see you in action to know what a badass you are."

This caused a round of laughter, all except from this Zach guy. He just continued to stare at Stephanie as though he was committing her to memory, molecule by molecule. It was unsettling, to say the least, but there was something else…something simmering just below the surface.

Stephanie swallowed hard. It felt like a roll of razor wire at the back of her throat. She straightened her shoulders, refusing to be intimidated by his scrutiny. *Who is this guy anyway?*

"Good to meet you, ma'am," Zach said.

*Ma'am?* She nodded and offered a hand, which he wrapped with a large baseball mitt–size paw that was warm and very rough.

Colton slapped Zach on the shoulder. "C'mon, bro. Let's get you settled in." Colt shouldered the huge duffel bag and headed off toward the room where he planned to settle Zach.

Zach hit her with his laser-beam eyes again and gave

a little nod before turning to follow his cousin. Misty and Mark trailed after them.

"He's had a rough time," Big Jim said. "My brother died while Zach was deployed, so he never got to say goodbye to his father."

"Oh, that's so sad," Stephanie said.

"He's a good boy. He's going to be just fine."

Stephanie agreed. *Fine*. That pretty much summed up the hottest guy she had laid eyes on in a long time…and she worked with the hottest men in the county.

---

Colt heaved the duffel on the bed and stepped back. "What do you have in that thing, Zach? Dumbbells?"

Zach managed a laugh. "Just what's left of my life." He opened the zipper and then began pulling things out and spreading them on the bed.

"Buddy, we gotta show you that there are other colors in the rainbow. Not everything is U.S. Army green." Colt gestured to the uniforms.

"Those are my ACUs—Army Combat Uniforms."

Colt shook his head. "Surely you have some other clothes."

That claustrophobic sensation wrapped around Zach and squeezed tightly. He had trouble drawing a deep breath. "Um—nope. My mom took the property I left at home to Fort Worth, and I didn't want to go through everything in her garage to find my stuff." He shrugged, trying to appear casual. "I figured if I hadn't needed it for the past ten years, I didn't need it now."

"Guess you're right. You can borrow anything you need from my closet, and we can go shopping anytime you like."

"That sounds good. I have plenty of money saved up. Nothing to spend it on."

Colt shook out the ACUs. "Do we put these on hangers?"

"Aw, just leave them rolled up and stick 'em in a drawer." Zach reached for his collection of olive-drab T-shirts.

"How about Stephanie?" Colt asked. "I'll bet she's the hottest girl you've seen in a while."

Zach quirked his head to one side. "No argument there. She's a babe, but a firefighter? C'mon. She must be the mascot or something."

Colt let out a hoot of laughter. "Don't let her hear you say that. She's a lot tougher than she looks."

Zach made a derisive noise in the back of his throat. "You must have forgotten the meaning of the word *tough*. Army Rangers are tough. Cheerleader-type chicks are not tough." He raised his brows. "No matter how hot."

Colt's joking demeanor suddenly changed. "Seriously, Zach. That pretty little thing has a spine of pure steel. When Misty was in trouble, Stephanie went down into an abandoned well to rescue her." A muscle beside his mouth twitched as though the memory haunted him. "And then she went back down to rescue an old man who had been shot and dumped there. I could have lost Misty that night if it weren't for Stephanie Gayle."

Zach tried to visualize this but couldn't. "Sounds like she knows what she's doing."

"Thank God!" Colt said fervently. "Stephanie had some specialized training where she learned to work in small spaces." He paused. "She's a part of the confined space team."

"That sounds about right," Zach said. "She's not all that big."

"She's almost as tall as Misty," Colt said. "Besides, you're huge now. You really have bulked up."

Zach made a scoffing noise. "You, too, Colt." He shrugged. "When we were eighteen, we were a couple of tall, skinny dudes, but I've been gone for ten years. We've both filled out a little."

"Ha!" Colt pounded him on the shoulder. "Bigger is better, right, bud?"

"As far as I'm concerned."

"Let's get you squared away and get back to the others. I'm pretty sure Dad has some steaks he's planning on grilling to celebrate your homecoming."

*Homecoming?* Zach's mouth went dry. *But I have no home.*

When they returned to the kitchen, Big Jim was placing thick-cut steaks on a platter that he covered with plastic wrap.

A pretty blonde woman was puttering around the kitchen. When she turned to face Zach, he could see that she was extremely pregnant. "You must be Zach," she said.

Big Jim turned with a wide grin. "Zach, this pretty little woman is my daughter-in-law Leah, and her young clone is sitting at the table." He pointed to a blonde girl, probably in grade school.

"Wait! I thought you were married to Misty." Zach looked at Colt for confirmation.

Colt met this comment with a loud guffaw. "Misty is my bride. Leah is married to Tyler. Remember my bratty middle bro? He scored the two blondes."

Zach tried to wrap his head around this. "Ty is married?"

Leah turned around, showing off her rotund physique. "And very happily married, I might add."

Zach rubbed his palm over his buzz cut. "I see."

"This is my daughter, Gracie. Say hi, honey." She pointed to the table where the girl was working on something with crayons and paper. The girl smiled prettily and raised her hand to wave.

Zach recalled Ty Garrett as being about sixteen when he had enlisted. He couldn't fathom that the guitar-strumming kid had grown up to become a responsible husband and father. He surveyed the room, filled with happy, loving family, but he felt distant, as though he were viewing the scene through an electronic device... spying on the normal lives of normal people.

He looked around again, wondering where the beautiful firefighter chick had gone.

As if reading his mind, Colt asked, "Where is Stephanie? She's not staying for dinner?"

"Nope," Big Jim responded. "Miss Gayle is devoted to those orphans. I gave her a little donation to try and help make their Christmas a bit better."

"Orphans?" Zach frowned. He had encountered enough orphans in Afghanistan to last a lifetime.

"Social services has a place for orphans and kids who have been removed from their parents for various reasons. Stephanie rescued a couple of young children, and she seems to feel responsible for them." Big Jim's fierce brows drew together. "Steph is a good girl."

Images of orphans crowded Zach's head.

# Chapter 2

STEPHANIE WAS DRIVING HER TWENTY-YEAR-OLD FORD truck—a well-known vehicle in the area. She'd had it painted bright fire-engine red with ornate gold curlicues, and the fire chief had let her install a siren and flashing lights. It wasn't an official vehicle, but whenever they called her in, it was because she was desperately needed.

Today, her bright-red truck contrasted with the snow-covered surroundings. The radio station out of Amarillo played nonstop Christmas carols, which she found quite cheering.

And she was eager to see Cody and Ivy, the children she was devoted to. As she drew closer to the state-run children's home, her heart felt lighter. She would cash the check and then make sure there was a special present for each child at the home. It was very nice of Big Jim to give her an extra two hundred dollars for Cody and Ivy. The kids had nothing.

Of course, Stephanie wanted to give them everything. When she looked at their little faces, her heart ached to give them love and security. She wanted to provide them with a safe haven…a home.

"Yes, Stephanie Gayle, notorious single woman, wants to be a mother." Saying it aloud made it real. She had an appointment to talk with the social worker tomorrow. She felt pretty positive about the meeting, certain that Miss Lorene Dyer, Licensed Social Worker, would immediately recognize Stephanie's desire to adopt the children. Surely she would appreciate the stable home life Stephanie could offer them.

True, she lived in a small apartment over a bookstore, but she had savings and could make a tidy down payment on a decent house with a fenced yard and trees to climb.

Stephanie turned on the defroster and swiped the back of her gloved hand over the windshield. The glass cleared quickly, giving her a view of the countryside. The flat, snow-blanketed pastureland was punctuated by fence posts and not much else. Miles and miles of nothing but miles and miles.

She slowed and made the turn leading to the children's center, only then letting her thoughts settle on Colt Garrett's handsome cousin, Zach.

Although she was surrounded with great-looking men at work, the Garretts' cousin was hard to ignore. Firefighters tended to be in great shape, and for some reason, most of them were calendar material, but there was something about Zach. She couldn't put her finger on it, but something about him reached out to her.

She laughed and shook her head. *Wishful thinking*.

But maybe she would see him again. Maybe he was thinking about her.

------

Zach sat at the long dining table surrounded by the Garrett family. He had been seated next to Big Jim, who presided over the meal as host. At the other end of the table, a small elderly woman was seated, with Leah and her daughter, Gracie, and a very jovial Tyler surrounding her. The elderly woman, Zach had learned, was Leah's grandmother, and she lived in the new house Tyler had built for his family there on the Garrett ranch. But, apparently, they spent a great deal of time at the original Garrett homestead.

"Did I get your steak right, Zach?" Big Jim asked. He looked concerned, and Zach realized he had not yet cut into his meat.

"Um—yes, sir. It's perfect." He sliced into the thick slab of beef and stabbed it with a fork. The steak was medium rare and quite tasty. The concern on Big Jim's face cleared to be replaced by a wide grin. He then dug into his own steak.

Colton and Misty sat across from Zach, with her younger brother beside her. They were having a conversation, but every now and again, Colt addressed a comment to Zach.

"Where's Beau?" Zach asked. When he had enlisted, Beau had probably been in middle school, maybe fourteen or so.

"Beau is with his wife and daughter," Colt said. "You remember that little red-haired girl who was always with him?"

Zach tried to recall someone with red hair, but mostly he was stunned that Beau, who he still thought of as a child, was married and had a kid. "He has a daughter?"

"That he does." Big Jim beamed from ear to ear. "And she is absolutely cuter'n just about anything. Red hair like her mother."

Zach scooped mashed potatoes into his mouth to prevent any expectation that he would comment. He was blown away that all three brothers were not only married but had families of their own. Somehow, the taste of his food flattened out in his mouth, and he found himself chewing without pleasure. He swallowed and reached for his tea, washing it all down and hoping to clear his mind.

How had his boyhood pals moved forward so quickly when he felt he had just been treading water? Slowly, he looked around the table, checking out each person. They all looked happy. Happy together. Happy to be a part of this family.

He was stunned that all this had been evolving while he had been deployed.

Big Jim was looking at him again, so he picked up his knife and fork to slice off another bite of meat. He made an appreciative noise and nodded at his uncle, which seemed to satisfy him.

After dinner Mark went to the den to watch a Christmas cartoon special on television. Big Jim shooed Leah, her daughter, and Tyler out the door, saying they needed to get home before it snowed more. By that time, Colt and Zach were clearing the table and loading the dishwasher.

Big Jim returned to the kitchen, rolling up his sleeves. "Just like old times, boys."

Zach remembered how often he had enjoyed dinner with his cousins, and afterward, all four boys had jumped up to clear the table and wash up. The Garrett brothers had been trained to show appreciation for the meals their mom slaved over by immediately pitching in to clean up and put away leftovers. Zach had always joined in, enjoying being a part of the family.

Big Jim opened the refrigerator and took out three longnecks, lining up two on the counter and popping the lid off the one he raised to his lips. "Good job, boys. Now let's retire to the den and see if there's a game on."

"I'm pretty sure there's nothing on TV but Christmas specials."

Big Jim grunted. "Well, that's fine. I'm pretty sure we three can enjoy a little male bonding."

Zach picked up one of the beers and flipped the cap off. He clinked the bottle against the one Colt grabbed and followed Big Jim to the den.

Much later, Zach was alone in the guest room. He peeled off his uniform, thinking how much his life had changed in the past week. He still felt like the odd man out around the Garrett estate, but his uncle and cousins were doing their best to make him feel at home. *It will just take a little time*.

He tried to put things in order before he turned off the light. Moonlight streamed in through the window, giving him plenty of light to see his way to the bed. He pulled back the covers and climbed in before pulling the handmade quilt up under his chin.

He realized his entire body was rigid. All of his muscles were tensed. He made an effort to take a deep breath and hold it for twenty seconds before releasing it. One by one, he consciously relaxed each part of his body. His feet and then his ankles and calves. Working his way up his body, he accompanied his freeing of tension with slow, even deep breathing.

Staring up at the ceiling, he tried to disengage from all the events of the past few weeks. He was no longer a soldier. He couldn't call himself a rancher, since the ranch he had anticipated returning to had been sold without him being consulted. Now he had nothing. Well, not quite nothing. He had managed to save a significant amount of money over all the years he'd been enlisted. He hoped he could get a job in the area. Maybe he could save up more money and find a little bit of land he could buy. He didn't have any other dreams or aspirations other than to be a rancher. It was what he was born to do.

—◆—

Stephanie had spent time with Cody and Ivy as well as the other children at the facility. It was unthinkable that so many children were without loving families, especially at this time of the year. Christmas was a family event, but these poor kids were alone.

Her visit had been depressing, to say the least. To see the drab facility hung with shabby and tattered Christmas decorations cast a pall over the whole visit.

Ivy had clung to Stephanie when she went to leave. Cody pulled Ivy away, taking responsibility for his younger sister. At four years old, he was used to a hard life. The social worker said he was "wise beyond his years." Stephanie hated that epithet. She wanted him to be a kid without the heavy burden he was carrying.

Now, tucked in at her apartment, she had showered and pulled on a pair of ridiculous flannel pajamas. They were red...with candy canes plastered all over. After she brushed her teeth, she retired to her living room to watch the news and brush her long chestnut-brown hair.

The apartment was cool. She liked it that way. But she also had an electric blanket on her bed and a ceiling fan overhead, both in operation in anticipation of retiring for the night.

She flipped on the television and pulled on a pair of wool socks. Her grandmother had knitted a whole drawer of socks for her. It was their thing. Stephanie wore the cotton socks inside her boots in summer and the wonderfully warm wool socks in winter. "Keep your feet warm, Steph," her grandmother would insist. "Mind you don't take a cold."

"Yes, ma'am," Stephanie whispered aloud.

A breaking-news banner flashed across the television screen. Stephanie turned up the sound.

The news anchor announced that a prison bus transporting accused murderer Rafe Neeley had been run off the road and the prisoner had escaped. He'd been on his way from the county jail in Amarillo to prison to be held until his trial.

Stephanie's chest tightened. She could feel her heart trying to beat its way out of her rib cage as the image of Rafe Neeley's angry face appeared on the screen.

She couldn't hear the rest of the news anchor's alert. His words seemed to be jammed together, but she gathered he was issuing a warning to the community to be on the lookout for this criminal, presumed to be armed and dangerous.

The hairbrush dropped onto the floor, but she didn't seem to be able to retrieve it.

Her stomach churned as the horror of the situation unfolded before her. The man who had murdered his wife, in front of his stepchildren, was no longer in custody. The vicious and abusive man was at large where he posed an imminent threat to the two children who had witnessed his crime. A threat to the little boy who had been recorded describing the horrific events he and his sister had witnessed. His recorded testimony was slated to be shown at Neeley's criminal trial.

Cody was a boy too young to be so old.

———ɯ———

The dream again…

*It was nighttime, and Zach was on patrol. Jeb was on point, and Leon was on his six. Zach couldn't see the rest of the team, but he knew they were there, alert and ready.*

*His hearing was super acute, every sound magnified a thousand times. The men's footsteps told him where each of them was located as the team policed the area. They were about three kilometers from camp when the first bullet was fired, taking out Leon, and then the next got Ray. Jeb discharged a burst of fire in the direction of the shooter.*

*"Did you see where the shots came from?" Zach murmured, his voice low.*

*Jeb was nearby, crouched low. "No, sir, I didn't see much. Just some sniper fire coming from up on that ridge." Jeb squatted beside him, peering into the darkness. They both fired into the general area, hoping they lucked out. Several others in their cadre fired into the ridge, but they were firing blindly.*

*The firing halted suddenly.*

*The silence that followed assaulted his ears with a hollow void. His own heart beat like hammer blows against his ribs. In the aftermath of the firefight, a sulfurous and metallic smell filled his nostrils, carried by the ultra-fine dust that permeated everything. This was overridden by an acidic, lingering, metallic odor that one could taste as much as smell.*

*He peered around, searching the darkness for his team, swallowing against the pungent, metallic flavor on the roof of his mouth. "Jeb? Leon?" he rasped out.*

*"Here, Sarge," Jeb croaked. "Leon's down…and Ray is gone…"*

Zach's body was wracked by a bone-deep chill. His skin tingled with the cold. Confused, he looked around.

Zach was standing outside in the snow. He became aware of his surroundings but had no recollection of how he'd gotten there. He hadn't felt the cold until now. But he had somehow come outside wearing only his shorts and T-shirt.

He was alone in the universe. Gazing up at the moon, he felt small in the overall hugeness of the cosmos. A light sprinkling of snow was falling. The silence was so profound he could hear the snowflakes as they hit the blanket of snow covering the ground.

He inhaled deeply, filling his lungs with the cold, crisp air. When he exhaled, a cloud of white mist formed in front of his face. He repeated this action several times, marveling that he, a mere shell of a human, could alter the universe, if only for a few seconds.

"Young man?"

He heard the small voice but wasn't sure he'd actually heard it. Maybe he was still asleep.

"Son?"

No, there it was again. He turned toward the sound and found a small woman gazing up at him. "Ma'am?"

"Aren't you cold?"

He heaved another sigh. "Yeah, I guess." He looked down at his bare feet, embedded in snow.

"I brought you this here quilt." The elderly woman held up a coverlet.

He had seen her with Tyler's pregnant wife…the grandmother. He groped to remember her name.

"I thought you might be gittin' cold out here." She waggled the quilt in invitation. "Why don't you jist lean on down here an' I'll wrap you right up."

"Um—yes, ma'am." Obediently, he crouched down to her level.

She tied the quilt around his shoulders and then gave a nod. "I wouldn't want a nice young feller like you to catch pneumonia."

"Yes, ma'am."

"Why don't you come on inside an' I can make us some hot cocoa. I must admit, I'm gittin' a mite chilled out here."

"Yes, ma'am. That sounds good." He accepted the small hand she extended to him and allowed her to lead him back into the house.

Once inside, she secured the front door and took him to the kitchen.

"Lordy, it's three in the mornin'. Hope we didn't wake nobody up." She gestured for him to sit at the counter and set about making two mugs of hot cocoa topped with miniature marshmallows.

Zach inhaled the rich aroma, feeling both gratitude and the ache of nostalgia. The first taste of the cocoa brought back memories of his childhood, when his father was alive and his mother cared about their home and land. He stirred the marshmallows into the hot creamy liquid.

The elderly woman slipped onto the stool beside him.

"I'm glad you made it home, Zach. I know the Garrett family is mighty fond of you."

"Thank you, ma'am." He paused for a moment. "You're related to Tyler's wife, aren't you?"

"That I am." Her face crinkled into a broad grin. "My name is Fern Davis. Leah is my beloved granddaughter, and Gracie is my great-granddaughter."

"That's nice. I don't remember Leah from when I was growing up."

She blew out a breath. "My Leah was raised in Oklahoma, but every summer she spent a lot of time here with her gran'pop an' me."

"That must have been nice." Zach was aware he sounded like a robot. He cleared his throat. "So when did she decide to move to Langston?"

Suddenly the lady looked incredibly sad. "She didn't exactly decide." She shook her head. "My poor girl had some trouble back in Oklahoma. She an' Gracie came here when they needed a place to be safe."

The skin on the back of Zach's neck prickled with gooseflesh. He set his cup down on the countertop. "Safe?"

"She had some feller after her, but it all worked out okay. Comin' here was the right choice…an' I sure am glad to have 'em here. They's the loves o' my life."

"That's nice." There was that robot thing again. He considered Tyler's wife, Leah. She was beautiful. It was hard to believe that she had been through some kind of trauma. Now she seemed to be happy and well-adjusted.

Maybe he would be able to break out of the compartment he seemed to have closed himself in. Maybe there was a job he would find meaningful. Maybe he would be able to feel again.

# Chapter 3

STEPHANIE GAYLE WORKED HER ENTIRE SHIFT THE NEXT DAY with her brain in turmoil. She kept tuning in to the news and checking online to see if Rafe Neeley had been captured. The news revealed that Neeley's two brothers were suspected of running the transport vehicle off the highway and carrying out the escape.

Her gag reflex was working overtime, and her stomach was tied up in a knot. Yes, she might have to hurl any minute.

She spent most of the day examining equipment and doing routine maintenance. It was a step-by-step procedure she had performed many times, but performing these tasks kept her from going totally off the deep end. Her options were limited. She couldn't exactly go looking for Rafe herself, but she hoped the law enforcement officers were tearing up the countryside searching for the Neeley brothers.

Stephanie called social services in Amarillo and spoke to the social worker, Miss Dyer.

"Miss Gayle, of course I'm aware of the escape. The sheriff's office contacted me immediately. The children are perfectly safe in the home. Don't worry."

Stephanie didn't think the social worker was taking the situation seriously enough. "You do realize this is the man who murdered Cody and Ivy's mother? Killed her right before their eyes?"

"Why, yes, Miss Gayle. I am aware of the circumstances under which these children came to be referred to my office. I assure you we will be extra vigilant in caring for them."

Stephanie let out a most unladylike snort. "Pardon me, Miss Dyer, but I'm not convinced. Those kids mean the world to me. I would like to adopt them and give them a permanent home."

It was Miss Dyer's turn to heave out a snort. "Miss Gayle, you are hardly qualified to be an adoptive parent."

Stephanie sucked in a deep breath. Miss Dyer's pronouncement felt like a physical blow. She experienced a gridlock of emotions. How could this woman find her to be unqualified? Stephanie was responsible. She was committed. She had a heart filled with love. "What makes you think I'm not qualified to adopt Cody and Ivy?"

*Silence.*

"Well, Miss Gayle, you are a single woman, you have no house, no support system, and you work in a very dangerous profession. These children deserve more."

If she had been punched in the gut, Stephanie could not have been more stunned. How dare this woman make assumptions about her qualifications for parenting? "I—I don't understand."

"Of course, we prefer to place children with couples, where they can have a good male and female role model...and you live in a small apartment, Miss Gayle."

Stephanie's frustration erupted. "Do you realize what a shithole those kids were living in? My apartment is a palace compared to that."

Miss Dyer huffed out an impatient breath. "Perhaps,

but we want the best for these children, so we will hope to find the ideal family situation."

"Good luck with that." Stephanie bit her lip. Best not to insult the woman who held the children's future in the palm of her hand.

When she disconnected, she was even more unsettled. Not only was she upset that she would not be considered parent material, but her fears for the children's safety had not been allayed. With Rafe Neeley and his brothers still at large, there was a real danger to the children… and apparently nothing Stephanie could do about it.

---

"Wake up, buddy. Time to rise and shine."

Zach awoke, surprised that the sunshine was pouring in through the bedroom windows. He usually rolled out of bed before the sun rose. "Yes—yes, Colt. I'm up."

"Come get some coffee," Colt said. "I'm going into town in a while. Make a list of things you need, bud."

"Sure thing," Zach called.

The events of the previous night were stirring in his brain. *The dream. Waking up outside. The little lady.*

He lay staring up at the ceiling for a few seconds before swinging his legs off the bed. Rubbing his eyes, he felt disoriented but rose to his feet and gathered clothing to put on.

Zach opened the door a crack and peeked down the hall both ways. Nobody coming, so he dashed across to the bathroom. He stepped into the shower and let the hot water carry away all his troubles. For a few minutes he succumbed to the physical experience. Numbness and pain slipped away. Needles of hot water prickled his skin.

He opened his eyes and hurriedly bathed himself before stepping out onto the bath mat and reaching for a towel. Pulling on yet another set of ACUs, he finished his grooming routine and headed for the kitchen.

Colt greeted him with a broad grin. "There you are. I was beginning to think you had rolled over and gone back to sleep." Colt gestured to Zach's appearance. "But here you are, fully dressed and I'm barely standing upright."

"I—I thought you wanted me ready to go."

"Sure. Now I need to get my ass in gear." He gestured to the counter. "Take a seat." When Zach slid onto a stool, Colt set a mug in front of him and filled it with coffee.

"Thanks." Zach picked up the mug and took a sip, recalling his early-morning visit with Fern Davis. "I talked to Leah's grandmother last night."

Colt grinned again. "Yeah, Miz Fern is quite a lady. She's got a little farm the other side of Langston."

"Oh?"

"Yeah. Nice little place. A little less than a hundred acres of land. Not much in the way of stock, but she has some cattle, chickens, and a couple of horses."

"Sounds like a good place. How come she's here?"

Colt leaned on the counter, cradling his coffee mug with both hands. "Tyler and Leah built a really nice home, and they have a suite for her. They're going to be joining the family for Christmas, but Miz Fern has gotten settled in here already. Because of the weather, they made the decision to wait until it warms up a little to haul her over there." He raised his cup to his lips. "And Big Jim just loves the hell outta her."

"She's—pretty smart."

"That's for sure." Colton set his cup in the sink. "Okay, let me get dressed and we can get to town." He disappeared in the general direction of the bedrooms, and almost immediately, Misty rounded the corner.

"Hey Zach. Hope you're hungry."

It was hard not to respond to her perky greeting. "Sure. Can I help?"

"Nah. You just sit there and keep me company while I get things started." In a matter of minutes, she had sausage patties browning in the oven while she popped toast out of the toaster and buttered it. A pot of oatmeal bubbled on a back burner while she broke eggs into a bowl and began to whip them with a wire whisk.

"Wow! You've got this breakfast thing down pat."

Misty threw him an amused glance over her shoulder. "Everything I know I've learned from Leah. She was throwing meals together for this bunch before I came on the scene."

"Glad you're taking care of the Garretts." Zach finished off his coffee just as Colt reappeared with Misty's little brother, Mark, in tow.

Big Jim followed with Fern Davis on his arm.

"The gang's all here," Misty sang out. "Take a seat. Breakfast is ready."

Colt motioned Zach to the table with a hand gesture. When they were seated, he and Misty placed the breakfast items on the table.

"This looks great," Zach said. "Can't believe you whipped this up so fast."

Misty looked pleased as Colt pulled out her chair and seated himself beside her.

The Garretts were apparently old pros at this

meal-service thing because they began to serve themselves and pass platters around.

Zach helped himself to scrambled eggs, sausage, and toast.

Big Jim ladled oatmeal into bowls and passed those around.

"Hearty breakfast," Zach commented.

Big Jim nodded toward him. "That's right, son. We all work hard, so we start out with some fuel in the tank."

"I see, sir." Zach recalled the countless meals he had eaten in Afghanistan, prepared by Army cooks serving uniformly tasteless food.

This meal was delicious and well-seasoned and had not been sitting on a serving line for an hour. The scrambled eggs were perfect, moist and tasty. Even the oatmeal tasted good. He ate with the typically efficient method he always ingested his food. When his plate was clean, he looked around and everyone was staring at him.

"Hungry, son?" Big Jim asked. "We got more. Colt, pass Zach some more sausage and eggs."

Zach felt a rush of heat to his face. "Um—no, sir. I'm fine. Guess I got in the habit of eating fast in the Army."

"No problem, son. I just wanted to make sure you had enough to eat." Big Jim lifted a forkful of eggs in a salute of sorts before sticking it in his mouth.

"Have some more coffee, Zach," Misty offered.

When the rest of the family had eaten, they carried their plates and utensils to the sink.

"You fellows have a good time shopping," Misty said. She stretched up to give Colt a kiss. "Buy me something awesome."

Colt grinned. "What makes you think I haven't already bought your Christmas present?"

Misty giggled. "Because I can't find it anywhere."

Colt's brows rose a bit. "Keep looking." He turned, and the rest of the males tromped out of the house behind him.

Zach looked back, and Fern Davis was smiling at him. She raised her small hand to wave, and he waved back.

When he caught up with the others, they were piling into Big Jim's truck. Big Jim directed Mark to sit up front beside him. "Colt, you and Zach can sit in back and talk to each other."

Obediently, Zach climbed in behind the boy, while Colt took his place behind his father.

"Where to first, boys?" Big Jim started up the diesel motor, giving it a little rev just for the thrill of it.

Colt jerked his thumb toward Zach. "Well, my friend here needs a whole change of wardrobe. How about the western wear store?"

"That will be the first stop," Big Jim promised.

Zach had thought they would drive into Langston, but once they reached the highway, Big Jim turned in the opposite direction.

"Amarillo?" Zach leaned close to Colt to ask.

"You bet. We need to do some serious shopping today."

Zach settled back in the seat. He watched the countryside whizzing by and felt somewhat reassured that things had stayed the same while he'd been gone. The fields were blanketed in white, punctuated with a blur of fence line. The cattle that would have been clustered around these same fields in the spring were gathered close to the places where ranchers had feeding stations. There would be hay and grain and water available.

But this cheered him. Something familiar. He relaxed and listened to the conversation coming from the front seat. Big Jim was talking to Mark, probing as to what he really wanted for Christmas.

"How about you, Zach?" Colton leaned toward him. "Anyone you want to look up? Maybe some special girl you left behind?"

Zach shook his head. "Can't think of anyone. I didn't want to leave any unfinished business when I enlisted. It just wouldn't be fair."

"No, I guess not."

In a while, Zach could see the city of Amarillo in the distance. This was due to the fact that the north Texas countryside was flat as a pancake. There were no hills, no valleys, and the highway was straight as an arrow.

The thing that did surprise him was how much Amarillo had grown. There were suburbs outside suburbs as they made their way into the city. Zach was craning his neck to see how things had changed.

Big Jim skillfully wove through traffic and wound up at a sprawling shopping center that had been nothing but open pasture when Zach had left. How could all this humanity have sprung up in the blink of an eye? When the truck had been parked, all four males climbed out.

Big Jim looped an arm around Mark's shoulders, hauling him along as he walked toward the mall. "What are you shopping for, boy?"

Mark grinned. "I want to get something for everybody, especially for my sister, Misty." His mouth tightened. "We had a pretty bad year, but things are better now."

"That's a very wise statement," Big Jim said. "Let's go to the western wear store, and then we can go to the fancy lady store at the other end of the mall."

Zach walked beside Colt, with Big Jim leading the way. They entered the western wear store, and Zach was immediately struck with the brightness of the interior. A country artist singing a Christmas song played on the sound system, and quite a few customers were pawing through the wares.

Big Jim headed to the back of the store. "Colton, you take Zach to pick out a good pair of boots. Every cowboy needs a good pair of boots, right, Mark?"

"Yessir," Mark answered. He kicked up a booted foot for emphasis.

"I'm pretty sure Mark needs a new pair. This boy is growing like a weed."

They spent some time trying on boots. Zach found a comfortable pair, and the clerk said he would hold them up at the register. Zach put his combat boots back on. He wandered over to a wall of denim jeans and looked for his size. He pulled out two pairs of Wranglers. *That should do it*. He had plenty of camo gear that was wearable, so the two Wranglers would be enough. He would need a couple of nice shirts because he would go to church with the family and he didn't want to reflect badly on the rest of the Garrett clan.

Colt joined him when he was pawing through a rack of western shirts. "That looks like a good one. It will bring out the color of your eyes." He assumed a falsetto voice.

Zach laughed and held up the hanger in front of

Colt's chest. "Danged right. Makes our Garrett eyes sparkle." Zach folded the shirt over his arm and sorted through the rest.

Colt pulled a couple more shirts out of the same selection, though Zach would have guessed Colt was bigger. *Maybe not*.

"A belt," Colt said. "You need a belt, bud." It took no time to select a belt and buckle, and when they made their way up to the cash register, Big Jim and Mark were waiting for them.

Big Jim slapped his hand on the box containing Zach's boots. "Put it down right here." He took the Wranglers, shirts, belt, and buckle from Zach and piled them on the counter alongside Big Jim's other purchases. He nodded at Colt, who placed three more pairs of Wranglers and three shirts he had pulled from the rack on top of the pile. Big Jim selected a platinum card and flipped it to the cashier. "How much do I owe you?"

Zach tried to refuse Big Jim's kind offer. "Oh, no, sir. I couldn't let you pay for my gear."

"Too late, son. I'm just glad to have you back home in one piece. Consider this an early Christmas present."

"Big Jim got me new boots!" Mark proclaimed proudly.

Zach thanked Big Jim, who waved him off. "No thanks needed, son. Just welcome home."

~~~

When they got back to the Garrett ranch, an old red truck was pulled up close to the house.

Zach noted the truck was in mint condition and waxed to a high shine. It looked great in spite of the gold-painted curlicues.

"Stephanie's here," Colt commented.

Zach was immediately interested. A picture of the beautiful Stephanie flashed through his brain. He was anxious to see her again. He gathered his packages and bags from the back of Big Jim's truck and trooped inside with them.

"Whoa!" Misty made an exaggerated surprised face. "The menfolk have been shopping. Anything left in the stores?"

"Not much," Colt said in passing. "Do not look in the hall closet."

"I wouldn't think of it," she shouted after him. Misty turned to Zach. "Well, look at you. You really must have bought out the stores."

"Well—I was just—" Zach shrugged, not knowing how to respond.

"Leave the boy alone," Big Jim bellowed. "He needed some civilian gear."

Zach spied Stephanie sitting at the dining table with a cup in her hands. She looked beautiful, but there was something going on…Was it fear he read in her eyes? He nodded at her, and she raised her fingers in a silent greeting.

Encouraged, he hurried to the room where he had slept and unloaded his bags and packages on the bed. He glanced at himself in the mirror and just saw his usual Army image. He was torn between changing to his new garb and hurrying back to visit with the beautiful Stephanie.

Zach shrugged out of his ACU shirt and pulled on a fresh tee. He was still dressed as a soldier but more casual.

He made it down the hall and rounded the corner into the spacious kitchen and dining room.

Stephanie sat on one side of the long Garrett dining table with Gran beside her at the head.

Misty was in the kitchen. "Coffee or tea, Zach?"

"Oh, uh—whatever you're having is fine."

Stephanie gestured to the chair next to her, indicating she wanted him to sit there.

Wordlessly, he obeyed, pulling out the chair and settling into it. He felt big and oversized next to Stephanie and Gran. He noted that Stephanie smelled great. Something light and floral. "Hi."

She flashed a smile. "Good to see you again, Zach."

"Good to be seen," he said.

"Here you are." Misty placed a cup of coffee in front of him. "Cream? Sugar?"

"Thanks, Misty. This is fine." He reached for the cup, glad to have something to do with his hands.

Misty sat down on the other side of the table. "We were just talking to Stephanie about some plans for Christmas."

Stephanie smiled but seemed anxious. "I appreciate your kindness."

"No problem," Misty said. "We're happy to have you."

Gran leaned over to pat Stephanie's hand. "Don't you worry about a thing. We want to make sure you an' those little children have a great Christmas." She shook her head. "Poor little things. They've been through a lot."

Misty chimed in. "They sure have. Poor babies."

Zach frowned. "You have babies?"

Stephanie heaved a sigh, her shoulders rising and

falling with the effort. "I wish I had babies. I just found out that I'm not good mother material."

Misty and Gran started protesting at the same time, but Stephanie held up both hands.

"I talked to the social worker about adopting or at least fostering the children—"

"The children she rescued from a murdering scumbag," Misty supplied. "Stephanie is a hero in every sense of the word. Trust me. I know firsthand."

Stephanie tried to brush it off, but Misty went on.

"I was attacked and thrown down an abandoned well. Fortunately, Colt found me and Stephanie was the one who came down to rescue me."

"That was plum amazin'," Gran said. "We wuz so happy to get her back."

"And there was a big man in the well too," Misty said. "He's about three times Stephanie's size, but she got him out too."

Zach gazed at Stephanie in admiration. He couldn't imagine how such a slender woman could manage those feats. "What murdering scumbag?"

Stephanie spoke slowly and distinctly. "I did not rescue the children. Their lowlife, abusive stepfather murdered the children's mother. The sheriff's office was called in, and they made the ultimate arrest, but I drove the ambulance, so I was first on the scene. The mother was dead, but I took the children to the hospital, as much for their safety as anything. The doctors checked them out and kept them safe while the deputies were doing their job." Her lower lip trembled. "But—I fell in love with them. I've been visiting them in the children's home and taking them little treats."

Gran's brows drew together. She peered at Stephanie through her glasses. "That sounds nice. I'm for sure dead certain them kids need someone to be nice to 'em."

"And I, for one, think you would make a terrific mother," Misty said.

Zach felt helpless in the wake of all this feminine sharing. He reached out to pat Stephanie on the shoulder.

She turned toward him and buried her face against his chest. "I don't know why everything has to be so difficult. I—I just want to give them a safe place and someone who cares about them." Her voice had risen in timbre.

"Uh, that sounds reasonable," Zach said, still rhythmically patting her shoulder.

"Th—the social worker told me that I couldn't adopt because I live in an apartment...and I don't have a yard for them to play in."

"Well, you could take them to the park across from the church," he said. "I presume there's still a park there."

"That's not all. She said my job was too dangerous and—and I'm a single woman."

"Why, that's ridiculous." Gran looked properly outraged. "My Leah was a single mother, and she did a darn fine job of raisin' Gracie." She shrugged. "Of course, everything is a whole lot better now that Leah and Tyler are married. They're so happy together, and Gracie loves Tyler just like he's her own real pa."

Stephanie uttered a miserable-sounding moan. "The social worker said they would try to find a family for the children. One with two parents." She pulled away from Zach. "Oh, I'm sorry. I didn't mean to fall apart on you. I've just been so upset."

"Why don't you marry Zach? He needs a wife." Gran gazed at them as though this was the perfect solution. "Just look at how good you two look together."

Zach and Stephanie sprang apart and began speaking at once, denying this was a consideration.

"Oh, Gran," Misty said. "They do look cute together, but they don't even know each other."

Zach laced his fingers together under the table, recalling the sensation of holding Stephanie for a moment. He had not held a woman in his arms in a long time.

# Chapter 4

RIDICULOUS. STEPHANIE WASN'T INTERESTED IN GETTING married, especially to a man she had just met. A man who seemed to be tongue-tied around her.

She glanced at Zach, surreptitiously, under her lashes. He had a strong and handsome face with the remarkable Garrett eyes, a luminous blue, almost turquoise, ringed with black lashes. His dark hair was cut short. He would have looked like a soldier even if he wasn't wearing camo pants and an Army-green T-shirt.

He caught her examining him, and they both looked away.

When she checked him out again, he was still looking toward the patio at the back of the house. It gave her an opportunity to admire Zach's extremely well-developed arms. *Talk about your big guns.*

Resolutely, Stephanie turned away from Zach and found both Misty and Gran grinning at her. They could read her thoughts.

"Okay," she said. "I better talk to Big Jim and get on my way." Stephanie pushed back from the table and thanked Misty for the tea.

Zach stood when she did. She liked that. Good manners were rare in her world, where her fellow firefighters thought of her as one of the guys. She held out her hand to him. "It was really good to see you again, Zach. I hope you have a wonderful Christmas holiday here with your family."

"Thanks. It's good to see you, Ms. Gayle." His big paw closed around hers. Warm and rough.

When he released her hand, she went to seek out Big Jim, the man who might be able to help her turn the social worker's opinion around.

She found him in his office, the room his sons referred to as his "lair." The door stood open, but she knocked on the doorframe. "Excuse me, Big Jim...I hope I'm not bothering you."

He looked up from his laptop screen and waved her to a chair. "Sit right down, young lady. What can I do for you today?"

She swallowed hard and then poured out her story. "I was hoping maybe a recommendation from you and a few of the other prominent people in town might hold some weight when they make a decision about placing the children."

He gazed at her, his ferocious dark brows drawn together in a frown. "Of course. I'd be mighty happy to write a letter or make a call. I think it's very admirable of you to want to adopt those little ones. Lord knows they've been through hell." He scratched his chin. "I can ask both Breck Ryan, our attorney, and his wife Camryn, the local doctor. I'm sure they would be happy to give you a good reference."

A kernel of hope bloomed in her chest. "Oh, that would be awesome."

"Maybe the preacher too."

Stephanie left the Garrett ranch feeling that, perhaps, she might be able to overcome Miss Dyer's objections.

—∿∿—

Zach felt a little disappointed after Stephanie's departure. He figured she had things to do and wasn't at loose ends like he was.

He sought out his uncle and found him in an office with his fingers on a keyboard. He peeked in, and when he saw that Big Jim was busy, he turned away.

"Hold up there, Zach. Come on back here." Big Jim waved him into the room. "Sit yourself right down here, and tell me what's going on."

"I just wanted to thank you, sir…you know…for springing for the boots and new clothes." He faltered. "And for having me here."

Big Jim closed his laptop and folded his hands on top of his desk. "Now, look here, Zach. You're my brother's only son. You've got to know I love you like you were my own because you *are* my own. I'm real proud of you for serving our country, but you're home now."

"Yes, sir. I appreciate that, sir."

"Whatever you want to do, I will support you."

Zach heaved a sigh. "That's the problem, sir. I don't know anything else but ranching." His chest felt tight. "I never dreamed my mom would sell the ranch, but I suppose she had a right to do that. It was her ranch too."

Big Jim looked grim, as though he was fighting to hold his tongue.

Zach hoped he hadn't said something to anger him.

Big Jim blew out a long breath. "Whooee! I hear that. I was pretty ticked off at Adele for selling the land. There were some tax issues, but…I mean, your daddy worked his rear end off for that ranch. I know he wanted you to take over someday."

"I know that, sir. I really let him down."

Big Jim leaned forward. "You did no such thing, boy. Your daddy was proud of you every day of his life."

"You're right, sir. But I should have come home. If I hadn't reenlisted the last time, I would have been here when he needed me. I could have helped out and saved the ranch." He shrugged. "It was just too much for my mom to take on by herself."

Big Jim huffed out a breath. "That's a very generous attitude, boy. I must admit that I need to stop being angry with your mama for not taking care of the property. She could have asked for help before it was too late." He sat back, giving Zach a long look. "You still feel the same way about ranching, don't you? Going over to that hell in the Middle East might have changed you…you know… Maybe you came back with different interests?"

"No, I don't think so, sir. I was planning on taking up where my daddy left off." He made a palms-up gesture. "But now I've got to start at the bottom…if someone will hire me."

"Well, don't you worry about that. You got a job right here with me, son. You can join the boys in taking care of the stock this winter, and then in the spring we'll start planting some grain crops."

"Seriously, sir?"

"Of course, son. I wouldn't have said it if I didn't mean it."

"But I don't want to take advantage of my family. I have some savings, so I'm not desperate or anything."

"Zachery Garrett. Now you listen here. I need your

help. With Tyler going off on tours and concerts now, it's hard to get things done. I really need you to work with us. Can I depend on you?"

"Yes, sir." Zach stood and reached across the desk to shake hands with Big Jim. He left, feeling significantly better. He didn't want to be a burden to anyone, especially his family.

---

*Artillery shells going off. Big guns rattling his bones.*

*He reached for his weapon, but it wasn't there. The ordnance was getting closer. Their position was taking direct hits. He was hit, arcing through the air and falling to the hard ground. The pounding in his head was deafening. Someone was yelling. Someone grabbed him…*

"Zach! Zach, wake up!" It was Colton who was shaking him. "Whoa, buddy. You almost decked me."

Zach opened his eyes. He was on the floor and tangled in his bedding. His hands were fisted, and every muscle in his body was tensed for action. He was breathing hard and sweating, though the room was cool. "Oh, God! Colt," he gasped. "I—I was just—"

"Relax, bud, it was only a nightmare." Colt had squatted down beside him.

Zach's heart pounded so hard it shook his entire body. "Sorry! I'm sorry…"

Colt's hand was on his shoulder. He looked concerned. "You're home with us. You don't need to be afraid. We're all here for you."

"I know," he said. "Everyone's been great." He took a deep breath, held it, and let it out and then another.

"Just take it easy, big fella." Colt gave him a couple of thumps on the shoulder.

"Everything all right in here?" It was Misty standing in the open doorway.

"Everything's fine, babe," Colt said. "Go on back to bed."

She nodded but looked doubtful as she turned away.

Zach tried to disentangle himself from the bedding. "Listen, man. I'm really sorry. I didn't mean to disturb you and your bride."

Colt stood and reached a hand out to Zach, hefting him up from the floor. "No problem... You were screaming out a name when I came in. It was Jeb. Does that mean anything to you?"

It felt as though Colt had punched him. A flash of lights blinded him. He stared into the void, seeing only Jeb's face. Young and eager. He was on his first tour, and the old-timers called him the mascot. Zach tried to swallow, but his throat was too dry. The result was a guttural murmur.

Colt was still looking at him, a question etched on his face.

"I can't talk about it."

Colt gave a slight shake of his head. "Are you going to be okay?"

Zach forced a grin. "Sure. Don't worry about me. I'll see you in the morning." He gave Colt a slap on the shoulder and sent him out of the room. He then gathered his sheets and the quilt and remade the bed, but instead of climbing back under the covers, he went to the window and stared out at the snow-blanketed view. The scene was bathed in moonlight, reducing everything to black and white.

He pulled an armchair up close to the window and leaned his head back. He stayed that way until the sky lightened and he heard people stirring in the house.

*My family.*

———

Big Jim made it a point to spend time with Zach the next day. "C'mon, boy. Get your cowboy on. It's time to ride."

Zach hurried to change into his new Wranglers and boots. When he emerged, everyone in the house applauded.

Fern Davis had a wide smile on her face. "There ya go! You look like a cowboy now, Zach."

"Thanks. This feels good." He reached for his Army field jacket and shrugged into it. "Can't wait."

"You'll need this, Zach." Fern reached up toward him, and he leaned down to meet her. She wrapped a wool scarf around his neck and tucked it into his jacket. "You stay warm now." She gave him a pat on the chest.

He thought he recognized genuine affection in her eyes. "Thanks a lot, Miz Fern."

"Well, let's get going." Big Jim made "hurry up" gestures.

"We're coming," Colt sang out. He took his Stetson off a rack and settled it on his head before motioning to Zach. "This one's for you...if you don't mind wearing a secondhand hat."

Zach had to laugh at that. "Naw, I'm happy to have a hand-me-down." He accepted the black Stetson and tried it on for fit. "Looks like your big bucket head is about the same size as mine."

"Looks good on you, bud." Colton followed his dad out the door, and Zach brought up the rear.

The trio trooped out to the stables and saddled three horses.

Zach sucked in a deep breath. The stables smelled like horses, and that was like perfume to him. He hadn't realized how much he'd missed this familiar odor until he got a snoot full of it. They led the horses outside and closed up the stables. One by one, the three men mounted up and headed out, with Big Jim in the lead.

Colton reined in so that Zach could catch up. Their breath formed a white vapor that trailed behind them. Other than the clop-clop of horse hooves, the countryside was totally silent and distinctly chilly.

Zach was glad for the secondhand Stetson and the warm wool scarf wrapped around his neck. He felt as though every molecule of his body was on high alert, but not in the way it had been in Afghanistan. More like he was alert for positive things. The chill air nipped at his ears and cheeks, but it was not unpleasant.

He reined in when he saw a cardinal in flight. It lit in a fir tree, its brilliant red a sharp contrast to the dark green of the tree.

Zach realized that Big Jim and Colt had pulled up a short way ahead of him. They were both grinning at him.

"Sorry," Zach said. "I haven't seen a cardinal in a long damned time."

"No problem, son," Big Jim said. "Fill up your eyes and your heart. You're home now."

They rode quite a distance to the place where a brick house sat, snugly surrounded by snow-covered landscaping.

Zach recognized the plantings as being relatively new. In the spring, the young trees and shrubs would thrive.

Christmas lights were strung along the roofline, and a wreath was hung on the door.

They dismounted, but before they could approach the door, Tyler came outside.

"Hey, guys! Get right on in here." Ty reached out to take the reins from Zach. "Let's take the horses around back." He led the way, ending up by opening the door to stables, where the three horses' saddles were removed and they were fed and watered.

Tyler closed up the stables and led them into the house through the back door.

"Come right in, gentlemen," Leah called from the kitchen.

The men took off their jackets and hung them on a series of hooks inside the back entryway. There was a washer and dryer as well as a pantry and storage area for seldom-used items.

Zach carefully cleaned his boots on a mat inside the back door. Then he removed the wool scarf and Stetson, hanging them on the same hook as his jacket.

When they entered the kitchen, they found Leah waiting for them. "What's your preference, gentlemen? We have coffee, tea, or hot chocolate." She smiled prettily. "Or would you like something else to warm your bones?"

"How about a hot cup of coffee? That should be enough to warm up these old bones." Big Jim gave her a hug.

"Coming right up. In the meantime, help yourself to some pie. I just baked it."

"Whooee! You don't have to tell me twice." Big Jim

took a seat at the kitchen table and pulled out another chair for Zach. "Park it right here, boy. Warm up and get ready for a real treat. Leah's pies are legendary."

Colt seated himself and made complimentary sounds too.

"Where's Gracie?" Big Jim asked.

"Right here, Grandpa." She came racing into the kitchen and straight into Big Jim's arms.

"And what did you ask Santy Claus to bring you, sweet girl?"

Gracie snickered. "Grandpa, there's no such thing as Santa Claus. That's baby stuff."

Big Jim made an exaggerated face, looking shocked. "What? There is no Santy Claus? But—but I asked for a new pair of mittens. How am I going to keep my hands warm if ol' Santy doesn't come through?"

"Aww…Grandpa."

Tyler was lining up mugs and pouring coffee while Leah brought small plates and forks and placed them in front of Big Jim with a serving utensil. "You can do the honors."

Big Jim held up his hands in a gesture of surrender. "I'll slaughter this beautiful pie."

"I'm busy," Leah said. "I'm making cookies for church. Everyone is bringing something to share, and my contribution will be cookies."

Ty slid an arm around her and winked. "Lots and lots of cookies."

Big Jim picked up the serving piece and cut the pie. "I don't know if you're going to have any leftovers after we get done with this pie."

Leah laughed. "Don't be silly. I made it special for

you. Misty called me to let me know you were headed this way, so I thought you deserved a little treat."

Big Jim's grin went wall-to-wall. "Well, how 'bout that? I told you to marry this girl, Ty." He served a large slab of pie to Zach and Colt before cutting a slice for himself.

"Yeah, that never occurred to me, Dad." Ty sat down at the table across from Zach. "You're looking great, Zach. More like yourself in western wear."

"Feeling more like myself for sure." Zach took another bite. "What's this about a singing career? Colt said you'd been touring the country and playing concerts."

Ty nodded. "Yeah, I was touring, but not again for a while. I'm thinking about cutting a Christmas album to release next year." He glanced at Leah, who was humming as she stirred something into a mixing bowl. "Now that we're having a baby, I want to be home for a while. Leah needs me to be here, for her and for Gracie." He pulled the eight-year-old onto his lap and gave her a kiss on her temple.

"I understand how you feel," Big Jim said. "It's good to have you home, son."

"When is your baby due?" Zach asked.

"January," Ty said.

"January tenth to be exact," Leah sang out.

Zach couldn't wrap his head around Colt's middle brother being married, much less his status as a step-father and father-to-be. "Sounds great. Congratulations." He finished off his pie while surreptitiously examining Tyler and Gracie. He sure did look comfortable in his new role.

By the time the trio took their leave and headed back to the main house, the temperature had dropped, and new snow was falling.

Zach pulled the wool scarf up to cover his ears and face, glad to have fallen heir to the Stetson. He trailed behind Big Jim and Colton, enjoying the peace and quiet and the familiarity of the scene.

# Chapter 5

STEPHANIE HELD HER PHONE FOR SOME TIME. SHE KNEW WHAT she wanted to do, but she couldn't bring herself to do it. If there were only some way to bring it about casually… but that wasn't an option.

"Don't be such a wuss," she chided herself. Resolutely she punched in the main number to the Garrett ranch.

"Hello?" It was Misty who answered.

"Hi. It's Stephanie." She hesitated. "Is Zach there?" *Silence.*

"Um, sure. Let me find him."

Stephanie heard the receiver being put down and, after a short wait, picked up again.

"Hello?" Zach's deep voice caused a tingling sensation low in her belly.

She cleared her throat. "Hello, Zach. It's Stephanie. Um—"

"It's nice to hear your voice. What can I do for you?" He sounded focused and upbeat. Not the way he had the last time she saw him.

"I know this is weird, but—I need to know… Can you dance?"

He chuckled. "Well, I don't know. It's been a long time since I stepped foot on a dance floor. What's up?"

"There's a Christmas dance here in Amarillo. It's sponsored by law enforcement and firefighters…for charity."

"Are you asking me to a dance?"

Stephanie swallowed hard, suddenly shy. "Well, the proceeds go to the children's home."

"But it's a dance?" He did sound interested.

"Yes, it's a huge formal dance... Would you be willing to go with me?" She cringed in preparation for outright rejection.

"Sure thing. When you say formal, you're not talking about western wear?"

She gnawed her lower lip. Now he would back out. "Unfortunately, no. But you can rent a tuxedo here in Amarillo. I'll pay for it."

He let out a scoffing noise. "Don't be ridiculous. I can pay to rent a tux." He heaved a sigh. "Tuxedo, huh? And what will you be wearing?"

"A dress. A long formal dress." She shrugged as though he could see the gesture. "I think you'll like it."

"And your hair? Are you going to wear it down? I really like your hair."

A flush of pleasure washed through her. Absently, she touched her hair. "I was going to wear it up, but... if you—"

"Down, please." The sound of his deep voice was causing strange sensations.

"Sure. I can do that."

*Another silence.*

"Can I ask when this event is to take place?"

"Oh, silly me. It's next Saturday." After giving him the important details, she disconnected, smiling and wondering how that deep, wraparound voice could lift her up so high.

"What was that all about?" Misty had obviously been eavesdropping.

He wasn't quite sure he wanted to share with her. "Just a phone call."

She smiled knowingly. "Like that, huh?"

He walked away with questions swirling through his brain. He couldn't imagine that a woman as beautiful as Stephanie didn't have men lined up three deep waiting to ask her on a date, but for some reason, she had chosen to ask him to this dance. He knew she was interested in the children's home, so maybe this charity event was extra important to her. But why not go with someone who meant something to her...a boyfriend?

*But she asked me...*

He came upon Fern Davis, and her features were wrinkled up in a frown. She waggled her fingers at him and appeared to be pacing.

"What's up, Miz Fern? You look upset."

She let out a deep sigh. "I just can't seem to git no help."

He drew nearer. "What do you need help with, ma'am? I'd be happy to help you."

She waved her hands. "Oh, no. I can't ask you to do this. It's too much."

"Tell me what it is, and maybe I can give some assistance."

"It's my ranch. I jus' can't seem to keep a hand there." She pushed her glasses up on her short nose. "It's winter time. All they have to do is see to the stock. Make sure they's fed and safe."

"Um, well, I'll ask Big Jim if I can borrow a truck and go check things out."

She gave him an appraising look. "Well, mebbe..."

—⁓—

Stephanie worked her shift, and it was totally quiet for a change. This gave her lots of time to worry about Cody and Ivy. She called the children's home on her break and was assured that there was no problem and the children were safe.

The assurances gave her no comfort because she knew how fast things could change. The children were so young and so vulnerable. She wanted to take them and tuck them away some secure place where they could recover from the trauma they had suffered and thrive like normal children.

Her fellow firefighters performed some regular maintenance tasks on the fire engine, but she chose to do maintenance on her own equipment. She replaced first aid supplies in her medical kit. Packing it fully, she felt confident that the supplies that had been depleted would be ready the next time she needed them. Nothing like being well stocked.

She considered her fellow firefighters. Generally, nice guys. Some were married, but some were single. At first, they had checked her out and acted flirtatious, but when she was adamant that she would not date any of them, they had backed off and begun to treat her as they would any other professional. Occasionally, one of them would make a run at her, but as long as she didn't give any encouragement, they would quickly lose interest.

Stephanie had taken special training to learn to operate in small spaces. At first, she had felt claustrophobic when she had been lowered into a cave or cavern or the occasional well, but she was a very important member of the confined space team. The fellows could operate the heavy equipment, but she was the one to crawl into tight places.

She expelled a breath. She could understand why the social worker thought her job was too dangerous. Maybe she could change positions. She could talk to the chief if she thought there was a chance Miss Dyer might overlook the other issues. Maybe she could at least rent a small house…with a yard…a fenced yard.

Her shoulders sagged. There was that other issue. Stephanie was single, and she was very good at it.

She thought about her decision to ask the big and hunky Zach Garrett to accompany her to the Christmas dance. Yes, it was pretty much self-serving. She knew that showing up with a tall, well-built man, whom the others might think was her boyfriend, would also keep them at bay…because, face it, Zach made most of the boys look downright puny.

"Whatcha smiling about, Gayle?" one of the firefighters called to her.

"Oh, nothing," she called back.

---

"Sure," Big Jim said. "We can go over to Miz Fern's place to check things out. Good that you want to help her."

Zach shrugged. "Who wouldn't want to help her? She's a really nice little lady."

"Agreed. I'm pretty fond of her myself." He reached for his jacket and the black Stetson that topped his crown of silver hair whenever he was outside the house.

They climbed into Big Jim's truck and idled for a

few minutes while the windshield wipers arced back and forth, clearing the glass of the soft snow.

"Beautiful day, isn't it?"

"Yes, sir. I haven't seen this kind of landscape since I left home." Zach felt a twinge of something close to pain when he said the word *home*. He still wasn't sure where home was, but at least it was more familiar here than at his mother's new house in Fort Worth.

He gazed out the passenger-side window, his breath clouding it instantly, but he swiped at it with the sleeve of his field jacket.

"So, how's it goin', boy? Are you getting settled in?" Big Jim shot a quick glance at Zach just before the truck rumbled over the cattle guard at the entrance to the Garrett property, He glanced both ways before turning onto the highway. "I know it's quite a change for you. All this quiet after all that fightin'… It's bound to take a little time to get used to things."

Zach heaved a sigh. *The old man hit the nail on the head.* "I'm really glad to be here, sir. It's great to be back on familiar territory…not looking for snipers or roadside bombs."

"That must be tough for you. I know Colt and his brothers are really glad you're home."

"Me too. Thanks for letting me stay with you. I'll figure out where I belong in time." He shook his head. "Right now, I'm just thankful that things don't seem to blow up around here."

A muscle in Big Jim's very square jaw twitched, but he said nothing.

The drive to Fern Davis's place was quiet. Zach kept staring out at the passing countryside. It was like driving through a sugar-crusted diorama. Not really real until his boots crunched into the snow…until the cold air bit his cheeks and ears.

Big Jim pulled onto a farm-to-market road and from there turned again. He was on a narrow unpaved road with fields on both sides. At the end was a farmhouse with some outbuildings at the rear.

"Nice little place," Zach commented. They sat in the warm, idling truck.

"You should have seen it before Tyler took his hand to it. Miz Fern's husband passed, and a mean old bastard and his sons tried to run her off the land." A smile broke out on Big Jim's face. "But Fern's a tough old girl. She stood her ground, but then Tyler got involved." He gave a rough chuckle. "I swear that boy is rough and ready for trouble." He shifted into park and turned off the motor. "Let's check things out, shall we?"

Zach nodded and opened the passenger door. The sudden bite of frigid air gnawed at his face. He tugged the wool scarf up around his ears and the back of his neck and pulled the Stetson lower. Definitely a big change from his time in Afghanistan. Yet when he drew the cold air into his lungs, he felt hopeful. Change was what he needed most.

Big Jim strode straight up to the house and mounted the steps to the porch. His boots sounded like hammer blows.

Zach followed behind, watching while Big Jim tried the door, found it locked, and peered in the front windows.

"Everything looks all right. Nothing disturbed."

Zach looked inside, seeing a small living room that looked as if it had last been updated in the 1950s but somehow seemed homey and comfortable. Beyond the living room he could see what appeared to be a dining room and probably a kitchen at the back of the dwelling. "It's quiet here."

"Yeah… Let's go check out back." Big Jim rounded the house with Zach on his tail.

There was a large barn with faded red paint. It appeared to be in good repair.

Big Jim opened the door and swung it wide. One wall was lined with bales of hay and bags of feed. There were several empty stalls on the other side with an old John Deere tractor parked in the middle.

Zach had to smile at the familiar scene. Several other pieces of equipment were parked close by and covered with tarps. He recognized a baler among them.

Big Jim closed up the barn and turned around. "Everything looks good. We can go check on the stock now."

"Isn't that a chicken coop?" Zach asked.

Big Jim grinned. "It could be. It was an outhouse a long time ago." He hooted out a single laugh. "But when the Davis family got indoor plumbing, this got rebuilt to become a chicken coop."

"Where are the chickens?"

"In their nice new coop behind Ty and Leah's house. I think they're mostly too old to lay and too tough to eat, so Gracie thinks of them as pets. It's her job to feed them."

"Sounds like everything's taken care of."

"Almost," Big Jim said. "Fern's got a small herd, mostly Angus. We'll just check on them and go back to the ranch."

Zach and Big Jim retraced their steps to the truck. It

was easy to see where they had walked previously, their footprints having imprinted in the snow all the way to the ground below.

In the truck, Zach was glad the heater came right on, but the windows frosted up immediately.

Big Jim, however, seemed content to sit in the idling truck while the defroster cleared the windshield. In time, he slipped the vehicle into gear and backed out onto the unpaved road. He turned the truck around and headed back toward the highway but took a right almost immediately onto another unpaved road. He drove about a quarter mile and stopped the truck. There were cattle in a snow-covered field. There was some kind of structure with a roof and open on two sides.

Big Jim left the truck idling and got out. He crossed the bar ditch and grasped one of the fence posts.

Zach joined him, noting that Big Jim seemed to be concentrating. He also noticed that there were hay and a trough of grain under the structure. Cattle were gathered nearby, and Big Jim appeared to be counting them.

"Damnation! I keep losing count. Could you tell me how many you see? There are supposed to be thirty-two in this field."

Zach counted twice, and indeed, there were thirty-two head of cattle.

They climbed in the truck and headed back to the Garrett ranch.

"I'm sure this will set Fern's mind at ease."

------

"Are you okay?"

Ivy's head bobbed up and down against Stephanie's

uniform shirt. Some days all she needed was to feel these two little ones' arms around her neck, and the problems of the world seemed to evaporate.

"How about you, Cody? Is everything all right?" She gazed at him as he shrugged.

His little face crumpled as he, too, collapsed into her arms.

"Aww...don't worry. We'll get things straightened out." She felt his shoulders shake as he gave in to the strong emotion pent up within him.

"But I wanna go home with you," he wailed.

This prompted Ivy to start whimpering as well.

"Honestly, Stephanie." Marilyn Phillips, a caregiver with a grandmotherly appearance, was shaking her head. "I think you and these children share some kind of special bond. Maybe things will work out for you." She gave a nod of her head in the direction of Miss Dyer's office.

Stephanie heaved a sigh. "I sure hope so." To the children, she presented a smile. "Hey, you two. I brought you presents. Don't you want to see them?"

Cody drew back, his eyes like liquid chocolate. "Pwesents?"

Ivy stared at her in a like manner.

Stephanie reached in her pockets and gathered something in her closed fists. "Let's see what's in here." She presented a fist to each child.

Ivy put her small hand on top of Stephanie's fist, and a timid smile played around her lips.

Stephanie smiled back and opened her hand, displaying a small stuffed toy elephant.

Ivy squealed in delight but didn't take the toy until

Stephanie assured her it was a gift for her. The child clasped the toy elephant, her eyes shining.

Cody patted her other fist, and Stephanie responded with a big smile and opened her hand to show a small truck. He wrapped his fingers around it while gazing into Stephanie's eyes as though she might take it away from him.

She swallowed hard, thinking that these children had lost so much. She assured them that these small presents were theirs to keep.

By the time she left the children's facility, she felt her visit had cheered Ivy and Cody, but being forced to leave them behind was painful for all concerned.

The sky was a dull gray, signaling another gelid night. Temperatures had dropped, and a light mist of snow was falling but evaporating as it hit the pavement. Stephanie didn't mind. It felt cool against her exposed skin, calming the raging emotions threatening to overwhelm her.

She was distracted when she walked across the parking lot to her truck. She unclipped the keychain from her belt loop, the place she habitually carried it. A variety of small tools were clustered along with her keys, but she clicked the remote to open the door.

She came to a complete stop when she reached her truck. Someone had scratched a message in the side of her beloved vehicle.

*You Dead*

Fear spiraled around her gut, causing her stomach to clench. Glancing around hurriedly, she saw no one. The parking area was deserted except for Stephanie. Yet someone had left this threat for her.

She had no doubt who had left it: Rafe Neeley or one of his brothers. The hair on the back of her neck was standing on end. He could be looking at her through the sight of a sniper's rifle.

With deliberate calm she turned and retraced her footsteps back to the children's facility. Her first instinct had been to jump in the truck and drive away as fast as possible, but instead she called the sheriff's office from inside the building and kept watch until someone arrived.

The first was a highway patrolman, and the second was a deputy out of Langston.

Deputy Dexter Shelton climbed out of his patrol car. "Hey, Stephanie Gayle. What's going on?"

"Hey, Dex. Someone vandalized my truck." She pointed to where her vehicle was parked. Now, flanked by the two armed and uniformed officers, she felt more confident, although she realized a sniper could take them all out in a matter of seconds.

"Damn! That looks serious." Dex frowned, resting his hand on his weapon. "Did you piss someone off, Stephanie?"

"Apparently." She turned to both men. "I know who did this. I called you in case there might be some kind of biological evidence or fingerprints."

The highway patrolman crossed his arms over his chest and gave her a skeptical look. "I can call in the techs, but I doubt they could pull fingerprints when your truck is covered with water from the snow."

"Probably not, but I'm going to make a report." Dex took pictures with his phone. "Tell me the name of your suspect."

"Rafe Neeley."

At the mention of his name, both officers started speaking at once.

"What makes you think he's involved?" Dex asked.

Stephanie pressed her lips together and took a deep breath before relating the morbid story.

Dex's brows drew together. "Yeah, I remember that incident. Terrible tragedy." He glanced at the children's facility. "Is this where the children are staying?"

She nodded, not trusting her voice to be steady.

The highway patrolman frowned as well. "And this guy is after you?"

Dex spoke up. "Stephanie was the first responder. She rescued the children, and so I'm betting this asshole blames you for something?"

Stephanie nodded. "The children witnessed the murder. The police took the boy's statement, actually filmed it. I guess Neeley wants to take his revenge."

"I think you should go home and lock the doors," Dex said. "I'll file this report and let you know if there's any news about capturing him."

"There's an APB out on all three Neeley brothers," the patrolman said. "This means they're still in the area."

Stephanie was wracked with a visible shiver. "I'm worried about the children, Cody in particular. Is there any way to protect him?"

"I'll talk to my sergeant," the patrolman said. "I'm sure he's going to okay some patrols of the area."

"Thanks. That makes me feel a little better." Stephanie allowed Dex to open the driver's side door and help her inside.

"You be careful, Stephanie. Sounds like this Neeley guy is a real nutjob."

With that comforting warning, Stephanie headed back to her apartment, but she did keep checking her rearview mirror all the way home.

—⁓—

The next morning, the Garrett men headed out to do chores. Zach and Colton tackled the stables, cleaning out the stalls and giving the horses feed and water.

"Thanks, Zach. This usually takes a lot more time. You're on fire today." Colton gave him a playful punch on the arm.

"Feelin' pretty good today." Zach mimed sparring with him. "I guess whenever you have time, I need you to take me to find a truck."

"You can always borrow my truck, bud."

"Thanks, Colt, but I'm going to need my own transportation. Might as well bite the bullet."

"Sure. We can check around online. Let's head for the house and fire up the computer."

Zach and Colt chased each other back to the house, pushing and shoving and Zach scooping up a handful of snow, forming it into a ball, and lobbing it at Colt. Colt flinched and formed a snowball of his own. They were yelling and laughing but sobered when they saw Big Jim lounging against the back door.

"I swear, you two are the same as you were ten years ago…maybe twenty."

"No doubt about it," Colt agreed.

"Just a little bigger now," Zach said.

"Dad, we're going to go online to shop. My friend Zach needs a truck." Colt strode past his father and into the warm kitchen, Zach and Big Jim hard on his heels.

Zach shed his field jacket and gloves. He followed Colt into the office and settled into the chair across from the desk. He watched Colt check area dealers and advertisements. They chatted about what he was looking for, finally settling on a late-model used Ford or Chevrolet four-door truck.

The list prices were a bit higher than Zach had hoped, but he thought he might be able to talk them down.

"That'n looks like a good'n." Big Jim leaned over his shoulder to poke a finger at the computer screen.

"Well, of course you'd like it, Dad. It's silver, like our trucks." Colton chuckled.

"Yeah," Big Jim agreed. "And it's a Ford…same model as mine…just a few years older. I think you should go check it out." He waved his hands to shoo them out of the room. "Go on, now. Before somebody else snaps it up."

Zach looked at his uncle, questioning his sudden change of mood. "Right now?"

"Right now. You boys go check it out." Big Jim drew Colt aside when Zach was shrugging back into his field jacket. Zach set the Stetson on his head and worked the gloves back onto his hands.

Colt gestured toward the front door. "Let's get on the road, bud."

He drove Zach to a small auto dealership on the outskirts of Amarillo.

About a dozen pickup trucks were lined up on one side of the lot, while SUVs and sedans were on the other. All the vehicles looked clean. The snow had been cleared off, and the wares were shining, even on an overcast day.

"That's the one we were looking at." Colt pointed to the silver Ford four-door.

Zach peered in the window, noting that the inside looked as clean as the outside.

"How you fellers doin'?" A shortish man came out of the sales office and sauntered up to them. He was wearing a bright-blue quilted jacket that gave him the appearance of a round blue balloon.

"Um—we're great." Zach said. "I'd like to take a look at this truck." He laid his hand on the hood.

"Oh," Colt interjected. "We'd like to look at that one too." He tilted his head toward a much older and much cheaper truck.

Zach tried to keep a straight face, realizing his friend was laying the groundwork for an excellent game of bargaining.

After a half hour of listening to the salesman disparage the less-expensive model and extol the virtues of the higher-priced vehicle, a test drive of the latter, and seemingly lost keys to the former, they found themselves sitting in the fusty, overheated office.

The price had been lowered somewhat, and Zach was thinking he could make a significant down payment and pay off the rest over time…and hoping he could find steady employment given his strengths and with access to reliable transportation.

"How much if we paid cash?"

Colt's question caught Zach off guard. He hadn't exactly shared how much he had in savings or if he wanted to blow most of it on a truck.

Then Colt asked the seller to knock a couple of thousand off that number.

Zach just sat back and let him handle the transaction. His bank information was in his jacket pocket, so when he was reaching for his checkbook, he was surprised when Colt sent him a subtle shake of his head.

"Then it's a deal," Colt said. He pulled a folded paper out of his pocket and wrote something on it. He pushed it across the desk to the salesman, who accepted it with a smile.

"Let me get you the title, Mr. Garrett."

"Make it out to Zachery Garrett. It's his truck."

Zach gave him a questioning look, but Colt waved his hand, warning him to be quiet. Zach wasn't sure what the plan was but figured he would be responsible for paying Colt once they got out of there. Not a problem. The price was much more reasonable than he would have gotten it for. He just needed to find a job immediately.

Once outside, the two best friends walked to the newly acquired truck.

"I'll pay you when we get home. Is that okay?"

"Nope." Colt tossed him the keys. "Merry Christmas. Dad paid for your truck."

Zach stopped in his tracks. "What? That's entirely too much. I can't possibly accept."

"Get in the truck," Colt directed. "And Dad said to tell you no arguments. You don't want to hurt his feelings, do you?"

"No, of course not, but this is just too much."

"Don't worry about it. Dad is not a man to be argued with," Colt said. "Now, get in your truck and let's get home 'cause I'm cold and I want to kiss my hot wife."

Zach grinned at him and got behind the wheel. He started up the truck and felt a sense of relief. He pulled out of the car lot, glad that he had been born a Garrett.

# Chapter 6

STEPHANIE HAD LAIN AWAKE MOST OF THE NIGHT, FLINCHING at any little sound. She awoke with a dull headache, but her first cup of coffee and a couple of Tylenol took the edge off.

When she got to work, her fellow firefighters gathered around, commenting on her injured truck.

One of the men, Wallace, drew her aside. "Listen, kiddo. The guys and me…we're all worried about you." He laid a big paw on her shoulder. "We been talking…" He glanced around at the other men.

She swallowed hard. The last thing she needed was pity.

"This guy—the murder guy—he's a really mean sumbitch."

"I know," Stephanie said.

"We all thought you needed some protection." He gazed deep into her eyes as though trying to project his sincerity.

"Thanks, Wallace. I appreciate all you men." She turned and waved, offering a totally insincere smile.

"You're gonna see a lot of us. Miller drew up a chart, and we're gonna take turns checking up on you at home. We'll be driving by and sometimes sitting on your apartment."

"That's great. You guys are the very best." She knew there was no point in trying to dissuade them. They were the very meaning of the word *zealous,* and they were very protective of her, their little sister.

She went into the station and clocked in. A quick call to her insurance company and she made notes on the instructions. Attacking her beloved truck had caused her more pain than if she had been attacked physically.

Unfortunately, the best body shop in Texas was located in Langston. It was run by a crusty old man. He was the only person on the planet she would trust her truck to. She called him, and he assured her he could get to it right after the Christmas holiday.

She disconnected, feeling dejected. *Happy holidays, my ass.*

Her shift dragged on. Only one small house fire, electrical in origin. When she and her squad returned to the fire station, she was in the process of putting away her gear when her cell rang.

"Good afternoon, Stephanie." It was Zach's deep voice that reached out and wrapped itself around her.

"Zach," she breathed, blushing when her fellow firefighters picked up on the change in her voice, and grinned. There were a few catcalls.

"I just wanted to find out where to pick you up and what time."

She liked that he sounded eager. She liked that he was planning ahead. "Let me just step outside. Too many interested parties at the moment." She smiled at her squad and sailed out to stand in front of the fire station under an overhang. "Still there?"

"You bet."

"Sorry. The guys were hanging onto every word."

"Sounds like they need to get a hobby."

Stephanie let out a whoop of laughter. "That's so funny. Most of these characters have too many hobbies. One of my buds is a knitter."

That brought laughter from Zach. "I can't picture a big burly firefighter with knitting needles."

"Picture it."

They conversed for a while, and she gave him her address and directions to get there. "Zach, I really appreciate you taking me to this dance. It's a really big deal, and I have to go." She leaned against the building, out of the wind that had picked up. "Last couple of years, I've just gone alone, but—"

"With all those guys, I would think they would be fighting to take you to a dance…or anywhere for that matter."

Stephanie shook her head, even though she knew he couldn't see. "I couldn't ask one of the guys. It would change the dynamic if they were to start thinking of me as a woman."

"Damn! I knew you were a woman the first second I laid eyes on you." He made an appreciative sound.

For some reason that pleased her immensely. "So, I'll see you on Saturday?"

"I'll be there with my tux on."

———

Zach disconnected, a wide grin on his face. Now, he needed to take his truck into Amarillo and find a place to rent a tuxedo.

He spent the rest of the day working with Big Jim, Colton, and Tyler. Whatever needed to be done he jumped into wholeheartedly.

He tried to gather hints as to what he might be able to

give them as Christmas presents. As far as he could tell, none of the Garretts were wanting for anything. It was difficult to shop for a group with no particular needs. Maybe he should opt for gift cards so they could each choose something they might really want.

Zach blew out a frustrated breath. Gift cards sounded pretty lame. *Too impersonal*.

"What's that all about, bud?" Colt asked.

"Nothin'."

"Seriously? Your face looks like someone just popped your balloon."

"Nah, just trying to think of something to get for your dad for Christmas. He's been so great to me. I want to get him a special gift."

"Dad is a tough one." Colt's brow furrowed. "If he wants something, he gets it."

"What did you get him?"

Colt's face morphed into a broad grin. "I'm off the hook. My lovely Misty did all the heavy lifting. Not sure what she got him or anyone else. That little scamp has all the presents wrapped and under the tree."

"Must be nice," Zach said. "Being married sure does seem to suit you."

"I've never been so happy. You ought to think about finding your own happiness. I'm sure there's a great girl out there just waiting for you."

Zach brushed that off. "I need to figure out what to do with my life first. I can't ask any sane female to be a part of it until I'm settled."

"You're settled," Colt pronounced.

"Job. I need a job." Zach laughed. "You know... income?"

"You're a rancher. We're Garretts. That's what we all do." Colt walked away, shaking his head as if that was settled.

Zach watched him leave, knowing nothing was settled. Still, he thought he might ask Leah or Misty for gift suggestions.

---

Stephanie's jaw was tight. She had been cruising the internet. Unfortunately, she'd found more than she wanted to find.

The Neeley brothers were not strangers to law enforcement. The oldest, Eugene, had served time for everything from petty theft to aggravated assault.

The younger brother, Curtis, had served time for armed robbery. And right smack dab in the middle, Rafe Neeley. It appeared that Rafe was the good brother... or perhaps he was less bad. That is, until he married a widow with two young children. There were multiple calls to the house for domestic abuse. The children had been removed from the home on two occasions, but for some reason, they had been returned.

Then, one night, Rafe and his wife got into an argument that ended in her death. She'd been shot with a small-caliber handgun, but she bled out before the ambulance arrived.

Stephanie had done the only thing she thought reasonable at the time. She had entered the building to rescue the mother but carried two very young children out of harm's way instead. The police had taken Rafe down easily enough, and Cody had related the entire story. His statement had been filmed because the social worker insisted that he was too fragile to be put on the stand. But the video had been presented as eyewitness testimony at the arraignment, so Rafe's claim of innocence had been discounted. His escape had been orchestrated when he was being transferred from the county jail in Amarillo to a secure prison to be held until his trial.

Stephanie had no doubt that it was Rafe who had scratched the threat into the paint of her truck. No one else hated her that much. At least, not that she knew of.

She was terrified that all three of the violent men were on the loose and might be focused on exacting revenge on the woman who had removed the children before they could be murdered too. No witnesses to belie Rafe's claim that his wife had been murdered by some stranger.

Stephanie made a disparaging sound and closed the laptop. No point in scaring herself even more. She had known how bad Rafe was, and now she knew it was a family business.

"Gayle!" It was Lieutenant Larsen, her supervisor, who poked his head into the break room. "You have a visitor." He jerked his thumb to indicate that said visitor was behind him.

Stephanie stood up when she spied Zach towering over her much shorter boss. She was aware that she was staring at the hottest man she had seen in a long time… and he was staring back at her…and smiling.

A warm flush swirled through her insides. It was the eyes that got her…and his grin…and his broad shoulders…

Stephanie took a deep breath. She didn't want to go all goony in front of her fellows. She consciously sobered and nodded to her boss. "Thanks."

He turned to glance at Zach again and then left them alone.

Zach came into the break room, his gaze fastened on her. "Hi." He gestured to her navy tee with the squad emblem over her heart and the dark trousers and heavy boots. "You look…awesome…and also really badass."

She chuckled, aware that she could look intimidating, but not to this fellow. "Thanks, I think. What brings you all the way to Amarillo?"

"I got a tux." He glanced away, as though embarrassed. "And I wanted to see you."

"I'm so glad you did. Want something to drink?" She gestured to the soda machine. "We serve nothing but the best here."

"Sure." He reached into his pocket, but she was faster, inserting coins into the slot.

"What's your pleasure?"

He looked even more embarrassed. "I usually don't let ladies pay for my drinks."

"Well, it's a new day, cowboy. I'm a woman, and I invited you to have a drink with me. Hope you're okay with that."

He shrugged. "Sure." He pushed the button, and a canned soda rolled out. "Thanks."

She huffed out a frustrated breath. "Sorry. As the lone woman on the squad, I tend to get a lot of patronizing. Don't get me wrong. The guys are great, but sometimes they're just…"

"I see." Zach looked back over his shoulder to where three of the firemen were hanging out close enough to observe them.

"Yeah, it's like having a bunch of big brothers, and I can't seem to have any privacy." She stuffed in more coins and selected a drink for herself.

"We could go somewhere."

Stephanie shook her head. "I'm on duty."

"Could we sit in my truck?"

"No, but there's an empty office. Let me show you." She reached out to take his hand, surprised that this big former Army Ranger was following her lead. She took him past half a dozen of her ogling coworkers, who went out of their way to check Zach out and roll their eyes.

Donnell, one of the newest additions to the squad, leaned forward and deliberately bumped his shoulder against Zach's.

What happened next left Stephanie breathless.

Zach rounded on Donnell, his hands fisted. The granite-hard countenance held no mercy.

The two men glared at each other, but Zach's expression was far more frightening.

Donnell stepped back, breaking the impasse. "Um, sorry," he murmured.

Stephanie put her hand on Zach's sleeve, noting that his arm felt like warm steel.

"Who's your friend, Gayle?" Wallace asked.

She raised her chin, meeting his gaze. "This is my friend Zach Garrett. And Zach, these…" She made a gesture, dismissing the men. "These are a bunch of asshats I work with. You don't need to remember them." She turned and led the way to the small office and opened the door. When she whirled around, Zach was on her heels, and the rest of the men in the room were laughing.

"I see what you mean," Zach said. "Tough crew."

"Asshats," she pronounced firmly.

"But they've got your back," he said.

"Yeah, I suppose so."

He sat down beside her, causing the small settee to jostle her.

She was very aware of his overall bigness. She reflected that she knew three ways to overpower a much larger attacker...not that he was going to attack her, but it felt good to know she wasn't some helpless little woman. "There was a moment there when I thought you were going to rip Donnell a new one."

"Sorry. My reflexes are still pretty taut." He flashed a sheepish smile. "I'm trying to gear down."

She gave a smile in return. "I'm glad you stopped by."

"I just wanted to see you...and I was in town." He shrugged, looking suddenly boyish and eager. "I hope I didn't interrupt anything important."

"Not at all. I was just doing some...research."

---

On the way home, Zach circled through the town of Langston and stopped at Fern Davis's ranch. It was actually a fair-sized piece of land, but when put beside the Garrett holdings, it was very small by comparison. Not many cattle left in the herd, but that could be built up over time.

He pulled up close to the house. It looked like a painting. A rustic winter scene. A layer of snow blanketed everything, so it appeared to be pure and untouched. The snow lent the illusion that everything was clean and fresh, not run-down and sadly neglected.

Zach shut off the motor and stepped out into the snow, marring the perfect surface with his boot prints. He trekked up to the house to check that the doors were still locked up tight. Peeking inside, he could spot nothing out of place from the previous visit with Big Jim.

The barns and outbuildings were the same, but there was a building Fern had called "the bunkhouse," and that was unlocked. Perhaps the previous tenant had left it open, but Zach stepped inside cautiously. The first room looked like an efficiency apartment, with a kitchen along one end. In the middle, an overstuffed chair and a bulky old-style television sat atop a bookcase on the opposite wall, with a bed and nightstand on the other. The bed was unmade, but the hired hand had probably not been a neat freak.

There was a door into a second room with a few more bunks and a bathroom. This room had a musty, unused odor, but the previous room appeared to have been recently occupied. He presumed this was the living quarters of Fern's various hands, but the last one had left the place a mess. There was trash on the small dining table.

Zach made another round of the area close to the house, looking for signs of recent disturbance, but everything seemed to be in order.

On his return trip to the Garrett ranch, he had a lot on his mind. The image of Stephanie Gayle's beautiful face kept appearing in his thoughts. Getting to see her at work had been a treat, but her fellow firefighters were very protective. They had closed ranks around her the minute he asked for her. They seemed to be very possessive of the woman.

Zach shook his head. She was beautiful and intelligent. Everything a man could want in a woman...but he was pretty sure he wasn't worthy of her. He literally had nothing to offer. Not to mention he was on edge all the time. He just couldn't seem to leave Afghanistan behind. *The dreams...*

He pulled up in front of the Garrett ranch house and sat inside his truck for a few minutes. It hadn't occurred to him to go out looking for female companionship...not yet. But meeting Stephanie had been pure happenstance. That his uncle had been funding her special project was just a coincidence. That he was suffering stirrings of passion and longing for something deeper with this woman was amazing to Zach. He had felt nothing but a void inside for so long.

Above all, he didn't want to do anything that might negatively affect Stephanie. He climbed out of his truck and crunched through the snow up to the front door, with his newly rented tuxedo carefully draped over his arm. He stamped the slush off his boots and wiped them on the mat before entering the house.

"Thanks," Leah greeted him. "I've been fussing at the men to clean their boots before they come inside."

"Let me know if you need some help with the cleaning," Zach offered. "I'll be happy to help."

Leah laughed and shook her head. "Are you kidding? My Tyler will hardly allow me to brush my own teeth, much less do any housework."

Zach hung the hanger with his tux on the coat rack and shed his field jacket and exchanged it for the tux.

"What do you have there?" Leah asked.

"It's a tuxedo I rented. I'm going to take Stephanie

Gayle to some fancy dance in Amarillo on Saturday. Um—she asked me."

"Zach, that's fantastic. Stephanie is such a great person."

He swallowed hard. "That was just what I was thinking." He draped the tux over his shoulder.

"And she ain't bad to look at either," Fern offered when she joined them. She was carrying a clear plastic bag of ornaments.

"Gran, what do you have there?" Leah eyed the bag.

"Well, I was just a-thinkin' that we need a little more Christmas cheer around here. So I'm puttin' up some decoration of my own...just to make things festive."

Leah met Zach's gaze over her grandmother's head. "Um, I don't know, Gran. Maybe Big Jim likes things more minimal. I know he's planning on getting a tree."

"Well, he needs a nudge then. We gotta get some holiday spirit goin'." She went into the living room and set her bag down. "I have a little Christmas village. I hadn't gotten it out since you was a little girl, Leah."

Leah blinked rapidly. "Oh, Gran. That's so sweet. I remember that little village. It used to set my imagination on fire. Let's set it up on the sideboard." She crossed the room to start clearing items off the surface.

Zach felt a warm stirring in his chest. This was what family was all about. "You ladies don't work too hard now." He started toward his room but turned back. "Um, Miz Fern, I went by your place earlier. Everything looks fine, except..."

Fern turned to him expectantly.

"The bunkhouse... It was open. Did your last employee turn in the keys?"

Fern's little face furrowed. "As a matter of fact, he said he left them under the old butter churn sitting on the back porch. They should still be there 'cause I ain't been out there." She peered up at him. "Why do you ask?"

"Just checking." He nodded and went down the hallway to hang up his tux.

———✦———

When Big Jim entered his home, he was greeted by the smell of something good. He couldn't put his finger on it, but the scent stirred some warm memories.

He hung his jacket on the rack, noting his nephew's field jacket was already there. He hoped the boy was settling in. Lord knows he had been through enough already.

It was sad that Zach's own father had passed away and that his mother had sold everything off and high-tailed it out of town. Big Jim had a moment of sadness that his brother hadn't lived long enough to see his only son come home from his deployment. Then he straightened his shoulders, determined to make sure Zach had a great Christmas in this house with the people who cared about him.

Big Jim heard voices coming from the living room and made his way there. He found his very pregnant daughter-in-law, Leah, along with her grandmother, Fern, drinking something in cups and talking. The lights were low, and twinkling Christmas lights had been arranged around the room.

"Well, hello, ladies. This looks plumb nice. You two have been busy."

"I hope you like it," Leah said. "My gran brought some ornaments from my childhood. Come look at this little village." Her eyes were shining as she motioned him closer.

There, on the sideboard, they had arranged a bunch of tiny houses with little trees and figurines. There were a church with a stained glass window and a Christmas tree outside on the roll of cotton batting serving as snow. A long strand of silver tinsel had been placed around the edges of the sideboard as some sort of border. The entire scene was lit up and looked very cheery.

"That is really nice," Big Jim said, noting how pleased Leah and Fern appeared to be. "I guess I better get that tree. Don't want to wait until all the good ones are gone."

"How about a cup of mulled cider?" Fern held up the cup.

"Is that what smells so good?" he asked.

"It's Gran's recipe, and it's fabulous." Leah's smile was so wide, her eyes crinkled up.

Big Jim took a seat in an arm chair. "I might try a cup."

Fern poured a cup from a china tea pot. "Here ya go, Big Jim."

He accepted the cup, wrapping his large hand around it. He inhaled the fragrance. "Just what makes this cider mulled?"

Fern laughed in delight. "Some nice apple cider with a little brown sugar, allspice, cloves, nutmeg, and cinnamon. Cook it up and ya got yer tasty hot mulled cider. Best thing to warm one's bones on a cold winter day."

Big Jim raised his cup in a salute. "Amen."

# Chapter 7

STEPHANIE ARRIVED AT HER APARTMENT AFTER DARK. SHE looked up and down the street, noting that the city had put up Christmas lights and some of her neighbors had decorations showing in their windows.

She rode the elevator up to her floor, feeling a particular lack of festive spirit. It was the children being held prisoner in the dour facility. It was Rafe Neeley and his thug brothers on the loose. It was the jagged threat scratched into the side of her truck. She heaved out a sigh as the elevator door slid silently open. It was going home to an empty apartment.

"Bah, humbug," she muttered, unlocking the door. Turning on the lights helped stave off the jitters that kept her on edge. She checked any area where a would-be attacker could hide. Fortunately for her, the apartment was small and neat, so it was easy to see that nothing was out of order.

Stephanie locked the door behind her and slid the safety chain into place. Somehow, this form of protection seemed feeble at best. She and her crew could break through any door, although their methods were not exactly subtle.

She still had the extra two hundred dollars that Big Jim had given her to buy presents for Cody and Ivy, and tomorrow was her payday, so she would have to find time to shop. Maybe that would help her to grow some Christmas spirit.

Turning on the television, she caught the end of the early evening news. There was a brief mention that Rafe Neeley, accused murderer, was still at large, but the weatherman was on next with a lot to say about upcoming heavy snowfalls.

Stephanie made a simple meal, opening a can of soup to go with her grilled cheese sandwich. She reflected that maybe she wasn't really such good mother material. She had never taken a home economics class or learned to cook at her mother's side. Stephanie's mom had been more interested in horses than hearth and home. That was fine with Stephanie. In truth, she wasn't interested in hearth and home until she encountered two young children who needed her.

She washed up her few dishes, all the while stewing. *Well, I can buy a cookbook or take cooking classes.*

With nothing appealing on television, Stephanie curled up on the sofa with a book. It was a suspense title, which probably wasn't the best choice given her current situation with a murderer carving threats in her vehicle's paint.

Finally, she closed the book and headed for the bedroom, but first she checked the locks again. She turned off the lights, thinking she might try to find a small Christmas tree. That might cheer the place up.

———

After dinner, at Big Jim's invitation, which Zach took as an order, Zach went into the living room. *The returned misfit must fit in.*

Some Christmas music show was on the television, and everyone seemed to be enjoying it.

Zach sat at the far end of one of the sofas and sipped a beer. He tried to smile or laugh at all the right times. He marveled at how happy Colton was with Misty, his pretty bride.

Colt was totally immersed in the relationship. The expression on his face was somewhat sappy when he was engaged in soft-spoken exchanges with her. Even her younger brother seemed to be wrapped up in the family-like unit.

Zach sipped his beer, not wanting to be conspicuous. *Just be quiet.*

He changed his focus to Tyler, the middle Garrett brother. Another totally sappy face. Except Ty was sitting with his arm around his extremely pregnant wife, Leah. You couldn't tell where one left off and the other one began. Ty's other arm was around Gracie, his stepdaughter. The girl was maybe seven or eight and looked like a carbon copy of her mom.

When Zach had enlisted, Tyler had been a sophomore in high school. Now, he had some kind of agriculture degree and was happily married with a stepchild and a baby on the way.

Zach was aware that someone was staring at him. Sure enough, when he looked around the room, Leah's grandmother was sitting in a high-backed rocking chair, crocheting something, but her eyes were locked on Zach. She smiled but said nothing.

It was as though they shared a secret. Both were peripherally part of the family…but not.

"How about another beer, son?" Big Jim took the

tepid beer from Zach's hand and slapped a cold long-neck in its place.

"Thank you, sir." Zach gave him a salute with the bottle.

Big Jim settled into an armchair, looking particularly satisfied.

"How is Beau doing?" Zach asked.

"My youngest son is doing quite well. He's nesting over at the Moore ranch with his wife and daughter. He is madly in love with Dixie, that red-haired girl he met in grade school...and have you seen my little red-haired Ava?" He tilted the bottle up to his lips and took a long drink. "She's about the prettiest little girl I've ever seen." Big Jim pointed at Gracie. "Right alongside this one. The Garrett family sure does have some fine-looking ladies."

Gracie smiled shyly.

Zach continued to smile and sip his beer. It was important not to be a pain in the ass to the only people who gave a damn if he lived or died.

When Tyler announced he was taking his family home, everyone rose to see them off. There were hugs and admonitions to bundle up against the cold. More snow had fallen, so Ty went out to start his truck and turn on the heater, but by the time Leah had suitably wrapped Gracie in jacket, mittens, scarf, and cap, and said goodbye to her grandmother, Ty was back to escort them to the idling vehicle.

Colton clapped Zach on the shoulder. "Heard you have a date with Stephanie Gayle. How did that happen?"

Zach was reluctant to talk about this. "Um, she asked me."

"That's good, bud. Glad you're getting out." He hooked an arm around Misty's neck and headed off to the kitchen.

When Zach returned to the living room, only Fern Davis was still there. She was straightening and rearranging her little Christmas village figurines.

"Good night, Miz Fern," he said in passing.

"Good night, Zach. Don't you worry. Everything is gonna work out just fine."

———

Zach endured the catcalls when he appeared in his tuxedo.

"I think you look hot," Misty said.

"You're going to be the prettiest one at the dance." Colton gave him a thump on the shoulder.

"Now you hush up, Colt. Zach, you look very handsome. You're gonna knock lil Miss Stephanie's socks off." Fern gave him a hug. "And you smell good too."

Zach moved toward the door, but Big Jim stopped him. "Now, son…you be careful out there. Don't drink so much you can't drive. We want you home safe."

"Yes, sir." He was touched that Big Jim was treating him as he would one of his own sons. "Thank you, sir."

Zach drove to Amarillo, feeling a little anxious and wondering why. He had gone on countless missions and patrols with perfect confidence and determination. But the mere thought of Stephanie Gayle brought a little flutter to his stomach.

When he was actually standing outside her apartment door, he was filled with misgivings. They were going to a dance. Did he still remember how to dance? Would the music be waltzes and tangos or rap? He raised his hand to knock on the door, but she opened it before he could make contact.

"Wow!" Nothing else came to mind.

"Thanks." She gazed up at him, wearing a wide grin and a long, slinky red dress. She was a little taller than the last time he'd seen her, but that was due to the spiky red sandals on her feet. Even her toes and fingertips were dressed in bright, shiny red.

"You—you look amazing."

"You cleaned up pretty well yourself." She checked him out from head to cowboy boots.

"The temperature is dropping," he said. "Hope you have something warm to wear."

She did a pirouette. "Aren't I hot enough for you?"

That made him laugh, and he felt the tension evaporate. "Yeah, you look plenty hot enough for me." *For me?* He realized this beautiful woman had done whatever women do to primp, and it was for him. The evening suddenly looked much more appealing.

Stephanie grinned and produced a really hideous but warm-looking quilted coat. "I know it's ugly, but it's filled with down and really warm."

He helped her put it on and zip the front. "Do you have gloves?"

She pulled a pair out of a pocket and slipped them on. "Ready to rock." She waggled her gloved hands in the air.

"Then let's roll."

Zach and Stephanie went down to the street level and stepped outside into the crisp, cold air.

She leaned down to pick up the hem of her red dress, giving Zach a show with her very shapely legs.

He, in turn, leaned down and picked her up, carrying her down the steps and crunching through the snow all the way to his truck. He used the remote to unlock his truck and then moved closer so Stephanie could open the door. He slid her onto the seat, feeling a little bereft over having to let her go.

"Thanks, Zach." She sounded a little breathless, but he had been the one slogging through the gunk.

When he climbed behind the wheel, her fragrance reached out to him. She looked beautiful despite the puffy coat. "Seat belt," he ordered.

"I can't reach it."

He leaned across her, getting another whiff of her perfume as he secured her in the passenger seat.

The windows had fogged up, but he turned on the defroster and sat idling for a moment until it cleared. Their conversation was stilted as she gave him directions to the hotel where the formal dance was to be held.

Fortunately, there was a parking garage adjacent to the hotel, so Zach was able to park without having to carry Stephanie through more slush. When they arrived at the right floor, they checked their outerwear.

Stephanie looked gorgeous in the red dress. Her hair was down around her shoulders, a warm cinnamon-brown.

He longed to touch it but held himself in check.

She turned to him with a big smile and reached out to take his hand. "Thanks for being with me. I don't think I could stand another of these things by myself."

"I'm pretty certain you could have any man you wanted." He gave her a wink. "I'm sure glad it's me tonight."

"Gayle!"

She turned toward the entrance to the ballroom. "Hey, Boss."

The man who held the door open was the lieutenant from the fire station. "Who's this big yahoo?"

She laid her hand on Zach's chest. "This is Zachery Garrett, my—er, my friend."

"Friend, eh?" He squinted up at Zach suspiciously.

She wasn't the least bit fazed but smiled brightly. "And this sterling gentleman is my boss, Lieutenant Larsen."

Zach offered his hand and received a firm handshake in return. "Good to meet you, sir."

Larsen's expression softened. "Military, eh? I could tell by the cut of you. Good to know you, Garrett. You two come sit at my table." He cocked his head toward the interior.

Zach glanced at Stephanie, and she nodded before leading the way into the ballroom. Heads turned when she entered. Zach recognized some of the firefighters as her coworkers.

The lieutenant gestured to a chair beside a woman his own age. Stephanie leaned down to give the woman a hug. "Mrs. Larsen. So nice to see you again." She introduced Zach and slipped into the seat, indicating Zach was to sit beside her.

He was introduced to the others sitting around the table, mostly brass from the fire department. There was one EMT sitting across the table, and he kept his arm around his wife. There was conversation, but mostly it was in reference to things related to their work and people they knew, so Zach sat and tried to appear attentive.

Mostly he was aware of Stephanie—how she looked and smelled and the sound of her voice.

Two men climbed onto the stage on one side of the room, where there was a podium with a microphone. They did all the things that nonperformers do with a mic, such as making it squeal and sputter loudly. Finally one introduced himself and began to speak. He introduced the other man, who gave a short speech meant to inspire the firefighters and police officers in the room. The crowd applauded while the meal service began.

First came a salad course with baskets of big, puffy hot rolls. Zach inhaled the food in front of him and the next course as well, not paying much attention to the speeches.

Stephanie glanced at him under her lashes, causing him to realize how fast he was putting food away. He put his fork down and consciously slowed his chewing. "Sorry," he whispered.

"No problem. I guess you're used to eating... efficiently."

He smiled. "That's a gracious way of saying I need to slow down. Sorry if I embarrassed you."

She squeezed his arm. "You didn't. Glad you're enjoying your dinner."

He chortled. "I've had worse."

The sound of her laughter eased his tension.

The person on the stage called out Stephanie Gayle by name. She sighed and folded her napkin. She put on a determined smile and rose gracefully from her seat.

"Go get 'em, Gayle," Larsen called.

Zach watched as she walked up onto the stage in her slinky red dress and super-high stilettos that made her legs look so awesome.

The speaker made a brief but glowing speech and presented her with a medal for extreme heroism.

Stephanie graciously accepted the medal and cited her wonderful and supportive team as equally deserving of the award. She received a standing ovation for this. When she returned to the table, she passed the medal in its velvet presentation box around the table for everyone to admire.

"You wear your heroism well," Zach said.

Stephanie blushed. "I was just doing my job."

"You must be doing it very well." He was filled with admiration for this slim, fine-boned woman. He couldn't imagine how she could have gone into an abandoned well to rescue two people and into a cave to rescue some lost and injured campers.

"It was nothing," she insisted. She picked up her fork and resumed eating her dinner, her eyes cast down.

He managed to make it through the rest of the meal without calling attention to himself.

While the tables were being cleared, Zach noticed musicians gathering on the stage. In no time at all they had finished tuning up and began playing a song for the few people who were dancing. A bar was set up on one side of the room, and quite a few men were gathered there, but they too had to turn to admire Stephanie in her red dress.

"Would you like something to drink?" Zach asked.

"Sure." She flashed a dimpled grin. "I'll have white wine…or a longneck. Whatever you're having."

He made his way to the bar and waited in a short line. Some of the men who had been served lingered at the far end of the bar and eyed him. *Yes, I'm the lucky man with Stephanie.*

One of the men made a lunge toward Zach, aiming to spill his drink, but Zach managed to straight-arm him, and the liquid spilled on the man himself, sending a stream of liquor down his pant leg. The man uttered a curse and reared back as if to have another go at Zach.

"I wouldn't do that if I were you." He spoke in a calm voice, but his expression let the man know he meant business.

The man stepped back, glowering, but left in the direction of the restrooms.

Another man laughed. "You got some pretty good reflexes there." He raised his beer in a salute of sorts. "I'm Slim Cullum. I've worked with Stephanie since she first signed on. She's quite a girl." The man was anything but "slim." The nickname must have started as a joke.

"That she is."

"But I have to warn you," Slim said. "If you do anything to hurt our girl, you'll have to deal with all of us. I don't care how big you are." He gestured to where Stephanie sat engaged in conversation with Mrs. Larsen. "She's one of us."

Zach regarded Slim with interest. "What makes you think I would ever do anything to hurt Stephanie?"

"Just sayin'." Slim nodded toward Zach and then tipped his longneck up to take a swig.

"Tell you what." Zach leaned closer and spoke in a lowered voice. "If I ever do anything to hurt her, you can kick my ass all around the block."

Slim let out a loud guffaw. He stuck his hand out to shake. "Deal!"

———

Stephanie tried to be casual in her surveillance of Zach as he chatted with some of her coworkers. There was a moment when she thought he was going to punch Reynolds after he had spilled his drink down his own leg. But that moment passed quickly.

Now Zach and Cullum seemed to be hitting it off. She liked that he was getting along with her fellows.

In time, he returned, bearing two longnecks and a white wine in a stemmed glass. He placed the wine and one of the longnecks in front of her.

"Mmm…I must be thirsty."

He sat beside her. "You seemed to be having trouble making a decision, so I thought I would give you a choice. Be prepared."

She slid the wine toward Mrs. Larsen. "For you, my friend."

They chatted a bit, and then the orchestra played a waltz.

Stephanie pushed back from the table and placed her hand on Zach's shoulder. "I've had about enough of listening to music. I want to dance."

"I should warn you that I haven't danced since high school."

"Okay. I stand forewarned. Now stand up because I need to dance. Have to dance."

"Is this a waltz?" He half rose, but she had already moved to the dance floor.

"It's a waltz." She was gliding around in circles.

He held out his arms, and she danced close, arranging him in a dance pose, then pulled him out onto the dance floor.

"I've forgotten more than I thought," he said. "I was under the impression the man was supposed to lead."

"Okay. You can take over. I just wanted to give you the idea." She switched gears and let him take the lead.

"Got it." His voice was deep, reverberating in his chest, annexing her as a part of him.

She gazed up into his eyes. Eyes so blue they were almost turquoise. Eyes that made her want to follow him wherever he was leading.

The music played on, and she was aware of the strong arm embracing her as well as the rock-hard shoulder she held. Altogether a perfectly formed human male. Being held this close was playing havoc with her hormones. All she wanted to do was bite his tuxedo off and let him know she was a woman. A woman who hadn't been satisfied in a long time.

Her focus had been on her job and recently on the children and their safety, but for the moment, all she wanted to do was climb this mountain of a man and give him a night to remember.

She wasn't naive enough to think this man would fall madly in love with her, but she did think there was enough electricity between them to sustain his interest for a while.

The next dance was a slow one, and the lights were lowered.

Zach still held her in the dance position. Other couples were moving around them, but he remained still, holding her.

Stephanie stepped closer, pressing herself against him and resting her face on his shoulder. "Dance," she whispered.

She felt him place a gentle kiss against her hair. "Yes, ma'am," he whispered.

A shiver rippled down her neck, and it had nothing to do with the temperature.

Zach pulled her closer and began to sway with her, taking enough steps to be able to call it dancing.

But to Stephanie, it was like making love while standing upright. She slipped her left arm around his torso, sucking in a breath at her own bravery, but he tucked her other hand against his chest and held it there. Definitely an embrace. Definitely the hottest and hardest body she had ever encountered.

"Cutting in."

She raised her head to see Donnell standing behind Zach, looking at her expectantly. "No," she said. "Go sit down."

When she looked up at Zach, he was struggling to keep from laughing.

"What? Were you anxious to get rid of me?"

He pulled her close again. "No way."

When the song was over, the lights came up, and Stephanie jerked herself from her reverie.

Zach's expression was smoldering. That alone sent waves of heat through her body. His hand at the back of her waist directed her to the table. When she drew near, she noticed that both her boss and his wife were smiling. *Glad I didn't climb all over Zach the way I wanted to.*

Zach pulled out the chair for Stephanie and seated himself beside her. "Would you like something else to drink?"

"I'm okay. How about you?"

"I'm driving…and I have precious cargo." He winked and took her hand.

"You two make such a lovely couple." When she turned, it was Mrs. Larsen who was grinning broadly.

"Um—thanks." She realized the entire squad was keeping her under surveillance.

They danced again. Stephanie gazed up into Zach's incredible eyes and felt sublimely happy for the first time in a long time. For a moment, she was able to lay her other concerns aside and just focus on the time she shared with this man.

"You look beautiful," he said.

"I'm glad you think so," she said.

"Everyone thinks so."

"Thank you." She took a deep breath and plunged in. "I've had about all of this gaiety I can stand. Do you think you could take me home now?"

The eyes scanned her soul, knowing everything about her in an instant. "Sure. If you've had enough dinner and awards and dancing, I'll take you home."

She could have danced all night in his strong arms but was tired of the crowd and the stares. She felt that she was entitled to some personal life without the entire squad being able to look on…and judge. She was not up for judgment at the moment.

When the dance was over, he walked her back to the table, where they took their leave and headed for the door. Zach gathered the big, ugly blue jacket and helped her into it. He leaned down and gave her a kiss on the cheek. "I'll go get the truck," he whispered.

She waited in the vestibule, pacing a little. When she turned, Reynolds and Slim were leaned up against the wall.

"Hey, Gayle. What's up with you and soldier boy?" Slim asked.

Anger flared in her gut. "Don't you guys have lives of your own?" She glowered at her two coworkers. "I have no intention of letting you share mine."

"Aw, Gayle," Reynolds said. "C'mon. Give us the lowdown. Who is this guy?"

"No one you need to worry about." She turned and went back to the door, hoping Zach would hurry up.

"Well, is it serious?" Slim asked. "You can tell us."

Zach burst through the door then, looking big and bad and cold. "I left the motor running with the heater on." He glanced at the two men. "Are you ready to go?"

"Yes," she breathed. When she turned to Zach, he lifted her in his arms, always a thrilling experience. She had to grin at him. "Home, James."

"Yes, ma'am." He swept out of the building and down the steps to his truck, where he eased her inside and closed the door.

She was still grinning as he rounded the truck and climbed in, making sounds to indicate he was cold.

"Thanks," she said.

"For what?" He flipped the heater knob to a higher temperature.

"For everything. For this evening."

"My pleasure." He started to shift into reverse, but she stopped him.

"Wait!" Stephanie leaned toward him, reaching out to stroke her fingertips over the side of his face. "Kiss me…and please don't say yes ma'am."

He chortled. "Yes…Stephanie." He threaded his fingers through her hair and lowered his mouth to hers, lightly brushing his lips over hers before deepening the kiss.

A ripple of passion swept through her as she

surrendered to the kiss. One kiss led to another. She had thought he was holding back, perhaps not interested… but now he seemed to be raging with passion and intent upon sharing it with her.

When she pulled away, she felt shaky.

He glanced up through the windshield. "Your friends are still trying to check us out."

She followed the direction he indicated and saw three of the guys hanging just outside the door, openly gaping. "Gah! Let's go."

"Fasten your seat belt." He waved at the onlookers and backed out into the street.

Zach's bravado spurred Stephanie to blow a kiss to the onlookers. "Sorry about that," she said. "The guys are just so—so—"

"Your fellow firefighters seem to think they own you." As he shifted into gear, the tires spun on the slushy ice then caught and moved forward.

The windows were fogging up, but he turned on the defroster, and they slowly cleared. By the time he arrived at her apartment, they were warm and toasty.

Stephanie's gut was tied up in knots. She wasn't sure what she had expected, but now that they were here, she was having second thoughts. Her panic level had climbed up into her throat and threatened to close off her airway.

Zach turned off the motor and pocketed the keys. "I'll come around and carry you to the building. Don't want to ruin those sexy shoes."

"Uh, no…I mean yes." She swallowed hard. "You don't have to carry me around all the time. I can walk."

"Don't be silly. I'm used to taking long hikes on patrol and carrying a sixty-pound pack."

"Doesn't sound like fun."

"Wasn't." He opened the door and slipped out. When he opened the passenger door and held his arms out to her, she gathered her handbag and leaned out to him. His strong arms lifted her, and she wrapped her arms around his neck. In no time at all, he had secured his truck and carried her up the stairs to the lobby of her apartment building.

"I can get down and walk," she said against his neck.

"But I've got you now, and I'm not letting go." He carried her to the elevator and deftly applied a thumb to the third-floor button. When the door silently slid open, he stepped out into the hallway and was standing in front of her apartment before she could compose herself.

"Oh, let me find my keys." She peered into her tiny handbag and extricated them.

Zach leaned down to allow her to insert the key in her lock and twist it. The door swung open, and he carried her into the darkness. He held her for a moment and then let her slide down until her sexy shoes touched the floor. He flipped on the lights and closed the door.

"Oh, that was...sweet," she said. "And here I am with nice dry shoes." They stared at each other for a few moments. "Um, would you like some coffee or hot cocoa?"

He grinned down at her. "Not really."

She ditched the blue puffy jacket and tossed her handbag on top of it. "Would you like to sit down?"

"Not really."

Stephanie swallowed hard. "Well, in that case, would you help me with this zipper?" She turned her back, showing the long zipper that started at the nape of her neck and went down to her hips.

There was a long silence, and then Zach's deep voice agreed, and his strong hands opened the zipper all the way down to her bottom. The sound of the zipper caused gooseflesh to whisper around her spine and her nipples to stand on alert. "Thanks," she murmured, her voice husky. She stepped out of the dress and, wearing only her red bra and panties, turned to face Zach.

He gazed at her without comment, and his expression was unreadable.

The silence grew, and she regretted her rash and uncharacteristic behavior. She was about to reach down to gather her discarded dress around her.

"I need to call the Garrett ranch," he said. "To let them know not to expect me. I don't want anyone to worry."

She didn't know whether to laugh or cry. She had been intent upon seducing this big man, and he appeared to be willing but was considerate enough to call those who might be concerned if he didn't show up that night.

She swallowed hard as he put his phone away and smiled at her.

"You are so beautiful. I don't think I've ever seen anything I can compare you to."

He spoke softly and reached out a hand to her. When she stepped closer, his fingers met the skin on her ribs and trailed softly down to her hip bone, leaving a tingling sensation in their wake.

Such a small gesture, but it awoke a chasm of longing deep within her. She sensed he was experiencing strong emotion as well. "I—I'm glad you're here with me, Zach."

One side of his mouth lifted in a wry grin. "Me too."

"I want you to know this is a first for me. I mean—I've never invited a man to my apartment… Not on a first date—"

"I don't happen to go home with every incredibly beautiful woman I meet either." He gave a little chuckle. "Of course, you do realize this is the first date I have been on in some time."

"Yes, I suppose I am taking advantage of you." She felt suddenly shy, dropping her gaze.

He gathered her in his arms, gazing intently down at her. "Please take advantage of me. I was thinking you might be feeling sorry for me, but I'm happy to be taken advantage of if that's what you're doing."

She slipped her arms around his waist and pressed her face against his chest. He didn't appear to be made of anything but solid muscle. "Zach, could you just shut up and let's go to my bedroom?"

"Yes, ma'am." He leaned down to pick her up, once again making her feel treasured. She pointed, and he carried her down the hallway, placing her on her bed almost reverently.

She patted the space beside her, and he let his jacket slide to the floor before sitting next to her.

He threaded his fingers through her long hair and kissed her, invading her mouth with his tongue, hesitantly at first and then with more confidence.

She leaned back, pulling him with her. Silently, she began to unbutton his tuxedo shirt, but he pulled away and very efficiently shed his shirt.

He tossed it on the floor beside his jacket.

Stephanie's breath caught in her throat. She had thought some of those firefighter calendars featured hot men, but she had truly never seen a man as ripped as Zach. His six-pack seemed to have developed into a twelve-pack. When he turned to remove his boots and then the tuxedo trousers, she got to admire a whole new anatomy lesson.

And then he was nude, standing before her, the bluest eyes in Texas seeming to devour her.

She couldn't speak but reached out to him and found herself wrapped in those brawny arms.

Just his breath falling against the skin on her neck brought a rush of moisture in her panties.

He kissed her hungrily. His large yet gentle hands roamed over her body, setting fire to her flesh as he explored. His kisses traveled from the side of her neck to her shoulder, where he paused to slip her bra strap down. His lips skimmed her flesh as he cupped her breast with his warm palm, fingering the lacy fabric of her bra.

A ragged whimper escaped her throat. She ached to feel her naked breasts pressed against his skin. She reached to unfasten the bra, but he released the catch and tossed the red bra on the pile of clothing beside the bed. Next, he slipped the red lace panties down her hips and disposed of them in like manner.

Zach gave proper attention to each breast, circling her nipples with his tongue before gently suckling them.

Deep in her belly, a fire burned out of control. She arched against him, opening her thighs, hoping her silent invitation got the message across.

If his hard maleness was any indication, he was ready for her. He was definitely erect and impressive.

"I hope you brought some protection," she rasped. *Oh, yeah. That was subtle.*

He pulled away, leaving her aching for satisfaction. Her skin felt chilled without his warm flesh pressed against her.

Zach reached into the pocket of his trousers and brought forth a wrapped condom. "Always prepared," he said.

"Good to know." She took the packet from him, tore it open, and then deftly fitted it over his magnificent member standing at attention for her.

When he entered her, she experienced a melting sensation, as though she was becoming a part of him. As though their coupling somehow created a bond between the two of them.

"Oh, Zach," she breathed as he stroked into her. She lifted her hips to meet his rhythm, sending a shock of pleasure into her body with each stroke.

He held himself above her, holding her tenderly, delivering thrust after thrust, taking her breath away.

Stephanie wrapped her thighs tightly around his hips, grinding herself against him. In what seemed like seconds, she experienced a spiraling of intense pleasure, sending spasms through her body as a huge climax left her gasping for air.

When she opened her eyes, Zach was grinning down at her. "I hope you're not done because I'm just getting started."

# Chapter 8

HE AWOKE, BREATHING HARD.

It took a moment for him to realize where he was.

The dream had been so vivid. He could still feel the heat, the sun beating down on the sand and reflecting back up into his eyes. Burning. Gritty. Hard to breathe…

The room was stuffy, and there was warm flesh pressed against his.

*Nice.*

His racing heart slowed back down to normal. Whatever normal was for a man still on the edge. He exhaled slowly. *On the edge?* No, he was clinging to it.

Stephanie stirred beside him.

Zach slowly turned his head, not wanting to startle her. The image of her lying disheveled in the early-morning light would be etched in his memory forever.

Her lustrous hair was fanned out around her, like a glorious aureole. Although her skin was fair to begin with, the winter light gave it a cool, translucent glow, like the inside of a shell.

"Like what you see?" she asked without opening her eyes. Her warm breath whispered across his shoulder, sweet as an embrace.

"Um—yes, of course." He leaned closer, his voice sounding rusty to his own ears.

Her eyes opened, and she gazed at him steadily. "Thank you."

"For what?"

"For everything." She stretched her arms, arching her back and straining the sheets with her lovely bosom. "I know that last night's gala was not your bailiwick, but thanks for stepping up." She raised up on one elbow to gaze into his eyes.

"Don't be ridiculous. I loved it."

Her expression was unreadable, but she placed her hand on his face in a soft caress. Then she leaned forward to kiss him on the lips. It was a sweet kiss. A soft kiss…but one that awakened his libido. Impossible not to respond, but what if she was just giving him a sweet morning kiss? What if he misread her greeting?

She solved the mystery by rolling onto her back and pulling him with her. "Is there somewhere else you need to be this morning?" Her voice took on a smoky quality as he fell under her spell.

"Nowhere else but right here," he said and set about the business of delivering morning pleasure to the beautiful woman in his arms.

Stephanie must have slept well because her energy level was through the roof. She had been a bit more subdued the previous night, but now she reminded him of a gorgeous and sleek animal, a wildcat or a puma. Her sweet body was a symphony of curves and muscle, and they were playing in unison.

Zach felt her grind against him and then grip him with her thighs as her body arched and spasmed. She let out a groan of pleasure.

With one last thrust, he joined her climax, relishing the rush of exhilaration.

"Oh—oh, that was—it was…" Her breath was coming in gasps.

He kissed her damp shoulder and neck and then her lips. "Yes, it was." He rolled onto his back and carried her with him. He could feel her heart thundering as fast as his own.

"Wow! You sure are—in good shape."

He laughed. This struck him as funny, since he had just been working hard to keep up with her.

"Where did you get this one?" She traced her forefinger over the small scar on his chin.

"That one was a football cleat in the face. It may have been Colt. I don't remember, it's been so long ago."

"With your dark beard, it looks like a little letter C has been branded on your face." She kissed his chin.

"Well, if you like that one, I've got a few more."

"I noticed," she said. "What was this one?" Stephanie examined a scar on his shoulder.

"Sniper got me when we were on patrol." He raised his shoulder to display the back side. "Through and through."

"Oh." Her eyes widened, and she swallowed hard. "I see... Well, what about this one?" Her fingers grazed an area on the side of his ribs.

"Shrapnel." He couldn't bear to tell her about the IED on the side of the road that had taken the lives of two of his buddies.

"That's too bad. They should give you a Purple Heart."

"They did...two of them. My mom probably has them in her garage."

Her brow puckered, but he kissed her again, not wanting to explain his strange family dynamic. "I hope all my dings and dents don't repulse you."

Her eyes opened wide. "Oh, no! I didn't mean—"

"I'm teasing," he said. "At least all the important parts still work."

She gasped and then burst into laughter. "That's for darned sure."

---~~~---

When Stephanie got to the fire station, she was greeted with a chorus of whistles and catcalls.

"Hey Gayle. Where's that red dress?" It was Donnell who got that one off.

"Her boyfriend's wearing it." That from Stanley.

She turned and went to the locker room without acknowledging any of their taunts. She knew better than to let them know they had gotten to her.

Putting her things away, she felt a wide grin spread across her face. She'd thought about Zach as she had last seen him. He had gotten dressed in most of his tuxedo and saw her off to work before he climbed in his truck and headed back to Langston.

Stephanie had watched him drive away from inside her red truck. Feeling warm inside, she reflected on their very vigorous bouts of lovemaking and somehow also felt bereft that they had parted. Without any particular plans to reconnect, she hoped she hadn't seen the last of him.

Drawing in a deep breath, she leaned over and expelled it. No reason to think he wasn't as involved as she was. But then it had been Stephanie who had asked him out. Perhaps he would never have asked her on a date if she had not been the aggressor.

She straightened up, making a discontented sound. It

was time to get to work and forget about how hot Zach Garrett was and how he had demonstrated his mastery of her body.

"Somebody got lucky last night." It was Schmidt, the newest member of the team.

Stephanie turned to give him a glare. "Shut up, Proby. You do not get to make personal comments to me or about me…ever!" She shoved him out of the doorway and left the locker room.

Fortunately, something in Amarillo was on fire, so the entire squad sprang into action. She jumped into her insulated pants and slid the suspenders onto her shoulders before shrugging into her turnout coat.

"Let's go, Gayle." Her boss jerked his thumb toward his vehicle, an SUV with his title emblazoned on the sides.

She was surprised but climbed in on the passenger side, clutching her helmet. "Sir?"

He cleared his throat roughly. "I heard the guff the fellows were giving you. Thought you could use a break."

"Um, thank you, sir."

Lieutenant Larsen cranked the engine and slipped the gear into drive. "And I really like that nice, clean-cut young man you brought to the gala last night. He was so proud of you during the award ceremony."

Stephanie thought about the previous evening and the way it had ended. She tried to hold onto her stoic expression. *No smiling. No blushing. No running off at the mouth.* "You're right. He's a very nice person."

The lieutenant cast a sideways glance at her and then pulled out of the station, hitting the siren as he turned into traffic. There was no conversation during the relatively short drive. Of course, the sound of two sirens would have made conversation difficult.

She wondered briefly what her fellow firefighters were saying about her riding with the boss, but it had been unexpected, to say the least.

When Lieutenant Larsen drew to a stop near a residence in an older neighborhood, she saw smoke rising and a family gathered near the curb.

There was a man with a vacant expression on his face standing next to a woman who was openly weeping. She held an infant wrapped in a blanket, and a preschooler clung to her legs.

Stephanie's heart went out to them.

"Go interview the family, Gayle," Lieutenant Larsen barked, thrusting a clipboard at her.

She gathered her jacket around her and climbed out of the vehicle.

Fortunately, there wasn't much to the fire, but the family appeared to be devastated. She took their information, noting that the father smelled strongly of alcohol.

The mother looked haggard, silent tears streaming down her cheeks. The infant in her arms slept through the chaos, but the toddler clinging to her skirt howled in counterpoint to the approaching sirens.

In a reasonably short time, the squad laid out their equipment, dealt with the smoldering fire, which had started in the bedroom, and were in the process of retrieving that same equipment.

Stephanie called a social worker, who arrived to distribute warm blankets and direct the family to a shelter where they could regroup and learn about the community resources available to them while they were out of their home.

"Gayle!" The lieutenant jolted her out of her reverie. He gestured for her to join him by his vehicle.

"Yes, sir."

"Let's beat the crowd and get out of here."

She glanced back at her squad, thinking that she should be doing her part, but then again, her boss just told her to get in his car. She removed her turnout coat and tossed it in the backseat before settling with the seat belt around her.

They pulled out into the slushy street, snow now awash with water from the fire hoses.

"So, what's your take on it, Gayle?" the lieutenant growled.

"Drunk husband smoking in bed?" She shrugged. "Don't mean to be judgmental, but his breath was definitely enough to set the whole place afire, and the wife is furious with him…from my observations."

"Good enough for me, Gayle." He turned onto the main street and made grumpy old man noises all the way back to the station.

Stephanie climbed out, secure in the knowledge that the city was not ablaze and that her fellow firefighters had performed well. Only the human part of her was concerned that a family was without a home due to one man's carelessness. She visualized the face of the crying toddler and the bereft mother, mourning their losses.

---

Zach spent the day helping his uncle and cousins around the ranch. He hauled hay out to the stock in one of the pastures. He cleaned stalls alongside Colt and Big Jim, all the while marveling that his ultra-rich uncle never pushed hard work off on others.

In the late afternoon, they returned to the ranch house, cold and hungry, having worked through the lunch hour.

Fern Davis greeted all three men. "I was wondering when you menfolk would decide to take a break."

"I'm pretty sure I'm broken," Colt said. "I can't feel my fingers."

The men removed their outer clothing and sat around the table.

Fern brought a mug for each man and set it in front of him. "I made some chili and cornbread for lunch. I thought you fellers would be in a lot sooner, but I kept it hot for you if you're hungry."

"Is that what smells so good?" Big Jim asked.

Fern's face crinkled into a grin. "S'pose so. Let me git you some."

Zach rose from his chair. "Now, Miz Fern…you don't need to be waiting on us. Let me help you."

"Aw, you fellers have been workin' hard all day." But she allowed him to deliver the chili and cornbread as she dished it up and pull out a chair for her to join them at the table.

"This is mighty nice, Miz Fern," he said as he took his seat beside her.

"Sure is," Big Jim agreed.

Leah's grandmother looked pleased. "I hope you fellers like it." She folded her hands on the table in front of her.

Zach spooned the rich, meaty chili into his mouth. "Delicious." He picked up the thick slab of golden cornbread and took a bite. It reminded him of meals he'd eaten with his parents when he was a boy…when he thought their way of life would go on forever.

"Zach, I don't know how you'd feel about this, but I gotta ask you…" Miz Fern pressed her lips together and heaved a deep sigh.

"Yes, Ma'am?" Zach responded. "What can I do for you?"

"I was wonderin' if you might like to take up residence at my place? I would feel so much more comfortable if you was stayin' there."

Big Jim did a double take, looking from Miz Fern to Zach and back again, but he didn't say anything.

Colton busied himself with spooning chili into his mouth, studiously ignoring the question hanging in the air.

Zach laid his spoon down, giving her his full attention. "I—I'm not sure what you're asking me, ma'am."

"I've hired several different men to be caretaker, but none of 'em have stuck around. I need someone who will be steady, and I thought maybe you might like to have your own place." She shrugged. "Just a thought."

"I'll have to think about it, Miz Fern. I need to help out around here too."

"I understand," she said, seemingly let down.

"But don't you worry, ma'am. I'm keeping an eye on things. In fact, after I eat this delicious chili, I'll drive right over to make sure everything is secure and the stock is okay."

She hesitated before thanking him, telling of her disappointment quite eloquently.

Big Jim wiped his mouth on a paper napkin. "I'll

ride along, son. Keep you company while you check things out."

"Great, Uncle Jim." Zach continued eating with his usual military proficiency. He arose from the table and carried his dishes to the sink. He gave them a quick rinse and set them in the sink before returning to take his seat at the table.

Big Jim scooped the chili into his mouth and sopped the last up with his cornbread. "Great meal, Fern. I was so hungry I could have eaten the south end of a north-bound mule."

A little smile played around her lips. "I'm mighty glad you liked it."

"Dee-licious, Miz Fern." Colt pushed his chair back. "Why don't you two get going and I'll clean up."

"Thanks, son." Big Jim rose and made a beeline for the front door.

Zach stood up abruptly, almost knocking his chair over in the process. He hurried to catch up with his uncle.

Big Jim had put on his warm fleece-lined jacket and was reaching for his Stetson.

Zach shrugged into his Army jacket and grabbed his Stetson, jamming it onto his head as they headed out the door.

"You want me to drive, boy?" Big Jim seemed impervious to the intense cold.

"Yes, sir." Zach swung into Big Jim's truck on the passenger side. The seats were cold. The air was cold.

Big Jim pulled out onto the road leading to the highway. When he turned onto the highway, there were no other drivers in sight. The entire countryside was covered in white. The truck's all-weather tires sounded loud when they made contact with the pavement.

Big Jim turned on the heater and the defroster at the same time. The windows immediately fogged up but began to clear just as quickly.

After a few minutes of silence, Big Jim cleared his throat. "How's it going with little Miss Stephanie? I'm mighty fond of her, y'know?"

Zach's smile went wall-to-wall. "Me too, sir. She's just—awesome!"

"That she is," Big Jim agreed. "You couldn't choose a nicer young woman."

"No, sir." He felt tongue-tied when it came to Stephanie. He wasn't sure exactly what their relationship was, and he didn't want to assume anything.

"You know those two little kids she's so fond of... they're orphans." Big Jim's voice suddenly got husky. "Stephanie rescued them when their stepfather moved up from abusing their mother to actually killing her."

"I heard about this terrible crime. Poor kids."

"And Miss Stephanie is hoping to adopt those two little children. Did she tell you that?"

"Um, no...she didn't mention that." He thought about the beautiful and strong woman whose bed he had shared. She was passionate and remarkable. In some ways, she terrified him in ways he had never been terrified before. He tried to imagine her as a mother... Couldn't.

Zach was hung up on her beautiful face and lush body. Her long, shapely legs that wrapped around him and drew him in. The smoothness of her skin, stretched over taut muscle.

"So, what do you think, son?" Big Jim jarred him out of his reverie.

"She's a work of art, sir."

Big Jim chuckled. "Yes, I suppose she is." He turned off the highway, heading for Fern Davis's ranch.

When they neared the property, Zach thought the house looked like a Christmas card. The snow covered a multitude of sins. He knew the house and outbuildings were quite run-down and that the various caretakers Fern had hired hadn't done much of anything to improve the property. But tonight it looked quaint and snug under its blanket of snow.

"You got the key to Miz Fern's house?" Big Jim called as he swung out of the truck.

Zach felt in his pocket, digging out the key Fern had given him. He followed Big Jim up to the porch. Both men stamped the snow off their boots on the wooden porch, the noise breaking the perfect silence of the scene.

"Cute little place," Big Jim said. "Too bad Miz Fern can't find someone solid to stay here and run things for her." He gestured to the front door. "Open up."

Zach unlocked the door. It swung inward without a sound.

Big Jim stepped inside, flipping on the lights as he entered.

Zach followed, noting the house was cold. Whatever kind of heating she had was turned off. He saw a small gas heater against the far wall and recalled seeing a propane tank located to the rear of the house.

"Look around. Check things out," Big Jim said. He hooked his thumbs in his belt loops and leaned against the doorway.

Beyond the comfortable-looking small living room, Zach could see a fairly large kitchen with a round dining table and four chairs pushed up to it. He glanced back at Big Jim, who nodded at him.

Zach took a deep breath and headed down the hallway that led off the living room. He turned on the overhead light and glanced in the rooms as he passed by. There were two smaller bedrooms, one slightly larger and a bathroom with a claw-foot bathtub. All the basic human needs could be dealt with in this little house. Not a bad place at all. He turned off the lights behind himself and returned to the living room. "Everything looks okay."

Big Jim flashed a smile. "Great. Let's go check on the stock. I'm freezin' my rear off." He returned to his idling truck and revved the motor a couple of times while Zach was securing the house.

Zach tucked the key back in his pocket and swung into the truck so they could continue their tour of the ranch. The bunk house was unlocked and still a mess, but they retrieved the key from under the butter churn and locked the door before tending to the animals. Zach was glad his uncle had decided to accompany him and glad he himself had taken on the responsibility of monitoring Fern Davis's property.

When they returned to the Garrett ranch, Zach called Stephanie. Just hearing her voice brought a rush of warmth to his chest.

"Hey, Zach. How nice of you to call. I was thinking about you."

He swallowed hard. "Yeah, I've been thinking about you too." He paused a moment too long, and it became a loud silence.

"Um, was there something special on your mind?" she asked.

"I—I, uh…" *Spit it out!* "I was hoping you might be free tonight… Maybe we could get a bite to eat… Catch a movie."

"Oh, Zach, that would be wonderful, but—"

He could feel his gut tightening up. *Here it comes…*

"I'm on duty tonight."

A flood of relief washed over him. "Oh, well… maybe another time."

"How about tomorrow night?" She sounded hopeful. "I would really love to see you again."

"Tomorrow's fine with me," he blurted out. "I mean—I'd love to see you again too."

They arranged a time and disconnected. Zach tucked his phone away. Things were looking up. He heaved a deep sigh, reflecting that when he had first arrived back in Langston, he had been a zombie… No feelings to feel…

But now he was beginning to feel that he belonged here. His uncle and cousins had welcomed him with open arms. Just performing a few simple tasks around the ranch made him feel competent and appealed to his need to belong to a team. Even the responsibility to look after Fern Davis's property made him feel useful.

And then there was Stephanie…

# Chapter 9

STEPHANIE TUCKED AWAY HER PHONE, SO RELIEVED THAT Zach had called to ask her out. That he had taken the initiative meant he really wanted to see her again. It wasn't all on her.

Things were still pretty loose and undefined between them. She couldn't call him her boyfriend yet. He was just a man she was dating. She expelled a long breath. Okay, he was the only man she was dating...the only one for a long time. *Talk about a dry spell*.

But when it came to breaking a dry spell, Zach had done so in style. She was amazed that the big guy had been such a tender and proficient lover...that he had found all the impossibly sensual places to kiss and touch her...touch her with those big, rough, but gentle hands.

She felt a rush of lust swirling in her lower body. *No! Think cool thoughts. Cool until tomorrow night when I will again jump on the magnificent Zach Garrett*.

"Hey, Gayle," Donnell shouted. "Dinner's ready."

"Thanks." She headed to the day room where her fellow firefighters lazed, watched television, played games, and ate.

There was a kitchen at one end and a few well-worn overstuffed sofas and chairs at the other end with a television mounted on the wall. In the middle was a long table with chairs lining both sides.

Stephanie lined up at the kitchen end to receive a

plate. "Chili mac?" She eyed the mound of pasta and meat oozing with cheese and thought of her waistline. "Don't you guys ever consider a salad? Maybe a vegetable?"

Climber, who had drawn cook duty, looked at her from the other side of the bar. "Nope. Never crossed my mind." He plunked two hot rolls on her plate with his plastic-gloved hand. "How about some chocolate pudding?"

She thought about declining, but he placed a plastic container of premade pudding beside her plate. "Um, thanks."

Climber looked pleased. "Enjoy." He had earned his nickname for his ability to climb almost anything with amazing speed, including trees to save cats and the extension ladder from the fire truck when it zoomed out to access a second or third story.

She took her plate to the table, sitting in the chair Donnell pulled out for her. Not that he stood up; rather, he slid the chair next to him back enough for her to be seated. All this without getting to his feet or without a lull in the rhythmic shoveling of food into his mouth. "Thanks," she muttered.

"So, how ya been?" he said between bites.

"Fine." She wasn't really in the mood for small talk.

Miller, who was sitting across from her, put his fork down and gazed at her intently. "How's your big boyfriend?"

*There it is.*

She gave him a cool stare under her lashes. "Trust me... He's fine." She drew the last word out for emphasis.

This was met with a howl of laughter and a barrage of questions.

"You guys are pitiful," she said. "Don't you have your own pathetic personal lives?"

"Well, yeah," Donnell said.

"So do I," Stephanie said. "And it's personal." She pushed back the chair and took her plate to sit in front of the television, leaving behind a murmur of discontent.

---

The afternoon wore on uneventfully. About seven in the evening, when the firefighters were just clearing away the remains of their evening meal, the alarm sounded.

Stephanie scrambled into her gear and took her place in the jump seat of the fire truck. Donnell, Climber, and Slim jammed in beside her. They rode facing the rear of the truck. No one spoke because the captain was speaking through the firecom system.

The captain sat in the passenger seat next to the driver in the front section of the cab. His voice sounded clear as he passed along information.

"House fire started in kitchen. Teen girl babysitting ran to neighbor." He spoke in his usual terse voice that boomed over the speaker.

The sirens wound down as the unit pulled to a stop. The firefighters sprang into action, exiting in reverse order that they had entered the vehicle. Before leaving, Stephanie grabbed a yellow pouch containing a mask from under the fold-down seats and an air pack that contained thirty minutes of air. She wasn't certain what she would need, but she would be prepared.

Due to her small stature, she rarely dealt with the

heavy equipment, but her squad mates were busy unloading and setting up equipment.

She settled her air tank on her shoulder and approached a couple of women huddled on the driveway next door. "Did you call in the fire?"

On closer inspection, she saw that it was a middle-aged woman and a teen girl holding a toddler.

The woman wrung her hands together. "Mr. Hudson is upstairs. Tammy got the baby, but the old man is bed-bound."

"His room is on the second floor," the girl whimpered.

Stephanie swallowed hard. Flames were shooting out the windows on the east side of the house. "On which side is his bedroom?"

The woman gestured, and Stephanie began to run in that direction.

"Gayle? Where are you going?" the captain called out.

"There's an old man upstairs." She didn't look back but raced toward the house.

The hoses had been set up, with Slim and Donnell walking them inside.

The front door stood open with smoke billowing out at the top, so Stephanie bent low to run inside. She spied the stairway at the opposite end of the room and ran toward it. The smoke was thicker on the second floor.

She opened each door. A nursery, a large bedroom, and finally a room with a hospital bed. A frail elderly man gazed at her with a frightened expression. He began to cough.

"I've got you," she said. Stephanie quickly loosened the bedding and used it to lower the man to the floor.

She discarded his pillows and wrapped him in the sheets and blanket. She gathered the bedding near the man's head and raised it before she began dragging him from the room. When she reached the stairway, the flames were shooting out from the kitchen area.

Donnell and Slim were engaged in fighting the flames, but Stephanie's only goal was to get the man down the stairs.

She kept his head elevated as she backed down the stairs, but the old man's heels hit the steps as she pulled him to the ground floor.

Once they had cleared the stairway, the heat was intense. As quickly as possible she pulled the man outside, still wrapped in his cocoon. Climber grabbed the other end of the bedding and lifted the man's feet. Together they delivered the man to the sidewalk, where an EMT team took over. They began examining the man, who was again coughing.

Stephanie removed her air mask and helmet. Bending over from the waist, she took deep breaths, keeping an eye on the man she'd rescued.

He was soon loaded into an ambulance and whisked away to the hospital.

Stephanie was still breathing hard when Climber leaned over her. "You okay, Gayle?"

She nodded. "Sure."

"Good job, Gayle," the captain said, giving her a pat on the back. "That is one lucky man you rescued."

She straightened and gave him a half smile. "Isn't that my job?"

"Yes, but you're supposed to wait for backup."

---

Zach drove to Amarillo, even though he knew Stephanie was on duty. He was conflicted, and he needed something to help him get centered...or someone...

He came bearing a gift as a way to justify his visit. Fern had baked an extra pie for him to bring as an offering.

When he arrived at the fire station, he was given a terse greeting by a young firefighter whose name tag identified him as S. Miller. He had been shoveling snow off the wide concrete area outside the bays where fire trucks were housed.

Zach realized that this S. Miller was acting as a road block. "I'd like to see Stephanie Gayle." He clasped the foil-wrapped pie in both hands.

Miller snorted. "I'll just bet you would, but she's out on a call."

"A call?" Zach regarded the surly young man.

"Yeah, a fire. This here is the fire department, and she is out on a fire truck fighting a fire."

Zach resisted the urge to pick Miller up by his ears and slam him against the wall, but he did narrow his gaze to send a silent warning to shut up. "I'll wait."

"Suit yourself." Miller did an about-face and resumed his shoveling.

Zach considered returning to his truck to wait for Stephanie's return, but it felt like a retreat...and he wasn't known for retreating.

He sauntered into the large bay that housed three fire engines. One shiny, big fire truck sat idle against the far wall, but there were two empty spaces.

He knew in his heart of hearts that Stephanie was a highly trained professional, but somehow he worried. This was Amarillo, Texas, not Afghanistan. She was in the company of her very tight squad, and he thought they were in the habit of working as a team. Not like his squad, where snipers were waiting to pick them off or roadside bombs were in place to blow them to hell.

He paced.

"Sir, can I help you?"

Zach turned, finding himself face to face with a gray-haired man. "Um—I'm waiting for my—my friend."

"Well, who's your friend?" The man cocked his head to one side, peering through his glasses as though Zach had dropped in from an alien planet.

"I'm waiting for Stephanie Gayle. She's my—friend."

"So you said. Well, Gayle is out on a call right now." The man was short and slightly hunched over, but he gestured to a side door. "Why don't you come inside to wait?"

Zach nodded. "Thank you, sir."

The man led him into the building, through a hallway, and into a large room that seemed to be some sort of recreation area. There was a long table with chairs pushed up to it, and there was an industrial-looking kitchen at the far end. The other side of the room was furnished with sofas and chairs and had a large television mounted to the wall.

"You can wait here if you want," the man said.

"Pardon me, sir, do you work here?"

The man broke into a smile. "I'm a retired firefighter, son. I work in the call center part time." He shrugged. "Keeps me off the streets." He walked off, chuckling.

Holding the pie, Zach settled into one of the chairs but kept his eye on the door to the garage bay.

In time, Miller, the surly snow shoveler, entered the building. He began shedding his gloves and the knitted hat he'd been wearing. He looked surprised to see Zach. "They're on their way back," he said.

Zach got to his feet and went to look out the door into the bay. He saw one fire engine had backed into the middle space, while another was backing with a loud beeping noise echoing off the hard surfaces. He felt enormously relieved.

When the truck had stopped, the doors opened, and people began climbing out. Two men and then Stephanie's much smaller figure exited the fire engine.

The two men looked familiar, but he couldn't recall their names. They nodded at him, letting him know they recognized him from the dance.

"Zach?" Stephanie spotted him and crossed to where he was standing. "What are you doing here?" She looked a little glassy-eyed, and her ponytail was disheveled, drooping to one side.

"Hey, I just wanted to see you." He suddenly felt foolish for coming. But her smile reassured him that his presence was welcome.

She surprised him by spreading her arms and giving him a hug in spite of the stares from her fellow firefighters. She smelled like smoke and had streaks of soot on her face. "I'm so glad to see you. We just had the best run."

He held the pie behind her back and patted her shoulder rhythmically with his other hand. "Best run?"

One of the men shook his head. "Superwoman is

probably going to get another medal for this run." He pushed on past into the building.

"What is he talking about?" Zach asked.

Stephanie took his arm and urged him inside. "Oh, it was nothing. Just a sweet old man who needed a little help."

The one called Slim came up behind them. "Another good run, Gayle." Slim pushed past, and when they got to the large recreation room, Zach saw that Slim had settled in one of the comfortable chairs and was flipping through channels with the remote while the other man had his face in the refrigerator. "Hey, Donnell. Grab me a soda, will you?"

The other man grunted and continued foraging.

"Is there somewhere we can talk?"

"Sure, we can talk here." She pulled him to a small table in a corner. There was a checkerboard and a deck of cards stacked neatly on top. "I'm sorry you had to wait." She sat down with her back to the other firefighters.

Zach placed the foil-wrapped pie on the table and took a seat beside her. He had expected her to be tired at this time, and especially after coming in from working a fire, but she was alert, almost electrified. "So, everything went well?"

"It was great…I mean, as great as a house fire could be."

"Don't mind her," Donnell said. "It's the adrenaline. Takes a little time to come down off the high."

Stephanie heaved a sigh. "He's right. It's like when a musician performs at a concert."

He understood this. It was like when he and his squad had been out on patrol. They had been so wired, it took a little while for them to come down.

Zach reached to take a strand of her hair and push it away from her face. He wiped at the smudge on her cheek. "I'm just glad you're okay. Are you hungry?"

"I suppose. I can see what's in the fridge."

"How about a slice of Fern Davis's pecan pie?" He nudged the pie toward her.

She looked at it as though she was noticing it for the first time. "Pecan pie? Oh, that sounds wonderful."

"Pie?" Slim turned around. "Did you say pecan pie?"

Donnell brought a stack of disposable plates and forks, and Slim brought a knife. They stood, looking hopeful.

Stephanie smiled. "I think we can share." She took the knife and served a wedge of pie to each of them.

"Thanks, soldier boy." Donnell took his pie and seated himself next to Slim on the sofa.

"Thank you so much for bringing this wonderful treat." Stephanie picked up her fork and dug in.

That she enjoyed the pie was worth the effort. Zach felt a sense of satisfaction.

"Had to share." He took a bite and sat listening to her prattle on about the fire and about a babysitter and an old man. Somehow, everything seemed to be right. Her comrades seemed to have accepted him. It was okay for him to be in her domain. He would be comfortable coming here when she was on duty. "Great pie, huh?"

---

Leah and Gracie were at the main Garrett ranch house early the next morning. Tyler had driven over and deposited them, saying they needed to entertain Gran while he got some work done. He was intent upon writing some new songs, and for some reason he wasn't able to concentrate with Gracie out of school for the Christmas holiday. This meant that the television would be on more and his girls would be twittering with holiday-themed projects.

Leah wondered how he was going to react to having a newborn in the house. But she was willing to grant him some alone time so she could spend the day with her beloved daughter and grandmother.

They had enjoyed a family-style breakfast, and then Misty had gone to work, and Big Jim, Colton, and Zach had gone out to do chores with Misty's little brother in tow.

Tyler kissed his wife and daughter and returned to their quiet house to create music and lyrics in solitude. He had allowed their dogs, Lucky and Eddie, to remain with him…providing they were quiet.

The big house seemed deafeningly quiet with just Leah, Gran, and Gracie sitting around the Garrett table.

"Do you need somethin' else?" Gran asked, reaching to pat Leah's hand.

"No, Gran. I'm full as a tick." She patted her belly, which seemed to have gotten even larger overnight.

"Almost time," Gran sang out. "And you, Gracie, are gonna be a big sister. Are you a-wantin' a lil sister or a lil brother?"

Gracie's brow furrowed. "I think I would like a baby sister." She shrugged. "I don't know anything about little boys except the ones at school, and they're awful. They're loud and rude, and sometimes they stink."

Gran considered her statement at length. "Well, yes… Boys can be a mite stinky. But they do have their good points."

Leah had brought craft paper for her daughter to work on and yarn for herself to crochet. "But sometimes those little boys grow to be the most amazing men. Look at your daddy. Ty is an awesome man, and his brothers are too. You know, you might have a wonderful little brother."

Gracie shook her head. "I'm pretty sure it's going to be a girl." She reached for a sheet of craft paper and cut it into a perfect square. "That way I can help her brush her hair and teach her all kinds of things. Like how to make origami swans." She began the intricate folding process she had learned as a Brownie Girl Scout.

"I'm going to go curl up in front of the television. That big old recliner is calling my name...and I better hurry up and get this baby afghan finished before this little one is born." Leah rose from the table, gathering her bag of yarn. "Just don't be disappointed either way, Gracie. Whatever it is, I just pray for a healthy baby as beautiful as you were."

Gran pushed her chair back and used both hands on the table to push to a standing position. "Amen."

———※———

That evening, Zach was on his own. He felt as though he was drowning in family kinship. Dinner had been delicious, and he had dutifully eaten it with his uncle, his cousins, and their families.

He envied the close and loving relationship his cousins had developed with their attractive wives. He caught the little exchanges going on between the loving couples. Hands touched. Voices spoke in lowered tones. Expressions softened.

Considering the austere conditions in which he'd been living, this was about as different as he could imagine. He drank the last of his coffee and pushed away from the table. "If you all will excuse me…" He took his dishes to the sink and rinsed them. When he turned around, everyone at the table was staring at him. "I thought I would just take a little drive."

This announcement was met with smiles and knowing glances. He realized they thought he would be going to see Stephanie. That was okay. Let them think that.

Zach shrugged into his jacket and set his Stetson firmly on his head. He stopped at the front door. Glancing back, he heard the sound of laughter and pleasant conversation emanating from the back of the house. Heaving a sigh, he realized he loved all the people in this house, but he was an outsider. As much as he wanted to be a part of the circle, he did not fit in…yet.

He opened the door and quickly stepped out, not wanting to allow the bitter cold to enter the house. The brisk wind that had howled around the buildings when he and Big Jim were inspecting Gran's place had died down. Now, the sound of his boots, crunching through the new-fallen snow, was the only sound to break the silence.

He climbed into his truck, as chilly as if he'd stepped into a giant refrigerator. He turned on the motor, letting the vehicle warm up a bit before starting out, but the windows immediately fogged up, so he turned on the defroster full blast.

Zach pulled his leather work gloves out of his pocket and worked his numb fingers into the folds. As soon as the windows were clear, he shifted into gear and eased out onto the drive.

The moon was almost full, reflecting off the snow that covered the landscape. While one part of Zach's brain could appreciate the beauty surrounding him, he was fixated on his destination. His mouth was set in a grim line.

He turned onto the highway and drove in complete silence, only his tires making a singing sound on the highway. The road cut a black line through the whiteness of the snow. As he approached the turnoff, his chest felt tight. He hated what he was doing, but he was incapable of changing his mind. Just something he had to do.

He made the turn onto the farm-to-market road and drove another mile before slowing to a crawl.

The house was dark, and there were no vehicles around. He turned into the short drive leading up to the home where he had been raised and rolled to a stop, the high beams washing the area.

He realized he wasn't breathing and heaved a huge sigh before idling the motor. He sat, staring at the house as though seeking an answer. But there was no response forthcoming.

Zach figured that if anyone were inside, they would have revealed themselves in some way. Turning on a light, perhaps. Or peering through the drapes. But no. He could detect no signs of life at all. He killed the motor and stuck the keys in his jacket pocket.

Resolutely, he climbed out, slamming the door and calling out, in case there was someone hiding inside.

He knocked on the door, but there was no response. He figured whoever bought the place would have had the house rekeyed, but he stuck his key in the lock, and the door swung open at his touch. The eeriness of the space caused a tingling sensation at the back of his neck…the same feeling he had experienced on patrol when something was just not right. "Hello?"

Receiving no response, he reached inside to flip the light switch, but the interior remained in total darkness. He swallowed hard and stepped over the threshold, his footsteps sounding thunderous hitting the hardwood floor and echoing in the cavern.

Zach chuckled. Hard to believe he let an empty house spook him, especially when he had been through hell and back with his men. He knew the address, and it was not in the Texas Panhandle.

The problem was this was not just any empty space. It was the place where he had grown up, where his father had carried him to bed when he'd fallen asleep in front of the television…where his mother had baked bread and served it to him after school with her homemade preserves. Now it was empty.

He understood why his mother had given up. After his father passed away, she had felt overwhelmed. He should have come home…while there was still a home to come to.

Zach raked his fingers through his hair. It was growing out. He would look like a pine burr if he didn't get a haircut. He strolled through the rest of the house. Without furniture or personal items, it was a little less painful. At least everything was safely moved to Fort Worth and under his mother's care. He pressed his lips together in a straight line. Better cut her some slack. He should go visit her before Christmas…maybe take Stephanie with him… *Naw, it's way too soon for that.* He still had no idea where their relationship was going… or if they even had one.

Taking one last look around, he closed the door and locked it back up. He stepped off the porch and into the frigid stillness of the night. Whoever owned this property now obviously had no use for the house. As isolated as it was, vandals might wreck it…but it wasn't his beloved home any longer.

He took a quick circle of the area, checked the empty barn and other outbuildings. No livestock in the yard. No horses. No cattle. Even his mother's chickens were gone. He followed up with a drive around the property, but no livestock was present in any of the pastures.

His breath made a cloud around his head as he huffed out a sigh. Apparently, whoever had bought the place just wanted it for the land. They had sold off the horses and cattle, the herd his father had so lovingly built up.

A hollow pain invaded his being. *This was a mistake. I shouldn't have come.*

Zach drove back to the Garrett ranch and managed to slip inside without waking anyone. He lay in bed for some time, staring into the darkness as the pain of losing his past enveloped him.

———~~~———

The next morning he told Gran that he would move into her house and take over the responsibilities of maintaining her property. He wasn't sure why he was doing it, but he needed to be in a separate space from his happily married cousins, and he felt a profound admiration for Fern Davis. She was like an elderly, female Yoda, sprinkling wisdom around and seeming to be the only person who actually saw him as he really was.

"I was a-hopin' you would decide to help me out."

She grasped his hand with both of hers. "I'm trustin' you with my place."

He patted her hand. "Yes, ma'am. I'll take care of everything for you." Seeing her smile made him feel certain that he had made the right decision.

He spent much of the day doing his tasks around the Garrett ranch. He was working with Colton and Big Jim, enjoying the camaraderie of his relatives.

Big Jim drew him aside and gave him a pat on the shoulder. "I really appreciate you for taking on Fern's place. I know she'll sleep a lot easier knowing you're there." His face split into a wide grin. "I suppose you know that the boys and I are mighty fond of that little lady?"

Zach broke loose with a grin of his own. "Yeah, she's pretty hard to resist."

"Well, I know you'll do a good job for her. Of course, I'm depending on you to keep working here too. Particularly since my youngest son, Beau, is neck-deep in fixing up his own place. He and his bride are working on the ranch she inherited, and she also owns the feed store in town." He heaved a deep sigh. "I gotta understand that he's got to take care of his new family and put their interests first." He turned and gave Zach another slap on the shoulder. "So you came home to us just in time, boy."

Having his uncle acknowledge his worth meant the world to Zach. He thanked Big Jim and received a hearty man-hug and shoulder pounding.

Zach finished his tasks and then moved his few belongings into the Davis ranch house. He figured he could spend the winter working for his uncle and still manage to keep Fern's place in good repair.

He turned on the gas heaters, which improved the interior of the house significantly and enabled him to be able to take a hot bath without stepping out to become an icicle. He dressed for his date with Stephanie, and turned the heaters off. He hoped to be spending the night at her apartment, snuggling the luscious woman in his arms.

# Chapter 10

STEPHANIE HAD BEEN LOOKING FORWARD TO SEEING ZACH again. Now she was dressed and pacing around her apartment, anxious for him to appear.

She was torn between a demure greeting at the door and jumping on him right out of the chute. Her flesh heated up whenever she thought of their sexual encounters, and she thought of them often.

What if Zach's interest in her was purely sexual? She stopped her pacing. She had been pretty easy for him, and he had been in the company of men, so perhaps any woman would catch his attention. Gnawing her lower lip brought her no great insights. She sighed and was in the process of reapplying her lipstick when she heard a tap on the door.

"Zach?" She called his name, hand on the knob, and waited for his response before opening it for him.

"Hey." He stood in the doorway gazing down at her, a smile on his lips, his incredible blue eyes devouring her.

"Hey yourself." A swell of warmth washed through her. She held out her arms, and he stepped into the room, closing the door behind himself. Stephanie found herself wrapped in his embrace. Very tender for a man built of such hardness.

"I—uh, I'm glad to see you," she managed to get out.

"Me too." He leaned back to look at her. "You look

very beautiful tonight. I hope I'm dressed well enough to be with you."

She laughed. "Don't be silly. You look—great."

"Hungry?"

The expression on his face sent a shiver spiraling around her spine. "Starving." Her voice came out all thick and husky.

Suddenly, they were a tangle of arms as they scooped each other up in a fierce embrace. His mouth was like fire, burning a trail from her lips to her cheek to her neck and back to her lips.

*Okay, I guess we're going to have sex now.*

His breath was hot against her cheek. "I better get you out of here," he rasped out.

"Outta here?" Her heart was throbbing against her rib cage, and certain parts of her lower anatomy were quite moist.

"Yeah, if you're hungry. I made reservations at a nice restaurant. I thought I would try to do this right."

"Oh, you're doing everything right." She stepped back and ran her fingers through her disheveled hair. "I—uh, let me get my coat."

When she returned with her coat over her arm, he took it from her and held it for her to don.

"It's cold out there. You better button up." He gestured toward the door.

"I'm ready." She grabbed her handbag and fished out her keys. She locked the door from the outside and tucked her hand in the crook of his arm.

When they stepped outside the apartment building, a blast of sleety air assaulted her face. Zach helped her into his truck and ran around to take his place behind the wheel. "Sorry to drag you out when the weather is so bad."

"Not a problem." She sent him a reassuring smile. *But we could have stayed inside and created some heat of our own.*

She was surprised when he took her to a very nice restaurant with valet parking. They dined on steak and seafood. By the time they left the restaurant, Stephanie felt pleasantly stuffed but still anticipated a night of passionate activity.

Zach seemed to be eager to get her alone. He leaned over to give her a kiss when they were stopped at a red light.

She felt almost giddy when they reached her apartment building and rode the elevator up to her floor. Laughing, she produced her key, but Zach seized it instead. When he tried to insert it in the lock, the door swung open silently.

A bolt of fear shot through her. Stephanie couldn't draw a breath. They stood in the hallway, gazing at the remains of her residence. The interior of the apartment was in ruins. Every piece of furniture had been shredded. Anything made of glass or ceramic was shattered. The destruction was thorough.

"My God!" Zach stepped inside, staring at the total demolition. "Who would do this?"

She had no doubt who was behind the devastation. Her lips trembled, and she couldn't form words. She stared around, feeling helpless for the first time she could remember. Her legs felt as though they had turned to rubber. She reached out to Zach, and he immediately embraced her.

"Careful," he said. "Do you want to sit down?"

Staring around, she saw there was no place to sit. "N—nooo…" she wailed.

Zach followed her gaze. "I see…Well, why don't you gather up what you need and come to my place tonight. We can sort this out tomorrow."

"I want to see my bedroom." She pushed away from him and tiptoed through the debris in the hallway. The bathroom was trashed. Cosmetics were crushed on the tile floor. "Oh, no!" She felt as though the breath had been knocked out of her. On the pale-blue wall, her lipstick had been used to write a message.

"What?" It was Zach close behind her.

The words DIE BITCH struck a new chord of fear within her.

"Let's get out of here. You don't need to be tormented by whoever did this."

"But—but I have to call the police. They have to see this before we touch it." She punched the numbers 9-1-1 and explained to the operator what had happened. In a matter of minutes, the sound of sirens split the air.

Stephanie buried her face against Zach's chest. "I'm sorry this date has been such a bomb. I had a great time…up until now."

He kissed her hair as heavy footfalls were heard in the hallway. "I'm not leaving you here. You are definitely coming with me."

The officers who surveyed the scene took notes and advised her not to touch anything. They called for crime scene investigators to come and look for clues.

"Do you have a safe place to spend the night?" the officer asked.

"She's going to be with me," Zach said.

Hearing these words rumble out of Zach's chest made her feel less fearful.

The officer urged them to leave, swearing the location would be secure.

"But my things. I need my things," she wailed.

Zach urged her toward the door. "We'll pick up new things. Let's go now and let the officers do their jobs."

"I—I guess so, but…"

He had her out the door and in the elevator before she could gather her thoughts. She couldn't think about what she might need but felt horrible just abandoning her possessions to the law enforcement personnel who were milling around her apartment.

When they hit the sidewalk outside, she saw another vehicle pull up with the words CRIME SCENE emblazoned on the side.

She was silent as Zach drove out of the city and headed toward the small town of Langston. She tried to clear her brain, but all she could see was the destruction she'd left behind.

"Are you going to be all right?" he asked.

She shook her head slightly. "No, I don't think so."

—◆◆◆—

Zach kept his outward calm in place, hoping to help Stephanie relax. Inside he was raging. He glanced at her from time to time, but she was too wrapped up in some inner turmoil to even notice.

He was furious that someone was threatening Stephanie. He was a warrior, but at the moment he felt impotent. How could some monster be threatening her?

His anger settled into a cold fury deep in his gut. He made a vow that, no matter what else, he would protect Stephanie Gayle, no matter how she protested.

When they reached the turnoff to the Garrett Ranch, he blew by it without slowing. Stephanie glanced up but didn't comment.

He turned onto the road to Fern's house and pulled up to the cottage then turned off the motor.

She gazed at him solemnly, her large eyes asking the question her lips were unwilling to ask.

"This is Fern Davis's place. I'm sort of looking after it for her."

She nodded and reached for the door handle and had slid down from the seat, embedding her shoes in the snow, before he could climb out to assist her. She looked down at her shoes but didn't seem to be too disturbed.

The house was dark, and he had turned off the heat because he thought he would be spending the night at Stephanie's apartment. *Change of plans.*

Taking her hand, he helped her to the front porch. "Here we go, just step up here."

She followed him into the house. He seated her on the comfy sofa and set about lighting the heaters and turning on lights. He brought a blanket from one of the bedrooms and wrapped it around her.

"Thanks." Her cheeks slowly warmed as the temperature of the room heated up.

"I can make a pot of coffee," he said. "That's about all there is in the pantry. I'll go to the store tomorrow."

"Thanks," she repeated.

Zach felt the need to do something for her...something more than he had done already.

She watched him move around the kitchen, obviously out of place in this environment, searching for ingredients and implements. But she knew he was trying to take care of her, and that alone warmed her heart.

He came to sit beside her. "Coffee will be ready in a couple of minutes. Are you doing okay?" He clasped her hand.

"As good as I can be with all my worldly possessions destroyed and I can't even check the damage."

"We'll have plenty of time to clean up your place. Don't worry about a thing."

That sounded reassuring. In spite of her situation, Stephanie felt heartened that Zach had jumped in with both feet. It would have been reasonable that he step away from a woman being threatened by a killer, but Zach was hanging in with her. "I—I appreciate what you're doing."

A hint of a smile twitched his lips. "And what am I doing?"

"Comforting me. Making me feel less afraid." She huffed out a sigh. "Protecting me from the reality that is my brutal life."

He put an arm around her and pulled her closer. "Listen, Stephanie. We're new together…you and me. But I think we are growing…you know…closer."

She leaned her head against his shoulder. "Yes, we are."

"So, I just thought… You know?"

"Yes, I think I know…but you can spell it out for me."

"Let me get our coffee. It's ready now." He hurried to the kitchen and poured two cups of coffee. "Cream? Sugar?"

Stephanie leaned her head back against the sofa and stared up at the ceiling. *Why are men so difficult?* "A little cream and sugar would be great." She closed her eyes, hoping it would all roll out as it should. When she opened her eyes, he was standing over her, holding two cups. She sat up and reached for the one he extended to her.

He placed his cup on the coffee table and sat back down on the sofa beside her. "I'm going to spell it out." His brow furrowed. "You know that I really like you?" He looked at her for confirmation.

"Yes, I like you too."

"Well, I was thinking maybe you might be willing to live here…with me."

Stephanie turned her full attention to him. "Here?"

"With me. I want you to live with me. I want to go to bed with you every night and wake up with you every morning." He gazed at her, the turquoise-blue eyes burning through to her soul.

Stephanie tried to play it cool and took a sip of her coffee. "That sounds good, but I work out of Amarillo. Sometimes my shift is overnight. The chief babies me, so he doesn't put me on overnight shifts often, but sometimes…"

He took her cup and set it beside his. "So, that means…you're willing to move in with me?"

She nodded. "Considering that all my remaining possessions are in my purse, I'm pretty sure I've already moved in with you."

His face split into a wide grin. "Great. We can get settled in here. Fern said I could do anything I wanted to the interior, so if you want me to paint or something, she's cool with that." He stopped talking but kept grinning.

"You can kiss me now." She leaned up toward him, letting the blanket fall away.

"Yes, ma'am." He kissed her tenderly, then again.

"So, how about a tour?" she asked.

He stood and pulled her to her feet. "I've barely checked it out myself. This is the living room."

"Really?" Her voice was heavy with sarcasm.

"And that is the kitchen and dining room all together." He pointed toward the rear of the house.

"Very efficient."

He put his arm around her shoulders and drew her with him as he turned on lights. "Down this hall, you will find the sleeping quarters and the bathroom…only one, so we have to share." He flipped on the light and brought her into the old-fashioned bathroom with him.

She considered what such sharing might mean. "I can do that."

He leaned close to her ear and spoke in a raspy whisper. "In fact, we might need to conserve hot water and share our bath."

"Oh! Well, that would be…" She put both hands over her mouth. "A claw-foot bathtub. I love it."

"Yeah?"

"I do," she said. "I love old-fashioned things. This is the real deal country décor."

Zach huffed out a laugh. "This is about as country as it gets."

"What else? Aren't you going to show me the bedrooms?"

Something in his expression sobered. "Right this way." He held out his hand.

Slipping her hand in his felt like an act of intimacy.

He flipped on the overhead light in the larger of the two small bedrooms. The walls were papered in a small floral print. The furniture was in good repair, obviously having been lovingly polished over the years. There was a small dresser with an oval mirror affixed to the wall. A couple of lacy crocheted doilies adorned the top and contrasted with the shiny dark mahogany. The bed was neatly made, topped with a handmade quilt.

"This is really…sweet." Stephanie realized the double bed was hardly big enough for Zach, but she supposed they could both occupy it if they slept very close together.

"Looks comfortable," Zach offered hopefully.

"Hmm…maybe." Stephanie crossed the room to sit on the foot of the bed. She made a show of bouncing up and down a little. "I'm not sure. I think we need a second opinion." She patted the bed beside her invitingly.

His eyes crinkled at the corners as his good humor took over. "I can give it a try." He unbuckled his western belt and slid it out of his belt loops. "But that quilt looks kind of delicate. Maybe I should take off all this extra stuff that might mess it up."

"I think that's an excellent idea. Do you need some help?" She managed a relatively innocent expression.

"That's mighty nice, but I was just going to offer to help you out of all that cumbersome clothing."

The timbre of his voice and the intensity of his gaze brought about a rush of excitement low in her belly. Suddenly, all the misery of the day faded away as she anticipated what was to come.

"Sure…I can use some help." She stood up beside him and slid her palms up his chest to interlace her fingers behind his neck. She lifted her chin, knowing Zach would kiss her. She was rewarded with strong arms embracing her and a kiss that warmed her down to her toes.

In no time at all, most of her clothing had been dealt with most expeditiously. The date dress she had so carefully selected lay on the floor, discarded. Stephanie acknowledged that any task Zach took on was carried out efficiently. Like the way he made love. She swallowed hard, recalling their previous coupling.

The blue eyes gazed into hers before he slowly lowered his mouth to hers.

Like magic she found herself horizontal, with the beautiful man beside her, kissing, caressing, and touching all the right places.

Just his nearness was enough to cause all her senses to come alive. She caught her breath as his warm gaze sparked a rush of excitement inside her.

He cupped her cheek and delivered a sweet kiss to her lips, her cheek, and her ear.

Her pulse throbbed rhythmically, her senses sharpened by the scent of him, the feel of him against her. "I want to live here, Zach," she whispered against his neck. His arousal felt like a hot rock pressed into her groin. She tried to resist the rush of passion flooding her insides.

"Just don't ever leave." He found her breasts with his mouth and hands.

She was on fire. Flames spread from her taut nipples, from his mouth suckling and teasing her, burning a path to her core.

When he reached for her, she pulled him down on

top of her, kissing and biting him with a passion she knew he hadn't anticipated. Her strong thighs encircled his hips, drawing him to her. "Please…" she breathed against his skin. "Don't make me wait any longer."

Zach hesitated a moment then reached for a condom in the bedside table. As he entered her, he gazed into her eyes. "You're so precious," he whispered. He surprised her with the ferocity of his lovemaking.

Stephanie let out a soft moan as their bodies connected and again with every stroke that reached deep inside her. She held him tightly, lifting her hips into his thrusts. When the first waves of orgasm washed over her, she went rigid, riding it out until she collapsed back on the bed, struggling for breath.

She whispered his name and held him tighter. Matching his thrusts as her passion built again. When she climaxed again, Zach groaned and ground against her, exploding with a force like an earthquake.

She kissed his neck, tasting the salt of his sweat, feeling his pulse beat against her lips as he pulsed inside her.

She held him tightly against her as tears slid from the corners of her eyes and into her hair. The losses she had suffered meant nothing compared to the joy of being loved by this man.

"Are you okay?" he asked, his rough fingers stroking the side of her cheek. "Did I hurt you?" His face was all concern.

"I've never been better," she whispered.

# Chapter 11

THE NEXT MORNING WAS CHAOS.

For Stephanie, it was a gleeful chaos of bare flesh, still tingling from a night of passion and tenderness. The aftermath brought about a sweet achiness. A longing spiraled deep in her core. It was such exquisite sadness she couldn't quite grasp where it was coming from, and she was afraid to examine it too closely.

She had awakened cradled in Zach's strong arms and held tightly to his chest, with her leg casually wrapped around his waist. Their private parts were dangerously close in proximity. A wave of heat roiled up from the wetness in her groin.

She stared at Zach's tanned face in repose. His handsome features were relaxed, which was a change from his usual state of hyperalertness.

And then his eyes opened.

Her heart picked up its pace as his electric-blue eyes gazed into hers. Without a word he read the emotions she was experiencing. He cupped her cheek in one hand and gave her a tender kiss and then another.

"Zach, I—I..."

His hand caressed her shoulder and then slowly swept down her side, stopping to give a squeeze at her hipbone.

It was just a little gesture, but she found it endearing... Also exciting.

They made love again. While nighttime sex had
been fierce, morning sex was languorous and rich in
sensation.

Stephanie's heart raced, and her breathing was
ragged, but she held onto Zach as though he might
evaporate.

"Good morning," he whispered, his voice raspy.
"What are you thinking about so hard?"

She had to give a little laugh at that. "Good morning.
I was just kind of waffling between being very happy
and very scared."

He looked at her long and hard. "I hope I'm the happy
part."

She swallowed hard. "You are."

"And the scared part?"

"Um, everything else…my apartment, my truck, the
Neeley brothers…the children…"

Wrapping both arms around her, he gave her a kiss
that definitely got her attention. "You've got to believe
things are going to work out. I mean…" He dropped
another kiss on her lips. "I mean, I'm here for you. I—I
care about you… Aw, hell!" he exploded. "I'm pretty
sure that I'm in love with you."

She stared up at him, her eyes wide.

One side of his mouth curled up in a wry grin. "How
sad is that? For the first time in my life, I'm totally crazy
in love."

Stephanie felt the sting of tears behind her eyes.
"You're in love with me?" The tears rolled down from
the corners of her eyes and into her hair.

His brows drew together. "Whoa! I didn't mean to
upset you." He brushed away her tears with his thumb.

"It's okay if you don't love me. I don't mean to assume anything."

She could hardly draw a breath. *Is this man actually declaring his love?*

"Don't worry about it," he said. "I didn't mean to put you on the spot. Just forget I said anything." He started to move away from her, but she grabbed his face with both hands.

She planted a kiss on him that she hoped made her feelings clear. "Don't even think about it. I heard you the first time, and I'll never forget."

He stared hard, his gaze penetrating her defenses. "I'm not reading you, but it's been a long time since I've been around a woman…I mean close…"

A giggle bubbled up from her insides, lifting her spirits considerably. "I meant to say, you are so very dear to me…I love you, Zach, just the way you are. But I had no idea you felt the same way."

"I figured you knew how I felt."

"No, you've got that strong, silent thing going for you." She gave a slight shrug. "I guess you'll just have to tell me you love me over and over again so I don't fail to recognize your feelings."

He grinned and leaned down to deliver another kiss. "I will be happy to tell you, over and over again, how much I love you."

She lay curled in his arms for a while and then jerked away. "Oh no! I have to call in. My boss is going to kill me."

Stephanie called Lieutenant Larsen and explained that her apartment had been shredded and that she had to try to see what was left of her possessions.

"Gayle! That's terrible. Take all the time you need." Lieutenant Larsen cleared his throat. "Um—do you need a place to stay? The wife and I can put you up for a while."

She felt her color rising. "Oh, sir. That's so sweet of you, but I—uh…" She glanced at Zach, who was staring at her intently. "I have a place to stay."

"I see… Well, just take care of yourself." Lieutenant Larsen disconnected.

She held her phone in both hands and gnawed her lower lip. *Now what?*

Her "date dress" was hanging in Zach's bedroom closet along with her pride. Now she wore several layers of his clothing. A T-shirt in a particularly unflattering shade called olive drab. *Yeah, it's all that.* She topped it with a red, long-sleeved plaid flannel shirt with the sleeves rolled up, but the hem kissed her knees. It was roomy, to say the least, having been purchased to hang off Zach's broad shoulders.

She had retrieved her own panties and bra from the floor, where they had landed the previous evening. At least something fit her. The rest of her body was covered with a pair of camouflage-patterned pants. Thankfully, Zach's lower half was nice and lean. The waistband caught neatly on her hips, mostly because he had found a big safety pin to bunch them up in the back.

The moment he had dropped to one knee to roll up the legs so she wouldn't trip, she had experienced a longing she couldn't identify. She was somewhat overwhelmed by the tenderness this giant of a man displayed. It felt like a hollow ache, and she couldn't identify the reason for her yearning. She couldn't claim to be in any kind of physical need since Zach had made sure she woke up in a good mood.

"What's up?" he asked, and she realized she had been staring right through him.

"Oh, uh…I just…" Her lips trembled as a tear rolled down her cheek.

Zach cupped her cheek. "Stephanie, honey…you don't have to be so damned strong all the time. You've had your place demolished…your things trashed. You've got a right to be mad and sad for a while."

*Exactly!*

He pulled her toward him, and she gave in to the need to let someone else be the strong one for a change.

Circling his torso with both arms, she buried her face against his chest and let loose with the ocean of tears she'd been holding back.

Zach cradled her head, whispering soothing words. His voice was like a balm to her tormented soul. When he told her things would be okay, she could believe that they actually might.

She snapped her head back, gazing up into his eyes. It was at that moment she realized she was really in love with him. It had never occurred to her that she, the iron maiden of the Amarillo Fire Department, could possibly really fall in love.

He kissed her, sending shots of hot electricity swirling around her lower regions. Just when she thought she would be divested of the garments so carefully applied, he pulled away.

"Are you hungry? I thought we could grab a good breakfast at the diner before we head to Amarillo."

"Like this? You want me to go out in public like this?" She gestured to the outfit she wore.

He gave her a wide grin and a deep chuckle. "You look perfectly fine, but you gotta be hungry, so let's get moving and find some food."

"Oh, I know you're right, but I look so…so—"

"Beautiful. That must have been the word you were searching for." He brushed an errant strand of hair away from her forehead.

*There! That feeling again.* How could her feelings be yo-yoing up and down every time he looked at her…or said something sweet…or touched her…

She sucked in a breath and tossed her hair. "Yes. Exactly. That's just the word. I was about to break out with a few bars of 'I Feel Pretty'."

He brought her coat and held it open for her. "You go right ahead."

And this was how Stephanie found herself sitting in Tio's Mexican Restaurant facing a large plate of something Zach had ordered for her. She eyed the plate, poking at the contents suspiciously. "And what exactly are 'migas'?"

Zach scooped up a bite and shoveled it in his mouth, making pleased noises. "Eggs…I don't know what else." He waved the waitress over. "Hey, Milita. What are the ingredients in migas?"

The attractive woman strolled over, grinning. "What? I thought you loved our migas, Zach."

"Love 'em," he mumbled before chewing and swallowing. "But my beautiful friend here isn't very adventurous and wants to know what she's about to take in."

Milita smiled at her. "Okay. Diced onions, peppers, tomatoes, eggs, cheese…and of course some spices."

Stephanie gazed at Zach, happily scooping this concoction into corn tortillas and adding some kind of salsa. There was a side of refried beans, and he scooped some of that into his tortilla.

"Some people fry strips of corn tortilla and add that into the mixture, but this is the way we do it. Some people prefer the flour tortillas." Milita shrugged. "But this is my father's recipe. It's a signature dish."

"I'll try it." Stephanie took a corn tortilla and scooped some of the egg conglomeration into the tortilla then took a bite. The flavor exploded on her tongue. She found herself making appreciative noises similar to Zach's. "This is wonderful."

Milita winked at her before turning to her other duties.

The creamy egg and cheese complimented the tang of the salsa and the crunch of the lightly sautéed vegetables. It was something like a Mexican version of spicy quiche wrapped in a corn tortilla instead of crust.

She opened her eyes to see Zach, still chewing but managing to smile anyway.

"Okay, you were right. This is delicious."

He swallowed. "You notice I'm not saying 'I told you so.'"

"Yes, and I appreciate that." Stephanie laughed, all the while wondering how she could be so happy, having so much fun, when her apartment had been trashed and her possessions destroyed. But somehow, sitting in this restaurant with Zach, she felt safe and uplifted.

When they had eaten, Zach loaded her into his truck and headed for Amarillo. The sky was gray. No clouds, but just a solid slate gray stretched overhead from horizon to horizon. It made her feel claustrophobic, as though an ominous dark tent pressed her down to earth.

Zach seemed to be aware of her heightened tension. He tried to engage her in conversation, but when she only gave one-word responses, he fell silent too.

Stephanie's anxiety grew the closer they got to Amarillo. Spending the night with Zach had been a respite, but now she had to return to the real world, and it was looming large.

By the time the Amarillo cityscape came into view, her stomach was tied up in a knot. Her mouth felt dry, and her back teeth were grinding together.

Zach reached over and squeezed her hands. "It's gonna be okay."

She looked down at his large hand wrapped around hers...the ones she had locked together in a death grip. Drawing in a lungful of air, she released it in a rush. "Thanks."

When he pulled up in front of her apartment building, he let the truck idle as they looked around. There was a patrol car and a van with a police logo on the side pulled up close to the entrance. The tightness in her chest returned.

"Ready for this?" he asked, and when she nodded, he parked and walked her up to the building.

But they were turned away. The police officer informed them that they could not enter the apartment because there were techs still in the unit. They were directed to go to the police department so she could make an official statement.

Zach's presence made her feel less stressed, although he spoke few words. Just having the big, protective man standing close by made it easier for her to get through the interview, where she had to go over the details of rushing into a burning house to rescue two young children whose mother had been murdered. She described the threats made by Rafe Neeley, the damage to her truck, and her belief that he and his brothers were responsible for the destruction in her apartment.

At the end, she shook hands with the detective. He instructed her to take extreme precautions until such time that Neeley could be recaptured.

"I'm not letting her out of my sight," Zach said. The two men shook hands. It was a guy thing. They were taking care of the little woman.

On the one hand, Stephanie was a little insulted, but she also experienced a moment of realization where she understood how those women felt...the ones who were loved and cherished...and taken care of by their menfolk. Then she huffed out a breath and came back to earth.

She was Stephanie Gayle, firefighter extraordinaire. She had special training and was an essential part of the team.

But she looked up at Zach and read the concern etched on his face. The intensity of his gaze caused any offense she had been harboring to evaporate. The blue eyes reached all the way to her soul. She knew she could trust this man.

--—--

They killed time, hoping to get into the apartment. She insisted on being taken to a mall where she could purchase some garments and personal items.

With Zach by her side, she selected underwear, clothing, and cosmetics.

"I have toothpaste," he offered when she was checking out the various brands.

This announcement made her wrap both arms around his torso and bestow a lingering hug. "Thanks."

He was laden with bags and parcels, so he couldn't properly reciprocate, but he did drop a kiss on top of her head. "I just didn't want you to have to spend your money."

"How sweet. It's not a problem. I do have renter's insurance, so whenever the police get done, I'll get in touch with my agent and have him come to assess the damage." She shrugged. "I'm pretty sure they're going to be cutting me a big check."

"Oh, well…that's good, I guess."

"I guess. I just hope they didn't destroy the things I treasure most. I can buy new dishes and clothes, but there are some precious mementos from my parents that cannot be replaced. My grandmother's painting. The necklace my mom gave me when I graduated from high school…" She bit the inside of her lip to keep from tearing up.

"I understand. Let's hope for the best."

He drove her to her apartment, and they were allowed to enter. The crime scene techs were just finishing their tasks and clearing up their equipment when Zach and Stephanie arrived.

Stephanie stood just inside the doorway, surveying the scene of the devastation. Her stomach was clenched like a fist.

Zach stood behind her and laid a hand on her shoulder.

"I think you're going to need some boxes. I saw a little grocery store in the next block. How about if I go see if I can scrounge some up?"

"Good idea. I'll just start picking up a little in here." Stephanie released the breath that had been stuck in her throat. She gave a weak smile and nodded to the one tech.

"Whoever did this," the tech said, gesturing around, "sure did leave a lot of...uh, biologicals around."

"Skin cells?" she asked.

The tech snorted. "Not hardly. The dickhead peed on things. Like it wasn't enough to rip up things with a knife, but he had to piss on them too."

This added indignity hit Stephanie like a blow. "I'm thinking it might have been more than one dickhead involved."

"Well, that explains a lot. We'll have to take that into account...but I think you're going to have to just throw most of this stuff out."

"I hear you." She looked around sadly. "I wasn't all that attached to the sofa anyway."

The tech fished out a pair of rubber gloves and handed them to Stephanie. "You better use these."

Stephanie sighed and drew on the gloves. She spied the one item she was most concerned about and picked her way across the room to where the painting lay on the floor. It was the painting her grandmother had made just for her. When she had left home to attend the fire academy, her beloved grandmother had made an oil painting of Stephanie's favorite place in her grandmother's garden, a place where the two of them had shared many hours sitting in a wooden swing attached to a sturdy oak tree. From this vantage point, young Stephanie had shared her innermost thoughts with the one person who had always understood her feelings. That painting had followed Stephanie to this apartment, and now she would clean it up and take it with her wherever she landed. Maybe Zach would find a place for it at his new digs in the meantime.

The painting wasn't damaged, but the frame was a bit wonky on one corner. Reverently, she placed it on the floor beside the front door. In the kitchen, she found that everything made of glass or china had been smashed, but she placed the utensils and small appliances on one section of the countertop, ready to box up when Zach returned. Her toaster had a small dent, but it heated up when she tried it. The microwave was in one piece, but the glass lid to her small Crock Pot had been shattered. She made a note of the damaged or broken items to turn in to her insurance agent.

She heard movement in the living room and presumed either the tech was moving around or Zach had returned. "That you, babe?" she called out.

There was no response. Must have been the tech. She turned to find one of Rafe Neeley's brothers standing in the kitchen. She recognized him from his mug shot on the news.

His eyes glinted like black onyx. He was tensed, like an overwound spring.

Stephanie's heart raced, and she fought a wave of light-headedness. It was like staring into the eyes of a coiled snake.

His fleshy lips peeled back to reveal large teeth. He wasn't smiling but rather leering at her.

"What are you doing here?" she asked, her voice a raspy whisper.

He huffed out a mirthless laugh. "You. I'm here for you." He took a step toward her. "You been a pain in the ass, y'know?"

"You have to leave," she said. "Right now. The police are here."

"I did not see them," he hissed. "It is jus' you and me." He raised his right fist.

Stephanie braced herself, thinking he would hit her. She ran through a list of possible weaknesses. She could launch herself at his eyes. That looked like his only soft target. She realized that he held something gripped in his hand.

A muscle near his mouth twitched. His thumb flicked against the item in his hand, and a six-inch double-edged blade thrust up from the handle accompanied by a sound of metal on metal.

*Snick!*

# Chapter 12

ZACH CARRIED AN ARMLOAD OF NESTED BOXES INTO THE apartment building. He was pleased that he had been able to grab them before the grocer had broken them down. Riding up in the elevator, he anticipated that Stephanie would appreciate his efforts then laughed at himself. *Good boy! You retrieved the boxes.* He visualized himself as a puppy on a leash, wagging all over when he was near Stephanie.

He hoped she had been able to recover some of her belongings, at least the ones she treasured most.

Zach stepped out of the elevator and turned to Stephanie's apartment. The door was standing open, but he presumed the crime techs were still working inside. He dropped the boxes beside the door and looked around. "Stephanie. I'm back."

He heard a thud and then Stephanie's voice. "Take your hands off me!"

Zach raced into the small kitchen and came to a hard stop when he saw a large swarthy man who seemed to be wrestling with Stephanie over something.

"Get back!" the man shouted. He wrapped a meaty arm around her neck, but she elbowed him in his substantial gut. He expelled a sharp breath, but it didn't faze him. He pressed a double-edged knife to her neck. "Get back, I said."

"No!" she shouted. "Get him."

Zach held his hands up. "Whoa! Just calm down. You let her go, and you can walk out of here."

The man made a scoffing sound. "Or what?"

Zach huffed out a sigh. "Or I'll have to kill you."

The man looked him over. "With what? You got a gun somewhere?"

"I don't need one."

The two men stared at each other silently.

Zach was barely breathing. He went into full warrior mode, his focus totally on his foe.

The man broke the silence with a huff. "Aww...you jus' tryin' to psych me out." He brandished the knife dangerously close to Stephanie's face.

She cringed away from the flashing blade.

Zach flicked his wrist, dislodging a piece of broken china off the countertop. It landed on the floor by his boots.

The man glanced down, giving Zach the opportunity to lunge forward, deflecting the knife and jerking Stephanie free of the man's grasp. Zach thrust her behind him and tried to disarm the man, but he held fast to the knife.

Zach twisted the man's arm behind him, but he was surprisingly strong and managed to wrest himself from Zach's grasp.

Zach stepped back, keeping himself between Stephanie and the man who had been threatening her. The man raised the knife, as though he intended to rush Zach, but Zach punched him in the face, sending him reeling backward to hit the edge of the counter and fall on the floor. The man rolled onto his back, and Zach could see the knife embedded in his side.

"I—I called 9-1-1," Stephanie said, her voice shaky.

"Who is this guy?" Zach asked.

"He's one of Rafe Neeley's brothers. Maybe the older one. I don't know for sure."

"Eugene! I am Eugene!" the man yelled. "I'm cut. You got to help me."

"Where is Rafe?" Stephanie glared at Eugene, but her lower lip trembled.

There were footsteps running down the hallway, and two officers entered the apartment, guns drawn.

"Back here, officers." Stephanie motioned to them.

Zach felt a moment of alarm when the first officer rushed into the kitchen, pointing his weapon at Zach.

"No, that's my boyfriend," Stephanie protested. "The guy on the floor tried to kill me, but my boyfriend overpowered him… He saved my life."

*There it is. She called me her boyfriend…twice.*

Zach couldn't repress his grin. "That's me. I'm the boyfriend. That guy on the floor is the bad guy. He has a knife in his gut."

The police officer holstered his gun, glaring at Zach. "You stabbed him?"

"Nope. He stabbed himself, actually."

Stephanie reached out to Zach, pulling him to where she stood in the small kitchen. "That's what happened, Officer. That man is Eugene Neeley. He threatened to kill me."

The second officer stood nearby, covering Eugene with his own weapon.

At that moment, they heard someone calling from the front door.

"Back here, guys," Stephanie called, as two EMTs appeared in the kitchen doorway.

"Dang, Gayle. Didn't know you lived here," the taller of the two men said. "Interesting décor."

"Shut up, smart-ass," Stephanie said. "We're going to get out of your way."

"Don't leave until we take your statement," one of the officers instructed.

"Hadn't planned on it." Stephanie seemed to feel more confident now that some members of the fire crew were on hand, or perhaps she just needed to put on some swagger in front of them.

"I brought boxes." Zach gestured to the pile by the front door.

"Good boy," she said. "Bring some to the bedroom. We can work in there."

He laughed, thinking this was just what he had imagined…without the presence of police, EMTs, or bad guy.

———※———

Big Jim was babysitting. He was in charge of his grand-daughters, Ava and Gracie, as well as Mark, Misty's twelve-year-old brother. The older kids were out of school for the Christmas holidays. Ava, his youngest son's daughter, was only four and eager to start kindergarten the next fall. She thought school was this magical place where everything in the world would become known to her.

The reason for Big Jim's captive audience was that the collective parents were on a trip to the city to purchase Christmas presents and did not want their little ones to be around.

But Big Jim took his duties seriously and had an agenda all mapped out. He had fed them a big breakfast of scrambled eggs and ham wrapped in flour tortillas with cheese, a bowl of fruit, and big glasses of milk.

Now, the children were in a food-induced stupor, collapsed in front of the television in the den.

Big Jim rinsed the dishes and stuck them in the dishwasher. He was very aware of his daughter-in-law Leah's advanced state of pregnancy. He insisted all the inhabitants of the house clean up after themselves so she would not take on any unnecessary tasks. Leah was almost freakishly neat and jumped on anything she saw out of order. Having married into a family of males, she had many opportunities to carry out her obsession.

But now Big Jim and the entire Garrett family were holding their collective breath, anxious to pamper the very pregnant woman.

"Honestly!" she would say. "You would think I was made of eggshell or something."

But Colton would assure her that they just wanted to give her plenty of time to rest up for the big event.

Other than the sound of the television, the house was totally silent. Even Leah's grandmother had ridden with the other adults to Amarillo, bundled in a puffy down coat with her shopping list clutched in her tiny fist.

Big Jim wiped down the table and hung up the dishcloth. Looking around, he was satisfied that the kitchen and dining areas were sparkling clean. Nothing for Leah to decide she had to do when she returned.

He went to the big glass sliding door that opened out onto the covered patio at the back of the house. As far as the eye could see, the land was blanketed in white. He and his sons had dealt with the horses early that morning, and the cattle in the pastures had plenty of fresh hay for their dining pleasure.

Big Jim stared out at the pastoral scene, but his brain was otherwise occupied.

His nephew Zach had been weighing heavily on his mind. Big Jim was concerned that since Zach had returned from his military service, things had not been quite right. Nothing he could put his finger on, but something was just a hair off-kilter.

Zach had been raised right along with his own sons.

Big Jim raked his fingers through his thick mane of silver hair. *Hell, Zach was like another son to me. He was, in fact, one of the Garrett boys.*

People in town couldn't tell one from another, since they ran in a pack. Zach and Colton, Big Jim's oldest, were the same age. They acted more like brothers than cousins.

Big Jim shook his head, thinking of the choices the boys had made, which seemed to have determined their outcomes. He thought if Zach had chosen to stay in Langston, he would have taken over the ranch when his father became ill and would have inherited the land and entire estate.

Heaving a huge sigh, Big Jim was grateful that Colton had made the decision to go on to college, earning an agriculture degree from Texas Tech University in Lubbock and then returning to the ranch to take his place in the Garrett dynasty of ranchers. By that time, Tyler was also attending Texas Tech and Beau was graduating from high school.

Big Jim knew that Colt had considered enlisting with his best friend but fortunately had made the decision to further his education.

Colt's decision had probably been influenced by his mother's tears more than anything Big Jim could have said to persuade him.

He said a silent thank-you to his beloved wife, who had passed on a few years previously.

Now, it was up to him to see if he could help Zach find a place in this world where he could be happy and comfortable…because he was certainly ill at ease in this one.

"Grampa?"

He turned to see Gracie staring up at him. "Yes, sweetheart?"

"We're bored. Can we go outside?"

Big Jim's face split into a wide grin. "Of course we can. Let's get you all bundled up, and Grampa will help you build the biggest, best snowman ever."

---

Stephanie was feeling pretty good, considering the events of the day. She figured it had to do with the man driving the big silver extra-cab pickup in her rearview mirror. She patted the steering wheel of her own truck, which would be fully restored by the body shop, complete with gold curlicues, right after the holidays.

All of her salvageable worldly possessions had been packed in the boxes Zach brought and were sailing along in the bed of her truck or Zach's. Not much had escaped the wrath of the Neeleys. Her furniture, clothing, and most anything breakable had been shredded or broken.

She touched the necklace her mother had given her at her high school graduation. When she had found it among the rubble, she had asked Zach to fasten it at the back of her neck. It was a gold heart-shaped locket with a small diamond in the center of the case. A tiny picture of her parents was inside. This was one of the few things she valued. The locket and her grandmother's painting were among her most precious possessions.

Stephanie called her insurance agent, who told her to take photos and gave her a claim number. She then informed her landlord of the attack and her subsequent immediate departure.

Zach had helped her lug all the debris to the dumpster and load the items she was able to salvage. Now they were heading to the cozy little ranch house where he was staying…where she was staying with him.

The countryside rolled by, a study in white. The temperature held steady, so they were looking at more frigid days ahead.

But, in truth, it was beautiful. Her grandmother could have painted it. A broad smile spread across her face as she glanced at the painting, firmly belted in on the passenger side.

She could replace her furniture, her dishes and glassware. She could buy new clothes. The one thing she could not replace was that painting, and it was safe and snug beside her. It seemed like some sort of victory that the Neeleys set out to destroy her belongings but had not gotten the few things she really treasured.

When they arrived at Fern Davis's place, Stephanie carefully removed the painting from the seat belt and smiled at it as though it might respond.

Zach knocked on the window. "Hey, it's cold out here. Let's get this stuff in the house."

She unlocked the door, and he helped her out, reaching for the painting. "I'll carry this," she said.

He looked puzzled for a second but reached into the bed of her truck for a box of books that had escaped the destruction. He juggled it to open the front door then stepped back for her to enter.

Stepping into the warm house was an immediate reprieve from the frigid temperature.

Zach placed the box on the floor. "I'll bring the rest of the boxes inside. You warm up." He was out the door before she could offer to help. She watched him gather boxes and head back to the house. He was so different from the other men she had known, especially the ones she worked with. And he truly cared for her.

Stephanie placed her grandmother's painting on a chair, setting it upright so she could see it and get used to seeing it in this cozy little room. Turning, she saw that Zach was tromping back with his arms full.

She opened the door for him, and he leaned down to kiss her before dumping his burden and slipping outside again. Yes, this was what she wanted. It became blindingly clear that being in this shabby little house with this magnificent man was all it would take to ensure a happy life.

She opened the door for him again as he brought in another load then darted back outside. By the time he had dumped the next load, he closed the door behind himself. "That's it. Everything is here." He gestured to the boxes. "What do you want to do with it? There's a spare bedroom. We could put everything in there so you could take your time going through it."

"Sure. That will work."

"What's this?" he asked, gesturing to the painting.

"Do you like it?"

"Yeah. It's great. Glad it didn't get destroyed."

"Me too," she said. "Me absolutely too."

---

Leah had been uncomfortable when riding in the passenger seat of her husband's truck. The seat belt made her feel as though she had been hog-tied. Her burgeoning belly took up a good bit of her lap space, and there just wasn't much room for these straps to be binding her.

She would have let the others go to Amarillo without her, but this was an important time of year. She owed it to Tyler. She wanted their first Christmas together to be memorable. It would be the first time that her daughter, Gracie, would be able to experience a real family holiday with her newly adopted father. Tyler had stepped right into the role he was born for.

Now, they would have another child, one made up of both their genes. This was what worried Leah the most. What if this new baby changed the way the Garretts felt about Gracie? Would she be the stepchild and the baby become the "real" child?

Colton and Misty were in the backseat with Leah's grandmother sitting between them. They were talking in low voices. Leah caught words here and there to gather the conversation revolved around plans for Christmas Eve and Christmas Day…about the kids…about Big Jim. They were discussing presents and items on the children's wish lists.

Tyler glanced at her, his expression one of concern. "You all right, Babe?"

She smiled at him. "I'm fine. Don't be such a mother hen."

He turned in to the parking area for the huge mall. "I'm just an anxious papa. Don't mind me." He reached over to give her a pat. "I love you, y'know?"

She squeezed his hand in return. "I know, and I love you right back."

Tyler turned the wheel and pulled up close to the main entrance to the mall. "I'm going to let you folks out right here and go park. I'll meet you inside... Take care of my little missus."

Colton climbed out of the backseat and helped his wife and Fern Davis out of the back and onto the covered walkway. Then he opened the front passenger door and very carefully assisted Leah to alight. He gave a wave to Tyler and gathered the three women in a seeming embrace. "Let's get inside. We can wait for Ty without freezing off any body parts."

Leah glanced back to see Tyler's truck turn down a long row of vehicles in his quest to find a parking place. *Good man.* She reluctantly allowed herself to be herded inside where the rush of warm air and chaotic noise greeted her. A lively Christmas tune was playing full blast overhead, but the crowd noise made it impossible to understand the words. "What's the plan, gang?"

"I think we should get the children's presents first," Gran said. "I counted out my money for each child." She gave a little headshake. "Don't want a one of them little critters to be disappointed come Christmas mornin'."

Leah gave her grandmother an awkward hug. "Don't you worry, Gran. The most important thing we have to give our kids is lots of love."

Colton leaned toward Gran. "Miss Fern, do you want me to get you a wheelchair? This place is huge."

Gran glared at him over her glasses. "No, Colt. Do you want me to get you one?"

Leah and Misty broke into peals of laughter, while Gran maintained her steely gaze.

Colton looked abashed. "Yes…I mean no, ma'am."

"Would you mind waiting here for my hubby while we get a head start?" Leah said. "I don't know how long I'm going to last standing on my feet." She leaned forward to announce in a stage whisper, "They're a little swollen."

Colt nodded. "Sure thing. Where will we meet up with you?"

"Gran and I will be in the big toy store. You coming with us, Misty?"

"I most certainly am," Misty said. "I need to go to the toy store too. Mark wants some electronic things, but I need to shop for the girls, so I need your input."

The three women walked toward the brightly lit store, which seemed to be teeming with people, most in groups of families.

Misty looked back to wave at Colton.

"Wow! Talk about a crowd." Leah felt a bit claustrophobic as she surveyed the mass of humanity pouring into and out of the store. She commandeered a shopping cart and passed it to Gran, who set her huge handbag in the top part.

Misty got a cart but passed it to Leah before getting another for herself. "I think we can plow through the other shoppers a little easier if we put a little metal between us and them."

"Great plan," Leah said. "I can use a little something to lean on. Let's make some kids happy."

"And don't forget," Gran said, raising one of her

small fingers. "We should all get a couple of extra presents for those young'uns that our little Stephanie is so attached to. I have a feeling they might be joinin' us for Christmas."

Leah looked at her in surprise. "Really? The kids who are in the children's home?"

"Yep. Them are the ones. If they don't come to Christmas, we can just give the presents to Stephanie an' she can figure out how to get 'em together."

"That's so sweet, Miz Fern," Misty said. "You're right. We should share with those who are less fortunate." She shrugged. "Not so long ago, I thought Mark and I were going to be tossed off our property, but by the grace of God, things worked out. I know I've never been so happy in my life." She nudged her cart into an aisle behind Gran.

Leah knew what it was to be living close to the bone. When she had fled Oklahoma with Gracie, she had been out of money and out of hope. All she was looking for was a safe haven…and she had found it in the arms of a man who loved her beyond reason. She swept one hand over her belly. A man who would forever be a part of her.

"Let's shop for the girls first," Misty said.

They were eventually joined by Tyler and Colton, who had little to offer in the way of advice on presents for girls, but when the procession turned down an aisle with racks of toys and games for boys around Mark's age, they were more enthusiastic.

"Honestly!" Gran exclaimed. "You two fellas are like little boys yourselves."

Leah chortled. "Very big little boys."

Tyler and Leah exchanged an amused glance. She

loved that quality about Tyler. His boyishness was quite refreshing and endearing. He was so very protective of her and Gracie. She was extremely glad he had come into her life.

He gave her a wink and silently mouthed *I love you*.

They selected some electronic games and other things Mark would like and several toys for the young boy Stephanie was involved with.

When they checked out, all three shopping carts were filled with items guaranteed to delight the youngsters.

Tyler and Colton hauled the packages to the truck and then joined the women for lunch at the food court. After eating, they split up, agreeing to meet at the entrance at a specified time.

Leah and Gran stayed together, choosing to spend their time in a large department store. Leah wanted to find something special for Tyler, especially since this would be their first Christmas together as a married couple. And maybe more important, this would be Tyler's first holiday as a father, since he had officially adopted Gracie. She wanted this Christmas to be perfect.

# Chapter 13

"How about now?" Zach had hung Stephanie's painting in the bedroom, where she could see it first thing when she woke up.

"It's a little higher on the left…just a hair." Stephanie gazed at the painting from across the room, nodding when he adjusted it slightly. "That's perfect." A wide grin graced her face. "Thank you so much for understanding how much this painting means to me."

"Happy to make you happy," he said. In truth, he longed to tell her how much he wanted to please her… to be her protector in every way. He was just glad they had been together when the Neeleys had entered her apartment and violently destroyed almost everything she owned. What would have happened if Stephanie had been there?

Would they have injured or killed her? He had no doubt that he might have lost her forever, the woman he loved.

He had seen too many people die. Now, when he had found this amazing woman and knew that his feelings were reciprocated, he had to hang on to her. *She loves me*.

All he had to do was keep her safe until all of the Neeleys had been rounded up and jailed. He swallowed hard. *One down*.

"What do you want for Christmas?" she asked.

"What?" He frowned, feeling confused.

She cocked her head to one side. "Christmas. You know…the baby Jesus? Holly? Mistletoe? Tall, pointy trees with lights? Presents?"

It hit him like a physical blow that it had been a long time since he had actually celebrated any holiday, let alone Christmas. An ache of longing enveloped him. He recalled the many Christmases he had celebrated with his parents and always with his cousins and his aunt and uncle.

But now, his father had passed away, as had his aunt, Big Jim's wife. His mother had sold their home and moved to Fort Worth. There was nothing left of his life as he had known it.

Stephanie came closer, sliding her arms around his neck. "What are you so serious about?"

But he couldn't find the words to tell her everything that was tearing his insides apart. "Um—thinking about the baby Jesus…and presents…we gotta have some presents."

She lifted her chin, demanding a kiss, which he was happy to provide.

"Yeah, I'm all for presents. What can I get for you?"

"Mmm…surprise me." She gave him a sassy wink.

"No hints?"

"You're on your own, cowboy."

"Well, I'll surprise you then…but no complaints."

She gazed up at him with an expression that made his heart melt. "You know that I will treasure any gift you might choose for me."

Her earnest expression caused a tightness in his chest. "I better do good, huh?"

"Doesn't matter. I'll love it." She cocked her head toward the front of the house. "Come on. Let's get the rest of my stuff put away. There's not a lot, so it shouldn't take much time."

"Let me take you into town after we get things straight around here. We can grab dinner and a few groceries along the way."

"I'm in."

Sadly, it took no time at all to find a place for her belongings, mostly kitchen items that had not been destroyed. She was especially glad her microwave had been spared, since Gran's kitchen did not contain any such newfangled contraptions.

Stephanie set her electric can opener on the tiled countertop. "What do you think?" She spread her hands.

"Everything looks great. Whatever you want to do is fine with me."

"I suppose we'll figure it out." Stephanie shrugged, but there was pain in her eyes.

Zach admired her for being so strong when she must have been devastated by the loss of her possessions. She seemed confident that her insurance would cover everything, but still...

They hurried through their tasks, and he drove her into Langston for a quiet meal at Tiny's Diner. Stephanie had expressed a desire for a cheeseburger and fries, so Zach had taken her to the place famous for those very items.

Stephanie held up a golden french fry with two fingers. "Yum!" she exclaimed before dunking it in ketchup and chomping it in half.

Crystal, a longtime waitress at Tiny's Diner, came to stand beside the table. "You sure do make those french fries look good." She planted her fists on her substantial hips.

"I just haven't had anything this tasty in a while." Stephanie chewed the rest of the fry and wiped her fingers on a paper napkin. "And this cheeseburger. How do you make it taste so good?"

Crystal let out a hearty laugh. "That's the cook's secret spice mix. He rubs it on the barbecue he has smoking out back."

"What's in it?" Zach asked.

Crystal shook her head. "Good luck with that. Junior is dead serious about the secret part."

"Just tell him it's really good," Stephanie said, chomping into her burger again.

"So this is a win?" Zach looked at Stephanie for confirmation.

"It's the best burger I've ever put in my mouth. I'm ruined for other burgers forever."

"My work is done here." Crystal gave a broad wink and rolled her weight from one significant hip to the other. "Enjoy."

Zach smiled at Stephanie as he stuffed the last of his burger in his mouth. He was happy that they could share a simple meal and put the horror of the day behind them. He was also concerned that she would be vulnerable once she left for work the next day.

---

The entire back of the pickup was filled with packages. Fortunately, the bed of the truck was covered with a lid of sorts. Tyler called it a bed cover, but it opened the same way the hood did, by lifting it up and closing with a metallic security.

Leah was glad their outing was coming to an end. She

had been a little antsy leaving Gracie with her father-in-law—not that Big Jim would fail to care for the children, but it was just that she and Gracie had been so close for so long.

The heater was going full blast, steaming up the windows at first, but the defroster was bathing the windshield with warm air, so at least the front was clear, and there was a built-in rear window defroster so the driver could see out both front and back.

The side windows were another matter. They were totally frosted over, effectively cutting off any hint of what was going on in the passing countryside.

Leah sat, belted in, with her hands gripped together.

Tyler reached over to cover her hands with one of his. "You okay, babe?"

She nodded, flashing a brief smile. "Yeah, why?"

"I don't know. You look tense. I was just checking on you." He put his hand back on the wheel. "I know this was a tough trip for you."

"I just wanted to do some shopping on my own. I'm fine."

"So you say," he said. "The doc still thinks we're a couple of weeks from our due date for baby Garrett."

She huffed out a sigh. "Baby Garrett will show up in his or her own good time." She rubbed her fingertips over her belly. "Don't rush us, and keep your eyes on the road. It's getting dark soon."

"Yes, ma'am." He drew her hand up to his lips, laying a lingering kiss against it.

"Hey, you two," Colton yelled. "Get a room."

Tyler cleared his throat. "That's how we got in this condition."

When Tyler turned in at the Garrett main entrance and the truck ran over the cattle guard, Leah felt like she was receiving hammer blows. Just banging over the rails made her tense. She couldn't wait for the truck to stop and to be released from the seat belt.

"Well, how about that?" Tyler stopped the truck and sat idling for a moment.

Leah gazed out the windshield and then began to laugh. There in front of the house were snowmen depicting every member of the family. It wasn't hard to pick out which one was supposed to be Leah since it was the only one with a belly.

---

Big Jim looked around the dining table at his young audience, each clasping a cup of hot chocolate with both hands. He noted that cheeks were a bit reddened from their herculean feat of building a whole family of snow people near the front door. His young sculptors had enjoyed the effort immensely, but he hoped he hadn't kept them outside too long. Gracie was the most adventurous, finding nature items to create the features and branches to form arms, while Mark and Big Jim provided the muscle to build the snow people.

Mark had kept Ava busy, adding snow to the mounds per her instructions. The sound of their laughter was like music to Big Jim's ears. He had enjoyed raising his three sons, but he also thought the sound of his grandchildren's voices raised in joy was the sweetest music ever played.

Ava had conked out early, so she was napping in Gracie's room before her parents picked her up. Big Jim had left the door ajar should she awaken, but as hard as she had played, he doubted she would pop back up.

Now he sat at the table with Mark and Gracie, munching cookies and drinking hot cocoa, feeling completely satisfied with his day. *This grandfather business is the best job ever.*

Big Jim heard a truck pull up outside. The diesel motor sat idling for a while before being shut off. Truck doors slammed shut, and he heard people stamping the snow off their boots on the front porch.

"Sounds like your mamas and daddies are home," he said. "Stay right here, and we'll all have some hot cocoa together."

Big Jim wondered which of his offspring had returned from their shopping expeditions. The front door opened, and his rowdy crew came through the entrance.

"We're back here," Big Jim yelled. "And we have hot cocoa."

Leah joined them, her cheeks and nose a bit reddened, and when she put her hand on Big Jim's shoulder, it was like an ice pack.

Big Jim took her hands in both of his and chafed them gently. "Welcome home, little lady. Where are your gloves? You need to warm up."

She shivered but was grinning ear to ear. "I don't remember where I left them. I'm just glad to be home."

He patted her hand. "Gracie, why don't you pour your mama a nice cup of cocoa with extra marshmallows?"

"Sure, Grampa." She gave up her chair and went to comply, and Mark went with her.

"That is one sweet girl," Big Jim said. "I'm so glad she's my granddaughter."

Leah sank into the chair Gracie had vacated. "Oh, Big Jim. Those are the words I most wanted to hear. I know you love Gracie, and she loves you so much. It's just—just so good to have family." Tears gathered in her large blue eyes, tugging at Big Jim's heart.

"Well, looky here, little lady. You and Gracie coming into this family was about the best thing I can recall." He reached out to pat her shoulder. "Heckuva deal. We got two for one."

Gracie returned with several cookies on a saucer, and Mark set the cup of steaming cocoa in front of Leah.

"Oh, this is lovely. Thank you both so much."

Tyler came to the table grinning. "I hope I can get a cup of cocoa around here too."

Both children scrambled to the kitchen to serve up more cocoa and cookies.

Ty exchanged an amused look with his wife. "I've stowed the presents," he whispered. "No nosy little critter will be able to find Santa's stash."

Leah smiled. "Good work. Santa's oversized elf is awesome." She turned to Big Jim. "Oh, I forgot to tell you. We all bought some extra presents for those children Stephanie Gayle has been giving some special attention to. Did I understand that you were going to invite her to bring them here for Christmas?"

Big Jim leaned back in his chair. "That was my plan—before Stephanie hooked up with Zach. They might have other plans now."

Tyler seated himself across the table from Leah, smiling as Mark brought a cup of steaming cocoa to set in front of him. "Thanks, man. That looks awesome. Oh, I love cookies." He reached out to give Gracie a hug.

When the children were out of earshot, he spoke again. "Yeah, Dad, I guess you better let Zach and Stephanie figure out what they want to do."

"You're probably right." Big Jim pressed his lips together, sad that the two orphaned children might spend their Christmas in a soulless institution.

———ᨆᨆ———

Stephanie lay awake in the dark. Her head was resting on one of Zach's muscled biceps. She wished she could be anywhere else but here, in bed with the man she loved. He had made love to her so tenderly and then fallen asleep while holding her in his arms…only to call out in his sleep for another woman.

*Jewel…*

Stephanie could only lie awake wondering who Jewel was and why she was on Zach's mind after he had shared an intimate night with Stephanie.

Stephanie was hurt. She was jealous. Whoever this Jewel was, she was too late. Zach had told her he loved her.

She pressed her lips together. There was no way she was going to cry. Stephanie Gayle was tougher than that. Only weak, insecure people were jealous. She placed her hand on Zach's chest so gently she didn't awaken him. His heart pulsed slow and steady under her palm.

She was glad he was sleeping so soundly. She wanted to scream at him. *Who is Jewel? What does she mean to you?*

But he slept so peacefully she wouldn't think of disturbing him. She eased out her breath and tried to let it go. *Everyone has old flames.*

Maybe Jewel was just someone from his past? Maybe she was happily married to someone else? Maybe she had six children and weighed three hundred pounds?

Maybe he still loved her?

———

The next morning, Zach noted that Stephanie seemed to be preoccupied. He couldn't judge her mood because she was playing her cards very close to her chest, answering most of his queries with one or two words.

She practically ran out the door to climb into her old red truck, allowing just a quick kiss.

"Be careful, Steph. There are still two bad guys out there."

She glanced back and then hopped up into the truck. "I know. I seem to attract the worst kind of men." She slammed the door behind her and in a few seconds was revving the motor before tearing out of the driveway.

*What did that mean?*

Zach climbed into his own truck and headed to the Garrett Ranch. He was still troubled when he arrived.

His uncle, Big Jim, was outside and raised one of his big paws in greeting. "Hey Zach. Good to see you, son." He enfolded Zach in a big hug accompanied by a few hearty thumps on his shoulder. "C'mon inside. The coffee's hot, and I'm freezin' my butt off."

Zach followed him inside, appreciating the central heating that embraced him.

Big Jim poured a mug of hot coffee and thrust it in Zach's hands.

"Thank you, sir."

"Now, I know you been in the U.S. Army for a while,

but I'm still your uncle, and you don't need to talk to me like I'm your sergeant."

Zach let out a whoop of laughter. "My rank was sergeant when I got out. I was a squad leader."

Big Jim's eyes widened, and he gave a curt nod. "Good for you, son. Have you had breakfast?"

Zach recalled the slice of toast he'd made, planning on making whatever kind of eggs Stephanie preferred, but she had grabbed the toast, mumbled something about work, and rushed out the door. "Um—no, sir…Uncle Jim." It was as though Big Jim's blue eyes had laser beams and could cut right through the bull. "Stephanie had to rush off to work, so we didn't really have a chance to—"

"I see," Big Jim said. "Well, I was just fixin' to make a mess of eggs to go with the biscuits." He shook his head. "Of course, I just banged them out of a tube because I didn't want Leah to go to any trouble." He brightened visibly. "But I was makin' breakfast for you and the boys before Leah came along."

"Yes. Whatever you're having, sir—Uncle Jim." He took a seat on the other side of the counter.

Big Jim placed an empty plate in front of Zach along with eating implements and the aforementioned biscuits, nestled in a linen napkin. "Help yourself, son." He placed a covered butter dish nearby.

The aroma of hot biscuits overwhelmed his senses. Zach had not eaten biscuits in some time. He reached for one, inhaling deeply before he split and buttered it. He must have made some kind of appreciative noise because Big Jim was grinning ear to ear.

"Enjoy!" Big Jim opened the refrigerator and removed a large ceramic bowl, half filled with fresh eggs gathered from the ranch chicken coop. "How about a big mess of scrambled eggs to go with those biscuits?"

"Sounds great." Zach managed to catch himself before he added "sir."

Big Jim made himself busy breaking eggs into a bowl and whisking them with a little milk. He seasoned them with salt and pepper before he stirred them into a heated skillet. He continued stirring until he turned and dumped half the eggs on Zach's plate and half on his own. "Dig in, son." He nudged a jar of peach preserves Leah had put up the previous summer close to Zach's plate. "We got milk and orange juice." He set a carton of each in front of the plates along with glassware.

"This is wonderful," Zach said. "I haven't been spoiled like this since—since before I enlisted." He scooped a forkful of eggs into his mouth. *Perfect*.

Big Jim sat down next to him and began eating.

"This brings back some good memories," Zach said. He remembered all the times he had slept over at his uncle's house after a day where he and his cousins had played themselves out.

Big Jim chuckled. "I recall when you and Colt ditched the younger boys and hid out down at the creek."

Zach smiled, flashing back to those days. "Now we're all grown up." He released a heavy sigh. "And your sons have got great families." He didn't add the obvious, but he felt it deeply.

Big Jim cleared his throat. "Um—I was just wondering... How are things going with Stephanie? You two doin' all right?" His eyes were fixed on his plate.

"Yeah, I think so. She's living with me, at least for the moment."

Big Jim turned to stare at Zach. "What does that mean…'for the moment'?"

Zach shrugged. "Her apartment was trashed last night. We went out on a date, and when I took her home, almost everything inside had been destroyed. The police came, and I helped her pack up the few things that made it through."

"Damn! That's terrible." Big Jim's face was a thunderstorm. "Does she need some money to help her replace things? I can help her out."

"I think she's okay. She said her renter's insurance will cover it all." He let out a deep sigh. "But in the meantime, she's staying with me at Fern Davis's place. I hope that's okay."

Big Jim flapped his hand at that. "I'm sure it's all right. Fern adores Stephanie, and she would want her to have a safe place to stay."

Zach nodded, feeling greatly relieved. Now if he could just find out what had caused her to run out of the house so quickly.

"So you and Stephanie are doin' okay? I mean, your relationship is…?"

Zach put down his fork and turned to gaze at his uncle. "Not sure what you're asking me."

"Well, son, I guess I'm just hopin' you and little Miss Stephanie have got something real goin' on. She's a fine person."

Zach frowned at his uncle. "Are you asking me if my intentions are serious?"

Big Jim frowned back. "Yeah, that's it. I just wanted to know if you'll be bringin' Stephanie to our house for Christmas. That's all." He picked up a biscuit and chomped into it.

"Uncle Jim, I'm sure Stephanie would love to spend Christmas with the Garrett family…I mean, more of it than just me."

"Whoa! That's a good thing. We all think the world of her…and just speakin' for myself…it sure is good to see you goin' out with such a remarkable young lady."

"Yeah, she's pretty special all right." Zach took another big bite of his eggs.

Big Jim poked at his breakfast again. "I don't suppose you know about those two little children she saved? She's the one who got their stepfather arrested for killin' their mother."

"Neeley," Zach pronounced.

"Yeah, that guy. They haven't convicted the bastard yet, but his no-good brothers helped him escape when they was transferring him to prison. So, I've been worried about Stephanie. Maybe this Neeley fellow is the one who tore up Stephanie's stuff…ya think?"

"Yes, one of the brothers showed up at the apartment after the police left. He—he's been arrested."

Big Jim nodded with satisfaction. "That's good. Hope they round 'em all up."

Zach raised his coffee mug. "Amen."

# Chapter 14

STEPHANIE THOUGHT ABOUT GOING BACK TO WORK, BUT Lieutenant Larsen wasn't expecting her, and she could use some time off.

Her emotions were being put through the wringer. She thought she had found the man of her dreams. The one true love a woman longs for. The man who rang all the bells and made her insides catch fire with a single soul-stirring gaze. She had let down her guard and been blindsided.

She stared ahead, driving without seeing the snow-covered countryside. Her fingers wrapped, white-knuckled, around the steering wheel. The vision driving her forward was of a tall, broad-shouldered man with laser-blue eyes.

The threat of tears tingled her eyes. "No!" She smacked the steering wheel with the heel of her hand. Stephanie Gayle was not some weak, wimpy woman who went to pieces over a guy…even an incredibly hot guy…who told her he loved her.

She smacked the steering wheel again. And then he'd called out some other woman's name in his sleep…after giving her multiple orgasms in one session of incredible lovemaking.

Her brain kicked in when she neared Amarillo. There were stoplights, traffic, and large vehicles clearing snow. She drove straight to the children's center and parked near the front entrance.

Maybe if she got to spend a few minutes with the children she loved, she could forget about Zach's fixation with this Jewel woman.

She climbed out and slogged through the slush, up the concrete steps and into the building. She was greeted with a rush of warm air, which momentarily stunned her.

Although she dreaded seeing the condescending social worker again, she heaved a sigh and made her way to the woman's office. She stood outside, staring at the gold lettering on the door. *Lorene Dyer, LSW*. Her stomach tightened, and so did her lips. Straightening her shoulders, she knocked on the door.

A frowning Lorene Dyer opened the door, holding a phone to her face. She appeared to be irritated. Irritated before she opened the door and irritated to find Stephanie on the other side. The crease between her brows grew deeper, but she nodded and motioned Stephanie inside, waving her to be seated.

Miss Dyer turned away, her voice terse. "No, you may not put me on hold ag—" She let out a stifled shriek. "Honestly!" She disconnected and stuffed the phone in the pocket of her jacket. She huffed out a breath and rearranged her facial features to something a little less fearsome. "And what can I do for you, Miss Gayle?" She took a seat then clasped her hands on top of the desk. A woman in total control.

Stephanie's stomach was twisting in a knot. Apparently she had chosen a bad time to drop in on the kids. "I—I wanted to visit Cody and Ivy."

Miss Dyer didn't quite roll her eyes, but Stephanie could almost feel it.

"Miss Gayle. The children are settling in quite well

here. I don't know if it would be a good idea to disturb their routine."

"Um, I was hoping to have the children with me for Christmas."

"That's impossible. I've already granted a request for Cody and Ivy to spend the entire week of Christmas with a very nice family."

"What?" Stephanie half rose from her seat. "Why?"

"Relax, Miss Gayle. I have only the children's best interests at heart. I'm hoping that this Christmas visit might end up in an adoption." She flashed a semi-sincere smile. "I'm sure you want the children to wind up with a wonderful family where they could have all the advantages."

Stephanie's voice seemed to be stuck in her throat. She opened her mouth, but nothing came out.

Miss Dyer leaned forward encouragingly. "Are you surprised that we found a family for them so quickly?"

"Yes," Stephanie gasped out. "I—I was hoping that I could convince you to let me adopt them. I mean, I love them so much." She swallowed hard before plunging on. "I'm living on a very lovely ranch now, so they would have lots of room to play, and the school district is really great."

A short huff of air again. "Listen, Miss Gayle. You're still single, and you have a very dangerous job. Not a good background for a prospective adopter."

"I—I just want to take care of them."

Miss Dyer's mouth pinched together. "I would think you would be thrilled that they could spend the holiday with a family as nice as the Garretts."

—⁓—

Stephanie could hardly breathe. She drove away from the children's center, her chest wrapped in a steel coil of emotion. Drawing a full breath was impossible.

Her jaw was so tight it was a wonder her back teeth didn't crack. How could the Garretts do this to her? They had everything. How could they take away the children she loved? Cody and Ivy had already been through so much. They needed something constant in their lives. From the night Rafe Neeley had murdered their mother in an alcohol- and drug-induced rage, the children had depended on Stephanie to be their constant.

First Zach, the man she loved, had called out for another woman in his sleep. And now a smug social worker had judged her to be unfit for motherhood. Her apartment had been trashed and her possessions demolished. *What else?*

Stephanie whimpered. *No, don't ask that. If there's something worse coming my way, I don't want to know about it.*

She turned off the main street and found a parking spot outside a small diner about a block from her empty apartment. She put the truck in park and stepped out into ankle-deep slush. It appeared a snowplow had cleared the street and pushed this brown mush close to the curb. She was extremely grateful for the lace-up boots that were part of her gear. Stepping up onto the sidewalk, she stamped off the goop and made her way into the diner.

It was warm inside, making her feel stuffy in the jacket. She slid the zipper open immediately upon entering, sorry she had pulled one of Zach's wool sweaters on over the shirt. She didn't see the man she was looking for, so she took a seat where she could watch the entrance.

When the waitress came to take her order, she ordered a bowl of the soup of the day, which happened to be chicken gumbo, with a side of cornbread. The toast she had grabbed for breakfast was long gone, and the soup should warm her up. The waitress set the bowl of soup in front of her with the cornbread on the side plate with a pat of butter. The aroma was heavenly, the best part of her day so far.

A few minutes later, her insurance agent, a balding, fifty-something man, entered the diner with a broad smile when his gaze lit on Stephanie. "Miss Gayle!" he called out, advancing toward her. He shook her hand and pulled up a chair across the table from her. "Sorry about the damage to your apartment. Let me see what I can do to help you replace your belongings."

Stephanie showed him images of the damage on her phone. She forwarded the images to his email, and he promised to process the information and that she would be receiving a check in the mail within the next few weeks.

Stephanie finished her now-tepid soup and pushed the last bite of cornbread into her mouth. Okay, so the whole day sucked, but maybe she would be reimbursed for her losses…at least the financial ones.

---

"Okay, I'm feeling like a complete sloth." Leah was propped on pillows on the sofa with her feet up. "First your dad is running around making sure I don't do any actual work around here, and now you're treating me like I'm made of eggshell."

Ty sat on the other end of the sofa with her feet in his lap. "Well, I might be inclined to agree with you, but these are some really fat little tootsies. Fat feet, *no bueno*. So you gotta rest and keep them up for a while. No arguments."

Leah pressed her lips together. It wasn't that she didn't appreciate all this babying, but she was antsy, and when she felt this way, her solution had always been to throw herself into some kind of task…but there was nothing they would let her do. "I just wish there was something—"

"Forget it. You'll have plenty to do after the baby arrives, so you'd best rest up while you can." He gave her a stern look.

"You realize that when I was pregnant with Gracie, I was fully functional all the way up to the time when I started having contractions?"

Ty let out a snort. "You know that old saying 'That was then and this is now'? Well, this is now. You are my wife, and I reserve the right to spoil you rotten. Just lean back and enjoy it." He proceeded to peel off her warm wool socks and began to massage her feet.

She had to admit it felt heavenly. But she could be working on getting their dinner prepped.

Fortunately, Big Jim had enlisted both Gracie and Mark to be his accomplices. She heard the sounds of pots and pans being banged around in the kitchen along with a few peals of laughter from the youngsters.

The fact that they were all pitching in to make her life easier should have made her feel better, but in fact, it hurt her feelings. Being an essential part of this family was the single achievement that gave her the most joy… She needed to be needed.

She crossed her arms on top of her baby belly and

expelled a deep breath. "Sounds like they're having a good time in there."

Ty grinned at her. "Sounds like it. But no. You're not going to join them. Your job is to sit right here with your feet up and a smile on your face. I'll probably have to go on the road again in the summer. My agent is pushing me to write some new songs…but I thought I would rework some of my favorite Christmas carols. You know, a mix of traditional and new songs."

She nodded, not sure what he was saying.

"I was thinking of putting out a new album for next Christmas."

"Oh, that sounds nice."

"And work up some new songs for another album. That should make my agent happy."

"That sounds like you want to spend more time here at home." She gazed at him for affirmation.

"I'll admit that I do. Our new home is going to be ready. Your grandma should be plenty happy with her accommodations, and I'll have a music studio, so I could record from right there."

"Oh, that's a wonderful idea. I hate to have you on the road for so long at a time."

He picked up one of her feet and planted a kiss on her instep. "Yeah, I'm kind of excited about spending more time at home with my wife and kids." He was very careful to slide each of her socks on her feet before allowing her to retract them.

Leah was grinning now. It felt as though her face might split wide open. "I'm so glad. Having you around is really the best thing ever."

He stretched to reach for his guitar. "Here's a little

something I've been working on. I thought you and the baby might like to get in the Christmas mood."

She thought she was ready enough, having spent the morning with Gran wrapping the presents she had purchased at the mall. Just being able to purchase such a big stash of gifts had given her great pleasure. The sad and frugal times in the past when she was only able to give her daughter one present and there had been no tree at all... Those times were past, and now they had been enfolded into this big, wonderful family.

Tyler strummed his guitar and then began singing a countrified version of "Rudolph the Red-Nosed Reindeer."

Leah sat with her feet tucked up under her, clapping out a tempo for her husband's music. He played several songs for her, and when she looked around, Big Jim and both children were enjoying the music as well.

"Well, ain't that nice," Gran said as she came down the hall from the bedroom wing. "I thought maybe the angels were a-singin', but it was my dear grandson-in-law a-playin' his sweet music. Lordy, this man has been blessed."

Ty set the guitar aside and reached for Leah's hand. "Indeed, I have been blessed."

―⁓―

Zach was a little antsy. He had spent most of the day with Big Jim and Colton. They had driven out to check on the herds and to make sure there was enough fresh hay and that there was water for them to drink. Each pasture had a shed, open on one side but with a roof to keep the grain and hay dry. The cattle were gathered around these feeding stations in winter, when in warm weather they would be grazing on the grasses now blanketed by snow. After the men returned to the Garrett ranch house, they gobbled up bowls of Big Jim's chili, which both warmed and filled them.

Zach returned to Fern Davis's place in the early afternoon and decided to cook something special for Stephanie. He figured that returning to work after having her apartment wrecked might have caused some stress, so he wanted her to be able to relax when she came home.

*Home?*

He knew she didn't think of this place as home, but maybe he could help her to feel more comfortable. There was no television, but he tuned in a country station on an old radio. Just some music softly playing in the background. Maybe that would soften the environment enough so she would relax.

What else would a man do for the woman he loved? *Food.* He would make sure she was well fed.

Zach peered into the refrigerator and selected items to prepare, glad they had shopped for groceries.

By the time he heard Stephanie drive up outside, he had their supper bubbling on the stove. He hadn't had much opportunity to cook in the past few years, but he did recall how to prepare a simple meal.

Zach went to open the door for her. "Welcome home."

She stared at him, her eyes hard. After a momentary hesitation, she stamped the snow off her boots and stepped inside.

He pulled her into his arms and gave her a kiss. Her

body felt rigid at first and then slowly relaxed in his embrace. "Hi, baby. I missed you all day."

She gazed up at him; her expression seemed sad. "Did you?"

He frowned. "Of course I did. I even made my famous spaghetti with meat sauce for your dining pleasure. I love you, you know?"

"Oh, Zach," she wailed. Her lower lip quivered, and she rested her forehead against his chest.

He stroked her hair gently. "Stephanie, please don't be upset with me. You don't have to eat the spaghetti. I can make something else…or we can go into town."

"I'm not crying," she said, but her voice was muffled, and she kept her face averted. "So, do you really love me, or is there someone else?"

"What do you mean, someone else?"

"Another woman," she mumbled.

He expelled a deep breath. "I've barely gotten home. I haven't been in the States for a long time."

She threw her head back, glaring defiantly. "I mean an old girlfriend."

He shook his head. "Any old girlfriend of mine is probably married and has a couple of kids by now. That's how it goes." He could tell she wasn't buying it. "Where did you get the idea there was someone else?"

Stephanie drew back and shook off his embrace. "I want to know about Jewel. The woman who seems to haunt your dreams…even after we've made love." She stared at him, accusation in her eyes.

"Jewel? Are you kidding me?" He let out an exasperated growl. "Jewel was our squad dog. She was trained to detect explosives." He took her hand and led her into the kitchen, seating her at the table.

"I—I'm sorry," she said. "I didn't know. You called out her name in your sleep."

"No, I'm sorry. I just felt terrible leaving her behind." He took a seat beside her. "My squad, we were trained in EOD…Explosive Ordnance Disposal. And Jewel was part of the team. She slept right beside me. I—I wish I could have brought her home with me."

Stephanie still appeared to be upset. "I feel so foolish for being jealous of a dog."

Zach smiled, stroking the side of her cheek. "She was almost as pretty as you are. A beautiful black German shepherd with big brown eyes."

"A German shepherd? I guess it makes sense that bomb-sniffing dogs would be German shepherds."

He shook his head and heaved a huge sigh. "Yeah. Most are shepherds. They have incredible noses." He picked up her hand and kissed her palm. "I can't believe you got jealous of Jewel, but it's kind of flattering too. You know I love you, don't you?" He cleared his suddenly husky throat.

"Yes—yes, I do." She took his face in both her hands and kissed his lips. "Can you ever forgive me for being so crazy jealous? I hardly slept at all last night. I just kept thinking there was some woman named Jewel."

"I'm not a liar, Stephanie. I would never have told you I love you if there was someone else. You're the only one." He pulled her into his arms, and they just held each other for some time.

"Hope you like pasta," he finally said.

"Yeah, the aroma is killing me. I'm starving."

"Great. Let's go eat." He got up and shepherded her into the kitchen. "By the way, Big Jim officially invited us to spend Christmas at the ranch. I hope you're okay with that."

To his surprise, she drew back and snarled at him. "I am so mad at Big Jim right now. Someone at the ranch is trying to adopt the two children I was hoping to adopt."

Zach held out one of the chairs, and she slid into it. "I don't know anything about that. Let's just eat dinner without worrying about anything else. You can ask him yourself." He turned to the stove and quickly filled a plate then placed it in front of her.

She appeared to be quite upset, but she huffed out a breath and pulled her chair closer to the table.

Zach served himself and joined her. She mumbled a few words about the tastiness of the meal but made no other comment. He remembered hearing something about her wanting to adopt orphans, he thought from his uncle, but couldn't recall the details. Now she was angry with Big Jim, and he wasn't sure he wanted to find out why.

---

The next morning, Stephanie logged onto one of the computers at the station. She wasn't sure how to get there, but she sure did know what she wanted.

The link she located took her to the ASPCA, where she found a way to see if she could connect with the site she needed.

There was a phone number, so she opted for that, since she didn't want to wait for someone to get around to responding to an email.

When she was finally connected to the right person, she settled into the big cushy chair behind Lieutenant Larsen's desk. Her boss's office was the one place she could have a private conversation without her coworkers hanging onto her every word.

She was surprised that the process was fairly easy, but she was concerned that the timing might not work out. She knew that the gift would be appreciated whenever it arrived, but she desperately wanted it to arrive quickly. It would be the perfect Christmas present for the man who had stolen her heart...the man who seemed to be complete without any particular needs or wants. After all, what would be the perfect gift for Captain America?

# Chapter 15

EARLY THE NEXT MORNING, TY WENT OUT TO START HIS truck and turn on the heater. He cleaned snow off the hood and windshield.

Leah had been ordered to remain inside where it was warm, but she peered out the window, happy that she had married such a fine man. She pulled on her fleece-lined gloves and adjusted the wool scarf around her neck.

"Be safe out there," Big Jim said. "Gracie's going to help me gather eggs in a while." He laid his hand on Gracie's shoulder. "I think she's got the makings of a first-class rancher."

Tyler came inside and shut the door quickly. "Brr... cold out there." He shivered and blew out a breath.

Leah kissed Gracie on the forehead. "I think you're right, Big Jim. My girl can do anything she puts her mind to."

"That's for darned sure," Ty said. "Our girl is smart as a whip and stubborn as a mule. That combination should land her anywhere she wants to go."

"Daddy!" Gracie laughed, leaning up for his kiss.

"Now, you take care of my daddy, y'hear? He's getting on in years and needs a lot of help getting around."

"You get outta here," Big Jim roared. "I'm fifty-five. That's young."

"Of course it is, Big Jim." Leah blew him a kiss as

Tyler hustled her out the door. The frigid air bit her cheeks like a hungry animal. "Oh, my!"

"Glad you bundled up," Ty said. He held onto her all the way to the truck and assisted her up into the cab. The heater was on and surrounded her with much-needed warmth.

Tyler swung up into the driver's seat. "Let me help you with that seat belt."

Leah chuckled. "You may have to get me an extension seat belt if I get much bigger."

He fastened the belt and gave her a squeeze on her arm. "Don't worry, Leah. It's all baby."

"I must be giving birth to an elephant."

The drive into Langston was uneventful, but Leah thought it was beautiful. The defroster kept the windows clear, and she could enjoy the beautiful landscape of north Texas in winter.

When Tyler pulled up in front of the doctor's office, he had to release her from the seat belt because between her girth and her warm layers she could not reach it.

The doctor was able to see them quickly, her nurse ushering them into an exam room.

When Doctor Camryn Ryan entered the room, she was all smiles. "Great to see you two. Merry Christmas."

"Thanks, Doc," Ty said. "Merry Christmas to you too."

She examined Leah and pronounced her well. "You're right on target, Leah. Looks like a New Year's baby or maybe a week more."

"Can't wait," Leah said. "Feels like I've been pregnant forever."

"I can't wait to hold this baby in my arms," Ty said, a wide grin across his face.

Leah let out a chuckle. "Yeah, it's about time you start hauling this kid around."

---

"Mommy, I gathered the eggs, and there were seventeen today. Grampa says that's a lot." Her face was glowing with pride.

Big Jim stood nearby, almost as proud as Gracie herself. "That's right. She's got the touch. My little Gracie is the chicken whisperer."

Ty squatted down on one knee to give her a hug. "That is a lot. Those hens must have seen you coming."

"I've got to lie down," Leah said. Her voice revealed her exhaustion. She had pulled off her gloves and stuffed them in her pocket but seemed to be having trouble unwinding the scarf from around her neck.

Ty sprang up and helped divest her of the bulky jacket and scarf. He draped them over a coatrack and put his arm around her.

Big Jim watched his middle son help his wife to the room they occupied in this house.

Gracie looked downcast and a bit worried.

"Why don't we fix a nice tray for your mama?" Big Jim suggested. "I think she would like some refreshment. What do you think?"

Gracie perked up immediately and agreed to help.

Big Jim heated water for some caffeine-free tea while Gracie arranged apple slices, cheese cubes, and ginger snaps on a plate. "That looks plumb delicious." He placed the cup of hot tea on a tray beside the plate. "I'll carry it, and you knock on the door."

When Ty called for them to enter, Gracie opened the

door, but Big Jim passed the tray to her and watched her carefully carry it to the bed, where Leah lay propped on pillows.

"Oh, Gracie. This looks lovely. Thank you, sweetheart." Ty lifted the tray onto the bed beside Leah since it would not fit over her added bulk.

Big Jim stepped away, thinking this was a private time for the three of them. He returned to the kitchen. He was almost as excited about the coming addition to the family as were the soon-to-be parents. Although he was crazy about Ava and Gracie, he was secretly hoping the baby would be a boy to carry on the Garrett name.

When he got back to the kitchen, Colton and Misty were sitting at the counter, drinking coffee together. Again, Big Jim felt as though he was intruding in his own house.

"Hey, Dad." Colton reached for another cup. "What's the program for the day?" He poured coffee into the cup and offered it to Big Jim.

"Maybe we can just let the horses out of the stables into the corral while we clean up in there a little. Then we can feed them."

Colt grinned. "That sounds good. The horses can exercise themselves while we clean the stalls."

Big Jim took a sip of his coffee. "That's what I was thinking."

"Could you take Mark with you?" Misty asked. "I really need to wrap presents, and he's been like Velcro lately. Just need a little space to perform my elfin magic."

"Sure thing," Colt said. "My dad is the Pied Piper for kids. Mark would follow him anywhere."

Misty let out a huff of laughter. "Mark would follow

you too. He feels so happy here." She sipped coffee. "I know it's not going to be so much fun when we get our house finished."

"He'll be back in school after the holidays," Big Jim said. "He'll get to be with his friends then."

Misty pressed her lips together, appearing to be very pensive. "I don't think he really has any friends. Our father died a drunk...and our older brother was murdered for blackmailing a murderer." She shrugged. "That's some pretty bad stuff. Kids can be so cruel."

Big Jim set his coffee cup down on the counter, frowning. "Surely you don't mean he's being bullied? Mark is such a great kid."

Misty sighed and set her cup down as well. "He's quite sensitive. It doesn't take much to hurt his feelings. I don't know how his classmates perceive him, but he's pretty much isolated."

Big Jim felt a rush of sympathy for the spunky youngster. "He's always a ray of sunshine around the ranch."

Misty nodded. "He loves working with the animals and feeling like he's a part of the family. He's needed a good male role model for a long time." She wrapped both hands around her cup as though protecting it. "And he loves taking on the role of big brother to Gracie and Ava. It's what makes him happy."

Big Jim considered the boy and all that he had been through the previous year. "He's quite a young man." His voice sounded husky. He wondered what he could do for Mark to let him know he was really a part of the Garrett family.

—◆—

Zach woke up feeling relaxed. Stephanie was asleep in his arms. He gazed at her in the dim early-morning light.

Her lashes lay thick and full on her cheeks, and her lips were slightly parted. She looked beautiful and also very vulnerable.

He was filled with the desire to protect her, which was hard to do since she fancied herself invincible. Her training and experience as a firefighter, where she rescued other people, made her think she could take on the world.

But there were actually bad people out there who were trying to hurt her. Threats had been made against her life.

He couldn't imagine that she would do what a normal woman would do…that she might take precautions and not put herself in danger. No, this audacious woman would run toward danger instead of away from it.

Zach had been involved in enough dangerous situations in the Middle East to last a lifetime. He considered himself fortunate to have come through.

Now, it was most important that this woman in his arms would survive. How could he convince her to be careful, to take precautions, and to wait for the authorities to capture the Neeleys and cart them off to jail?

"You sure are thinking hard, Zach." Stephanie spoke without opening her eyes.

"Maybe," he said. "Just wondering what you really want for Christmas."

Her eyes opened wide. "You don't have the power to give me the one thing I want for Christmas." Her lips trembled before she tightened them. "Just some stuffy old social worker who seems to think that kids need a mother and a father and a fenced yard to play in…and the mother can't be a firefighter because it's too dangerous."

He took a moment before responding. She seemed to be so sad and yet angry just under the surface. "Well, there are a lot of kids at the mall. We could probably find some there."

A reluctant smile graced her face. "Oh, you're so funny. Yeah, that's what I want to do…go to the mall and kidnap kids."

He rolled her over onto her back. "In that case, we can make our own. Some will be gorgeous like you… and some will be fierce like me." He kissed her neck, her ear, and her shoulder.

Stephanie arched up toward him. "I'm fierce."

He caressed her, putting all his emotion into his kiss. "Yes," he breathed. "You certainly are."

———

Big Jim made it a point to spend some time with Mark. The idea that this fine young man was being bullied had gnawed at his gut since he first learned of it.

He followed the boy out to the stables when Mark went out to feed and groom his horse. "Hey there, Mark. How are you doin'?"

The boy turned, and his face split into a big grin. "I'm okay."

"I was just wondering what you might want Santy Claus to bring this year." Big Jim winked at him.

"Aw, you know I don't believe in that baby stuff no more." He gave the big Appaloosa's flank another sweep with the curry brushes.

"I see…" Big Jim adjusted his Stetson. "I heard you talking to the little girls about Santy Claus."

"I was just talking," Mark said.

Big Jim took one of the curry brushes and began to brush the horse. "Nice of you to let Ava and Gracie keep believin'. You seem to be taking responsibility for the girls when the three of you are together."

"Aw, they sometimes need somebody older to make sure they don't get hurt."

Big Jim nodded. "Like a big brother? That's the way Colton always looked after his little brothers."

Mark's brow furrowed, and he kept his gaze fixed on the horse.

"I heard you were taking a little heat from your classmates. I don't like to think about nobody bullying you."

Mark's mouth tightened, but he didn't give any other response.

Big Jim laid his hand on Mark's shoulder. "You're part of this family, you know?"

He felt Mark's spine straighten, but the boy only nodded.

Big Jim selected his words very carefully. "When your sister, Misty, married my son, her last name changed from Dalton to Garrett. And now, with your daddy and big brother dead, you're the only one around here with the last name Dalton."

"I know. When my daddy was sick, I guess I had time to get used to the idea that he would be goin' away." He swallowed hard but kept his gaze averted. "I always thought my big brother would be here."

"I'm sure that was tough to deal with."

"An' all the stuff my brother was doin'…that was—"

"Yeah, well"—Big Jim suddenly found his throat tight—"don't you worry about that none. What he done don't reflect on you at all."

For the first time, Mark raised his tearful face to Big Jim. "Yes, it does. They all say things…about…about…"

Big Jim heaved out a deep sigh. "I see. Well, you know, your name is a very important part of you. I'm gonna tell you somethin' that's jus' between you an' me…unless you want to share with the others."

Mark sniffled and drew the back of his hand across his eyes. He gazed up at Big Jim. His dark eyes tore a hole in the big man's heart.

"I was thinkin' maybe you'd like to be a Garrett. It wouldn't take much for your name to be changed. I know you've been a Dalton all your life, and that may suit you just fine…but you think about it, boy. If you want to be a Garrett, I'll make that happen."

His offer hung in the air as Mark appeared to be digesting the possibilities.

―∿∿―

Stephanie climbed into her truck, which was still scarred after the Neeley attack. At least she would be able to get the damaged body repaired after the holidays. She shut the door with a thunk. The windows were frosted over, and she felt as though she had shut herself in a refrigerator. Her breath came out in big, puffy clouds as she struggled to insert the key into the ignition, her fingers clumsy in her fleece-lined leather gloves. The motor growled a bit but finally grabbed, purring to life.

She sat for a moment but turned on the windshield wipers to brush soft snow off the glass. Two semi-clear arcs appeared in front of her, and she could see Zach standing on the porch, watching her leave.

*Such a sweet and passionate man.*

He had been rabidly opposed to her returning to her job in Amarillo, but she couldn't allow his fear to obstruct her purpose. She was a firefighter, and her purpose was to save lives and put out fires. *Yes, that's it.*

She turned on the heater and defroster, immediately frosting the windows and isolating her from those incredible blue eyes staring at her, heating her insides even when her outsides were frigid.

Stephanie sucked in a deep breath and blew it out, but now that the interior of the truck had warmed, her breath no longer made vapor clouds. She wrapped her gloved fingers around the steering wheel, and when the defroster had done its job, she put the truck in gear and backed away from the house. She did a dramatic turn and sped off, chastising herself for trying to show off.

Once on the highway, she focused on the drive but admitted to herself that, in spite of her defensiveness to Zach, she was afraid. Two of the Neeley brothers were still on the loose, and instead of making a clean getaway, they seemed to be intent on making her life miserable. Her truck had been damaged and her apartment demolished.

What more could they do? She shuddered, envisioning Rafe's vicious expression. She definitely did not want to find out what more they could do.

When she pulled into the parking area at the fire station, she found a slot right next to the lieutenant's big diesel truck. Maybe her old, bright-red truck could just hunker down between the big boys.

She locked it carefully and grabbed a backpack filled with a few new personal items. She looked around before entering the building, where she was greeted profusely by her fellow firefighters.

"Hey, Gayle! How was the vacation?" Miller called out.

"Lookin' good, Gayle." This came from somewhere above her.

She looked up to find Slim standing on a ladder, cleaning out the air ducts. He had a mask over his nose and mouth and his sparse hair tied under a do-rag. He had peeled off his outer clothing and stood staring down at her. He was well-muscled, but after she had spent time with Zach, Slim looked downright puny to her.

"Gayle!" It was Lieutenant Larsen. He motioned her into his office and pointed to a chair. "How are things? You okay?"

She dropped into the chair, allowing her backpack to slide onto the floor. The backpack belonged to Zach, and of course it was olive green. "I'm okay. Just a little down, you know? I didn't know how attached I was to my stuff."

Larsen gazed at her over the top of his glasses. "Of course you were. That's only normal."

"What's been going on while I was out?"

"A couple of fires. One was a home fire due to faulty Christmas lighting, and the other was at the city's posh-est restaurant."

"Kitchen fire?" she asked.

"Yeah, but after the restaurant had closed. They think it was a couple of homeless guys who broke in and stole some food. They may have set the fire to hide the theft, or it may have been an accident."

Stephanie considered this information. She stood up and picked up the backpack, slinging it over her shoulder. "Thanks for catching me up to speed, sir. I better go get myself squared away."

Lieutenant Larsen nodded, and she escaped to the locker room. She was stowing her stuff when Miller and Donnell came to lounge just inside the door.

"So, where ya stayin' now, Gayle?" Donnell asked. "If you need a place to stay, I'll toss out my roommate, and you can move right in."

"Or with me," Miller said. "I've got my own place. No roomies."

Stephanie looked them both over and shook her head. "I would rather eat glass."

"No, seriously," Donnell said. "We're all here for you." He shrugged. "Just wanted to let you know that, you know…"

"Yeah," Miller said. "You can bunk in with any of us anytime."

Stephanie sucked in a deep breath. "I'm staying with…my boyfriend."

Donnell and Miller exchanged a look.

"Ahh…the big boyfriend." Miller made a face and swung his arms loosely, imitating an ape.

"Careful," Donnell said. "Big guy might beat your ass."

"Nah, he's a pussycat." Miller waved him off. "He's all polite with that 'yessir' 'nosir' stuff."

Stephanie leaned back against her locker and crossed her arms over her chest. "You know my boyfriend was a U.S. Army Ranger? He could kick both your asses without even breaking a sweat." She was pretty sure she was smirking.

Donnell raised both hands, waving her a "calm down" motion. "I'm sure he could. He sure did make a good impression on the boss. He was commenting about the guy after the awards banquet."

Stephanie raised her brows. She recalled how Zach's manners had charmed her boss and his wife. "Okay, get outta here. I need to change."

Donnell gave her a mock salute and jerked Miller by the arm so they both exited the locker room.

Stephanie grabbed a change of uniform and put it on after carefully locking the door. No reason to invite an unexpected audience.

As the day wore on, they received only one emergency call, and it had to do with a vehicular accident in which one had skidded into another. Now someone was trapped inside. Donnell used the Jaws of Life to pry open the door so the driver could be removed and loaded into an ambulance.

If the weather had been warmer, the crew would have washed the spilled oil and gasoline out of the street, but since it was so cold, they followed the wash down with a generous strewing of sand to keep vehicles from sliding on ice.

Not a big day, but at least something satisfying in the way of work. They had pried a guy out of a freshly compacted car, and he was on his way to the emergency room.

The combination of frigid weather, water, and wind meant she was chilled to the bone, her cheeks were raw, and her lips were chapped. Worst of all, her nose was running. Ick!

She climbed into the interior of the fire engine, glad to be out of the wind.

Slim climbed in beside her. "Whooee! Aren't you glad you decided to become a firefighter?"

"Um, yeah. Rethinking my career decision right now. I could have been a kindergarten teacher."

Slim shook his head. "Nah, I can't see you with a room full of little rugrats. You don't have the temperament to deal with kids."

Stephanie felt as though she had been punched. "Wha—I don't understand why you'd say that. I'm a nice person."

"Yeah, but you're not patient. Not like a teacher…or a mom. Maybe start out with a houseplant. If you don't kill it, go for a cat."

The rest of the crew filled the engine, and Lieutenant Larsen took off. They returned to the station and proceeded to clean and return equipment to its proper place.

The rest of the afternoon she felt glum, wondering if that was the kind of vibe she gave off. Maybe that was why Miss Dyer, the social worker, had not believed that she would be a competent mother.

"Gayle! Phone! You can take it in here." Lieutenant Larsen hollered at her from his office. He gestured to the phone on his desk with the blinking button. He grabbed his coffee cup and left the office.

Stephanie thought it might be Zach calling to check up on her, so she was smiling with she answered the phone. "Hello," she crooned into the receiver. But then it dawned on her that he would have called her cell. Her grip on the receiver tightened.

There was a silence that met her cheery greeting. The kind of silence that made the hairs on the back of her neck tingle. She knew that Zach was not on the other end of the line.

"You gonna die."

Stephanie swallowed hard, but something caused her to straighten her spine. She didn't want to let him know he had spooked her. "Mr. Neeley. You need to give yourself up to the authorities. They have your older brother, and they will catch up to you. It's just a matter of time."

There was a sound somewhere between a scream and a growl. "You—you got no time." He hung up abruptly.

Stephanie, on the other hand, stood frozen in place, trembling and gripping the receiver with both hands.

# Chapter 16

BIG JIM SCOOPED LADLES OF CHILI AND FILLED LARGE BOWLS. Colton and Zach were arranging other items on the table. There was a carton of sour cream and a bag of grated cheddar, along with a small glass bowl with green onions.

Colton pulled a cast-iron skillet out of the oven, and the aroma of the freshly baked cornbread filled the kitchen. "This looks good, Dad."

"Smells good, too," Zach said. He removed a gallon jug of milk from the refrigerator.

"Let's eat while everything is hot," Big Jim invited.

Misty had taken Gracie and Mark into Langston to spend their savings on Christmas presents, and Leah had eaten some custard earlier but was now taking a nap.

It was rare that the three men ate a meal together without female companionship or without the presence of children.

"What's the agenda for Christmas?" Zach asked. "I appreciate you inviting Stephanie and me to share your holiday."

"Aw, son," Big Jim said. "You're a part of this family, so you can just consider your invitation to last a lifetime… for you and anybody you see fit to bring with you."

Zach saluted him with a spoonful of chili. "I'm pretty sure it's going to be Stephanie, at least for as long as she will put up with me."

"You love her?" Big Jim gazed at him intently.

"Guilty. I've never known anyone like her."

"She's one of a kind, all right." Big Jim sprinkled more cheese on top of his chili.

Colton had been listening to this exchange and let out a loud huff. "Easy, bro. You haven't exactly been in a place where you can meet nice hometown girls. You were in the middle of the freaking desert for years. Stephanie is the first attractive single woman you've seen in many years." He slathered more butter on his cornbread. "Just don't go overboard. I don't want you to get burned."

Big Jim saw a muscle in Zach's jaw twitch, and he figured he was trying not to go off on Colt in front of his father, so Big Jim thought he should step in. "No, you need to back off, Colt. Stephanie Gayle is a remarkable young woman, and any man would be lucky to be in a relationship with her." He reached out to give Zach a pat on the shoulder. "Your cousin here has been through a lot, and I'm sure he knows what he's doing. Just let Zach and Stephanie figure it out for themselves. They may be dating for the next ten years…or the next two weeks. It's all up to them."

A muscle in Colt's jaw tightened, but he picked up his cup and saluted his father with it. "Yes, sir."

The three men managed to eat their meal in silence… a strained, uncomfortable silence.

───※───

"What's the matter, Stephanie? You can tell me." Zach had welcomed her home and could see her agitation.

"Matter? What makes you think there's anything

wrong?" She had a grim attempt at a smile on her face, but she didn't quite meet his gaze.

He helped her out of her down jacket and hung it on the old-fashioned bentwood coatrack. "Everything… Just tell me, okay? No games."

She huffed out an irritated snort. "I don't play games."

Zach felt his own temper rising and worked hard to keep it in check. "In that case, you're lying to me."

Stephanie whirled around, her face reddening. "I can't believe you said that to me. I don't lie."

Zach fisted his hands on his hips. "Well, what is it you're not telling me about? It's obvious you're really upset. Just spill it, and we'll figure it out."

She glared at him for a moment before her lower lip trembled. "Oh, Zach. I didn't want to burden you. I—"

Zach pulled her into his arms and kissed her. He kissed her until he felt the tension ease from her body.

Her arms slipped around his waist as she pressed close to him. When she leaned away, her face was distorted with unshed tears. "Oh, Zach. I'm so scared."

"Scared? What happened?" He pulled her toward the sofa and eased her down beside him.

"It was Neeley. He called me at the station."

Zach frowned. "Did you call the police?"

She nodded. "I did, but I don't think they really thought it was all that big a deal."

"An escaped murderer is stalking and threatening you. That's a big deal."

She drew a breath. "I—I'm okay now. I guess I just needed to get home and have you hold me tight. I feel safe with you, Zach."

He squeezed her, amazed that she knew he would

protect her. "Don't worry. I'll take care of you. Let me take you to dinner at the steak house. We'll just relax and enjoy our meal."

She nodded, brushing at her eyes with the back of her hand. "I'll just freshen up a little and be right back."

While she was busy, Zach made a quick phone call. When she was ready, he drove her into Langston to the steak house and shepherded her inside.

They were shown to a booth on the far side of the restaurant, where Zach slid in on the same side as Stephanie. She smiled up at him. A real smile and not forced.

They were perusing the menu when a friend slipped onto the seat across from them.

"Dex!" Zach called out.

"Zach Man!" Dex responded. He was tall but not as muscular as Zach. "And I think I know this lovely lady." He sat gazing at Stephanie with a wide grin on his face.

"This is my friend, Dexter Shelton. We went all the way through school together." Zach wrapped his arm around Stephanie. "Dex, this beautiful woman is Stephanie Gayle."

Dex stroked his chin, covered with a bit of scruff. "Seems like I've heard that name before." He snapped his fingers. "I know! You're that amazing hot firefighter chick."

Stephanie laughed. "Shut up, Dex." She started to wave off his compliment, but Zach jumped in.

"She's the one! My girlfriend wears a cape."

Dex held up a finger as though another thought had just struck him. "And there was something else. Didn't you have something to do with the Neeley murder?"

Stephanie's face froze. "And just why are you here again?"

"I'm still good old Dex Shelton. You know I work with the sheriff's office."

"I know who you are." She drew back then glanced from one man to the other. "So this was a setup? You and Dex cooked up this little meeting?"

Zach covered her hand. "Yes, I called Dex. He's a friend, and he's pretty smart... I swear, Stephanie...if anything happened to you, I don't know what I would do."

She softened a bit. "You guys are sweet. Nothing's going to happen to me...I hope."

"You see, Dex, this guy is threatening to kill her, and she won't stay home with me where I can protect her." He shifted his attention to her. "Just tell me how I can protect someone who thinks she's invincible?"

Dex shook his head. "Tough gig!"

Zach raked his fingers through his scruffy hair. "You're telling me."

"Oh, stop it," Stephanie said. "I cannot go into hiding just to humor you two idiots. I have a job. I have a life."

Dex grimaced. "That's what your boyfriend wants you to have...a life." He leaned forward, elbows on the table. "I know you want that too, so don't be so stubborn. It's okay to take a step back, at least until we catch this Neeley creep."

Stephanie's lips moved as though she wanted to argue but thought better of it.

"Are you folks ready to order?" The waitress appeared, pad and pen in hand.

"Yes, we are." Dex handed her a menu. "My friend here is buying me prime rib tonight."

Zach grinned at Dex. "Make it three."

Stephanie protested that she couldn't eat that much, but Zach whispered, "Doggie bag."

During the meal, Dex continued to throw out little tidbits, advising Stephanie to lie low until Neeley was apprehended.

At the end of the meal, Dex stood and took his leave. "You be careful, Stephanie Gayle. My man Zach doesn't lose his heart to just anyone."

"I'll do my best." She raised a hand to bid him goodbye.

When Dex had gone, Zach lifted her hand to his lips. "How about dessert?"

"Totally stuffed," she said.

He waved for the check, paid, and walked her out to the truck. When he had the motor running, he sat idling to warm up the engine. He glanced at Stephanie, but she was staring out the window, seemingly deep in thought. He reached over to take her gloved hand. "We'll have some heat in a minute and clear the windshield."

"I'm in no hurry."

"I hope you paid attention to Dex. You're in danger, you know?"

She shrugged. "What made you get him to gang up on me?"

He gazed at her sadly. "Because, my stubborn darling, you weren't paying attention to anything I said to you. I thought the local sheriff's office should know that this Neeley had contacted you at work and threatened you again…and I figured you might actually listen to someone from that office."

Stephanie pursed her lips, looking pensive for a

moment. "I know you're right. I just don't know how to ratchet back. I've always been used to going full throttle."

"Just for a little while," Zach assured her. "I'm sure your boss will understand. He wouldn't want you to risk your life."

This seemed to strike her as funny because she threw her head back and laughed. "You do realize that I'm a firefighter and we risk our lives on a daily basis?"

"Not the same thing."

"It's exactly the same thing. We're highly trained, but accidents do happen. In fact, my job is so dangerous the damned social worker won't even consider letting me adopt two really unfortunate orphans." Tears shimmered in her eyes.

"Aww...I'm sorry. Don't cry, baby." He reached out.

She brushed him away. "You don't understand," she insisted. "Your uncle, Big Jim Garrett...he's trying to adopt the kids. Or maybe he's helping one of his sons to adopt." Her voice broke. "Lord knows any of them would make the perfect family...at least according to Miss Lorene Dyer. They're all happily married. They have property where kids can play outside. They don't have dangerous jobs..."

Zach shook his head. "That can't be right. All of Big Jim's sons are married and have their own families. I don't believe Big Jim would want to take on the responsibility of little kids when he has just gotten to a place in his life where he's free. He enjoys his grandchildren, but I seriously don't think he's in the market to start a new family."

Stephanie leaned her temple against the window, her face a portrait of sadness and loss.

"Come on, Steph. We're just a few days from Christmas. Let's focus on spending a great holiday together and keeping you safe. I want you to give me one special gift this year."

She turned to meet his gaze. "What is it you want?"

"Just call Larsen and tell him you need to take some time off…until Neeley is captured. That's all I want." He brushed his fingertips along her cheek. "I just want you."

―⁘―

The next morning, Stephanie called Lieutenant Larsen and explained that she had been threatened by Neeley and that Zach had convinced her to lay low for a while.

"That young fellow you're going with has a good head on his shoulders. Glad he's taking care of you."

Stephanie's back teeth gritted together as she tried not to respond with the snarky sarcasm trying to break free. *The big strong men will take care of us helpless little women.* She rolled her eyes. "Yeah, he's one in a million."

"Don't you worry about a thing. We've got it covered on this end. Just enjoy your Christmas holiday."

"Yes, sir…but you can always call me in if you need me." She hated that pitiful tone in her own voice.

"Thank you, Gayle, but you don't need to worry. We'll be just fine without you."

She hung up feeling distinctly disappointed. Something about not being needed.

Zach, for his part, was looking extremely satisfied. He had been managing a cast-iron skillet filled with sizzling bacon while she made the call. Now he was actually grinning at her. "How do you like your eggs? Over easy?"

She glowered at him for a second. "That sounds good. Bacon smells great."

"I talked to Big Jim. He gave me a few days off to be with you."

"Oh, great. So I don't get to go to work, and you're going to be babysitting me?"

"Yeah, don't make me spank you." He was breaking eggs into the skillet now.

"I'd like to see you try," she said. "Do you have a death wish?"

He turned to give her a long and solemn stare. "Nope. I've seen way too much death. I made it back here, and I'm focused on the future."

Stephanie swallowed hard. What was it about this guy that just rocked her back on her heels? "Sorry," she whispered.

"Not a problem. Sit right down because your breakfast is coming in for a landing." He flipped her eggs over and then eased them onto a plate, which he placed in front of her. He broke more eggs in the skillet, and while they were cooking, he set the plate of bacon and another with buttered toast on the table.

"Wow! Where did you learn to make perfect eggs?" She reached for a piece of toast and bit into it.

"My dad. He was the one who took the time to teach me." He flipped his eggs onto a plate and joined Stephanie at the table. "By the way, my uncle invited us to go over and hang out at the ranch this afternoon."

"Oh!" Stephanie froze, a bite halfway to her mouth. She wasn't sure she wanted to be around the man who was planning to adopt Cody and Ivy. But she wondered what the hell he was trying to do. "I—I guess that will be okay."

Zach saluted her with a glass of orange juice. "Great. We'll have a good time."

She nodded. "Yeah…good time."

———

Leah was propped up on the sofa in the living room. Her feet were raised on a pillow, and she was tremendously bored as well as tremendously huge.

"You need anything, honey?" Tyler stepped into the room, looking every bit the doting husband.

"Maybe some tea? You know, that decaf kind that Gran got for me?"

"Sure. I'll be right back." He turned as if to leave.

"Wait! Come sit down for a minute." She patted the chair beside the sofa.

Ty came over and kissed her forehead before taking a seat. "What's up?"

She heaved a sigh. "I'm just lonely. Everyone seems to have something to do except me. I don't even know where my daughter is."

"Don't worry about Gracie. The kids are with Dad. He's determined to teach them how to be ranchers, and he's starting with the small stock."

She had to laugh. "I heard all about it from Gracie. She's so proud that she knows how to gather the eggs. And she's named all the hens."

"Don't tell her, but Dad ordered some Lavender Orpington chicks from the feed store. He thought Gracie might like to show one for 4-H."

"Sounds impressive," Leah said. "I'm sure Gracie will love it. She idolizes Big Jim."

The doorbell sounded, causing Ty to jump to his feet.

"Must be Zach." He left her to go to the front and then shepherded Zach and Stephanie back to the living room.

Leah struggled to move her feet. "Hey, Stephanie and Zach. Come sit down. My beloved husband was just going to get some tea for me, but we have coffee and hot cocoa as well."

"Remember to tip your waiter," Ty drawled.

"Hey, I'll help you out," Zach said. He turned to wink at Stephanie before following Ty to the kitchen.

Stephanie came to sit in the chair Ty had abandoned. "How are you doing, Leah? Got a couple more weeks before the baby arrives?"

Leah placed her hands on her belly. "That's what Dr. Ryan tells us, but I swear, I never got this big with Gracie."

"Not that I've ever experienced motherhood first-hand, but I understand each pregnancy is different." Stephanie shrugged. "Maybe someday."

"Oh, I'm sure you'll be a mom someday. Maybe you and Zach—"

Stephanie's brows rose high on her forehead. "Mr. Bossy Pants?"

"Uh-oh. Sounds like trouble in paradise."

"Not really. It's just since my truck got damaged and my apartment got trashed and then yesterday I got a death threat from this guy—"

"Oh no! That sounds awful." Leah reached out to squeeze Stephanie's arm.

Stephanie patted her hand. "It's okay, really. I'm sure he's just trying to scare me."

"Oh, I would be terrified." Leah couldn't imagine how Stephanie could be so cool about what had been happening.

"And Zach is so protective. He would like to stuff me in a closet and sit outside guarding me…but I love him for it, no matter how crazy it makes me."

Leah smiled. "Yeah, I get that. You would think this baby was the first one ever. Tyler treats me like I'm made of glass."

Tyler and Zach came in, each bearing two cups. Ty handed one to Leah, while Zach did the same for Stephanie.

"I do not treat you like you're made of glass," Ty said, taking a seat next to Leah. "I treat you like you're made of everything I love, and it's my job to make sure you get whatever you need to have a good life." He grinned and patted himself on the chest. "I happen to believe that's me."

Leah reached out to him with both arms, and he leaned close to embrace her. "Love you," she whispered.

"I love you more," he said.

They heard a stamping of feet and noise coming from the back of the house along with voices raised in joyous chaos.

"Sounds like Big Jim has come back with Gracie," Stephanie said.

"Yes, daily egg gathering has become quite an event."

Gracie came running into the room, her cheeks reddened from the cold. She held the hand of a small boy. "Mommy! We had the best time. Cody got to bring in an egg all by himself."

"Oh!" Stephanie half rose. "Cody!" She knelt down on the carpet, and the small boy ran to her arms.

Leah was amazed to see the ever-cool firefighter with tears rolling down her cheeks as she rocked the small boy in her arms. "Stephanie, are you okay?"

Stephanie drew back, gazing at the boy, who also had tears spangling his dark lashes. "Yes, it's just—"

Big Jim came around the corner with an even smaller girl in his arms. "Hey, Stephanie. Look what Santy Claus brought you."

Stephanie let out a soft whimper. "Ivy!"

Big Jim set the girl on her feet, and she ran to Stephanie. For a few minutes there was no other sound except the three people who were hugging and blubbering.

Leah realized that Big Jim had tears in his eyes too.

Zach was standing beside him with a broad grin. His gaze was fixed on Stephanie and the two young children in her embrace. A rush of warmth filled Leah's chest. She could see the love reflected in Zach's expression. Big Jim gave Zach a slap on the shoulder and urged him to join the group on the floor.

Zach approached hesitantly. He appeared to be so big compared to the fine-boned firefighter and two small children. He reached out to cup her cheek, and she kissed his palm.

"How long have you been keeping this secret?"

He shook his head. "It was a surprise to me too. My uncle knows how to keep a secret."

"Big Jim," Stephanie began. "I don't know what to say. I went by to see the kids at the children's shelter, and the social worker seemed to think you would be adopting Cody and Ivy."

Big Jim spread his hands. "I didn't say that. I just told her we wanted to make sure the kids had a good Christmas, and I asked her if we could let them have a weeklong sleepover. She was real nice to me."

Leah let out a whoop. "Seriously, Dad. Who's not going to be nice to Big Jim Garrett?"

Big Jim looked confused.

"I mean, this social worker would have to be from another planet not to know who Big Jim Garrett is." Leah made a flapping motion with her hand. "You're a big deal around here."

"That's for sure, Dad," Ty said. "You make us all proud."

Big Jim looked pleased. "I know how much these children mean to Stephanie. I just wanted to be sure they got to spend a great Christmas together. I'll do whatever I can to help that social worker understand what a good person you are."

"Thank you, sir," Zach said.

Stephanie hugged both children. "Best Christmas ever."

# Chapter 17

IT WAS VERY DIFFICULT FOR STEPHANIE TO LEAVE THE Garrett ranch that evening, yet she allowed Zach to walk her to his truck and drive her away. She was so thrilled to have unrestricted access to the children she adored. Ivy had fallen asleep in her arms, and Stephanie had tucked her in bed in the room where Gracie slept. Cody was still awake but drowsing by the time she left.

Perhaps there was a chance that she would be able to adopt Cody and Ivy. Surely if Miss Dyer could see how happy the children were when they were with her... Surely Miss Dyer would want them to be cared for by someone who loved them.

"You look happy," Zach observed. He had turned onto the main highway going to the Davis ranch.

"I am," she said. "And relieved. I thought I was going to have to fight Big Jim Garrett for those children." She shook her head. "And all the while he was trying to help me adopt." She let out a little yelp of joy.

"I sure do hope it all works out the way you want."

Stephanie looked at Zach. Such a fine man, but she didn't know anything about his long-term goals. She didn't even know his plans for their relationship. Was this just a comfortable state wherein he had convenient sex? No, she believed he truly cared for her, but was he looking for anything more? After years of enlistment, was he capable of making a lifetime commitment?

"You're awful quiet," Zach said. "What are you thinking about?"

She made a humming noise. "Just thinking."

"Want to share?"

"Not yet."

He cast a concerned glance at her before heaving a sigh. "Well, if you decide you want to talk, I'm always available."

"Always?"

"Yes, ma'am."

That was something. He said she could count on him always being available…but for what?

<hr>

*It was late afternoon, but it felt like dusk. The air was thick with ash from the earlier firefight and the smell of burnt-out humanity.*

*Zach was on patrol, searching through the village for any remnants of the snipers his team had been chasing. Jewel was by his side. She was excited but under control.*

*Smoke billowed up from several burned-out buildings, but all was quiet except for the boots of his squad as they made their way through the village, each member on high alert.*

*A sound…*

*The voice of a woman wailing. Then more rubble falling. The team crept toward a corner and lined up behind Zach, waiting for his signal to move on.*

*He peeked around the corner. A few civilians were rummaging through the rubble, searching for any human remains or precious belongings.*

*Casualties of war. The price of conflict.*

Zach's stomach was in a knot. He hated these missions…after the shelling and shooting stopped, there was this bloody aftermath. The fine dust filtered into his lungs along with the metallic aftertaste of fine shards of shrapnel still lingering in the air.

Jewel pulled at her leash.

"Okay, girl. Go find 'em." He felt sure that if there were any enemy forces lying in wait for his team, Jewel would root them out.

Jewel raced straight for a partially demolished building, in the gaping doorway, and down a dark hallway.

Zach and Jeb raced after her, with the rest of his team positioning themselves to guard them.

Jewel barked once, pawing at a door. Zach tried the door, but it was blocked with something heavy on the other side. He envisioned enemy forces behind that barrier. He glanced at Jeb and got a thumbs-up before he put his shoulder to the door and pushed through the barricade. It was dark inside, but the light on his helmet illuminated a small area. He led with his rifle, his finger on the trigger. Anyone lurking in the shadows would be dead in a heartbeat. Zach was barely breathing, his heart thundering in his chest.

There!

He heard a noise and whirled around, his light illuminating three figures huddled together in a corner. Jeb sprang into the room, his rifle pointed at the group.

"Stop!" Zach shouted.

Jewel had found three young children, wide-eyed with fright. Small, brown-skinned children with large and terrified eyes.

*Zach expelled a lungful of air. He had almost shot children.*

*"Damn!" Jeb stood beside him, his mouth agape. "Damn!"*

*"Yeah." Zach called Jewel off and looked around. There didn't seem to be any adults or remains thereof.*

*Zach slung his rifle over his shoulder and leaned down to pick up the smallest child and then the next smallest. He nodded for Jeb to gather the remaining child. Together they trooped outside, carrying the now-whimpering children. Jewel trotted by his side, her leash dragging through the debris.*

*He called for the children to be picked up by an ambulance, standing watch as the little girl stared at him with her haunting gaze.*

*"Sad, huh?" Jeb asked. He was too close. Zach could feel his warmth against his own skin.*

*He could hardly breathe; the warmth was suffocating him.*

He jerked awake, lying in the dark, breathing heavily.

Amazingly, he hadn't awakened Stephanie. She lay naked and warm against his skin, her breathing regular.

He hadn't had a dream in a while. He didn't know what had triggered this one.

Oh, yes…it was the eyes. The large dark eyes of young children. Eyes that had stared at him earlier that day.

---

Stephanie had begun her search online only a few days previously. She had learned what would make the perfect Christmas present for the man she loved. The man who loved her. Stephanie's lips curved upward. This was the one thing she knew would bring him joy.

Sadly, she was pretty sure she would not be able to find what she was looking for or, if it were available, she couldn't make it happen before Christmas…but she searched nonetheless. *No harm, no foul…*

Stephanie stared at the screen. "Joint Base San Antonio," she said aloud. *San Antonio, Texas?* At least the answer to her question was close at hand. There was a phone number listed, so she picked up her cell and punched in the numbers.

"Hello. I would like to know how to go about adopting a military service dog."

She spent the next hour being passed from one office to another and making the same request. Finally she got to talk to the person who could fill in the blanks.

Stephanie answered some of the questions and made note of information she would have to supply. "So, do you think there's a chance we could make this happen?" she asked. "You know, in time for Christmas?"

There was a long pause, where she could hear the rapid clicking of fingers on a keyboard.

Finally, the person on the other end of the line cleared his throat. "Well, you're in luck. I've located Jewel, and she is with a volunteer in Houston who is fostering her." There was another pause. "You do know the dog was injured, don't you?"

Stephanie drew in a sharp breath. "Oh, no!"

"So you don't think the dog's former handler would want to adopt her since she's handicapped?"

"I didn't mean that," she assured him. "I'm just sorry for the dog…that she was injured. But—but we want her."

The man sent a form to her email that she was to fill out and return. She looked it over, wondering where she could find the information without Zach's knowledge. Her mouth drew up into a scowl as she stared at the blanks. She had no idea what Zach's middle name or initial might be. In truth, she didn't know any of the little details about Zach's life. Only what he chose to tell her, and he was rarely forthcoming.

She tapped her fingers on the edge of the keyboard. This would take some serious reconnoitering on her part. Perhaps Zach's best friend, Colt, might have the answers. Or maybe Big Jim could help her fill in the blanks.

She wandered around, wishing she could get a look at Zach's driver's license and any other pertinent information that might be in his wallet, but short of mugging the big guy, she was stymied. Then her gaze fell on the items on the bedside table on Zach's side of the bed. A shiny metal object caught her eye.

*Zach's dog tags.*

She picked them up, feeling a little burst of joy in her chest. There it was.

*Garrett, Zachery W.* And his service number.

Stephanie hurried back to the computer and finished filling out the form, sent it, and followed it up with a phone call.

It seemed that Santa Claus would be coming to town after all.

———

"The airport?"

"Yeah, I thought you could drive me...you know... because I'm a helpless little female and need a big strong man to take care of me." She clasped her hands together in supplication and batted her eyes at him.

"You are such a brat…but I would be happy to drive you to the airport." Zach reached for his jacket. "You're not leaving me, are you?"

She threw her head back and laughed, exposing her pretty neck. "Not hardly. I've been working so hard to get you trained. Almost there."

"Oh, you think so, do you?" Zach found himself laughing too. She was in a great mood, and this was a good thing, considering the damage to her truck, the loss of her possessions in the apartment, and the threats to her life. He was proud of her for being so strong but concerned that she was such a risk taker. "Maybe I'm getting you trained?"

He was surprised when she melted into his arms, gazing up at him soulfully.

"I think we're getting used to each other and just naturally bending to each other's will."

He stared at her for a moment before kissing her. "That was a beautiful thought."

She grinned impudently. "So, take me to the airport."

He reached for her jacket and held it open for her to slip into. Once they were in Zach's truck and on the way to Amarillo, he noted that Stephanie was really excited. She could barely hold it in. "So, can you tell me why we're going to the airport? Are you meeting your old boyfriend?"

Her dimples flashed. "I do have a guest coming in. I hope you like her."

"Is your friend going to stay with us at Fern Davis's place? There's another bedroom, so I guess it will work." He glanced at her to find that she was barely able to control her gleeful expression.

"Oh, I'm sure you're going to love her. You're going to want to keep her around."

Zach just shook his head. He couldn't imagine that he would find some other woman that enticing. All he wanted was to find a way to make a real home for Stephanie. A home of their own.

In time, the Amarillo city skyline rose on the horizon. Zach followed the signs directing him to the airport.

Stephanie was grinning, her face practically glowing with joy.

Zach felt a twinge of jealousy, hoping that he could give her as much happiness as the arrival of her girlfriend.

"Do you want me to let you out and wait while you meet your friend?"

Her eyes opened wide. "Oh, no! You have to come inside with me."

He left her off under a portico and went to park the truck. When he joined her inside, she was still grinning.

She threaded her hand through the crook in his arm and told him the arrival gate where her friend would be meeting them. "We're a little early, but I wanted to be sure we were here in plenty of time. You're going to love her."

Zach loved having Stephanie on his arm. He thought they were growing closer together. His immediate problem was what to give her for Christmas. He knew it had to be something significant. He was savvy enough to know that this present had to come straight from his heart. The problem was she was not forthcoming with any suggestions. *No clues. No hints. Nada…*

"Here we are," she sang out. "Gate five, and her flight is right on time."

They sat down close to the arrival gate. Zach wondered how Stephanie had been able to get them through security, but she seemed to have things well in hand. Perhaps her guest was some important or famous person.

He was pleased that Stephanie kept a tight grasp on his arm. This felt good. Better than good.

The flight was announced, and Zach noticed that a photographer was standing by, as though he too was waiting for this flight. This confirmed his suspicion that Stephanie's friend was some sort of celebrity or something.

A line of passengers began to pour from the passageway. Family and friends met some of them with shouts of joy and hugs, probably home or visiting for Christmas.

Stephanie got to her feet and pulled Zach closer, where they would be able to spot her friend.

The rush of passengers thinned out. One gentleman was wheeled out in a wheelchair, and he seemed to be the last one out. He was greeted by a young couple and whisked away.

Zach glanced at Stephanie, who was still gazing at the passageway with a rapt expression.

Someone appeared at the doorway. It was a man in uniform. There didn't seem to be a woman nearby, so Zach was wondering if Stephanie's friend had failed to make the plane.

There was a dog…

It was a dark German shepherd. The dog barked, or rather shrieked, and jumped in excitement.

Zach felt as though he'd been sucker-punched.

*Jewel...*

"Jewel!" he shouted, and the dog broke free, dragging her leash behind her.

Zach fell to his knees, but Jewel knocked him over. She barked and made a noise like a squeal as she licked him and danced around him.

The photographer was snapping pictures, circling around them, but Zach was only peripherally aware of him. It was all about Jewel.

His chest felt tight, and his face was wet with tears. Thankfully, Jewel was licking his face, so he didn't have to acknowledge the emotions he was experiencing.

Jewel was wagging all over, her tail sweeping the air like a fan. She made little whimpering noises that let him know how much she had missed him too.

The soldier leaned down to shake Zach's hand. "Sergeant Garrett. It's a pleasure to meet you, sir. Jewel is a wonderful dog. We're so glad to reunite the two of you."

"I—I don't understand how this happened," Zach said, struggling to his feet.

"Um—a lady named Miss Gayle got things rolling, and she paid for me to fly in a bulkhead seat so Jewel had enough room by my feet and didn't have to ride in baggage."

Zach turned to see Stephanie gazing at him with tears in her eyes. "You!"

She shrugged but grinned anyway. "I hope you like your present, Zach."

He didn't know how he could love her any more than he did at that moment. "And Jewel is your girlfriend?" He lifted her chin and laid a quick kiss on her lips.

"I'm sure she will be."

Zach picked her up and swung her around, while Jewel danced around them and the photographer clicked away.

When he set her on her feet, he picked up Jewel's leash and shook the hand of the soldier who had accompanied her. "So, what are you going to do now, soldier?"

The young man grinned. "Catch my return flight in about forty-five minutes, sir. My assignment was to escort this canine hero to her final post." He presented Zach with a large brown paper envelope, which he said contained all the paperwork related to transfer of ownership of the dog.

The photographer started to leave, but Stephanie called him back. "What are you going to do with the photos you took?"

He explained he was with the newspaper, and this was a "feel-good" story that might get national coverage. He took a couple more photos of Zach and Jewel, wrote down their names, and got some quotes for the story. When he walked away he was grinning.

Zach wasn't sure how he felt about that, but he thought it was worth it to get Jewel back. He put his arm around Stephanie and whispered, "Thank you for doing this. It's the best thing ever."

"Merry Christmas," she said.

~~~

"You and Jewel are like Velcro," Stephanie commented, noting that although Jewel was in the backseat of the truck, her large head was on Zach's shoulder.

He leaned his cheek against the dog's muzzle. "I can't even begin to tell you what this means to me."

"Don't forget to put this someplace safe." She handed him the large brown paper envelope containing all of the transfer information.

Zach opened the envelope, letting the papers slide out. He rifled through them and then pulled one up, his brow puckering. "What's this? It says Jewel was wounded."

"Oh, yeah. I forgot to tell you about that." She shrugged. "I didn't think it would make a difference. You do want her, don't you?"

He made a scornful sound in the back of his throat. "Of course I do. I just hate that she had to suffer." He held up one page that showed that part of Jewel's right forepaw had been reconstructed and that one of her vertebrae had been replaced. "Well, girl, I've got a few scars myself, so we make a perfect team."

Stephanie reached to stroke the dog's head. "Oh, her ears are so soft."

Zach started the truck and headed for the highway, Jewel's head firmly on his shoulder. He seemed to be quite comfortable driving that way.

Stephanie thought this image would be engraved on her heart forever.

He glanced at her. "Haven't you ever had a dog before?"

"No…" She shook her head, thinking about her childhood. "My parents would never agree to a dog. I had a series of house cats. My mother thought it was easier to take care of a cat than a dog because we usually lived in an apartment. Nobody had time to walk a dog."

"That's kind of sad," he said.

"Different strokes," she said. "It appears that you and I

had a totally different upbringing. My dad got transferred a lot in his job, but we always lived in cities. And you grew up with all that annoying fresh air, country boy."

"That I am. I had never been away from home until I enlisted. That was my big adventure."

She studied his profile as they drove toward home. "What made you choose the Army over going to college? Your cousins all went to college, but you chose a different path."

He considered her question for a moment. "I suppose I thought I was being patriotic. And I really didn't want my dad to have to pay for my education. I figured I would earn an education through the GI bill." He reached over to grab her hand and bring it to his lips. "But in reality, I never wanted to be anything other than a rancher."

She felt a surge of pity for him, although he didn't appear to pity himself. "I'm sorry you didn't come home to your own ranch."

Zach heaved a sigh. "Me too, but I'm hoping to save up some money and buy a little place. It will take time, but that's what I want to do." He glanced at her again, this time more intently. "How does that sound to you?"

This caught her off guard. She sensed that her response was important to Zach, but she wasn't quite sure what he was really after. "I think that's a wonderful goal."

"So, you're okay with me working my tail off, trying to recover some of what I've lost?"

"If that makes you happy." She knew this future ranch was the perfect setting for Zach and that he wouldn't be truly happy anyplace else.

"But what makes you happy?"

"Me?" She considered for a few moments. "I'm happy when we're together. I'm happy at work." She gnawed her lower lip.

"And…" he offered.

"I'm happy when I'm with those two little kids. The way I met them was horrific. I know they need me…" She moistened her lips. "Or someone like me."

"How did you get on the Neeley brothers' radar?"

She felt her throat tighten but swallowed against it. "I was first on the scene. I rode with the ambulance crew, and I identified Rafe Neeley leaving the scene, covered in blood." She sucked in a deep breath and expelled it. "My testimony put him away."

A muscle in his jaw twitched. "So you really bonded with the kids?"

"Yes. I didn't even know I liked kids until I felt Ivy's little arms around my neck or looked into Cody's big brown eyes. How about you? Do you like kids?"

"I suppose so. Lately the only children I've seen have been in some kind of danger. Brown-eyed Afghani kids who look hungry and scared…and who might have a bomb strapped to them." He slowed the truck and turned off toward the Davis ranch. "I guess I finally had to turn off my emotions when it came to children. You hand them a candy bar and hope they don't blow you up."

"That's horrible. How can people use children like that?"

He shook his head and turned onto Fern Davis's property. "Don't ask me. But I've seen so much horror on a daily basis…" He shook his head again and parked the pickup close to the house. He turned off the ignition but made no move to get out of the vehicle. "Stephanie, I've seen enough pain and suffering to last a lifetime."

"Oh, Zach, I'm so sorry. I'm sure it was terrible."

He released his seat belt and turned to put his hand on her shoulder. "When I got here, it was like I was sealed in plastic. I couldn't feel anything. It was as though I was observing but couldn't really get close enough to be a part of anything. My uncle and cousins were great. They went so far out of their way to welcome me and make sure I knew I was still part of the family." He brushed her cheek with the back of his hand. "But I couldn't feel anything...until I met you."

Stephanie's heart beat a little faster. She could hardly breathe. His pain was so visceral she could feel it too.

"I was like a block of ice, but you thawed me out. Steph, you've made me whole again."

"Oh, Zach. I don't know what to say."

"I don't want to lay all that on you," he said. "You're not responsible for my feelings or well-being, but...I know what it means now when people say they found their better half. You do make me whole again."

The tears that had gathered in her eyes spilled down onto her cheeks as he leaned closer to deliver a tender kiss. This kiss was interrupted when Jewel laid her paw on Zach's shoulder and emitted a soft whine.

"Let's go inside and show Jewel around," Zach said. He got out of the truck, and Jewel jumped over the seat to get out with him.

Stephanie could have opened her own door, but she knew by now that Zach would come around to open it for her and help her down. *Sweet*.

# Chapter 18

"CAN I GET YOU SOMETHING?"

It was Misty, her sister-in-law, who hovered over her.

Leah struggled to sit upright and swung her legs down off the sofa. "I'm okay," she mumbled. "Just feeling huge and grumpy."

"How about some cocoa and cookies? I was going to have a little snack myself." Misty looked so sincere Leah had to smile.

"Don't pay any attention to me. I'm just feeling sorry for myself. This is the first Christmas with Tyler as my husband and Gracie's daddy. I wanted to be able to do so much for everyone." A solitary tear drooled down her cheek. "I wanted to be baking and making ornaments with Gracie. I just wanted everything to be special."

"Aww." Misty gave her a hug. "This is just the first of a whole lifetime of holidays you're going to spend with them…and now you'll have this new baby. Gracie will have a little sister or brother."

Leah sniffled. "I know, and I'm very happy about that." She huffed out a sigh. "I'm just feeling huge and useless."

Misty shrugged. "I wish I was in your situation. I can't wait to have our first baby." She wrinkled her nose. "Colt wants us to have our own house first…so I suppose I'll have to wait a while."

"Your time will come." Leah heaved a sigh. "Our

house is essentially finished. We have a nice wing for Gran, and Gracie can't wait to get to decorate her own bedroom."

"Sounds very nice."

"It will be…but since our house is situated a little further into the Garrett ranch, Big Jim convinced Tyler that we should all be under one roof. He was thinking of Gran too."

Misty grinned. "Your grandmother is a sweetheart. She made the gingerbread cookies you may be smelling." She giggled. "I must admit I sampled a few."

"That's my gran. I'm so glad we're all together." She thought about the circumstances under which she had fled Oklahoma with Gracie. It was an amazing stroke of luck that Tyler Garrett had happened by when her old beater of a car had died on the side of the road. Although they had gone through a lot to be together, somehow it had eventually worked out, and they were very happy together. Thankfully, Tyler had understood that Leah was part of a package deal that included her daughter, Gracie, and her small and frail grandmother, Fern.

"I heard you young'uns a-chattin' in here, so I thought I would bring you a little snack." Gran appeared in the doorway bearing a tray with a teapot and a plate of cookies.

Leah leaned forward to clear a space on the coffee table. "Right here, Gran."

Gran walked slowly toward them, but Misty sprang up off the sofa to relieve her of the tray. "I was telling Leah about your fabulous cookies."

Gran's wrinkled face split into a wide grin. "I'm so glad you like 'em." She settled herself into her favorite rocking chair, which Tyler had brought from her house. It was smaller and didn't swallow her up the way the rest of the Garrett man-size furniture did.

Misty helped herself to a cookie. "Seriously, Miz Fern. You ought to open a bakery. I'm sure you'd be swamped."

"I made us some hot cocoa, if you girls are a-wantin' somethin' to wash them cookies down."

Leah gave her grandmother a smile. "I'd love some, Gran."

"I'll pour," Misty offered.

"Put some of them little marshmallows in the cups first, an' then pour the hot cocoa on top. It should get nice an' melty."

Misty obeyed and passed a cup to Leah before pouring a cup for Gran and herself.

Leah inhaled the sweet and rich chocolaty aroma and took a sip. "Delish, Gran. I didn't know I needed chocolate until you brought this wonderful cocoa."

Misty sipped hers and smacked her lips. "This tastes different."

"Gran has her own recipe. She makes it from scratch."

Misty laughed. "I thought I was making it from scratch when I opened a packet into a cup of water and nuked it…but this is better."

Gran, for her part, appeared to be pleased. "Glad you ladies are enjoying it. I made some for Mark an' Gracie an' also them little orphans too. The children are in the kitchen drinkin' their cocoa an' munchin' on cookies."

Leah groaned. "I guess you better pass me a cookie. I'm wasting away here."

The look on Gran's face was worth all the extra

calories she was ingesting. Leah understood her grand-mother's need to be needed. It was just that Leah needed to be needed as well.

—∿—

Jewel inspected all areas of Fern Davis's house. The dog was bright and alert but checked out every corner and under every bed and chair.

Zach removed her leash and found a place to hang it beside the front door. They had purchased a large bag of premium dog food before leaving the city as well as large stainless-steel food and water dishes. He busied himself peeling off labels and giving the bowls a rinse before filling them.

He called Jewel and showed her where her food would be located in a corner of the kitchen. She ate the food, and then Zach took her out. He thought, given her training, that she didn't need the leash but started out with it anyway.

The temperature was dropping, so although he was sure Jewel would have eagerly explored all the outbuildings, he hurried her back inside once she had finished her business.

"Brr," Stephanie said. "You didn't put on your jacket. Come sit down and have some coffee while I forage for dinner."

He sat at the table and cradled the mug of hot coffee in his cold fingers. "Just what I needed."

"Come in out of the cold, cowboy." She gave him a look that warmed his insides faster than the coffee.

After dinner, they wanted to watch television for a while. When Zach sat down on the small sofa, Jewel jumped up to sit beside him.

Stephanie cocked her head to one side and raised an eyebrow. "So this is how it's going to be, huh?"

"Um, no. Here, Jewel. Get down, girl." He pointed to the floor, and the dog climbed down off the sofa.

Zach grinned at Stephanie and patted the space beside him. "Here, girl."

Stephanie squinted her eyes and gave him a murderous look.

He laughed and held out his arms to her, but when she neared, Jewel jumped on his lap.

Stephanie gave a slight shake of her head. "Aww. Seriously, Zach, I don't want to hurt Jewel's feelings. I don't think she's used to sharing your affections."

"Down, girl. Down." Zach struggled to get Jewel back on the floor. "Seriously, Steph, come sit down and let Jewel get to know you. She's a good dog."

"I'm sure she is, but I don't want to rush her."

Zach looked at first one and then the other of his female companions. "Let's do this, then." He slipped off the sofa onto the floor beside Jewel and pulled a cushion down for Stephanie to sit on. "Let's be together."

She smiled and lowered herself to sit beside him. "This is good."

Jewel moved closer to Zach, first laying her head in his lap and then creeping closer with her paws draped across his thighs. She gazed at Stephanie intently.

"Hello, Jewel," Stephanie crooned, reaching to stroke the dog's head. She continued to pet the animal, who slowly relaxed and laid her head down in Zach's lap.

Zach embraced Stephanie with one arm, pulling her closer to rest her head on his shoulder. "Thanks so much, Steph. Jewel is the best present anyone has ever given me."

Leah had been fed, her dishes carted away, and her swollen feet lifted onto a pillow. For the moment, she was alone...and she could stop trying to pretend to be jolly. *Merry Christmas*.

She should be baking cookies at least. Her pumpkin pie recipe was epic...but she supposed Gran would be up to her elbows in goodies.

Leah heaved a sigh.

All the presents were wrapped. The house was decorated inside and out. There was nothing left to do. At least there was nothing to do that Leah was capable of doing.

*Oops!* There it was. The baby kicked her.

She placed her palm over the spot on the side of her belly where her baby's foot was kicking around in circles. This brought a smile to her face and a warmth in her chest. *This is my child. The life I'm growing inside my body*.

"Hey, little one. I'm here. I feel you."

The little foot kept circling.

"Pretty soon, I'm going to evict you from your habitat and force you out here so we can get better acquainted."

She looked up to see her husband leaning against the wall by the doorway.

"Hey, gorgeous. What's up?"

"You mean, 'Hey, fat and frumpy'? That's me." She was aware that her lower lip jutted out a little.

He pushed away from the wall and came to stand in front of her. He stroked his hand over her hair. "Aww, baby. You're not fat. You're carrying my precious child. That's a beautiful little love bundle you got there." He knelt down and pressed his lips against her belly, encircling her hips with his arms.

"Sorry. I was just feeling sorry for myself." She raked her fingers through his thick, dark hair, wishing she could lean down to kiss him.

"You are my everything," he said. "You and Gracie… and now we will add this new little person to our family." He gazed into her eyes, and he shook his head. "I'm sorry if I somehow haven't told you that enough."

"You have. It's just me and these pregnancy hormones making me weepy. I know how blessed we are."

Ty eased onto the sofa beside her and drew her into his arms.

Leah felt the tension slipping from her shoulders as she relaxed against her husband's muscled torso. She took a moment to reflect on how much better her life was during this pregnancy compared to her previous childbirth, where she had been alone and desperate. She rested her hand on Tyler's thigh, and he covered it with his own. "I love you. I love everything about being your wife." She heaved a loud sigh, hating that it sounded so pitiful. "I just wanted to be able to do more to get ready for our first Christmas as husband and wife. I wanted to make this so special for you and Gracie."

Tyler embraced her with both arms. "You're giving me the best Christmas of my life. Next year you can run around like crazy if that's what makes you happy. But this one is all about our baby. We'll just relax and have a good time. Trust me, my dad will make sure everyone enjoys themselves."

"Really?"

"Absolutely," he said. "My dad always has a few

surprises up his sleeve, so just chill and let everyone else run around like crazy. You can be crazy next year."

Leah smiled, letting Ty's infectious enthusiasm penetrate her prickly defenses. "I suppose you're right. I'm just having trouble being so inactive."

"It's only a couple more weeks. After the baby is born and we get moved back into our own house, it will be easier." He kissed her temple. "Please be patient with yourself."

"I'll try," she said. "It's just that patience is not one of my virtues."

—◆—

Stephanie did take a little more time when she prepared herself for bed. Zach had taken Jewel outside for a last trek around the yard. She felt lighthearted and was quite proud of herself for pulling off such an exquisite surprise for Zach.

It was obvious that he and the dog had a deeply emotional attachment. Stephanie hoped to make friends with Jewel, but she had no experience with dogs and wasn't certain how to proceed. In the meantime, she observed how Zach and Jewel interacted and hoped she could slide into the equation somewhere along the way.

Stephanie brushed her hair out and spritzed on a little cologne in strategic locations. *That should do it*.

She went into the bedroom they had been sharing. She turned down the covers and plumped the pillows. Hearing Zach reenter the house, she flipped off the harsh overhead light and turned on the small lamp on the bedside table.

"This is as good as it gets…here." Stephanie hopped into bed and waited expectantly for Zach to join her.

She heard him moving around, and finally he came down the hallway to take his turn in the bathroom. Waiting for him to get ready for bed only increased her anticipation. She wondered if he was as eager to join her as she had been while making herself presentable for him.

She heard the shower running and heard Jewel's toenails on the hardwood floor in the hallway. Apparently Jewel was pacing. Perhaps she was anxious too.

Finally the water was shut off, and in a short time the bathroom door opened and Zach emerged. He appeared in the bedroom doorway, breaking into a broad grin as he gazed at her. "Hey, you look beautiful."

Stephanie felt her face reddening, although his reaction was exactly what she was hoping for. "Thanks. Come keep me warm." She patted the bed beside her.

He moved toward the bed, but Jewel zipped into the room and onto the bed in one leap. She turned around and lay down facing Zach. Her tail flailed against Stephanie's arm.

"Um…I'm not up for a threesome. Can you tell your other girlfriend that I get to curl up with you at night?"

Zach slapped his hand against his thigh. "Jewel, get down. C'mon, girl. Off the bed."

No response from the dog. Alert, she gazed at Zach, her front paws hanging over the side of the bed.

"Your fur friend is ignoring you." Stephanie leaned back against the pillows and crossed her arms over her chest.

"Yeah, I noticed." Zach went back to the living room to retrieve his jacket. He placed it on the floor beside the bed. He pointed to the jacket and said firmly, "Down, girl."

To Stephanie's surprise, Jewel jumped down and turned around a couple of times before settling down on top of the garment.

Zach slipped onto the bed and pulled the quilt over his legs. He reached for Stephanie, leaning close to nuzzle her neck.

She slipped her arms around him, feeling a rush of heat swirling through her belly. Scooting lower in the bed, she looked up at him, the aching need growing stronger. She saw it in his eyes. His rock-hard body leaned over her, radiating a heat of his own. She wanted to wrap her thighs around him right away but also wanted to experience every molecule of the warm-up. *Oh, yeah!*

There was a whine, and Jewel placed her paws on the bed.

Stephanie blew out a deep breath. "Okay, I give up. Let's just get some sleep." She leaned over to flick off the light and then turned over.

"Aw, I'm sorry, Steph. She just needs to get used to us. This is all new for her."

"I really do understand, Zach. It will all work out."

He kissed her on her cheek and spooned her.

Stephanie felt some satisfaction knowing that she was not the only one disappointed tonight, judging by the hard erection nestled against her back side.

---

The next morning, Zach woke up with his arms still around Stephanie. She smelled so good, but he smelled something else. It dawned on him that Jewel was plastered against his back, and she was softly snoring.

He was so grateful to Stephanie for locating Jewel and for arranging for her to be escorted to Amarillo… and to become a civilian. Now Zach was officially a dog owner.

He was just worried that, in reality, Stephanie would not like living with Jewel. Maybe she just wasn't a dog person?

He tried to nudge Jewel and scoot her to the floor, but she was having none of that. The dog did an elaborate rollover and ended up with her muzzle propped on Zach's hip. He had to smile. This would be hilarious except he didn't want Stephanie to know the dog had snuggled with his backside all night.

When he turned back to Stephanie, she was gazing at him with an amused expression on her face. She reached out to let Jewel sniff her hand and then proceeded to stroke her head. "Oh, such soft ears you have."

"She really likes to have her ears rubbed," he offered.

"Is that a doggie erogenous zone?"

"Yeah, pretty much."

She continued to pat the dog, and Jewel's long tongue snaked out to lick Stephanie's wrist. At first it startled her, and then she chuckled. "Do you suppose Jewel would eat little children?"

"No, of course not. Jewel has rescued quite a few children in her glorious career." Zach dribbled little kisses along Stephanie's bare shoulder. "She's trained to go after bad guys on command…and if someone is threatening the team, she'll attack and take them down."

"Good, because I was going to try to spend some time with Cody and Ivy today if that's okay with you."

"Of course. I mean, it's more than okay with me.

Jewel likes—I mean, I like those kids of yours—I mean, the orphans." He drew in a breath and released it. "I would be very happy if you were to spend time with the children today. I can share you."

"Thanks, Zach. I do hope you like Ivy and Cody because I would really love to adopt them. They've been through so much. I just want them to know somebody loves them and will give them a stable home."

His throat suddenly became tight. "I hope that will happen, Steph." His voice came out all thick and raspy. Holding her in his arms, he knew his future happiness would be woven together with hers. If it entailed adopting two unfortunate orphans, he would embrace that role as well.

"You know what?" She glanced up at him.

"What?"

"We're going to need a bigger bed."

# Chapter 19

"I'M GOING OVER TO THE GARRETT RANCH," STEPHANIE announced after breakfast. "I want to spend as much time as I can with the children."

"Sure," Zach said. "Why don't you bring them over here? Maybe they'll like it in this small place. They can run around and be wild without wrecking anything."

She was pulling on her clothes in preparation for going out into the chilly countryside. She pulled a sweater over her head and then fastened her jeans. Over that, she donned her thick jacket. "Where are my boots?"

He shook his head, grinning. "Right where you left them."

She pursed her lips in a mock pout. "Well, if I remembered where they were, I'd go get them."

Zach chortled. "Oh, yeah! I forgot I put them in the closet right beside mine."

"Who would have thought," she said and headed back to the bedroom. As she passed, she wondered how this little house would accommodate a family. There was only one bathroom and one other bedroom, but it would do just fine for a while...

She sucked in a breath, stopping herself from venturing down that path. *No reason to think there is even a chance of that happening.*

In the bedroom, she spied the boots and sat on the bed to pull them on. She laced them up and got to her feet, smoothing out the covers under which she and her lover had slept.

It struck her as somehow sad, she supposed because it felt too fleeting. For her, Zach was the most perfect male on the planet, but she was pretty sure he would be completely satisfied if their relationship remained just as it was. Lots of hot sex and fun. No particular responsibilities. Just coasting along in a state of bliss.

Stephanie knew that her anxiety was born of her desire to offer a home to Cody and Ivy. To adopt them… To become a mother in every sense of the world. She wanted to build a nest for these two whose security had been taken from them so violently.

She was eager to make a commitment to them, but it seemed premature when the man she wanted to nest with was totally silent about any future plans.

When she reached the front room, she took her gloves out of the pocket of her heavy jacket and pulled them on. "I'll be back in a flash."

Zach came out of the kitchen. "Kids like macaroni, right?"

She felt as though she was smiling all over. He was thinking of the children. "Sure do."

He wrapped her scarf around her neck and pulled the knit cap down over her ears. "You stay warm and be careful out there. The roads are slippery, and it's so hard to find girlfriend replacement parts…especially parts like yours." He gathered her jacket in both fists and pulled her toward him for a kiss.

He started to walk her out to her truck, but she shooed him back. "I'm fine. I'm perfectly capable of climbing into my own truck, Zach Garrett. Thanks anyway." She stroked Jewel's head as a means of saying goodbye. "You take good care of our boyfriend, y'hear?"

Zach gave her another kiss and watched her step off the porch. "Be careful. Don't take any chances." Jewel stood by his side, her tail wagging.

Stephanie waved goodbye and trudged through the ankle-deep snow out to her truck. It took a minute to start up, growling and complaining, but it finally caught. She let it idle for a while before pulling out onto the road, eventually making a turn toward the Garrett ranch.

Big Jim and two of his sons were working with the livestock, but Fern Davis greeted her and brought her back to the kitchen. "C'mon in, and set yerself right down here. I'm gonna pour up a cup o' hot cocoa for you with these little teeny marshmallows." She gestured to a chair.

Stephanie shed her jacket and let it slide to the floor behind the chair. She smiled as Fern brought her cocoa with a saucer of home-baked cookies on the side. Thanking her profusely, Stephanie looked around for the children.

Cody was sprawled on the floor, busily scrubbing crayons onto the page of a coloring book. He grinned at her but did not stop his coloring.

"Where's Ivy?" Stephanie asked.

"That little one is not feelin' up to snuff. She's got a good case o' the sniffles." Fern let out a scornful huff. "Probably too much playin' out in the snow with Big Jim." She shook her head. "I swear that man is just a great big ol' little boy."

Stephanie sat up, feeling alarmed. "Oh? Does she have a fever?"

"Nope. Just sniffles and her little cheeks are chapped somethin' fierce." Fern gestured to the bedroom wing of the house. "She's down for a nap right now, but I'm sure she's gonna be up and at 'em pretty soon."

"Oh, good. I'll look in on her in a bit." She took a sip of her cocoa and nibbled a cookie. "How is Leah? I wanted to see her too."

Fern chuckled. "Well, you come at a good time, but you caught her in a nap, too. Gracie and Mark are checking out pictures of chickens and other livestock they might want to show. Gracie is lookin' at chickens, but Mark thinks he might want to show a calf."

"That's really nice." Stephanie was feeling decidedly antsy. She glanced down at Cody and acknowledged how happy he appeared to be. She realized he was usually charged with looking after his little sister, but at the moment, he was just being a happy little preschooler.

Stephanie enjoyed her refreshments while talking to Fern, who wanted to know how her property was faring over the winter.

"Zach is taking his duties very seriously. He makes sure everything is in good repair."

"I knew I could trust him. That young feller is one nice and responsible man."

After she finished the cocoa, Stephanie stretched out on the floor beside Cody. She complimented him on his artwork, and he proudly held it up for her inspection.

"That's beautiful, Cody. I'm sorry your sister isn't feeling well, but I hope you're okay."

He shrugged. "I'm okay."

"Good. Do you think you might like to take a little drive with me? I was going to show you where I live now."

He put his crayon down and sat up, looking at her expectantly. "Yes. I want to go at your house." He reached out to hug her. "You be my mommy."

Tears stung her eyes, but she blinked them away. "Oh, Cody. I would love to be your mommy and Ivy's too. But I have to see what the lady says. I have to have a good house for you and so many other things."

Fern gazed down at the two and shook her head. "I can't imagine a better mother for these two little 'uns. It's easy to see how much you care for them."

"I do," Stephanie said, hoping that Miss Dyer would be able to see that she would be the best mother for these children.

With a lot of noise and boot stamping, Big Jim, Tyler, and Colton came through the back door.

Big Jim hailed her enthusiastically. "Well, looky here. What you got there, Cody? Looks pretty good to me." He examined Cody's artwork and declared it worthy of a place of honor on the refrigerator door.

Stephanie noted that Cody was beaming with pride.

Big Jim ruffled Cody's thick hair and took him to the fridge to find just the right placement for the picture.

She noted that Big Jim had some sort of kid mojo that made them follow him around like puppies. In her heart of hearts, she hoped that Zach had some of that same kid charm.

"I was going to see if I could take the kids over to Fern's house for a little while," she said. "But I didn't know that Ivy wasn't feeling well."

Big Jim looked a little sheepish. "It's my fault. Fern and Leah have beaten me up over having the kids outside too much. We built the snowmen in the front, and they've been going out to collect eggs every day." He shook his head. "But the other kids are fine. Hope little Miss Ivy will bounce back. Misty gave her something for the sniffles, but it made her sleepy."

"I'm sure she's going to be fine. Don't want her to be sick on Christmas Day."

"Oh, absolutely not." Fern's brow puckered. "That child deserves a wonderful Christmas here with people who truly care for her."

"Why don't you take Cody to visit? I'm sure that will make him feel pretty special." Big Jim nodded to his oldest son. "Colt, why don't you get the kid seat I got for Cody out of my truck and put it in Stephanie's? We want him to be safe on his little outing."

Colt caught Big Jim's keys in midair and shrugged back into his jacket. "Keys?" He held out his hand to Stephanie.

"Thanks so very much." She retrieved her fallen jacket and fished her keys out of the pocket. She turned to Big Jim. "You bought a car seat?"

"Sure. I got one for both the kids. I wanted them to be safe when I brought them here from that children's center." He made a face. "Not exactly a cheery place."

"That was so kind of you," Stephanie said, wondering how she could have misjudged his motives.

When Colton returned, he tossed her the keys.

"All set. But you know that you're supposed to have him in a backseat…which you don't have."

"Oh, I didn't know." She gnawed her lower lip.

Fern waved her hand. "I'm sure it will be okay. We used to have kids standing up in the backseat while we was drivin', and they all lived through it. Just take it easy."

Big Jim nodded. "The roads have been cleared, so you should be all right. Just drive slow."

Stephanie nodded, pulling her cell out of her pocket to give Zach a call. She told him she was on her way with Cody and should be home soon.

"Be careful, baby." Zach's deep voice resonated through the phone.

"I will." She disconnected, smiling. When she turned, she found that Fern and Big Jim were smiling too. She returned the phone to her pocket and zipped it closed.

Cody was dressed in warm clothing with Fern fastening his cap on his head. "Here are your mittens, sonny."

"He looks so cute," Stephanie said. "He's wearing so many layers he can hardly get his arms down to his sides."

"I'll help you get him in the car seat," Colton offered. He spread his arms, and Cody jumped into them eagerly. Colt gave him a boost in the air and then carried him out to Stephanie's truck. He got the boy fastened into the car seat while Stephanie said goodbye to Fern and Big Jim.

"See you in a few hours." She climbed in beside Cody, checking out the car seat and thinking how many things she did not know about parenting. Starting the truck, she revved the motor and waved goodbye to the people gathered to see them off.

"Here we go, Cody. Zach is waiting for us."

Cody grinned and stretched his legs out. "We go home now."

"Well, I'm taking you to the place I'm living right now." She bumped over the cattle guard at the main gate and pulled out onto the highway.

"I wanna live with you, Steffy." Cody kicked his feet some more, and his lower lip jutted out.

"Um, well, that's what I want too." She adjusted the defroster since the windows were fogging up. She saw headlights in the rearview mirror, and the driver was coming way too fast. She tapped the brakes to get his attention, but he was still racing up on her. There was really no room to get over since the shoulder of the highway was loaded with snow that had been cleared from the road itself.

Surely the speeding driver would swerve around her, since there was no traffic coming from the other direction. She was braced for an impact, and indeed, when the other truck passed her, there was a rush of air that felt like a physical blow.

She exhaled, thankful that the driver had passed her by, but then she slammed on her brakes since he had skidded to a stop, blocking the road in front of her. She jerked the wheel, and the truck did a stomach-turning slow-motion slide into the other vehicle. Her truck crunched into the side of the parked truck and rebounded into a snowbank. She gripped the wheel, her heart trying to beat its way out of her chest. "Whoo! Are you okay, Cody?"

He gazed at her with a horrified expression on his face, his mouth open in a silent howl, which became an ear-splitting cry.

"Are you hurt, Cody?"

But he continued to cry.

A sharp cracking noise against the driver's-side window caused her to turn. A man in his twenties was plastered against the window, a revolver in his hand. His expression was feral, his teeth bared.

She let out a little yelp, but it was unheard over the

din Cody was making. She stared at the grimacing man, terror swirling through her gut. It wasn't fear for herself but fear that Cody was with her.

"Get out!" the man screamed. "Open the door, and get out."

She eyed his hand gun. "Look, I don't know you, but I have a little boy here who needs to be home. Leave us alone."

"Get out of the truck, or I'll shoot you right now." The man's face was intent, and he appeared to be crazed by some strong emotion. "Now!" he demanded.

She glanced at Cody, now in full voice. "Settle down, now, Cody. I need you to be my big boy and stop crying. I'm going to step out and talk to this man. You just sit right here."

The truck was still running, so Stephanie made sure it was in park then slid out of the running vehicle, leaving her keys inside. Whatever happened to her, she did not want Cody to freeze to death out here on the highway.

"What do you want?" She glowered at the man, hoping her bravado would draw attention away from the small boy inside her truck.

The man hissed at her, grabbing her by the arm in a bruising grip. "You come with me."

She tried to jerk her arm away, but he held her fast. "Let go. You're hurting me."

He made a scoffing noise and dragged her around to the driver's side of his old truck. He stuck the gun in the back waistband of his pants but kept her mashed against his vehicle while he opened the door. "Get in my truck." He shoved her against the metal running board, bruising her shins.

"What are you doing?" she asked. "I don't have any money."

He gave her a push up into the cab, and she was forced to grab the steering wheel to pull herself up.

"Get over," he said, rudely shoving her into the passenger seat.

She struggled to reach the door handle, but her captor had pushed the childproof door locks. She exhaled, trying to find a way to escape.

He backed up, turning the wheel sharply and then skidding his tires on the wet pavement. He peeled out, fishtailing before heading toward Langston.

Stephanie grappled for the seat belt, thinking she would fare better with it fastened than not. "Who are you?"

Her captor did not respond but kept his gaze locked straight ahead on the long straight highway. A muscle in his jaw twitched, giving another clue to his disposition.

"Look, I don't have much money, so if you're after a ransom, you're fresh out of luck."

"Shut up!" he snarled.

"Why me? Surely you could have hijacked a Cadillac or a Lincoln and have more luck. I work for a living."

"I know who you are." His hate-filled voice sent shivers down her spine.

He slowed and turned off on a rutted dirt road, much worsened by the recent roller coaster of snow and thaw.

The road was narrow and overgrown. No houses along this roadway.

Stephanie's panic level was rising by the second. She kept hearing her captor's voice over and over in her head. *I know who you are…*

# Chapter 20

ZACH HAD BEEN LOOKING OUT FOR STEPHANIE'S TRUCK. ITS bright-red paint job was one of a kind. Even though it had been damaged, she would get it restored right after the holidays. He knew she had had the gold curlicues added just for the fun of it looking like an old-fashioned fire engine. But she seemed to be taking her own sweet time.

He was a little nervous about entertaining the preschooler. He hadn't exactly had a lot of experience with children, let alone really young ones. But this kid was very important to Stephanie, so he would become very important to Zach as well.

He loved her, but they hadn't talked about future plans. He knew she longed to make the two children a part of her family, and if their relationship continued, he knew they would become a part of his family, that now included Jewel. He leaned down to scratch her ears. "Good girl."

He paced around a little, glancing out the front time and again. Jewel accompanied him on his rounds. Maybe Stephanie had changed her mind. Maybe something had kept her at the Garrett ranch, but surely she would call to let him know.

He took out his phone multiple times to call her but didn't. He thought it would be distracting if she were driving.

Finally, he called the Garrett ranch landline, and Leah answered. "Hello, Zach. How are you tonight?"

"I'm fine. I was just wondering if Stephanie is still there. She hasn't made it home yet, and I'm getting worried."

"Oh, no. I didn't get to visit with her. I was taking a nap. Sorry."

He heard the regret in her voice. "I'm probably being paranoid, but I just wanted to check and see if she left later than I thought."

"Let me see what time she left. I was totally out of it."

Zach heard her stirring around and then the murmur of conversation.

"Zach?" It was Big Jim who returned to the line. "Stephanie left here almost two hours ago. She took little Cody with her."

A sick, twisting sensation roiled through Zach's gut. "She should have been home long ago."

"Tell you what, son. I'm going to get in my truck right now and head your way. Hope she didn't break down in that old truck of hers."

Zach heaved a deep sigh, knowing she would have called if she were able. "And I'll start driving from here. Hope we find her somewhere in the middle."

"Good goin', Zach. See you in a little while." He hung up abruptly.

Zach tossed on his jacket and grabbed his gloves. He worked them onto his fingers as he strode out the door and approached his truck, Jewel by his side. He held the door open for Jewel before swinging up into the cab. He started the motor, revving it several times. He should have let it warm up a bit but was too anxious to take the time. "C'mon, baby," he whispered and shifted into reverse. He backed the truck in a wide arc and shoved the gear into drive to head out to the main road, and when he reached the highway, he turned in the direction of his uncle's ranch.

His windows fogged up immediately. He turned on the defroster and wiped a clear space in the middle of the windshield with the back of his gloved hand.

The windshield wipers were beating out a rapid tempo, but not as fast as his heart was drumming.

Then, just ahead, Zach saw red and blue lights flashing. He slowed and pulled off the road then stared at Stephanie's red truck. It appeared to have run off the road into a snowbank.

Zach sprang out and sprinted to the truck, Jewel at his side.

"Wait! Hold on there, buddy." A Texas highway patrolman held up both hands, stopping him from getting closer.

"That's my girlfriend's truck. Is she okay?"

"What's your girlfriend's name, sir?" The patrolman blocked his way, although Zach towered over him.

"Stephanie Gayle. She's a firefighter out of Amarillo."

The patrolman nodded. "Come with me, sir." He gestured toward an ambulance parked on the other side of Stephanie's truck.

Zach fell into step alongside the officer, dreading what lay ahead but anxious to be there.

"This guy says he's the truck owner's boyfriend." The patrolman flicked his thumb toward Zach.

Zach turned toward two ambulance attendants and a firefighter standing together at the back of the ambulance, where one held a small boy wrapped in a blanket...*Cody*.

"Where's Stephanie?" he asked the men.

"That's what we'd like to know." The firefighter was one whom Zach had met at the awards banquet, but he couldn't recall his name.

That's when Big Jim pulled up behind the fire engine and got out with Colton and Tyler. The three large men came stomping through the snow, their expressions grim. "What's going on, Zach?" Big Jim demanded.

"I just got here," Zach said. "But where is Stephanie?" He gestured to the inside of the ambulance, but the attendant shook his head.

"She wasn't in the truck when we arrived." He shrugged. "Donnell here used a slim jim to open the truck and get this little boy out."

Donnell frowned, eyeing Zach and the three new arrivals. "Who are you?"

"We're family," Big Jim said, frowning much more fiercely. He went straight over to the attendant who was holding the boy and lifted him out of his arms. "Here you go, Cody. You're all right now."

The boy reached out for Big Jim, who cradled him in his arms.

"Please tell me where Stephanie is," Zach said.

Donnell let out a grunt. "That's what we're all wanting to know. When we arrived, the truck was running, and this little fellow was locked inside."

"But what happened to Stephanie?" Big Jim thundered. His gaze landed on the patrolman who had hung back. "What do you have to say, sonny?"

"Sir? They're thinking there may have been an abduction." He called another officer over. "These people are the victim's family."

The second officer came to where the Garretts were standing. "At this point, we believe that the victim was run off the road and that she was abducted. It appears that she managed to lock the vehicle with the heater running for the sake of the child."

Hearing the woman he loved referred to as "the victim" was like stabbing Zach in the heart. He could hardly draw a breath. "Wha—what's going to happen now? How are we going to find her?"

The older officer looked at Zach sternly, as though assessing his worth.

"Please, sir. If she's been abducted, then you have to tell me how we'll get her back."

Colton stepped forward and stood with his hand on Zach's shoulder. "We want to help."

"The best thing you gentlemen can do is to go home. Leave your contact information with this officer, and let us clear up the scene and determine if a crime has taken place."

A flash of rage erupted in Zach's chest. "No, sir. That's not going to happen. There is no way Stephanie would abandon Cody unless she had no choice. If someone forced her off the road, it's pretty clear she wanted to protect this little boy."

"That sounds exactly like what she would do," Donnell spoke up. "She's like that."

"There was some guy after her," Zach said. "A man she had testified against." His gaze fell on Cody, and he lowered his voice. "The man was this boy's stepfather and murdered his mother."

"Neeley," Donnell said. "You know the case, officer?"

The older officer's brows drew together, as he exchanged a glance with the younger one. "We know the case." He lowered his voice to a growl. "We shot at the bastard last night, but he got away."

––––––—

The truck rolled to a stop at the end of the narrow, rutted road.

Every fiber of Stephanie's being was on high alert.

She flicked a glance at her kidnapper, but he shifted the truck into park and got out of the truck. "Get out!" he ordered.

She was frozen in place, her eyes wide, searching for a means of escape…but to what?

The kidnapper's boots crunched through the snow around to the passenger side. He wrenched the door open. "I said get out. Now!" He reached toward her, but she flinched away.

"I'm getting out," she snapped. "Where are we?"

"It ain't none a yer business. Just get out here."

Stephanie slid down to the snow-encrusted ground, her boots embedding in a few inches of a freshly fallen layer.

Her captor motioned for her to follow as he strode up to the shack and opened the door.

She felt her cell phone vibrate in her pocket and fought the urge to pull it out and scream for help. Somehow, she knew this would probably be the end of her. At least if she had the cell, she might get a chance to use it…or not…

She walked up onto the porch, where rotting planks threatened to give way. "What is this place?" She hoped it was not to be her execution location.

"Get in here," he ordered. "You got work to do."

She stopped in the doorway, her eyes getting used to the darkness. A small kerosene lantern gave scant illumination to the single room. There was bedding thrown on the floor, and there, propped in a corner, was a dark figure.

She was barely breathing as she stared at the man. Long, dark hair and beard shuttered his downcast face. There was a stench of unwashed bodies and something else…something antiseptic.

Her captor shoved her toward the man. "Fix him!"

When the man raised his face, she realized it was Rafe Neeley.

"You!" she gasped.

"Yeah, it's me." He had a ghastly pallor and appeared to be sweating, although the room had no heat. "Good work, little brother. This is the woman who can fix me."

"Fix what?" she asked, trying to take in everything about the small space.

Rafe groaned, apparently in pain. "Curtis, make her fix me."

She realized her kidnapper was the youngest of the Neeley brothers.

He gripped her arm, forcing her to squat close to Rafe. "Make him well. You got to save him. Isn't that what you do?"

Stephanie refused to show her fear. She huffed out an impatient snort. "Well, I need some light. I can't see a thing in here."

Curtis brought the lamp closer and turned up the wick, showing that Rafe's stomach area was covered in a dark stain…and that he held a handgun.

"Wha—what happened to you?"

"Highway patrol," he rasped out. "One of 'em got me..." He sucked in more air. "But I got one of them too."

A violent shiver coiled down her spine. "You got in a firefight with the Texas Highway Patrol?"

"There were only two of them," Curtis said. "My big bro handled himself real good."

"Yeah, I can see that." She stared at the dark stain spreading across Rafe's white undershirt. "Don't you think you better take him to a hospital?"

Curtis backhanded her across the face, causing her to fall on the gritty floor. He cursed her, calling her names and circling the small room as he ranted.

Her cheek throbbed where he had struck her, and fear kept her from trying to get back up.

"Don't be stupid," Rafe said, his voice wheezy. "We don't need no hospital when we got you."

---

Big Jim had commandeered Cody and the car seat. He insisted that he and Tyler should return to the Garrett ranch to await word about what was happening with Stephanie and so Ty could be with his very pregnant wife.

Zach sat in his own truck, letting it idle as he watched the latest crew of techs go over Stephanie's vehicle, looking for clues. Jewel hung over the seat and gave Zach's ear an encouraging lick. She could sense how enraged he was and stood ready to go into battle at his side.

"Sorry about all this, bro." It was Colton, who had climbed in beside Zach.

"It's just not fair," Zach said. "Stephanie's the sweetest woman on the planet. I can't believe anyone would kidnap her."

Colt shook his head. "Me neither, but this Neeley fellow has been giving her grief for a while. He killed his wife in some kind of rage, and her two little kids were there to witness the crime." He gave Zach a squeeze on the shoulder. "What kind of animal would do something like that? As I understand it, Stephanie was with the first responders on the scene. She tried to save the woman and had a confrontation with the killer herself, and then she rescued the two kids."

Zach felt hollow…the way he had when a roadside bomb had exploded, sending him thirty feet across the field. Then it was only his body that had felt the pain. Now he was filled with a soul-wrenching pain that penetrated every fiber of his being.

*Stephanie…*

If he had been with her, he could have prevented her abduction. Indeed, had he been with her, he would have defended her with his very life.

His trance was interrupted by a sharp knocking on the passenger-side window.

Colton rolled it down. "Hey, Dex!"

"Hi Colt. Hey, Zach. I heard about Stephanie."

Zach recognized his old friend, Dexter Shelton. He nodded at him. "Dex."

"Get in," Colt instructed. "Before you freeze your butt off." He indicated the backseat.

"Whoa!" Dex opened the back door but recoiled as Jewel loomed above him. "Nice doggie."

Zach called her down so that Dex could climb in.

Dex settled himself, and Zach got a good look at him. He must have been on duty because he had on a uniform and wore a holstered gun at his side.

"What can you tell us?" Colt asked him.

Dex shook his head. "Not much at this point. They're just gathering clues." He jerked his head toward the group working around Stephanie's truck. "It's the Texas Highway Patrol. They're pretty territorial…but then the guy they're after shot one of their own."

Colt turned to Zach. "Dex here's the sheriff's right-hand man."

"So he tells me." Zach was not in the mood for old home week. He just wanted to find Stephanie.

"You and Miss Stephanie make a pretty fine couple." Dex let out a low whistle. "Pretty fine lady."

Colt frowned and shook his head at Dex. "We're very worried about her. Zach is about to climb out of his skin."

Zach struck the steering wheel with the heel of his hand. "I just wish I could do something!" He wished he had access to some of the tools he had used in Afghanistan when tracking an enemy. Of course, he had Jewel…but he also had drones with infrared electronic tracking to transmit images.

"Easy, bro," Colt said. "We'll just sit tight until we know something."

"You don't understand." Zach raked his fingers through his cropped hair. "I was always the one hunting the bad guy. I led my team to track down insurgents and rescue hostages. Now that it really matters, I can't help her."

"She just disappeared between the Garrett ranch and the Davis ranch," Colton said. "She left with the little boy and was on her way to meet up with Zach."

"Hmm…no word since then?"

"No," Zach said. "I didn't want to call her while she was driving." He shrugged. "You know, with the icy roads, I didn't want to distract her."

Dex leaned forward. "She had her phone with her?"

"Yeah," Zach said. "I finally called her after I talked to Big Jim and he told me how long ago she'd left. I thought she might have had trouble with her old truck. It went to voicemail."

Dex cocked his head to one side. "There wasn't a phone in the truck. She must have it on her."

Zach turned to face Dex. "So, you can track her through her phone?" He heaved a huge sigh, realizing that the real world had kept up with the technology he was used to. "That's a good thing."

"That's a very good thing."

---

"I need supplies," she said. "And lots of gauze."

The bullet had gone completely through Rafe's body, entering in his lower gut and exiting just above his pelvic bone. With the amount of blood he had lost, she was doubtful that she could save him. He needed to be in a hospital.

Curtis dropped a plastic bag filled with bandages on the floor at her side. "I got all this stuff at the drug store. You better make sure he pulls through." The threat in his voice was clear.

Stephanie eased Rafe back onto the pile of bedding. "Just try to relax and let me look at your wound."

"Ay!" Rafe let out a cry as he leaned back.

She carefully raised the undershirt, exposing a wound

that was oozing dark, thick blood. She suspected that the bullet that ripped through Rafe had also ripped through some vital organs. Definitely liver. Probably upper gastrointestinal tract as well. She could smell it. The chances that Rafe would live through the night were slim to none.

All she could do was to attempt to stanch the bleeding and try to convince Curtis to call for an ambulance.

She glanced up at Curtis, who was rocking back and forth anxiously. She wondered if he was on something.

Now she was jammed between two nutcases, and either one could go off at any moment. "This is going to hurt," she said. "A lot."

Rafe nodded, his eyes closed and his teeth gritted. "I am a man," he gasped out. "I am a stallion."

She jammed some of the gauze into the gaping hole in his gut.

Rafe screamed, and Curtis let out a sympathetic whimper. "Do you have to do that?" he asked.

"No. We could call for an ambulance or load him in your truck and take him to the hospital." She eyed him steadily. "In a hospital they would have anesthetic and your brother wouldn't be in pain. Your choice."

"No!" Rafe shouted. "No hospital. No ambulance."

"I'm doing the best I can," she said. "But I don't have anything to anesthetize the wound. I'm trying to stop the bleeding."

Rafe gazed at her, panting out his stale breath. "You go ahead. I'm a man. I can take it." He leaned his head back against the wall. "You jus' go on ahead and stop the bleeding."

She nodded. "You need to turn over so I can work on the exit wound."

To his credit, Rafe attempted to turn but was unable to do so.

Stephanie tried to lift him, but in the end, Curtis had to hold him while she worked on the hole.

"Now what?" Curtis asked.

"We let him rest, and I monitor him for changes." She arranged some of the bedding around Rafe to try to keep him warm.

Curtis was glaring at her, but she did a fast cleanup, gathering the bloody used gauze and stuffing it in the plastic bag. She poured alcohol over her hands to clean them...sort of.

Stephanie leaned against the wall near where Rafe rested. His eyes were closed, and his breathing was easier.

"You fixed him, right?" Curtis asked.

"Not yet," she said. "I stopped the bleeding. We'll wait to see how his body reacts." She gave him a shrug. "Hopefully, he'll improve."

Curtis gave a grunt and settled on the opposite side of the small room, only to slide down to sit with his back against the wall. He held the handgun now, letting it dangle off his fingers.

Stephanie wasn't exactly able to relax, but she wanted to give the appearance of being chill. She had no idea how she was going to get away, but she knew she didn't have a chance as long as Curtis was staring at her so intently.

She made a show of stretching and then drew her knees up. It was cold in the room, but she was dressed warmly; her thick thermal-lined jacket was keeping her fairly well insulated against the temperature. Now, all she had to do was bide her time and look for an opportunity to escape.

# Chapter 21

ZACH'S ANXIETY LEVEL WAS THROUGH THE ROOF, BUT HE gave off the impression of calm intent. He was definitely focused, paying attention to every step of Dexter Shelton's process.

Dex stood outside his patrol car, his phone to his ear, while Zach and Colt circled around the area, pacing and trying to stay warm. Dex had called in to the sheriff's office to see about pinging Stephanie's phone.

Zach had only minimal information, but he heard Dex use words like *triangulate*, so he figured law enforcement knew how to handle tracking Stephanie's cell phone. In the meantime, Zach was practically crawling out of his skin.

"Chill out, man," Colton said. "Dex will locate her."

Zach shook his head. "Not fast enough."

Jewel stood on alert, right on Zach's heels no matter where he paced. Just having her there gave him the impression that he had some control, but his entire body was taut, ready to pounce, if only there was a hint of where the bad guys might be.

"We got her," Dex announced.

"Where?" Zach and Colt rushed to look over his shoulder at a screen with various lines and dots.

"I have the coordinates, so we can get under way. Let's go!" Dex was on the move. He slid into his patrol car and pulled out with Colt beside him and Zach in the backseat with Jewel.

Two additional patrol cars pulled out behind them, sirens blaring. The procession screamed along the highway, heading west.

To Zach, it seemed as though they were crawling along, but the speedometer said otherwise.

Every fiber of his being was urging Dex onward.

"Now, Zach, I gotta warn you…" Dex glanced at him in the rearview mirror. "We located her phone, but that don't mean we located her."

Zach's mouth felt dry. "What do you mean?"

"It means that maybe whoever abducted her found the phone and just tossed it out. Don't go all crazy on me."

"You've got to find her!" Zach gasped out, afraid of what they might find at the end of their quest.

"We'll find her," Colt growled.

Dex silenced the sirens, and the procession turned onto a side road, obviously rarely traveled.

Zach slowed his breathing in preparation for whatever action was to come.

---

He was dead.

Rafe Neeley's lifeless form was resting against Stephanie's arm.

She glanced at Curtis, sitting on the floor across the room. He was still slumped against the wall with his knees drawn up and head drooping against his crossed arms. He appeared to be sleeping. The gun was on the floor between his feet.

Stephanie knew she didn't stand a chance of making it across the room to grab for the weapon, but she couldn't think of anything else to do.

At least she hoped Cody had been rescued by now and that he was safe. She visualized his sweet face and the way he had said he wanted her to be his mommy. She couldn't stop the lone tear that rolled down her cheek. Perhaps one of the Garretts would consider adopting Ivy and Cody if she didn't make it out of this mess.

*Zach!*

Her throat felt tight with emotion. She had been such a loner. All her life she had worked to survive and had gone into the survival business. She was able to operate within a team, but she remained apart. The lone woman on the team. The one with special training, able to perform special tasks.

Now, when her life had turned around...when she had connected with the perfect person...the man she wanted to share her life for eternity...

She understood what was meant when someone said *You complete me*.

Zach was her other half.

He was just coming out of his shell, leaving behind the darkness that he had experienced in Afghanistan. Leaving behind the death and destruction. What would happen to him if he lost her?

"Hey! How is my brother?" Curtis had roused himself and spoke with a thick sluggish voice.

"He's okay, but it's cold. I'm just keeping him warm." She snuggled closer to the remains of Rafe Neeley. "Get some rest and we'll see how he's doing in the morning."

Curtis struggled to his feet. He unwrapped the ragged blanket from around his own shoulders, offering it up. "Here. Put this around him."

Stephanie reached for the blanket, but Curtis stepped past her.

"I'll do it myself." He shoved her aside, leaning over Rafe's body. "Hey! He ain't breathing!"

For a moment, both she and Curtis remained motionless, but that quickly passed.

Curtis leaned down to gather Rafe in his arms, making a strange feral sound, something between a growl and a moan. "You let him die!"

Stephanie sidled out of the way, hoping to reach the handgun he had left behind. "I told you he needed a hospital. You should have taken him." She made a lunge for the gun.

Curtis unceremoniously dropped Rafe and turned on her like a rabid animal.

Just as her fingers closed around the cold metal, Curtis grabbed her ankle and pulled her toward him across the rough and filthy floor.

She grasped the gun in both hands and pointed it toward the man looming over her, but he collapsed down on her, crushing the breath out of her body.

His hand wrapped around hers, forcing the muzzle toward her.

She screamed, but it sounded muted inside the hut. "Get off me," she rasped.

"You killed him!"

"You killed him," she countered. "He needed serious medical attention."

Curtis's eyes were closed into angry slits. "You let him die." He sucked in a ragged breath. "And now you're gonna die too."

Her finger was on the trigger, but the big ham-like hand wrapped around hers prevented her from pulling it.

Curtis's other hand went for her throat, which was well insulated with layers of sweater, scarf, and coat.

The image of Zach wrapping the scarf around her neck flashed into her brain.

Stephanie's jaw tightened as she struggled to squeeze the trigger, hoping to hit her attacker.

There was a furious scratching at the door.

Curtis jerked his head in that direction just as Stephanie gathered the strength to pull the trigger.

The loud explosion deafened her, but another crash sounded as the door to the hut splintered inward and Jewel romped in, her fangs bared. She sank her teeth into Curtis's arm, but Zach lifted him off Stephanie and body-slammed him to the middle of the floor.

More men poured into the room, bringing with them a cacophony of voices shouting and boots falling hard on the wood floor.

Stephanie, still clinging to the handgun, inched away from the melee taking place before her. Suddenly strong hands gripped her, lifted her, and held her sheltered from the conflict.

"Steph! Are you all right? You have blood on you. Where are you hurt?" Zach let out a fierce growl. "I will kill that guy."

"I—I'm okay, Zach. It must be his blood."

Zach heaved an audible sigh and gripped her against him. "I've been going crazy. I can't lose you."

Stephanie's arms gripped Zach's neck, the handgun still in one hand.

"Whoa! Let me take that," Dex said as he gently disarmed her.

She buried her face against Zach's chest and let the adrenaline calm down.

He patted her rhythmically and rested his cheek against her hair. "I'm so sorry, baby. I should have gone with you to pick up Cody. I'll never let you out of my sight again."

She raised her face in horror. "Oh no! Cody! Is he all right? Did you find him?"

He gave a gentle chuckle. "Sure did. Right where you left him."

"Ooh," she huffed out her relief. "Where is he now?"

"My uncle confiscated Cody, so he is under the fierce protection of Big Jim Garrett himself."

The deputies were in the process of removing Curtis from the hut. He had been wounded in his shoulder, bleeding but defiant. He still yelled and struggled, but he was in handcuffs, and several armed lawmen had their hands on him. When he was outside, the noise level dropped considerably.

Dex leaned over the pile of bedding. "Hey, this guy's dead." He looked over his shoulder at Stephanie. "Did you kill him? Just askin'…"

She managed to compose her face, brushed away the tears, and glowered at Dex. "No, I did not. I swear I'm going to smack you, Dex."

Dex turned around, grinning. "Well, from what I could tell, when we entered the room, you were the one holding the gun, and you got off a shot at that lunk in the squad car." He cocked his head. "Pretty tough, girl."

Reluctantly, a smile spread across her face.

Zach pulled her even closer. "Hey, Dex. Lay off. My girlfriend wears combat boots."

—◆—

Dex dropped them off at the Garrett ranch, where
Stephanie was reunited with Cody, who cried and
wouldn't let go of her. This set off Ivy, who also started
wailing, so Stephanie just sat on the floor in the dining
room with both children in her lap.

Zach leaned up against the wall, gazing at her. He
felt limp and hollow, all emotion having been wrung out
of him, but his attention was focused on the beautiful
woman cradling small children in her arms. He knew his
future would forever be tied to hers.

Leah sat at the table nearby. "We were all worried
about you, Stephanie. I'm so glad you're all right."

Jewel settled right next to Stephanie, resting her head
on her paws. To most people she would appear to be at
rest, but Zach knew Jewel was in guard mode.

Stephanie stroked her hand over Jewel's head. "You
were such a brave girl. Did you know she ran in and bit
the bad man on the arm?"

Cody's eyes grew round. "She bited the bad man?"

"Yes, she did. Jewel ran in and got him." She glanced
up at Zach and winked. "Of course, Zach was right
behind her. He helped too."

"Hey, I kicked in the door…so Jewel could run in
and bite him."

Big Jim and Colton sat at the table across from Tyler
and Leah. Fern Davis was bustling around the kitchen
with Misty. They were preparing food for Stephanie, as
well as Zach and Colton, who had been too busy with
her rescue to eat.

"Well, I'm just thankful that we're all here together,"

Big Jim said. "Do you realize tomorrow is Christmas Eve? Beau and Dixie are bringing Ava over to celebrate Christmas with us." He raised his coffee cup to Stephanie. "I'm glad you're with us."

Zach let out a grunt. "Glad to be here, Uncle Jim. Of course, my truck is still at the sheriff's office, so we'll have to impose on you until someone can run me over to pick it up."

"Not a problem," Big Jim said. "Stephanie, your little truck got some front-end damage, so I had it towed to the mechanic over in Langston. You can check with him, but he's gonna be closed up until after Christmas."

Stephanie's lips tightened. "I think I'm giving up on that truck. It was fun, but I think I would like something newer…with a backseat."

"Good plan," Zach whispered.

Big Jim nodded. "You two just make yourselves comfortable. I want you to stay over through Christmas. We're all going to church together…as a family."

"Yes, sir," Zach said. He smiled at Stephanie, aching to be alone with her…knowing they would not be alone for a while.

"You young folks come sit down here at the table, while Misty an' me get your vittles served up." Gran carried a basket of hot rolls and a covered butter dish to the table, followed by Misty carrying three filled plates.

"Hope you like it," Misty said, a hint of pride in her voice, as she placed a plate in front of her husband. "I made the meatloaf."

Zach pushed away from the wall and lifted both children off Leah. "Let's eat. I'm starving."

She climbed to her feet. "Me too, and I love meatloaf."

She took a seat next to Leah. "Oh, this smells fantastic. Seriously, Misty, this is awesome."

Misty beamed with pride. "Miz Fern is teaching me how to cook." She looked at Colton, who was digging into the meatloaf.

He gave her a thumbs-up. "It's great, babe." And he continued stuffing his face.

Fern also looked particularly pleased.

When Stephanie picked up her fork, Zach handed the children off and took a seat beside her. She surreptitiously slipped her hand onto his thigh to give it a squeeze.

*Oh, yes…*

Stephanie noticed Leah's lips were pressed tight together and her breathing was somewhat ragged.

Stephanie removed her hand from Zach's thigh, turning toward Leah. "Are you having any discomfort?"

Leah's brow furrowed. "Not exactly pain. Just a little uncomfortable. Maybe I overate." She flashed a smile. "That meatloaf was excellent."

Stephanie nodded but still looked concerned. "Maybe you ought to check in with your doctor. Have you been seeing Cami Ryan?"

Leah cocked her head to one side, smiling. "Who else? We're pretty lucky to have such an awesome doctor right in Langston."

"Amen to that," Big Jim said. "And a doctor willing to make house calls." He nodded at Tyler. "Maybe you ought to give Dr. Ryan a call…just to check in?"

"Sure, Dad. Just to check in." Tyler pulled his cell phone out of his shirt pocket and selected the right number. All this with his left hand, while his right continued to rub little circles in the middle of Leah's back. "Voicemail," he said. He waited a second and then began leaving a message. "Doctor Ryan, this is Tyler Garrett. Just checking in with you. Leah is a little uncomfortable. Just wanted to let you know." He pushed a few more buttons and slipped the phone back in his pocket.

"I'm sure she'll call us back soon," Leah said.

Big Jim had been holding Ivy, who was not quite asleep on his shoulder, but Fern Davis approached with her arms outstretched.

"Let me put this little 'un to bed," she said. "She's out for the night."

"I think we wore her out," he said. "I'll carry her. Just open the doors for me." He slipped off the chair and followed Fern down the hallway to put the little girl to bed.

Colton shook his head. "Good thing you're having this baby, Leah. I think Dad is loving playing grandpa to those two little houseguests."

"Well, he can be grandpa all he wants," Ty said. "Gracie is ready to play big sister too." He gave Leah a kiss on her temple. "We may have to take a number to get any time with our new son or daughter."

Leah leaned her head against his shoulder. "That sounds good to me. I can't tell you how happy Gracie and I are to be a part of this family." She grimaced and straightened, reaching to grip the edge of the table.

"Are you having contractions?" Stephanie asked.

Leah smiled and shook her head. "No way. I'm not due until after the first of the year." She rubbed her lower back. "I just did too much today. Gran's been trying to sit on me, but I got to do a little decorating today. I put up some strands of tinsel on the tree and tried to give the room that Cody and Ivy are staying in a little Christmas spirit."

Ty looked at her, concern etched on his face. "Take it easy, Leah. You know you're supposed to be resting."

"Oh, a woman can only take so much *resting*." She made quote marks in the air. "I just wanted to be a part of the holiday preparations. Is that a crime?"

"I understand," Stephanie said. "Getting ready for Christmas is almost as much fun as Christmas itself." She gave a cute little shrug that Zach found endearing.

Leah heaved a deep sigh. "Thank you. I'm glad somebody understands."

Stephanie pushed her empty plate away. "I wish somebody would explain to me what happens during a Garrett family Christmas. What are the traditions I should expect?"

"Yeah, that would be good for me, too." Misty sat down beside Colt and looked up at him with a loving expression. "My little brother Mark and I are new to the Garrett family too."

"Aw, honey." Colt was still shoveling food in his mouth. "Nothing special happens. You know after our mother passed away, the joy was just sucked out of the holidays."

Ty nodded. "Yeah. When we were little kids, it was all-out for Christmas, but without Mom, we just went to church, exchanged gifts—mostly very practical, by the way—and that was about it."

Colt pointed his fork at Tyler and squinted his eyes. "You know, I think it's all about the women and children. Dad hasn't been all that much into holidays for just the Garrett menfolk."

Tyler leaned back, a little grin on his face. He spread his arms in a wide gesture. "You're right. The old man wants to make the holidays special for the kids and for the women." He circled his arm around Leah. "See what you did, baby? You kick-started our papa. Got him right in his heart."

Colt nodded. "Yup. Leah started it all. She kept Tyler from abandoning the ranch, and she brought Gracie into his life." He embraced Misty with both arms. "And then I brought Misty and Mark into the family."

Ty gave him a thumbs-up. "And finally, our little brother, Beau, reconnected with his long-lost high school sweetheart...and found out he was a father. Ava was like the cherry on top of the cake."

"That sounds like a nice story," Stephanie said. "So all three sons are married with children, one way or another."

"Man with three sons now has a family of nine," Zach said.

"More than that," Colt said. "When your mom sold off the ranch, Dad was pretty ticked. His brother had worked that ranch most of his life, and your father wanted to pass it on to you, Zach...so now that you've come home, Dad feels like the Garrett family is all together again." He spread his hands. "Like it or not, bro...you're one of us."

Zach shrugged. "I'm good with that. When I was a kid, I hung out here more than I did at home...but I always thought I would have the ranch. It kills me that she sold it."

Stephanie grabbed his hand. "So sorry. I didn't realize—"

"I just always thought I would come home and be a rancher. Other than being a soldier, it's all I know." The image of his squad with all the original members played in Zach's brain. He heaved a deep sigh, regretting the men lost...the men injured. He swallowed hard. "And now I'm home."

Stephanie was watching him. "I'm really glad you're here." Her voice was soft and turned Zach's insides to jelly.

When Zach and Stephanie were alone in the room they had been assigned for the Christmas holiday, he lost no time in offering to help her remove her excess clothing. She sat on the bed and gazed up at him expectantly.

Jewel lay on the area rug beside the bed. He hoped she would stay there and not jump into bed with them. At least it was a queen-size bed, so it would be roomier in case it became a threesome.

He knelt on the floor in front of Stephanie. He unlaced her boots and removed them, holding her feet in his hands for a moment. "How do you manage to walk on these little things, anyway?"

"It's a balancing act." She laughed and leaned back on her elbows. "That feels good. You can rub my feet for as long as you want."

"Yes, ma'am. I can do that." He massaged her feet, watching as she relaxed and let the horrors of the day slip away. "You know I'm happy to be with you, but you're wearing entirely too much clothing."

"You're one to talk. Let me get you out of that flannel shirt. Come here, cowboy." She grabbed his shirt with both hands and pulled him toward her. Slowly, she unbuttoned his shirt and pushed it off his shoulders.

He stood up to finish removing it, exposing his

muscled torso clad in a white cotton sleeveless undershirt.

Lifting the bottom edge of the undershirt, she rubbed her fingers over the taut ridges lined up along his abdomen.

Her touch stirred him. So did the way she smelled. Something floral with spice.

She kissed him just above his navel, her tongue exploring his abs.

*Oh, yeah!* Zach's libido surged into overdrive. He couldn't believe he was being seduced by this beautiful woman. Could she possibly want him as much as he wanted her? Fumbling under her clothing, he managed to get everything unhooked, unbuttoned, and discarded in short order. Her beauty astounded him.

He caressed her long, soft hair.

She looked up at him and leaned her cheek into his palm. "I am so in love with you."

"Oh, Stephanie. I'm in love with you, too." Then he threaded his fingers through her hair and leaned down to kiss her.

She unhooked his belt buckle and stripped the belt from his jeans then slid the zipper open. He took over from there, divesting himself of his boots and jeans.

When he reached for her, she leaned back onto the bed, drawing him down on top of her. He caught himself in time to keep from crushing her. He kneed her legs apart, and her silken thighs opened then embraced him as she drew him closer.

Zach kissed her lips and her neck and worked his way down her body, paying homage to each breast with his mouth and tongue. She arched up to him, making little sounds of pleasure. But he kissed down her ribs and her flat stomach. She was trembling when he investigated further, gently exploring the moist folds. He found her tiny bud and abraded it with his tongue, urging her to climax. Her gasps and whimpers spurred him on.

When her luscious body tensed, and little spasms overtook her, he intensified the pressure until she relaxed back onto the bed, breathing heavily. "Oh, that was—that was so good."

Zach chuckled as he donned a condom. "I'm just getting started." As he entered her, Stephanie's warm, wet flesh devoured him. Each thrust took him to a new plane of delight. Their bodies were attuned to each other's pleasure.

When they were done, they lay together, enmeshed in a tight embrace, a puzzle of arms and legs wound together. They were spent but unwilling to break apart the magic that they had become.

# Chapter 22

STEPHANIE'S HEART WAS STILL POUNDING WHEN SHE SETTLED into Zach's arms. This day had brought so many different emotions together, from anger and fear to joy and passion.

Zach held her close, cradling her in his strong arms.

She was safe. She was loved because wherever Zach chose to be, that was where she would be as well. Her future was forever bound to his.

There was a sudden pounding on the door to the bedroom.

Stephanie's first thought was fire. She rose up out of bed and grabbed for her jeans.

"What's going on?" Zach called out.

"It's Leah," Ty said. "I think she's in labor... She wants Stephanie."

"I'll be right there." Stephanie had most of her clothes back on. She pulled a sweatshirt over her head as she went to the door, her feet bare.

"I'll be right there," Zach said as he too scrambled for his quickly discarded items of clothing.

Stephanie threw the door open to find Ty pacing back and forth in the hallway.

"Please, she wants you." He grabbed her by the hand and almost dragged her to the room he shared with his wife.

"Did you call Doctor Ryan?" she asked.

Ty raked his fingers through his thick, dark hair.

"Yes, but it went straight to voicemail. I—I guess we could call an ambulance to take us to Amarillo...but—"

"But that's a long way." Stephanie paused in the doorway, surveying her friend who was obviously uncomfortable.

Leah was in bed, and she looked scared. "Hey, Stephanie. Thanks for coming down. I don't remember feeling this bad when I gave birth to Gracie."

Stephanie sat on the edge of the bed and patted Leah's arm. "I think it's natural to forget the discomfort. It's nature's way of ensuring that the species continues."

Leah tried to laugh, but it sounded more like a whimper. "Oh, I'm just sorry that I'm feeling this way. I'm not due until after the first of the year."

"Babies come when they come." Stephanie shrugged. "Are you sure you're in labor? It could be Braxton-Hicks contractions."

"I don't know... Maybe. I—I need to go to the bathroom." Leah struggled to swing her legs off the bed.

"I'll help you." Stephanie and Tyler helped her to her feet.

She made it to the bathroom, but on the way back, she reached out for the wall. A gush of fluid stopped her in her tracks. "Oh! My water broke!"

Stephanie grinned. "Well, that settles it. You're definitely in labor."

"What shall I do? Do you want me to go warm up the truck?" Tyler asked.

"Not unless you want your wife to give birth in your truck. Now let's get her back to bed." Stephanie was hoping that Leah's childbirth would not have any complications.

—◦◦◦—

Big Jim measured coffee into the coffeepot. It would be a long night, and his middle son was a basket case. He was thankful that Zach was standing by, calm and dependable…as always.

Leah's grandmother and Stephanie were with Leah. It seemed that the town doctor was making a house call with another patient. Big Jim turned to see his oldest son, Colton, exchange a glance with Zach and shake his head.

"You need to calm down, little brother. The baby is going to come when it's going to come. That's what Stephanie said." Colton waved Tyler over. "Come on and sit down. You're wearing out the floor."

Tyler turned to him with an anguished expression on his face. "You don't understand. She's in pain…and I can't do a thing about it." He slumped onto a chair across the table from his brother.

Big Jim sent Colt a slight shake of his head before turning to address Tyler. "Listen here, boy. I know how you're feelin' right now. I watched your mother give birth to the three of you rascals, and it don't get much easier." He carried the pot of fresh coffee to the table.

Zach took a seat beside Ty and gave him a slap on the shoulder. "I think you two had great timing. It's wonderful that we will have a baby for Christmas."

There was a moment of silence while each man considered the implications of that statement.

"You're right," Big Jim said. "I think there's an important precedent for Christmastime births." He refilled all the cups before placing the coffeepot on the counter.

"Come sit down, Uncle," Zach said. "It's after midnight, so take a load off." He pulled out a chair for Big Jim.

"Christmas Eve." Big Jim sat beside Zach and reflected on the fine young men in his family. "I wonder how they're doing in there."

Fern Davis came down the hall so silently no one heard her until she was near the table. "You need to come be with your wife, Ty. Leah is askin' for you."

Ty looked like he might pass out. He was decidedly pale. "Is something wrong?"

Fern waved her hand to indicate he was way off base. "Oh, pshaw! She's jus' fine. Leah jus' wants you to be with her. Y'know, ya did have somethin' to do with this situation." She let out a raucous laugh. "Ya might as well be in on the big finish." She grinned from ear to ear and made her way back to the bedroom wing.

"What are you waitin' for, son?" Big Jim asked. "Go be with your wife."

Tyler stood up uncertainly.

Big Jim realized that this was probably the first time he had seen his rebellious middle son exhibit real fear. "Leah needs you, Ty. You gotta be strong…for her."

Tyler sucked in a deep breath and expelled it forcefully. "For Leah," he said and headed down the hall to follow Fern.

The three men remaining at the table stared at each other.

"How about you and Misty?" Zach asked. "Any kids in your future?"

Colt shook his head. "We've talked about starting a family, but Misty is pretty young, so we'll probably hold off a couple of years."

Another long silence.

"What about you, Zach? Any plans with Miss Stephanie?" Big Jim gave him a questioning look. "You two seem to be quite an item."

A muscle in Zach's jaw twitched. He took a sip of his coffee. Big Jim thought he was stalling for time.

Zach carefully set the cup down. "I think the world of Stephanie. I just wish I had more to offer her. She deserves a lot better."

Big Jim felt a rush of compassion for his nephew. He recalled when he and his wife were just starting out. They had nothing but hearts filled with love and willingness to work for a better future. He wanted to encourage Zach, but he knew he was comparing himself to Colton, Tyler, and Beau, who were recipients of their father's hard work. His mouth tightened. He couldn't fault his sons. They had always done their share of work on the ranch. They had definitely paid their dues, and he was certain they would continue to work their butts off for the family.

"Don't you worry yourself about it, Zach. I'm pretty certain that beautiful little firefightin' lady would think you were a pretty good catch, judging by the way she looks at you."

That elicited a slight smile as Zach stirred his coffee. "She's the best," he said.

"Don't you think you owe it to her to give her the choice? She's a pretty smart young woman. She knows what she wants."

"You trying to get me married off, Uncle Jim?" Zach looked up with a smile.

Big Jim stared at him long and hard. "Believe me, son. All I want is for you to be happy."

—⁓—

"It's a boy!" Stephanie announced. She held the newborn and looked around at the others.

Leah lay back on the pillow, exhausted. "Oh, he's beautiful!"

Tyler held her hand, and Stephanie could swear she saw tears glinting in his eyes. He kissed Leah's fingers and then leaned over to kiss her forehead. "Love you, babe."

"Aww…ain't that tha purtiest lil boy you ever seen?" Fern stood beside Stephanie, gazing at the infant with tears rolling down her cheeks. She clutched a large bath towel to her chest.

"Can I have that towel?" Stephanie asked.

"Shore thing." Fern unfolded the length of towel and offered it to Stephanie, who wrapped the perfect little human in it.

"There you go, little one." Stephanie gazed at the baby, feeling both pride and envy. She had brought forth a human life, but now she wanted to have a child of her own. Swallowing hard, she wished for a Christmas miracle where she would be able to become the mother that Ivy and Cody deserved.

But Miss Dyer was right.

Stephanie was single, and she didn't have a home of her own…and there was no doubt that her job was dangerous.

"Do you have a name picked out for your son?" Stephanie handed the baby to Leah, who cuddled him against her shoulder.

"Oh, isn't he just the sweetest thing?" She looked up at Tyler, who placed one of his big hands on the baby's head, just gently cradling it.

"Yes...yes, he is." Ty's voice sounded thick and filled with emotion. "Um, we talked about names but never really nailed anything down."

Stephanie shrugged. "It will come. You'll figure out the perfect name."

Leah was beaming with pride. "I just can't believe we did this."

"Look at all that dark hair," Fern said.

Stephanie tilted her head to one side. "Do you think you should tell the other people who are waiting for the news?"

"Sure," Leah said. "Invite them in."

"I'll go git 'em," Fern offered. "If they's still awake." She left the room.

Almost immediately the door opened again, with Big Jim filling the doorway. "Where's the new Garrett?" His face was almost bursting with a wide grin.

"Here, Dad," Tyler said. "Come see your new grandson."

"Hot damn! A grandson." Big Jim reached out a finger to stroke the baby's small hand. "Amazing! Best Christmas present ever. A son for you, Tyler."

"And a grandson for you, Dad."

Stephanie felt a pang of longing. She wasn't envious of the happy new parents, but she hoped that there would come a time in her life when she could enjoy the same experience.

Zach came into the room, silently slipping his arms around her.

She was overcome with exhaustion, and let her head rest against Zach's strong chest.

He kissed the top of her head, cradling her against him. "You did it," he whispered.

"I had to," she said.

"I know what his name is," Leah said. She looked at Tyler, grinning. "This is our son, James Tyler Garrett."

Tyler seemed to consider this and then nodded. "I like it."

Big Jim made a quick swipe of his eyes with his thumb and wiped it on his shirt. "I think that's about the nicest thing anyone's ever done for me."

"Merry Christmas to all," Stephanie said. She reached her arms out and herded everyone toward the door. "And to all a good night."

---

They slept late.

It was the aroma of bacon and coffee that awoke them.

"I'm starving," Stephanie murmured.

"Me too," Zach said. "Let's see if they cooked enough for us." It was difficult to consider getting out of bed. Waking up with Stephanie in his arms, cuddled in the curve of his body, gave him more pleasure than he could ever recall. Reluctantly, he threw off the comforter and forced himself to peel away from her body.

"Rise and shine." Stephanie gasped. "I'm so tired. My body feels like it's made of lead."

Zach grazed his palm down her shoulder all the way to her hip. "Feels pretty good to me. Soft and smooth."

"Do not turn me on," she said. "I'm dead meat."

Zach chuckled and traced a line of kisses down her neck and shoulder. "I know you're exhausted. Late night last night."

"Late night this morning," she responded. "I need food. It's Christmas Eve, and I need to be up." She slid her legs off the bed and pulled herself to a sitting position, her eyes still closed.

Jewel sat up and whined softly.

Stephanie reached out to ruffle the fur around the dog's neck. "G'morning, Jewel."

"Um—maybe I can bring you breakfast in bed."

"No, thanks anyway. I have to spend time with Cody and Ivy. I want them to have a great Christmas."

"I understand," he said. "Whatever you need to make that happen, you can count on me." He kissed her forehead.

She opened her eyes, gazing up at him with such a beautiful expression that he was filled with a warmth in his chest.

He recalled the words Big Jim had said to him last night. He wondered just how deep her feelings ran. In his heart, he wanted to be able to offer her more.

"Steph, you know that I love you. Right?"

She looked a little puzzled but nodded. "And you know I love you. Right?"

He grinned. "You bet."

"So, what does that mean?"

"I just wanted you to know that I'm serious about you. When I get my life figured out, I want us to think about…about…"

"Your life?" She expelled an impatient breath. "Don't be such a wimp. There are no guarantees in life. Just tell me what you're thinking."

He looked around the room, taking in the unmade bed, their hastily tossed aside clothing. Not what he pictured as a romantic setting. "Well, this is not how I pictured it…" He gave a slight shake of his head. "No, you deserve better. I'll wait for a better time."

"If I weren't starving and wanting to see the kids, I would so beat it out of you." She gave him a playful punch on the arm... Still, it packed a punch.

Zach rubbed his bicep as Stephanie got up out of bed and headed for the bathroom. "Merry Christmas."

---

When Stephanie and Zach made it to the kitchen, they were the last to arrive.

"How do you want yer eggs?" Fern called by way of greeting. "I kin make 'em over easy or scrambled. What's yer favorite?" She stood at the stove with a skillet and spatula in her hands.

"Um—whatever is easy," Stephanie said.

"Same here." Zach snagged a slice of bacon from a platter on the table.

"You kids set yourselves right down, an' I'll bring your plates." Fern pointed them to the table with her spatula.

Stephanie took a chair beside Cody and across from Big Jim. Cody was sitting at the table on a thick book, while Big Jim held little Ivy on one knee and was bouncing her gently.

Zach watched as Stephanie interacted with the two young children. Her face glowed as she chatted with them both. She was a natural born mother.

He wondered if she would be willing to have some kids with the last name of Garrett. *Yes*. He could picture his future with her...with them because it appeared it would be a package deal. Well, he came with some baggage of his own.

He sat at one end of the table and patted his knee.

Jewel settled herself close to his chair and rested her face on his thigh. He listened to the conversations going on around him, basking in the wealth of being a part of a great family. *A Garrett is a Garrett.*

Misty carried their plates to the table. "Eat up," she advised. "Everyone else has cleaned their plates." She took a seat beside her husband, and Colton reached for her hand.

It was easy to see that they were deeply in love.

Zach lifted his glass of orange juice and saluted Stephanie with it.

She gave him a wink because Cody was talking to her and Zach didn't want to interrupt their moment. He would have lots of time with her, but he wasn't sure what was going to happen with her quest to adopt. From what she had said, it seemed hopeless, but he would support her.

He ate silently, listening to the others. Misty's younger brother, Mark, was engaged in conversation with Gracie. She seemed to be thrilled to be a big sister.

"He's just the sweetest little baby," she said. "But I don't know what little boys like to play with."

Mark assured her he would help her figure it out.

Tyler sat sipping his coffee and chatting with Big Jim about his new son, James Tyler Garrett. It seemed that Leah was already referring to the newborn as *JT*. "She thought it was better than calling him *Jim* or *Jimmy*." He made a face. "Or, God forbid, Little Jim."

Big Jim cocked his head to one side, as though considering this. "That sounds reasonable."

Stephanie seemed to be recovering from her late-night endeavors. "So, what's the drill around here?" she asked. "Do you celebrate together on Christmas Eve or Christmas morning? I need to get my presents over here," she whispered.

"Well, we go to church on Christmas Eve," Big Jim said. "And we wake up on Christmas morning to find out what Santy Claus brought us." He reached over to tickle Cody on the tummy. "I wonder what Santy is gonna bring you, big boy?"

Cody giggled but reached out to Stephanie. "Mommy!" he said.

Everyone at the table looked at Stephanie.

She pressed her lips together and gave Cody a pat on the shoulder, then became very focused on her food. It seemed she couldn't respond to that term. Maybe she wanted it too much.

Zach finished his breakfast. "I need to take Stephanie to get a change of clothes and pick up some—uh, some other things." He didn't want to say the word *presents* with the little ones so attentive.

Stephanie nodded. She gathered their dishes and took them to the kitchen while Zach collected their outerwear.

It was cold outside but still. Not a breath of air stirred the tree branches. It looked as though they had stepped into a beautiful winter painting…a very cold one.

Their breath left trails of vapor as they trudged through the snow to the truck. Once inside, Zach apologized for failing to warm it up first.

"No problem," she said. "I'm well insulated." She held up her gloved hands.

He pulled out onto the highway and headed for Fern's small ranch.

Stephanie pulled a CD out of her pocket and slipped

it into the player. "Tyler gave me one of his releases. I've only heard a couple of these songs on the radio."

The first was a romantic ballad, and Zach could appreciate that Tyler actually had a great voice. It had been a surprise to him that Colton's tagalong little brother was a country music star.

When they arrived at Fern's little place, it looked especially forlorn. Snow was piled on the roof and had drifted onto the porch.

Stephanie was gazing out the windshield. "Do you think we're going to be able to stay here, Zach? I mean, for the long haul?" She blushed prettily. "I—I guess that it was pretty presumptive of me to assume that you would want to share a long haul with me."

"Of course I want to be with you. Silly girl." He let the truck idle, putting off going inside the unheated house. "Look, Steph. I wish I had more to offer you. I thought I would have my parents' ranch when the time came. My dad always talked about how much he wanted me to carry on there…but it's gone."

"I'm so sorry. I know that must have meant a lot to you."

He swallowed hard. "I just need to figure out what else I can do. It's not fair to you, when my future is so uncertain. I want to build a future with you, but you deserve so much more."

"You do realize I would be dead if you hadn't kicked in the door to that shack? Talk about a future. I had none." She gave a slight shiver.

He slipped an arm around her. "I was a crazy man. I couldn't imagine life without you." He paused. "So, do you want to spend your lifetime with me?"

"Wait a minute. Is this a proposal?"

"Pretty lame, huh?"

She rested her head against his shoulder. "Yeah, but kinda sweet too."

"I can do better. Just give me a little time."

"Yes."

"You'll give me time to get this right?"

"No, I'm saying yes. I want to spend my life with you, but I hope you know that I am going to try to adopt Cody and Ivy. Is that part of your plan?"

"Sure is. I hope you include Jewel in our future. She was my first love."

Stephanie laughed, her voice filling the interior of the truck, swelling Zach's heart in his chest.

"So, we're good?" he asked.

"We're fantastic, but we better run in and get our stuff. I want to spend as much time with the children as possible…you know, before they have to go back."

# Chapter 23

STEPHANIE HAD BEEN ON AN EMOTIONAL ROLLER COASTER. She had been run through the wringer enough to last a lifetime.

But she was elated.

She and most of the Garrett family were in the very packed church, singing a hymn. Due to the frigid weather, Cody and Ivy were snugged into bed under Fern's watchful eye. Leah and Tyler stayed at home with their new son, but Gracie stood beside Big Jim, who had his hand on her shoulder. He looked every bit the proud father and grandfather.

Colton and Misty were sharing the same hymnal, but Mark had his own. Stephanie thought they made a very attractive family.

She glanced up at Zach, who had a surprisingly good baritone voice. He held their hymnal for her to follow, but he seemed to know all the words to the song by heart.

Stephanie had been alone in one way or another most of her life. Now she had a chance to be merged into a large and loving family.

*Married.*

She was afraid to say the word aloud. Afraid that would break the spell. Afraid that she had been mistaken and perhaps Zach hadn't meant to propose. He asked for more time to "get it right," but she had pushed.

The hymn ended, and people were taking their seats.

Zach put his arm around her shoulder, and this made her feel safe and secure. She blinked fast to keep from tearing up.

The preacher began his sermon, one perfectly chosen for the night before Christmas, but Stephanie was silently praying for her own Christmas miracle.

---

Christmas morning Zach took Jewel out early. The crisp, frigid air burned his lungs and bit his cheeks, but Jewel was invigorated.

Zach wished he had a ball to throw for her but made a tight snowball and threw it for her to chase. He thought the dog was grinning.

"Come on, girl. Freezin' my cojones off. Let's go inside."

She fell into step beside him immediately, returning to her military-dog mode.

He reached down to ruffle the thick fur around her neck. "Good girl."

Walking inside through the back door felt as though he had penetrated a heat barrier. The heat was painful against his chilled cheeks and ears.

"You look cold, cowboy." Stephanie slipped both arms around his torso. "I'll warm you up."

"Merry Christmas," he said.

"Right back atcha. So are we engaged now?" She was grinning, but Zach sensed his response was very important.

"We're engaged to be engaged." He gave her a quick kiss. "When we're engaged, you'll know because of that official engagement ring on your finger."

She tilted her head to one side, looking decidedly disappointed, but she plastered on a smile. "I guess that will have to do, then." She turned away and crossed the room to open the refrigerator. "I thought I might start breakfast, since Leah is recovering from childbirth and Fern is helping with the baby."

"You mean James Tyler Garrett?"

She laughed. "Yeah, that guy. Sounds very imposing." She took a pound of thick-sliced bacon out of the refrigerator. "I wonder if they're going to call him Little Jim."

Zach laughed at that. "I sincerely hope not. He'll probably be a moose like his father and grandfather."

"And you? You're pretty moosey too." She laid strips of bacon on a baking sheet.

"It's a Garrett thing. How about if I make coffee?" He set about this task and had just gotten it started when Big Jim came into the kitchen.

"Merry Christmas," he said. "Glad you two are up early. Zach, I wanted to talk to you." He gestured for Zach to follow him.

Zach and Stephanie exchanged a glance, but he trailed behind his uncle to his private office.

Once inside, Big Jim took his seat behind the big desk and motioned Zach to a chair across from him.

Big Jim was so serious that Zach wondered if he was in some kind of trouble. "What can I do for you, sir?"

Big Jim smiled and folded his hands on top of his desk. "I just wanted to have a little talk, son…just the two of us." He took an envelope out of the top desk drawer and arranged it carefully in front of him. "I know my brother wasn't planning on passing on at such a young age…" His brows drew together, and he huffed out a breath. "And I know he was planning on you taking over the ranch. He said that from the time you was born."

"Yes, sir. He always talked about me continuing to work the land."

"And then—" He heaved out a huge sigh. "Your mother didn't let me know she was having problems right away."

"Problems?" Zach leaned forward, frowning.

Big Jim gave a little shrug. "She said she wanted to sell off everything and go live in Fort Worth." His expression grew even darker. "But the truth was she had gotten way behind in the taxes." He shook his head, his mouth tight. "And she owed a lot of people. The feed store. The propane company."

"I—I don't understand," Zach said. "We never had a lot of debt as a family."

Big Jim's gaze softened. "I know, son. But it was your father who was managing the ranch. When he got sick, Adele just couldn't handle it...but she didn't come to me until she was really under water."

Zach shook his head. "It wasn't her fault. I should have come home when Dad passed away. The ranch was just too much for her. I understand why she wanted to get out from under everything."

"Yeah, I can understand too. Just too much for the woman, even though I told her we would help her." He gave a slight shake of his head. "You got a good heart, boy." Big Jim slid the envelope across the desk toward Zach. "But in your father's will, he deeded the entire property to you, with me as your adviser and sort of guardian in your absence. Adele had a life interest in the ranch, but essentially, the land was to be yours. My job was to look after your interests."

Zach pointed to the envelope. "What's in here, sir?"

"It's the deed to your ranch. It's all your property."

Zach half rose and then sank back into his chair. "But my mother told me she had sold the ranch. She wouldn't lie to me."

"She didn't lie, son. I arranged the supposed sale through the bank. She thinks a big corporation bought it." He shook his head. "She had no idea about the value of the property, but she wanted to get to Fort Worth so bad, she really didn't quibble about the price."

"I—I don't understand."

Big Jim spread his hands. "My brother didn't expect to die young. He deeded the ranch to you directly because he knew you'd take care of your mama. You owned the property from the moment he passed on."

"But my mother—"

"I just gave her money to get relocated and buy her new place. Your daddy made sure there was an insurance policy that would provide her an annuity for life. She'll be fine."

Zach swallowed hard. "I—I didn't know anything about all this."

"Your papa set it all up after you enlisted. He just wanted to make sure you were taken care of and your mama too." Big Jim leaned back in his chair. "When you first came back, you were just—different. Like you were in a daze or something. I didn't tell you about the deed because I was hoping you'd settle in and get back to being yourself. I thought maybe you had that PTSD I been hearing about."

Zach hung his head. "Yeah, maybe I do. I've been having dreams...nightmares really." He shrugged. "About the guys who didn't make it home...but since I met Stephanie... I dunno. Everything's better."

Big Jim laced his fingers together, and his countenance morphed into the usually good-natured uncle Zach had always known.

"What about the money you gave my mom? I need to pay you back for that."

Big Jim pushed back from his desk and rose to a standing position. "How about we arrange a long-term loan just between the two of us?" He extended his right hand.

Zach jumped to his feet to shake hands with his uncle. "Yes, sir. I'll pay you back. I promise."

"Merry Christmas, son. Let's go see if our breakfast is ready."

# Chapter 24

STEPHANIE WAS ALTERNATELY SPOONING OATMEAL AND SCRAM-
bled eggs into Ivy's mouth. The little girl's tiny teeth were
chomping the food, and she was delighted to be fed. Her
dimples flashed after she finished a bite, and then she
opened her mouth like a baby bird, ready for the next one.

"That's my Ivy. You're such a big girl now."

"I a big boy," Cody insisted.

"Yes, you are," Stephanie dabbed her napkin on his
mouth. "Eat up, big boy."

She looked up to see both Zach and Big Jim standing
nearby and smiling at her.

"You look mighty good with the children," Big Jim
commented.

"Feels mighty good," she said. "Come on, you two.
Sit down and fill your plates."

Fern motioned them to the table. "Our little Stephanie
made our breakfast all by herself, an' it's real tasty."

"C'mon, Dad." Tyler sat, holding his son and looking
quite satisfied with himself. Leah sat beside him, eating.
"These eggs are just the way I like them, Stephanie.
Light and fluffy." He took another bite. "I hate it when
the eggs are dry."

Stephanie felt pleased that she had gotten breakfast
rolled out for the Garretts but didn't want them to know
that, as a firefighter, she had taken her turn prepping
meals for the entire crew.

Zach sat down beside her and kissed her temple. "Looks great, babe." He reached for the platter of eggs and spooned some onto his plate.

Big Jim settled himself at the head of the table with Tyler on one side and Colton on the other. He filled his plate with bacon, toast, and the eggs when Misty passed them down. "Merry Christmas, everybody. Better fuel up. We got a bunch of presents under the tree. You're gonna need a lot of strength to open them."

Stephanie smiled when Cody's big brown eyes opened wide.

"Pwesents?" he said. "Ivy, they got pwesents."

This set off a round of gentle laughter around the table.

Big Jim picked up a strip of crisp bacon and took a bite. "Great breakfast, Stephanie. I just have one question for you."

She looked at him expectantly.

"Are you going to marry my nephew and make an honest man of him?"

There was an audible gasp around the table and then silence as everyone turned to stare at Stephanie.

She felt her cheeks flame, which was a rarity for Stephanie Gayle. She glanced up at Zach, and he was trying to hold back a smile but gave up, beaming at her.

"Thanks, Uncle Jim, but Stephanie and I have been discussing that very question."

"Good," Big Jim said. "Are you two closing in on a decision?"

"We'll let you know," Zach said. "What's the hurry, Uncle Jim?"

Big Jim sat back, grinning. "Well, I was just wondering

what to tell Miss Lorene Dyer, the social worker. I would like to let her know that there will be a wedding. She seems to be a hardnose about letting single people adopt little children…" He looked at her expectantly.

Stephanie sucked in a breath. "Oh my! You talked to Miss Dyer?" She reached for Zach's hand and gripped it tightly.

Big Jim couldn't seem to stop beaming. "Oh, we may have had a few discussions. We seem to have some of the same interests." He saluted her with his glass of orange juice.

"Big Jim!" Leah said. "You've been flirting with the social worker."

He shrugged. "I don't know if you would call it flirting."

"You have!" Tyler said. "You rascal. I'm sure you got that lady's heart going pitty-pat."

There was a general round of laughter, but Stephanie couldn't stop hoping that the handsome, silver-haired rancher might be able to change the dour Miss Dyer's mind about approving Stephanie's adoption application. She couldn't imagine anyone saying no to the affable yet powerful man.

Zach raised her hand to his lips and placed a soft kiss against her fingertips.

It was such a sweet gesture that Stephanie could hardly breathe. Right here, in front of all the Garrett family, Zach was openly showing affection.

"If my opinion matters, I think you two make a great couple," Misty said.

Fern peered at them over the rims of her glasses. "They's about as cute as a bug's ear."

Colton put his arm around Misty. "My cousin is a great guy. I hope you're going to marry him, Stephanie. He needs you to be with him all the rest of his life. Like Misty is with me."

Big Jim pushed his empty plate away and folded his arms. "So, how about it, Stephanie? Will you marry Zach and the rest of this cockeyed family?"

Zach waved them off. "Back off, family. Don't pressure the girl."

"No, please," she said. "I would be delighted to marry you, Zach...and become a part of the Garrett family."

He kissed her then, amid a chorus of catcalls, applause, and even a little boot stomping.

Colton and Tyler high-fived each other.

Big Jim sat at the head of the table, grinning. "I think this is going to be about the best Christmas we've had in a long time."

---

Two days after Christmas, Zach drove Stephanie to his ranch. His chest was flooded with emotion as he pulled into the driveway. He let the truck idle for a few moments as he tried to sort out his feelings.

Jewel stood up in the backseat, her tail flapping against the upholstery.

The house looked the same. Blanketed in snow, the sprawling ranch-style house would probably need some maintenance, but for the time being, it looked like a Norman Rockwell painting.

Mostly, the pain of losing his father was revisited. He was so grateful to his uncle for preserving the estate for him. He would make sure to repay Big Jim for his outlay.

He was not looking forward to entering the ranch house. Memories of his dad flooded his mind. It hurt that he was not going to be inside to greet him.

"Are you okay?" Stephanie's voice broke through his reverie.

"Yeah, I'm great." He unfastened his seat belt but made no move to open the door.

Jewel whined softly.

"This is a gorgeous house," she said. "It's so large. And you were an only child."

"Yes, I think my parents wanted more children, but it didn't happen." He heaved a sigh and stepped out, tucking the keys in his pocket. He closed the door before pausing to take a look around.

Beyond the house, he saw the series of outbuildings including a large barn, where he imagined some of the equipment was stored, or perhaps Big Jim had moved it. His uncle had kept a tally of the number of cattle he had merged with his own herd to make it easier to take care of them. Big Jim promised to cut out the same number from his herd in the spring and return them to his nephew.

Stephanie was waiting patiently for him to ground himself. He was grateful for her sensitive nature. She always seemed to be able to read him.

Zach opened the back door to allow Jewel to make a graceful leap into the snow. She looked up at him, waiting for his orders. "Go play, girl." He leaned down to stroke her head.

He gave Stephanie a smile and trudged around the truck to help her out. Normally, the independent woman would have jumped out before he could reach her, but he figured she knew he needed her to go slowly today.

"Brr...it's instant freeze out here." She slid down into the ankle-high snow.

"I'll do my best to keep you warm." He reached for her gloved hand as they trudged toward the house. "It's not going to be much warmer inside, but we can light the gas stoves, and maybe there's some dry wood for the fireplace."

At the front door, he dug the keys out of his pocket and let the door swing open, unlocking a floodgate of memories.

"Come inside, ladies." He gestured to the interior, and Jewel rushed in, intent upon policing the area to make sure no bad guys were waiting to jump on them.

Stephanie stepped inside eagerly. "Oh, this is lovely."

He had momentarily forgotten that the room would be empty but quickly got his disappointment under control.

Stephanie was staring around, wide-eyed.

"It's empty," he said, closing the door behind him. "My mother has some of my things stored in her garage, but it's not furniture...just stuff from high school and outgrown clothes."

"But it's so large and airy," she said. "I love the fireplace."

"There's another one in the den...that's in the back of the house."

She twirled around, spreading her arms wide. "This is just the greatest house."

He tried to envision it as she was seeing it for the first time and not as the empty hulk of his childhood home. "Glad you like it."

She threw her arms around his torso, giving him an enthusiastic squeeze. "No, silly. I love it. I was so in love with you I was willing to marry you and live in Fern's tiny house, but this—this is a palace by comparison." She took him by the hand. "Quick. Show me the kitchen. That's the heart of a home."

He followed along as they went through the seldom-used formal dining room, where his mother had entertained her friends when her turn came to hold Bible study.

There was a cozy dining spot in the large kitchen, and that was where the family had eaten most meals. It had a bay window that looked out onto the back of the property.

Stephanie's face was alight as she explored. "This kitchen is like the Taj Mahal of kitchens." She gave a little jump up and down. "A dishwasher! I'm so thrilled there's a dishwasher. And is that a freezer beside the fridge?"

He had to smile at that. "Of course. On a ranch, we always had plenty of beef and chicken on hand, and my mom would freeze some of the vegetables and fruits from her garden."

"A garden. I'd love to learn how to grow something that we could eat. I know the kids would like to help." Stephanie squealed like a schoolgirl. "That is so very cool."

He opened the door to the spacious pantry. "This is where she stored the things she canned."

Stephanie pressed into the space. "Oh, I've got my work cut out for me."

When she emerged, he swung her into an embrace. "And all this can be yours, Miss Gayle. All you have to do is marry me." He planted a kiss on her luscious lips.

She snuggled against him, smiling. "Well, let me see. I can give up the single life, marry the man of my dreams, and become a woman of property just by saying those two little words—*I do*?"

"That's all it takes." He gazed down at her expectantly.

"I'm so in love with you. I would marry you if we had to live under an overpass."

"I would never let that happen," he assured her. "I'll always take care of you...and the children."

Tears filled her eyes. "Oh, Zach. I hope you'll grow to love them as much as I do."

"I'm getting there. They'll grow up as Garretts, so that means they'll have to deal with everything that entails." He shook his head. "Sometimes that's quite a lot to live up to."

"I'm not worried," she said. "They will have you as their role model. I hope they can get over all the horrors they've lived through."

"I hope so too. Big Jim is not letting them return to the place they were staying...that child care home for orphans."

"Big Jim is a hero, but so are you. I'll never forget how you saved me from the Neeleys."

He led her to the bay window in the back of the kitchen that looked out over the property. "This was where we ate most of the time. Sometimes Mom let us eat in the den in front of the television, but she believed a proper meal was served at the table." He let out a little huff. "Now all we need is a table."

"Oh, I can do that. You remember that I have a check on its way from the insurance company to replace the stuff in my apartment. We've got this covered. At least I can help with a little of the furniture."

"Great. I've got some savings. We'll be fine," he said. "Don't worry."

Stephanie knelt down to where Jewel had settled at their feet. "One thing for sure. We will need to have a king-size bed."

Zach joined Stephanie, stretching out on the carpet beside her. He stroked his hand over Jewel's thick fur. "One other thing we need." He reached into his pocket and took out the ring box from the jewelry store in Amarillo.

Stephanie's eyes opened wide. "Oh, my. That's a friendship ring, right?"

Zach chuckled. "Not hardly. This is my way of offering you a lifetime of being loved by one big kinda rough-around-the-edges ex-soldier cowboy."

"I can go for that, especially if it comes with jewelry."

He opened the box and offered it to her, hoping it was a good choice, hoping she would like it.

Her lips trembled, and then she pressed them together for a moment. "Oh, Zach. It's just beautiful."

Relieved, he took the ring out of the box and placed it on her finger. It looked perfect. He raised her hand to kiss it, but she grabbed his face with both hands and kissed him.

"I'm so happy," she said. "We need to call the church and find a date for the wedding...or maybe we should just go to the courthouse?"

"Oh, no, you don't," he said. "Garrett weddings are proper church weddings. I'm dragging you down the aisle to the preacher. It's a given."

"I'll get down the aisle under my own steam, thank you very much." She raised her brows, giving him an expression that screamed that she meant business. "Let's go to the church tomorrow and reserve a date."

"Sooner rather than later."

—⁓—

It was the first Saturday in February, and Stephanie stood before the full-length mirror, surveying herself. "Does my hair look okay?"

"No," Leah said. "Your hair looks gorgeous." She was sitting on a small settee, breast-feeding JT. "I hope I don't leak on this outfit."

Misty chuckled. "I think JT is doing his part to solve your problem." She held the bodice of Stephanie's gown open so she could slip into it without mussing her hair. "Here you go. Just dive in."

Stephanie managed to get her arms in the armholes, cringing while Misty held the rest of the dress away from her hair so it would remain in place. She straightened, and Misty zipped it up.

"I can't believe you found this great dress on such short notice," Misty said.

"I can't believe you got the church on such short notice." Leah placed JT in his carrier and fumbled to close her nursing bra.

"I ordered the dress online," Stephanie said. "Pretty good fit, huh?"

"Amazing," Leah agreed. "Gracie, could you hand me that bag?" She gestured to a roomy diaper bag that seemed to be filled to the brim.

"Sure, Mom." Gracie handed it off and then took a seat close to her new baby brother, gazing at him adoringly.

Leah sighed, removed a roll of paper towels from the bag, and tore off two large squares. She folded each one several times and arranged them in the cups of her nursing bra. "Hope this works. I ran out of nursing pads."

Misty raised her brows. "Well, you certainly look... voluptuous."

"Shut up." Leah laughed as she buttoned her jacket. "Your turn will come."

Stephanie smoothed the dress, pleased that it fit so well.

There was a knock at the door, and Mark's voice could be heard in the hallway. "They told me to tell you it's time to line up."

"Okay," Misty yelled back. To Stephanie, she said, "Let's get you married off."

Stephanie's stomach was in a knot. She took several deep breaths and straightened her shoulders. "Let's do this."

When they emerged, Mark was gone, but two of the church ladies were standing by to get the women arranged in their proper places.

When they stood together, listening to the organist play behind the closed doors, Stephanie tried to calm her jitters. "I want to thank you all for everything you've done to make this happen. You're the best friends ever."

"Nah," Leah said. "We're family. That's even better."

Tyler appeared through a side door and reached for the infant carrier. "You ladies look gorgeous, but my son and I are going to sit this out with Dad and Mark." He gave Leah a kiss and told her she was beautiful.

Leah watched him walk back through the door

leading to a side aisle. "I love that man so much, but I hope I'm not leaking."

Misty handed out the bouquets, a small, delicate one to Gracie and then one for Leah and another for Stephanie, before taking up her own.

Stephanie inhaled the fragrance and brightened when she spied Lieutenant Larsen heading toward them.

"Hope I'm not late," he said. He wore his dress uniform, resplendent with all his medals.

"You're right on time," she said. "Thank you for giving me away."

He reached for her hand and patted it. "I'm so proud that you asked me. It's an honor."

"Aww, Lieutenant. You've been like a father since I joined the fire department. Thanks for believing in me." She tucked her hand in the crook of his arm.

The organist was playing something light and lyrical. Gracie was thrilled to be leading the parade. She glanced back at her mother, who murmured something encouraging.

Misty seemed to be antsy, tapping her foot but faster than the tempo of the music.

They were all excited...excited for Stephanie... excited for Zach...just excited for all the preparations and buildup.

The church ladies opened the doors to the center aisle of the church.

For her part, Stephanie was paralyzed. She knew all she had to do was walk down the aisle and great things would happen. For a moment, she wondered if she were worthy of all these great things. She had survived a lot of tough situations and remained a loner. A loner among her fellow firefighters.

Now she would become a part of a whole. A woman lawfully married to the best man on the planet. A woman mothering two small orphans. A woman about to be enfolded into a wonderful, strong, and loving family.

At a signal from one of the church ladies, Gracie started down the aisle, followed by mother and aunt, all at a leisurely pace. Smiling... They were smiling...

Stephanie supposed she should smile too.

She moved forward, waiting for her cue to proceed.

The music changed, and the organist struck a dramatic chord before breaking into the traditional wedding march. The entire assembly rose to their feet, turning to look at her, smiling. Big Jim held Cody and Ivy in his arms so they could see, while Tyler held his infant son.

That was the moment that her eyes met Zach's.

He stood at the altar, between the preacher and Colton, his best man. Zach looked so happy and so proud. Such a good man, and he was hers.

A flush of pleasure filled her chest. She took one faltering step down the aisle. The next one was steadier and the next stronger still. She was on her way to a wonderful new life with her forever man.

*Don't miss the captivating beginning to
June Faver's Dark Horse Cowboys series!*

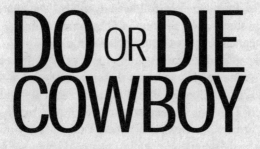

# DO OR DIE
# COWBOY

*Available now from Sourcebooks Casablanca*

TYLER GARRETT DROVE AWAY WITHOUT LOOKING BACK. Truth was, he was afraid to even glance in the rearview mirror for fear he would turn his big Ford extended-cab truck around. Of course, he was hauling a trailer with the finest quarter horse ever bred, so turning around on that two-lane road might have given him a little trouble...but then, trouble was what he did best.

Ty was the middle son. The one who invented the word *trouble*, at least, according to his dad. No one could deny that "Big Jim" Garrett thought the world of his three sons, but somehow it was always Ty who inspired him to call out, "Here comes trouble."

*Well, here goes trouble, Dad.*

He placed a hand on Lucky's head. The two-year-old golden retriever regarded him with trusting eyes. "We're going to be fine, boy." He reached the end of the farm-to-market road and idled, looking both ways for traffic, but of course, there was none. With a deep sigh, he hooked a wide right, allowing the trailer to arc out behind him as he pulled onto the interstate. He straightened his shoulders and thought about his destination.

*Dallas.*

Dallas, where Ty would take the first step in making his own dreams come true. Where he could polish his talent and live up to his mother's aspirations for him as well.

He frowned, his grip on the steering wheel tightening. *Too bad Mom didn't live to see this day. She always believed in me.*

A lump formed in his throat as he pictured her sweet face. She was the one who never failed to show up at the talent shows, looking pleased and applauding like crazy. Making her proud had been one of his prime motivators.

Big Jim, on the other hand, had just shaken his head and said, "That singin' stuff is nice and all, but you need to concentrate on your true callin', boy. You were born to be a rancher. It's in your blood."

Ty sucked in a deep breath and blew it out. Well, he'd done what he could to make that happen. He'd graduated from Texas Tech University with a degree in agricultural economics and range management. He'd devoted years of his life to making his dad proud of him, but ranching just wasn't in his heart.

His mother's last words to him were branded into his memory. She had placed her hand on his cheek and gazed up with love in her eyes. "Follow your heart, Ty. Not many people are blessed with the talent the good Lord gave you, so you need to make the most of it." She had lapsed into a coma and passed away the following day.

Ty owed it to her to make it big. And Dallas was just the launching pad. His friend Will had a recording studio and was going to cut a demo for him. Then, Ty was set to try out for the *Texas Country Star* television show. If he made it through to the state finals, he would go on to compete in the Nashville Idol contest. He was pretty sure he had a good shot.

Ty's departure was taking place a few days earlier than planned. Will had studio time available the beginning of the next week, but after the morning's blowup with Big Jim, Ty had decided to head for Dallas and just hang around at Will's.

He drove east, oblivious to the flat, northern Texas countryside. His head was someplace else, but without much effort, he filled the truck with his strong voice, singing one of his mother's favorite gospel tunes. He could see himself onstage, performing for the Nashville audience. For the world…

After a while, the town of Langston appeared on the horizon. He thought he should stop and grab lunch before the long drive to Big D. It was a fairly small town, so there weren't many choices. He passed a Dairy Queen and Tio's, a Mexican restaurant, before pulling in at Tiny's Diner. It was late, so the lunch crowd had already been and gone. Not too many cars outside. He parked where he could keep an eye on his rig and climbed down out of his truck, leaving the windows cracked for Lucky.

Funny to think he was really on his way. With all his
dad's wealth, Ty had only taken what was important to
him—his horse, his dog, his guitar, and a few clothes.
*'Cause I'm sure not going back.*

A metal cowbell clanked against the glass door when
he entered the restaurant. The aroma of good food hit
him like a fist. He hadn't realized how hungry he was,
since he had forgone breakfast in his rush to leave the
sprawling Garrett ranch that morning. The Circle G,
with its rambling, Spanish-style ranch house, the many
barns, stables, and outbuildings; with thousands of acres
of fenced pastureland for the beef cattle and horses; with
the long heritage of the Garrett family steeped into the
land. Not a problem. Surely his older brother, Colton,
or his younger brother, Beau, would pick up the slack.
They could take over running the spread when Big Jim
was unable. They could provide for future generations
of Garretts to carry on the tradition.

"Hello, Tyler," Crystal called out. She was a fixture
here at Tiny's. A big lady with a big heart. "Table or
booth?" She grabbed a menu and cocked her head, waiting for his answer.

"Table near the front window would be best."
Removing his Stetson, he raked his hand through his
thick, dark hair.

She walked him over to the window and placed the
menu on a table for two. "Here you go. Iced tea?"

"That'll be good." He set the Stetson on the other
side of the table and took a seat facing the door. When it
opened, he had to check out the new arrival.

*Man!*

His breath caught as his gaze fell on one of the

prettiest women he had ever seen. She wasn't exactly what one could call hot, but when she paused in the open doorway and took a look around, he felt like he'd been kicked in the gut.

Her large, wide-set brown eyes reminded him of a fawn, or perhaps it was her blondish-brown curls, swept up in an untidy gob at the crown of her head. Definitely had the air of a skittish animal, not quite tame. Her threadbare jeans had a rip on one thigh, and she wore a tank top with an oversize blue work shirt on top. She swept the room carefully, as though alert for something, then turned back in the open doorway and motioned someone through.

A young girl stepped forward, pausing when the woman's slender hand came to rest on her shoulder. The girl looked like a replica of the woman, with lighter blonde hair and a big cast on her forearm.

The kid had that same half-wild expression on her face, like she would turn and bolt from the restaurant if something spooked her.

Crystal came to slide Ty's iced tea on the table and then went to greet the newcomers. Apparently, the woman wanted to keep an eye on whatever was out there too, since Crystal seated them at the table next to Ty's, where she sat facing the parking lot. The girl was on her right, facing Ty.

He watched the woman carefully peruse the menu and then reach in her purse. She drew out a wallet and did a quick count of the bills inside. Ty felt a surge of pity, never in his life having to count his money before ordering.

When Crystal came to take his order, he ordered for

three. "Just deliver the other two meals to that table," he said under his breath.

Crystal winked at him and went to turn in the orders. When she returned a few minutes later, she sat a salad on his table and also in front of his two guests.

"What? I haven't ordered yet." The woman pushed her chair back, gazing up at Crystal with a frown.

"The gentleman paid for your meal, ma'am." Crystal nodded to where Ty sat.

The woman regarded him icily, her soft mouth forming a straight line of disapproval.

"Pardon me for being so forward," he said, "but Tiny makes the best chicken-fried steak, and I thought you might like to enjoy it with me." She started to protest, but he cut her off. "It would be a shame to pass through Langston without experiencing the best chicken-fried steak in all of Texas." He grinned at her encouragingly.

She pressed her lips together again and nodded curtly. "Thanks." Her voice came out low and gravelly, and a blush tinged her cheeks.

"I'm Tyler Garrett, ma'am. Just showing some hospitality."

---

Leah Benson swallowed hard. The cowboy was grinning from ear to ear. *He must feel real proud of himself for springing for our meal.* "We appreciate it."

She glanced at Gracie, who was staring at her wide-eyed. When she nodded, Gracie picked up her fork and speared the cherry tomato on top of her salad. She popped it into her mouth and closed her eyes when she bit into it. Such a simple pleasure and yet one that had been denied them for a while.

The waitress came back with a carousel of bottled salad dressings.

"Oh, ranch!" Gracie said, as though that particular dressing was a rare treat. She grabbed the bottle and tried to open it, the cast getting in her way.

"Here, let me." Leah opened the cap and set the bottle in front of her daughter.

Gracie squirted a generous glob onto her salad and commenced eating like she'd been starved.

Leah exhaled. Well, it had been a long time since they had eaten in a restaurant of any kind, so this was a treat. She squirted the dressing on her salad and took a bite. The tangy dressing complemented the fresh and crispy salad. *Yes, this is good.* She and her daughter had run out of the sandwiches Leah packed before they left Oklahoma. She'd thought they could make it all the way to Gran's without having to stop for food. Lord knows the high cost of gasoline had devoured her small hoard of cash. But they were close now. Less than thirty miles to go, and then they would be safe.

The cowboy had stood and was walking toward her table. *No way! If he thinks he can buy us a meal and then come over here—*

"Pardon me, ladies," he said in a deep, mellow voice. "I could use a little of that ranch dressing, if you're done with it." He looked at Gracie, and she nudged it toward him. "Thank you," he said.

Leah tried to keep her eyes averted, but his clean, masculine scent seemed to wrap around her like an embrace. She watched him return to his table, noting the wide set of his shoulders and how they tapered down in a nice V shape to his well-filled-out Wranglers. When he took his seat, he met her gaze with a dimpled grin.

*Oh no! I have no business noticing cute cowboys, not when I can't seem to get rid of the last one.*

She picked up her fork and concentrated on her salad, studiously ignoring the attractive man at the next table.

When the waitress returned, she brought large platters, each filled with a huge portion of chicken-fried steak and mashed potatoes, all covered with creamy white gravy. There were small bowls of seasoned green beans on the side. A basket of golden-brown cloverleaf rolls completed the array.

Gracie was staring like it was Christmas, and Leah had to admit the aroma had her salivating. She cut some bites for Gracie, thinking the huge serving might make a good dinner as well.

The waitress placed the same meal in front of the cowboy. Some light banter passed between them, and then he set about enjoying his food.

Maybe his generosity was just a random act of kindness. Leah had heard about them but never experienced any firsthand.

As long as they made it to Gran's before nightfall, they would have a safe haven. A place for Leah and Gracie to recover from their wounds, both emotional and physical.

Leah glanced at the cast on Gracie's left arm. *A broken wrist.* Leah's stomach seized up with guilt, but she hadn't known Caine would be paroled and that he'd show up unannounced.

Heaving a sigh, she reflected that she should have

left long ago, but they really hadn't had the money to relocate. Well, this latest disaster had set them on the road, ready or not.

She hurriedly gobbled everything on her plate, barely tasting the delicious food.

"Gracie, maybe you can eat that in the car," she said and hailed the waitress. "Do you think we could get this to go?"

When the waitress brought a Styrofoam container and a paper bag, Leah scooped the contents of Gracie's plate into the divided carton and snapped the lid on tight. After she slipped it into the bag, Gracie emptied the basket of rolls on top.

Leah went to the cowboy's table. "I want to thank you for your kindness, Mister—"

"Ty…Tyler Garrett," he supplied, rising to his feet. "Think nothing of it. It was my pleasure."

He had blue eyes, ringed by dark lashes. Dark like his hair. His eyes, blue as a summer sky, a sharp contrast to his deeply tanned face. He reached out to her and, without thinking, she found her hand enveloped in his much larger one. It was callused and warm. "You have a safe trip now."

"Um…thank you." Leah turned, but Gracie also extended her hand.

"Thanks for the meal, Mr. Tyler. It was delicious."

He bowed deeply over her hand. "You take care, little lady."

She smiled, the first real smile Leah had seen on Gracie's face since they had left Oklahoma. "My name is Gracie, and my mama is named Leah."

"Well, I'm happy to meet you, Gracie and Leah." He gave her another courtly bow.

Leah tried to quell the strangling sensation in her throat, hustling Gracie out of the restaurant and into their loaded vehicle. When her daughter was belted in and their small, terrier-type dog, Eddie, had calmed down, Leah pulled out onto the road.

Gracie continued to eat, and she shared a roll with Eddie, so they were content. Gracie's nose wrinkled up, and she made a face. "Ewww!" she shrieked. "Eddie!"

Leah sighed and opened the windows. "Honey, he can't help it. He's old. Every once in a while, he just has to…"

"He farts!" she exploded. "All the time."

Eddie, for his part, hung his head and thumped his tail on the floorboard.

"It's okay. The car is all aired out now."

"Eddie, please don't fart while I'm eating." Gracie gave him a stern look.

Leah had to laugh. Her daughter glowered, while her dog feigned innocence. If a flatulent dog was the worst obstacle they had to face, their future would be sublime.

The long, straight West Texas highway stretched out in front of them, like an arrow pointing the way to safety.

Leah heaved a deep sigh and tried to loosen her grip on the steering wheel, all the while thinking about the cowboy, whose blue eyes seemed to see all the way to her soul.

―――

Tyler gazed out the window at the woman and child as they scrambled into the old beater of a car. He shook his head. Something about those big brown eyes. He could read the fear there. Someone somewhere had caused her a lot of pain. There was no trust in those eyes.

He watched her pull out onto the interstate and hoped they were headed someplace good. Someplace where somebody gave a damn about them.

Crystal came to refill his iced tea. "That was real nice, what you did for them, Ty."

He frowned, dipping his dinner roll in the cream gravy. "It wasn't a big deal."

Crystal snorted. "It was to them. That woman had bruises on her arms. When I was serving their plates, her shirt fell back, and it looked like handprints on her shoulders too. Somebody gave them a rough time." She set the tea pitcher on his table and went to clear the one so recently vacated.

Crystal's words stabbed into his consciousness. *What kind of man would hurt a woman?* No matter how controlling his father was, he would never have raised a hand to his wife. He had worshiped her, in fact. Since his mom died, it had seemed his father was even more driven to cement Ty to the ranch, to quash any hope he had of making it to the big time.

Ty heard his father's voice reverberating in his head. "Just forget all that music nonsense. This is your life, right here on the land."

He stared out the window in the direction the brown-eyed beauty had gone. It appeared they were headed in the same direction. He hoped her dreams would come true as well as his own.

# About the Author

June Faver loves Texas, from the Gulf coast to the pan-handle, from the Mexican border to the Piney Woods. Her novels embrace the heart and soul of the state and the larger-than-life Texans who romp across her pages. A former teacher and healthcare professional, she lives and writes in the Texas Hill Country.

## Also by June Faver

DARK HORSE COWBOYS
*Do or Die Cowboy*
*Hot Target Cowboy*
*When to Call a Cowboy*

# MISTLETOE IN TEXAS

Bestselling author Kari Lynn Dell invites us to
a Texas Rodeo Christmas like no other!

Hank Brookman had all the makings of a top rodeo bull-
fighter until one accident left him badly injured. Now,
after years of self-imposed exile, Hank's back and ready
to make amends…starting with the girl his heart can't
live without.

> "This talented writer knows rodeo
> and sexy cowboys!"
> **—B. J. Daniels, *New York Times* bestselling author**

# COWBOY FIREFIGHTER CHRISTMAS KISS

---

The firefighting cowboys of Wildcat Bluff County take Christmas VERY seriously in Kim Redford's Smokin' Hot Cowboys series

When Ivy Bryant arrives at Wildcat Hall, she goes from website designer by day to honky-tonk manager by night. How to handle it all? Enter Slade Steele—rancher, firefighter, and proprietor of the Chuckwagon Café—who offers his services. Add his award-winning pies and a fiery chili recipe to the menu and folks will stream in the front door. It's an offer Ivy can't refuse, even though the passion between them is already at the boiling point...

"Cowboy Christmas reading at its very best."
**—Carolyn Brown, *New York Times* bestselling author**